Lake County Sheriff Bud Blair meets force with force when an international jihadist bent on revenge hires a biker gang to kill the Reverend TJ Wildish.

When three members of the gang are arrested and jailed, a gang of armed bikers threaten to destroy the small town of Lakeview unless their friends are released. Correctional officers, a dozen cowboys, and Bud's old partner join the sheriff and his six deputies to meet the threat.

In Portland, a rogue FBI agent sends Special Agents Wilcox and Brandt on the hunt for a human trafficking pipeline. What they find will unleash a wave of panic in the city.

Not Before Midnight is an international crime thriller, but it's also a love story. When Nancy Sixkiller breaks her engagement and flees to Yakima, Bud's reaction may cost him his job. But when Nancy returns, six months later, the town is taking bets as to how long it will be before the two are married.

The story covers the Pacific Northwest ... from Central Oregon, to Portland, Seattle, and Ketchikan. These landscapes strongly influence the character of the people living there and serve as a rugged backdrop to a realistic, page-turning novel — fifth in the Sheriff Bud Blair series.

Not Before Midnight

The Sheriff Bud Blair Oregon Mystery Series
Volume 5

Rod Collins

BRIGHT WORKS PRESS

Not Before Midnight
Copyright © 2017 by Rod Collins
Bright Works Press

Print ISBN- 978-0-9965394-9-4
eBook ISBN: 979-8-9895768-7-6

Cover designed
Zachariah Sturgil

Interior Design:
Eva Long
longonbooks.com

Printed in the U.S.A

to Vi

CONTENTS

1

What You Wish For

A GRAY WATERPROOF CARHART SWEATSHIRT KEPT THE spring chill at bay as Dell BeBe, retired detective, Portland Police Bureau, eased his canoe in against a bed of water lilies near the east shore of Dog Lake. He flipped a four-inch black plastic worm, rigged Texas style, into an open hole in the lily pads, watched the worm sink, and then counted to three before setting the hook on a bass that picked up the bait.

"There we go!" He lifted the limber bass rod as high as he could, trying to force the fish away from the tangle of water lilies. And then his cell phone started buzzing…

"Not now," he grumbled.

As the fish tired he worked it closer and lifted it into the boat. "You're not as big as I thought. I swear I caught you yesterday." He released the little bass and sighed. "Enough of this."

His cell phone buzzed again, and he pulled it from his shirt pocket. *I've got to remember to turn this thing off when I'm fishing.* It wasn't a number he recognized, but he answered anyway.

"This is Dell BeBe."

He heard Cletus Falls say, "You ever answer your phone?"

"Not when I'm fishing," BB growled. "Is that you Cletus? I didn't recognize the number."

"Once upon a time I was Cletus, but the way things be here in the big city of Portland, I may have to change my name. Word on the street is some radical Muslim dudes is coming after your friend Reverend Wildish. They seem to think he ratted them out to the FBI and help set up that big raid on their mosque last year.

"And the snitch that told the reverend? The guy with all the nice pitchers of those AK's in the basement of the mosque? He's dead. Hit and run. My friends in the FBI tell me it weren't no accident. They say he was tortured before they tossed him in front of a city bus.

"The reverend don't want to use his phone, so he asked me to call … tell you he be down later today."

"Down here?"

"I told him to leave town while the FBI sorts this business out and makes some arrests … if they ever do. He don't have no place else to run to … no safe place. I don't think they know you be friends."

His heart rate increasing with each deep breath, BB said, "They might. Wildish and I got arrested for some minor vandalism once … back in middle school. Juvie records are supposedly expunged, but I guess we'll see. I also emailed him several photos of my new house. I hope they don't find those."

BB paused and then added, "Thanks, Cletus. You watch your back. Those are evil men. Kill you just for fun."

"I will. Word is that some of them be black dudes – converts to Islam. And there's one more thing, the reverend don't have no money or car. He don't even have a credit card. So, I rented him some wheels and loaned him five hundred. I expects you to be good for it."

"You sure it was five hundred? You didn't add in a little interest on top?"

"You ask him yourself when he get there. I be straight."

"I will, Cletus. Now what are you going to do? Maybe you should come down here and help me catch some fish, stay away from Portland for a while."

"I don't like it out past the burbs. Too dangerous."

BB shook his head, knowing that – for Cletus – being more than five or six miles from downtown Portland was uncomfortable. It was foreign turf.

"Well, tell your mama hello, Cletus. This number work if I need to call you?"

"No. Use my old number. This is a junk phone … and I've been on line way too long. Good bye, Mister BeBe."

BB listened to dead air, and then ended the call. He shook his head and picked up his paddle. *Not good*, he thought. He powered the canoe back across Dog Lake, the memory of the first time he met Cletus still bright and clear in his mind…

2

Cletus

IN TROUBLE ... AGAIN ... BECAUSE HE WAS the subject of an article in The Oregonian about "Detective Dell BeBe of the Portland Police Bureau" and "police brutality," undeserved in BB's opinion. The Captain pulled BB off a homicide investigation and assigned him to look into a complaint about an outlaw vendor at the Rose Garden. The complaint said this vendor was selling cheap knockoff Blazer gear.

Big deal, a cynical BB thought.

He found the seller set up near the entrance to the home of the Portland Trailblazers. Wearing low rider, sag-around-his-butt baggy jeans and new Nikes, a small teenager, whose ancestry appeared to be a mix of Asian and black, was hawking counterfeit Blazer gear from a folding card table.

The stand held stacks of sweatshirts, numbered jerseys for fans partial to an individual player, caps, banners, and one legitimate autographed jersey with the number 22 dating back to the Clyde Drexler era – that one with a "Silent Auction" tag.

When BB walked up behind the sixty-five-inch Cletus and put a big hand on his shoulder, Cletus started and turned to look up at him.

"Who you?"

BB chuckled. "Why bro, if this was a bad movie I'd say I was your worst nightmare. But this isn't a movie, so I'll let that pass." He flipped his badge wallet open, then slipped it back into his pocket.

Cletus just stared at him, then said, "Let me see that again."

BB sighed, but held out the badge again. Cletus studied the badge at length and asked, "What for is a big-city detective rousting an honest businessman?"

BB shrugged. "Good question, but I still need to see your license."

"Don't need one."

BB sighed. "Not true. The city says you do."

Cletus turned serious, "If you let me go, I'll tell you something a lot hotter than an unlicensed vendor."

BB looked skeptical, but took the bait, "What you got, Bro?"

"See that tall black dude with the white chick on his arm? He be the pimp and she be the trick. And that ain't all they do. He be a big-time blackmailer. Gets the John into a room, let's the girl do the trick, and takes pitchers. Then shakes the John down for lots of cash money.

"Right now, they be prospectin' the crowd, looking for an out-of-towner willing to play around a little."

BB stared hard at Cletus before deciding he was telling the truth. He reached into his pocket, pulled out a roll of cash, and slipped a fifty-dollar bill into Cletus' hand.

"What's your name, boy? And don't give me no shuck and jive bullshit. I want a cell number and an address. Otherwise I'll take you downtown."

Cletus hesitated, but he complied. BB thumbed the number into his cell, hit Send, then listened to the phone in Cletus' pocket start playing a musical jingle.

"Okay. Gather your stuff and split. I don't want to see you here again."

"For another fifty, I got more information you might like."

BB used his cell phone to take a picture of the man and woman, and when Cletus laughed, he gently kicked him on the rump. A full sixty seconds ticked off the clock before Cletus had his folding table in one hand and a battered suitcase full of cheap imitation Blazer gear in the other.

BB shook his head and stared as Cletus swaggered around the corner and out of sight. He resisted the temptation to follow and see if Cletus had simply moved around the block and set his table up again.

"You need a daddy," BB growled.

When he shared the tip with an old friend who worked vice, he discovered Cletus had already sold that information … twice. BB just grinned, knowing he'd found a new snitch.

All of which led to a growing friendship between Detective Dell BeBe and the teenager Cletus, who dealt in street information as well as bootleg knockoff Blazer gear. Cletus worked pro bono as a snitch for BB, giving the big detective useful street info in exchange for an occasional dinner … and for not arresting him in the first place. Cletus endured BB's nagging and finally applied to be a licensed vendor. It wasn't much longer before he passed his GED.

But Cletus wouldn't give up the business of selling information to members of the Portland Police Bureau, Multnomah County Sheriff's Office, DEA, FBI, ICE, and whoever else would buy. His specialty was selling the same information to different people in each agency.

"Gots to pay for my education somehow," he'd say every time BB chided him for his scams.

In truth, BB thought of Cletus as a foster son, and he was pleased when Cletus announced that he, Cletus Falls, had graduated from Portland Community College with a 4.0 GPA in business administration … and was now enrolled at Portland State University. "Gonna get me a bachelor's degree."

BB eyed him and when it was obvious Cletus wasn't going to say anything more, asked, "What are you going to major in?"

Cletus grinned, spread his arms expansively and said, "Well, my man, here's the plan. First, I get a degree in criminology. I'm already sort of specialized that way, if you know what I mean.

"Then, I get a job as a big-city detective. Have to take a cut in pay when I do that, but at least I won't have some bad-ass cop peeking over my shoulder all the time."

BB was startled. It had never occurred to him Cletus would ever do anything but hustle. BB shook his head, tried to say something, and finally settled for reaching across the table to offer his hand. Finding his voice, he said, "Way to go, Cletus. Way to go!"

Cletus looked smug. It was the first time he had surprised his closest and best friend. "Yeah," he said, "but you ain't heard all of it. And then, after I rid the city of all the bad guys, I'm gonna go to law school. Be a big-time lawyer."

BB grinned and asked, "What does your mama think about all this?"

"She be proud of me. She says to tell Mr. BeBe he's a good man. Been a good father to Cletus." He stopped because he was afraid he would start blubbering, and that would not do, not for a hustler like Cletus Falls.

*****

BB SHOOK LOOSE FROM THE MEMORY of Cletus. He towed the canoe onto the newly green grass under the scattered pine trees that sheltered the west shoreline. He turned it upside down, slipped a light chain through the handle in the bow of the boat, wound the chain around a twelve-inch pine tree, and locked the ends with a Master Lock.

He picked up his fishing pole and followed the dim path from the lakeshore through the open scatter of young pine trees playing host to his new log home. BB still marveled at his good fortune in finding the five-acre lot, liking the sight of the reddish-stained logs, still looking fresh – even after a season of winter abuse. The house sat solidly on a point of land overlooking the lake.

I think I better call Dutch Vanderlin … if he's still the SAC for Portland. Find out what the FBI has on this. And I best air out the guest room for Wildish. I wonder if he even knows what fresh air smells like?

3

The Watcher

CLETUS ENDED THE CALL WITH BB, stuffed the cell phone in the belly pocket of his bright orange OSU sweatshirt, and then took a deep breath. He felt a degree of fear that was new and unsettling. It was one thing to get pounded on by bigger kids when he was growing up in north Portland. He developed a wariness. But you only got hurt; it wasn't fatal. And in time, you had a chance to get even.

It was an entirely different matter when someone wanted to kill you. He leaned back on the bench at a bus stop on MLK Boulevard and suddenly felt very naked and very exposed.

How did they find Reggie? And what did he tell them?

He spotted a man wearing a dark hoodie watching him from the window of a McDonald's across the street. *Don't know him. Why's he staring at me?*

Restless and edgy, Cletus jumped at the sound of squealing brakes. A Tri-Met bus was making a quick stop two blocks up the street. He looked back at McDonald's in time to see the watcher head for the front door. When the man reached the sidewalk, Cletus saw him look for a break in the traffic.

Hands in his sweatshirt pockets, the tall bearded black man skipped off the curb and started across the busy street in the direction of the bus stop. When he was halfway across, the man hollered, "Hey, boy. You Cletus?"

That was enough to push Cletus from wary to panic. He jumped up off the bench and ran as hard as he could up the sidewalk, running parallel to the street. He looked back in time to see the man pull a silver pistol from the belly pocket of his sweatshirt.

Later Cletus would tell BB he didn't actually hear any shots, but the gun was all the motivation he needed.

"I saw the bus start down the street, and I just ran in front of it and into the middle turn lane. I got lucky. No cars hit me, and he couldn't see to shoot at me with the bus in the way.

"Anyway, I catch me a break in traffic and run like hell up the other side and onto Knott Street. Ran until I thought I'd puke my guts out. Ran all the way to the Lloyd Center.

"Figured to get lost in there, hide in the back of a store. I bought a gray hoodie and ditched that orange one. Figured he couldn't watch all the exits. Figured maybe I could sneak into a car in the parking garage and hide.

"And then I see an old black woman carrying way too many packages. I gives her my winning smile and offers to help her to the bus. She's suspicious at first, but she finally nods and says it would be fine.

"I nearly crapped my pants when I see the same dude, the one with the gun, watching the door. But I ducked my head and walked right behind that old woman. Must have looked like a grandson helping his granny.

"The dude never even looks at me. I was shaking so hard I thought I'd drop the packages. Anyways, I just follows that old woman up the steps and onto the bus. Finds me a seat on the far side and rides away.

"That's when I called my FBI friend Sara. I knew I had to get off the streets.

"I called Mama and told her to go visit Aunt Elsie up in Seattle and stay there until I called again. I didn't want them coming after her.

"And Aunt Elsie's husband, George … he keeps a loaded shotgun behind his closet door."

4

Nancy Sixkiller

Normally, the twenty-five-mile drive from his A-Frame cabin on Dog Lake back to the town of Lakeview managed to cheer him up. But this wasn't one of those mornings. Not even the sight of a big mule deer doe down in the willows along Drews Creek could work its magic.

A chestnut horse grazing in a pasture brought memories of his first manhunt in Lake County. Bud still felt bad about the horse, dead from a .30-06 slug intended for himself. But that was long past. The present was his major concern.

Molly, his little black Lab, was sick. For years he'd talked to Molly while he drove, sort of trying out his thoughts on her. In good weather she sat upright on the passenger seat of the pickup, head out the window, ears floating in the wind, nose searching for scents, looking back and grinning at him from time to time … like she understood what he was saying.

Henry (Bud) Blair, sheriff of Lake County, worked the kinks out of more than one case that way … and the kinks out of his love life – which, at the moment, wasn't much to talk about. The vet had kept Molly overnight, and the pickup felt empty without her.

He liked to think he was a tough-minded, practical person, but he didn't like what the doc told him yesterday. Molly was getting on in life and looking it: muzzle turning gray and gimpy in the hips. When the vet said "might be cancer," Bud's heart just dropped. He glommed on to the "might be" part, but he knew the doc was right. He was ashamed to admit his first sorrow was for himself, but he got that worked out in a hurry and started feeling sorry for his old canine partner instead.

For another thing, Nancy Sixkiller's call last night knocked him off kilter, not a good thing for a cop. Distractions can get you killed.

Bud gloomily thought, *So far, I'm zero for one in the marriage department and zero for one in the engagement department.*

After the divorce from Linda, his first wife, it took most of a year and building his cabin on Dog Lake to get back to feeling like a normal person. And it took Nancy Sixkiller to put the bounce back in his step. For a while he had a picture of being married to the beautiful Yakima Indian woman, maybe having a child, living a normal life ... whatever that was.

"Damn," he said to no one in particular. He stomped the county's pickup into passing gear, took it up to seventy in a short burst, and then sighed and let his speed drop back to a safer fifty. "I'm not mad at this pickup. No sense in abusing it, or in killing a deer."

Last year, a long tall woman wearing a black jumpsuit and carrying a machine pistol punched a lot of holes in the windshield, the right-side doors, and the pickup box of the truck. His shotgun and a load of double-ought buckshot put a stop to that, but not before she shot a hole in the meaty part of his left shoulder.

That particular slug also punched a hole in his engagement to Nancy Sixkiller. After Nancy found Bud had been shot – again – she decided her mother needed her more than Bud did. She said it was because her mom had suffered a stroke. But she also said she couldn't stand the notion of being married to a cop ... specifically to Bud Blair. Too much "stress and worry" that he wouldn't make it home at night. She concluded that conversation with the news she was moving back to Yakima, Washington.

So, he took the engagement ring she handed him, put it back in its little velvet box, and then unhappily tucked it away in the safe he kept hidden at the cabin.

He was so busy for a while, tracking a killer and fending off a bomb-wielding drug cartel assassin, that he didn't have much time to think about Nancy or of what had transpired between them.

Or maybe that should be "expired" between us, he thought. But now that Lake County was living through a relatively peaceful spell, he had time to do a proper job of feeling sorry for himself.

Her voice on the phone last night brought all that business flooding back.

"Bud?" she asked when he answered.

"Yeah?"

"It's me. Nancy."

"Okay. What do you want?"

"I want to hear your voice, and I want to let you know I have my old job back."

Nancy thought he sounded startled when he said, "Here … in Lakeview?"

The sound of her old happy giggle and the vision of her dusty complexion, her beautiful green eyes, and her shiny auburn-flecked black hair tore his heart.

"Yes." She paused, and then said, "Bud, I want to see you. I think I have some explaining to do."

He was suspicious about what she had to say, but he suckered in anyway. "When?"

"How about tomorrow tonight … at the cabin?"

"Why?"

He heard the catch in her voice when she said, "Because I love you. Because I'm sorry. Because I worry about you as much as if we were married. Because … I just miss you. Are you going to be an asshole about this?"

That was a lot of territory to take in, especially after he thought the broken engagement was behind him, but he said, "Okay. Make it about seven. I'll burn us a steak." He didn't know if it was the hint of tears or the hint of the old fire in her voice that reeled him in, but there it was. The rumors were true. Nancy was back.

He kicked himself several times for his lack of spine, but it didn't dampen his excitement at all. He got busy picking up the newspapers and magazines that cluttered the cabin, sweeping the hardwood floor for the first time in a month, shaking out the area rugs, putting books back in the bookshelves, doing a week's worth of dirty dishes, making a quick pass at the bathroom, and bagging all the paper plates and plastic forks he was living with.

He fired up his little CD player and listened to "Take Five" and Dave Brubeck's marvelous syncopated rhythm while he tidied the cabin. He realized it was the first time in months he'd listened to any of his old jazz music.

Even as he cussed himself for being spineless, he used Windex and a kitchen towel to tackle the windows that looked out at the narrow north end of Dog Lake and the mass of willows that hid his small boat dock.

After Nancy left to go back home, it just hadn't seemed like housekeeping mattered much. Feeling a bit pressured, he had to ask himself why it mattered now? He knew, but he didn't want to admit it.

BB, his old partner from his detective days with the Portland Police Bureau, nagged him about letting things "go to hell." And he wasn't kind about the tummy bulge Bud was growing. "You need to get off your ass and start walking," he'd say. "Or get a bike and start riding, if you're too sorry to walk."

Bud's initial enthusiasm over BB's plans to build a new log home on a pine-covered lot next to Bud's A-frame faded after BB took to nagging him. It wore the shine right off his welcome. They were still friends, but they were working up to another fist fight, like the one years ago at The Greek's, a cop bar in Portland.

His friendship with BB was starting to read like a scene from the film, *Grumpy Old Men* … only he didn't know whether he was Jack Lemmon or Walter Matthau.

Between the new mountain bike he found leaning against his garage door yesterday – which he didn't doubt for a minute was BB's doing – and the phone call from Nancy, he knew his days of self-indulgent pouting were about to come to an end. And he wasn't sure he wanted them to. There was a certain amount of freedom in just not giving a damn.

5

Fussed

BUD PULLED INTO HIS RESERVED PARKING spot in the rear of the county courthouse, a flat-roofed, two-story, brick veneer building sheltered by tall deciduous trees of some variety. He admitted his lack of knowledge when it came to ornamental trees.

A dozen California quail, dark plume feathers bouncing, skittered across the lawn in front of the library entrance and east up Bullard Street in the direction of the town's swimming pool.

When he opened the metal entrance door, the first thing Karen Highsmith said was, "Have you heard that Nancy Sixkiller is back at her old job?"

He lied and shook his head because he wanted to hear what Karen thought about that. "No."

"Well," she sniffed. "I know she's pretty good at running the Emergency Services Center, and I suppose the Colonel will be glad to retire again, but I'm not impressed with the way she treated our sheriff."

She paused and looked up at Bud over the booking counter, her light brown curls bouncing a little as she shook her head and pursed her lips. "If she comes crawling, are you going to take her back?"

He just frowned and said, "As if that's any of your business."

"If it affects you and interferes with the way you run the Lake County Sheriff's Department, I think it is. Not that you've been paying much attention to your job these past few months anyhow."

She paused … and Bud waited … because he knew there was more to come. She worked as Bud's technical deputy in charge of the jail, and she also worked as his unofficial administrative assistant. Mainly, what he knew, she knew … and she knew what to keep to herself. Most of the time. It gave her license to say things Bud wouldn't allow any other person.

Native to the town of Lakeview, Karen was a fountain of information about who was doing what, with whom, and why. Between her, Agnes Lynch-Connor, and Police Chief Augustus Hildebrand, there wasn't much chance of anything staying secret for very long in the little town of Lakeview.

They did miss the business of a local banker killing old man Goodman, but that was the only miss he could point to. And he didn't feel too bad about that, because he solved that homicide with only a minor error in logic.

Karen took a deep breath … and in a softer tone said, "Bud, we just don't want to see you hurt again. You need a girlfriend, but not Nancy."

He tried not to growl and settled for a glare instead. "You got anybody in mind?"

He knew that was a rotten thing to say. Michelle Trivoli told him, when she was still working as a Lake County deputy sheriff, that Karen had a hard crush on Bud. All his nasty remark accomplished was to make him feel small and mean. But he didn't like all the interest Karen was showing in his empty love life.

Finally, he broke eye contact and just felt bad. "Oh, hell, Karen. I'll admit I haven't been much of a sheriff since Nancy pulled out."

"You've tried to act like it didn't matter," she nodded, "but your heart hasn't been in your work."

He nodded in agreement, remembered the mess at the cabin, and thought she was probably right … but settled for, "Enough, Karen. I'm back in the saddle, so you watch my dust."

Karen looked skeptical, but stayed silent.

"Where's Bea and Lonnie?" Bud asked, mainly to break the silence and put some sense of normalcy back in the conversation.

Karen looked at her notepad. "Bea is in Adel investigating a break-in at the store. Amy O'Fallon called and said she was burglarized last night."

"Doesn't Amy live in the back of the store?"

"Yes, but she said she stayed here in town last night. Too many deer down along Deep Creek to chance a trip back home. Says her eyesight isn't what it used to be."

Bud admired Amy O'Fallon, a small Vietnamese woman who married Army Sergeant Patrick O'Fallon in the fine city of Saigon many, many years ago. O'Fallon sent Amy home to his parents in the USA, and when he was discharged, he used his GI Bill to buy the Adel Stage Stop Tavern and Store in the isolated Warner Valley.

Bud still didn't know why O'Fallon never lost his liquor license, since his habit was to drink his way through each day. He finally had the good grace to die before making himself and Amy totally destitute. After Patrick's death, Amy worked the store alone. Recent rumors said one of Amy's granddaughters was coming to help.

Changing the subject, because he wanted Karen's opinion on something, he asked, "What do you think of Bea?"

Karen looked thoughtful before answering. "The thing I have to remember is that Beatrice Tusk is no Michelle. That doesn't make her worse or better. She's just different from Michelle. But I like her, and she seems to like us."

"Good. I like her too. I miss Michele some days, but Beatrice will do just fine. Dad met her when he came down from La Pine for a visit. He summed it up when he said, 'She's a pistol.'

"So … what have I missed, Karen?"

"You remember Lonnie talking about writing a grant for the funding to hire a new deputy?"

"Did he do that?"

"Yes. And the judge signed it … since you weren't here much."

"Ah yes, guilt, the gift that keeps on giving," he grumped. "And?"

"Well, we're getting a one-hundred-twenty-five-thousand-dollar grant."

"A onetime grant?"

"Yes."

"Hmm. So, what's the catch? The feds always tie strings to these things."

"One rationale Lonnie used was cleaning up old cases."

"Good, said Bud. We've got one dating back nearly thirty-five years." He suddenly grinned, looking happy for the first time in months. "I know just the gent for this."

Karen broke in, "Dell BeBe. Then he won't have time to pester you so much. Right?"

Bud studied Karen for a good five seconds before asking, "How do you know these things?"

"I heard you on the phone with Sonny Sixkiller. When you said you "wished he would just butt out," I knew you meant your friend BB."

Bud glared and stumped down the hall to his office. Just before the door slammed, Karen heard him utter a muted, "Women!"

"And Lonnie is working a wreck between Paisley and the hot springs," Karen shouted down the hall. She shook her head. "Bud just isn't focused. That's got to change."

BB's cell phone rang twice before Bud heard him say, "What do you want, honky?"

"Want a job?"

"Working for you?"

"Sort of. The feds are giving us a one-time grant to clean up old cases and take care of some other business. I figure you won't have so much time to mess with me if you have something useful to do for a change."

"Anything interesting?"

Bud nodded into the phone and said, "How does a thirty-five-year-old cold case sound?"

"What kind of case?"

"Homicide. Oregon State Police took ownership of the investigation and never reported back. When I checked with the OSP, they had no record of the homicide. What we do have is a report from the Lake County deputy sheriff who was first on the scene."

His tone serious for once, BB said, "You know, I could use a change in routine." He paused, and then asked, "You gonna be at the cabin this evening? There's somebody you should meet."

6

Dutch

BB ENTERED HIS TWO-STORY LOG home through the laundry room off the garage. To call it a 'mud room' was to besmirch BB's nearly fanatic need for cleanliness and order. If he hadn't worn a coat or jacket for six months, out it went. Sparse was a good choice of words for the décor. No bottles of detergent or bleach sat on the counter surrounding the laundry tub, no dust settled on the window sill. The foot rug was clean enough to use as a bath towel.

"OCD," he muttered as he opened an inner door into an open-beam family room, complete with a wall-mounted sixty-inch flat screen TV. "Or just too damned much time on my hands."

One wall played host to a floor-to-ceiling fireplace faced with gray river stones, each side flanked by built-in bookcases. A mahogany leather recliner and a matching leather couch fronted the hearth. Tall windows overlooked Dog Lake.

Above the mantle hung a 34x45-inch framed photo of Marine Sergeant Brian Dell BeBe, wearing a big grin and desert camo. He held a photo of his dad in one hand and a rifle in the other, an APC in the background.

BB had written Brian a letter of congratulations when he spotted the stripes on his son's sleeves. "Hey, Sarge! Looks like you intend to make a career of this military business. I'm proud of you, but if you are going to career-out in the Marines, at least apply for OCS. Officers live a whole lot better than enlisted men."

A copy of Teressa Foster's "Settlers in Summer Lake Valley" lay unopened on a polished oak writing desk, home to a printer, PC, and telephone.

BB sighed, the silence suddenly oppressive, cold, lonely.

He shook the feeling off and snorted. "To work," he said, and took the stairs two at a time up to the main floor.

***

DUTCH VANDERLIN, PORTLAND FBI SPECIAL AGENT in charge (SAC), was – in BB's opinion – a throwback to an earlier time. For starters, he answered his own phone, and unless he was online with someone, he almost always answered on the first ring. "Vanderlin," he growled.

"Dutch, this is BB. Do you know anything about some radical Muslims going after a local minister … a Reverend Thomas Jefferson Wildish?"

"Hold on." BB heard Dutch say, "Smitty, you got anything about radical Muslims moving against a local minister?"

Whatever Smitty said was muffled by the sound of paper rustling.

"BB," said Dutch, "I'm putting you on speaker. Okay?"

"Who's with you, Dutch?"

"The leader of our joint terrorism task force, Joseph Smith – 'Smitty' here at the office."

"Mister BeBe," Smith asked, "how did you come across this?"

"A loyal snitch."

Dutch broke in, "Are you talking about that little guy … what's his name … Cletus?"

"You know, Dutch, he's still pissed off about that last snatch-and-grab you pulled on him."

"Yeah, but he's alive."

BB shook his head. "He might not be for long. I understand his source, the one who fed us the disc with all those nice pictures of arms in the basement of the mosque, is dead – victim of a hit-and-run … but it wasn't an accident."

Dutch looked across the desk at Smitty, who nodded. "Confirmed, but we don't have enough evidence to make an arrest. The investigation is ongoing."

"And you suspect whom?"

Smitty shrugged his shoulders. Dutch shook his head, and then said, "You don't have a need to know."

Suddenly BB was angry – for the first time in months. "That's just bullshit and you know it. I'm bringing you information, and you have the gall to tell me it's none of my business."

Smitty's voice rose half an octave when he started to say, "Now listen, you ass…"

Dutch cut him off. "Truth time, BB. You have a history of using what I would term unconventional methods of investigation. If I tell you who the suspects are, I'm not sure I can trust you to leave them alone while we work the case." Dutch stopped and then asked, "Where in the hell are you, anyway?"

"Home."

"Home Portland or home Lakeview?"

"I don't have a Portland home."

"Don't go blowing smoke up my ass. We know you still keep a high-rise apartment here in Portland."

"Dutch, I know you are tracing this call as we speak, so you don't even have to ask where I am. But, because we are old friends, I'm about twenty-five miles west of Lakeview."

"And I'd guess you're going to hide your friend, TJ Wildish, out there in the pucker brush?"

"Well … it's been nice talking to you Dutch I guess you already know everything anyway."

"Hold on. Hold on." Smitty said. "How far are you from the Lake County Airport?"

"About the same twenty-five miles."

"If I sent an agent down there, would you meet her there and pick her up?"

"A woman?"

"Yes."

"Good looking?"

"Irrelevant," Smitty snapped. "She's one of the brightest agents on the task force."

"Give me a name."

Smitty said, "Special Agent Miranda Wright."

BB snorted and said, "Miranda Rights? Are you kidding me?"

"That's Wright – W-r-i-g-h-t. – no 's.' And I'm not kidding you. We'll have to call you back with the details, but I want her to interview your friend, Reverend Wildish. Maybe he can help us find out who leaked the information that got our informant killed. You know the drill: who talked to whom … work it backwards."

"And I was getting bored," BB said. "Dutch, I'd like someone to go get the reverend's computer. I emailed him some photos of my new house … and the directions to find it."

"Oops. Not good. Smitty, get somebody over there now."

BB heard Smitty ask, "Which church?"

Dutch said, "I've got the address. It's the Rock of Ages Church in Northeast, near Grant High School."

"I'll get Agent Wright headed your way. She'll need to stay over. Let her use a spare bedroom, BB, or you can put her up in one of the motels in town. I'll leave that up to you."

After BB hung up, Smitty looked at his boss and asked, "How well do you know this guy?"

Dutch laughed and said, "Pretty well … he's godfather to my children, and he was one hell of a detective for the Portland Police Bureau. Retired last fall. Now he's the only black man living in Lake County, Oregon."

Dutch paused, then added, "BB and I have had our differences. He's a hard man to love, but we're still good friends. That said, his best friend in the whole wide world is the sheriff of Lake County."

"Bud Blair."

"You've been doing your homework."

"We study his methods in dealing with drug cartels and terrorists … and in dealing with the press."

"Learn anything?"

"Yeah, like how not to do it. Who in his right mind sets himself up as bait for a trap? And it seems like he always goes out of his way to tee off reporters."

Dutch raised his eyebrows and stared at Smitty. "He gets results, though, doesn't he?" It wasn't a question. "I want you to find Cletus Falls and offer him protective custody. We can stash him at our safe house in West Hills. Make sure he understands we aren't kidnapping him again.

7

Newcomers

Bud was slightly ashamed of himself for being so mean to Karen, but he wasn't very good at apologies, so he settled for cleaning off his desk. He tried to concentrate on bulletins he'd ignored for several weeks, then went over two reports from the local interagency task force meetings – meetings he'd missed. Those dealt with child welfare issues: things like child abuse, domestic violence, runaway children, foster care, child support payments … or lack thereof.

He shook his head, put the stack of papers back in his inbox, and rocked back in his old wooden captain's chair. He sat there staring at the big map of Lake County pinned to the cork board covering the wall. Red stick pins marking closed cases, green ones on-going cases.

He said, "Enough," and turned back to his desk. "Yep," he decided. He looked up the number of the local flower shop and ordered a dozen roses, to be delivered post haste to Karen Highsmith at the Lake County Sheriff's Office.

"Have the card say something like … no, I changed my mind. No card. She'll know who it's from."

The pile of after-action reports from his officers was a week old, but he forgave himself for being tardy and started working through the stack.

Deputy Sheriff Beatrice Tusk had written a speeding ticket to an Idahoan who thought the open highways of southeastern Oregon were an invitation to play race car driver. She clocked him at ninety-five on her radar. She'd also taken a report of a missing thoroughbred stallion from a ranch owner, whose place sat between Highway 395 and Goose Lake, south of town. Bea sent a BOLO with a picture and a useful description of the horse to neighboring police jurisdictions.

Officer Lonnie Beltram was investigating the shooting of a steer in the Rabbit Hills, northwest of Plush. He was waiting on ballistics from the slug he and the rancher dug from the carcass. There was also a picture of tire tracks in a mud hole near the shooting. Lonnie was using pictures of the tracks to search for a tread match from tire manufacturers. *Good solid police work*, Bud thought, *but not much chance of success.*

Only one of the ongoing cases piqued his interest: a drive-by shooting in north Lake County, just a few miles west of the tiny town of Christmas Valley. There were no injuries.

In his report, Deputy Sheriff Roger Hildebrand included a photo of a dark blue bandana wrapped around a rusted rural mailbox wired to the side of a faded lodgepole pine fence post. A dirt lane led out through the sagebrush to an ancient single-wide trailer. The trailer, perched on cinder blocks, stood as companion to a faded, derelict VW bus parked next to what looked to be a slapped-together outhouse.

Bud pulled his cell phone from his shirt pocket and called Roger's number.

"That you, Boss?"

"One and the same."

"Good to hear your voice. I was beginning to think you were MIA."

"Are you going to start in on me, too? Karen already took care of the butt chewing. I called to see what you think about this drive-by shooting."

"You know, Boss, the bandana makes me think it could be gang-related."

Bud nodded. "It smacks of my days in Portland. You want a hand with this one?"

"No. But if you are finally through feeling sorry for yourself, you need to make the rounds. Go see the judge, talk to the Lake County News … contact your friends. Word is that a wealthy rancher from Montana bought the Z-BAR and is very interested in removing you from your job come the next election.

He plans to run his ranch foreman, an Iraq war veteran – decorated hero – for sheriff. Said you weren't doing your job, you're using antiquated methods and so on, and so on. Made a big splash at a Paisley town meeting night before last. He didn't run you down exactly, just implied you were old-fashioned … like that was some kind of cussword. I think he plans to run this county as his own personal fiefdom."

"You're kidding me."

"Afraid not, Boss. I know you aren't much of a politician, but you'd better learn how the game is played, or you'll become last year's news – despite all the good you've done. You know the old saying: 'What have you done for me lately?'"

"I don't know if I want this job anymore."

Roger ignored that self-pitying remark and said, "You do know Nancy is back?"

"Yes. Yes, I do."

"Pitiful."

"What do you mean by that?"

"I mean people are giving odds that you'll be married before the month is out."

"Don't bet on it."

"It won't hurt your chances of being re-elected, Boss. And don't tell me you don't want to keep your job."

"Well, damn. You're just full of good news. Go talk to whoever is living in that wreck of a trailer again, and see if there's gang trouble brewing."

"Hard to believe, isn't it?"

"Four or five years ago, I would've agreed. But when the cartels came after us, I started thinking anything was possible."

"By the way, Boss. We need to hire a new deputy. Larae said she was determined to be a stay-at-home mom."

"Well, damn." Bud took a deep breath … then said, "Okay. Ask her to think it over. And if she's still serious, I'll need a formal letter of resignation. You know, Roger, I'm wondering if Gar, I mean John Bernard, would work for us?"

"Doubt it, Boss. You want me to ask?"

"Do it. And keep me posted of any progress on this drive-by shooting."

"One more thing, Boss. You'll be getting a call from Sonny. He and Carol Connor are getting married, and she plans to keep on running the Lake County News. It means he wants his old job back … and since you never got around to hiring an undersheriff…"

"I've been waiting for you to ask for that job."

"I like it up here in North County."

"Tell him to call and the job is his."

Bud hung up and was reaching for the phone again when Karen knocked and pushed his door open without waiting. She put a vase with a dozen long stem red roses on his desk. "These just came. No tag."

"No tag? Well, dang. They're for you. An apology."

She put her hands on her hips and stared for a long ten seconds. Somehow, she reminded him of his mother when she was about to give a much younger Bud Blair the "What for."

Karen slowly shook her head. "Bud, you are just about the dumbest man I know when it comes to women. You should only send flowers in the good times, and keep your mouth shut in the bad."

Bud frowned, reached for the flowers, then dropped them, vase and all, in his wastebasket. "Okay. Lesson learned."

Karen stooped to retrieve them and glared at the sheriff. "Well, we can't waste these beautiful roses." Then she whirled on her heel and took them back down the hall.

8

Molly

B UD FIDDLED WITH UNINTERESTING PAPERWORK, DRANK a second cup of coffee, and stalled off the dreaded trip to see Molly … and the vet. He finally snagged his tan Stetson off the hat rack and walked up front.

"Karen, I have to be gone for a bit. I'll be on the radio if you need me."

She started to say, "That'll be a welcome change," but something in his eyes stopped her. She settled for a nod. "Okay."

He knew it had to be done, but he also knew he wasn't going to like what was coming. He wound up circling the block twice before pulling into the parking lot. He sat and stared at the white concrete block building that housed the veterinary, at the chuckhole in the asphalt paving leading around back to the barn and the stables, and at the orange tabby perched on the window sill, soaking up the morning sun.

Brenda Brown, Doc Saunders' lanky, redheaded assistant watched until she saw Bud open the pickup door. She walked to the back and said to the big gray-haired, crewcut man stitching up a wounded cat, "Doc, the sheriff's here."

"Okay. I'm finished with this guy," he said, pointing to a sedated tomcat that lost a fight with a bigger tomcat. "Give this old-timer his antibiotics and wrap him up."

He peeled off the blue latex gloves, stuffed them in the disposal, and sighed. Saunders liked being a vet. He didn't like sheep or goats, but he liked doctoring when he could actually save someone's beloved milk cow, horse, dog, hamster, ferret, Myna bird … or tomcat.

But that wasn't the case this time, and he dreaded giving Bud the bad news.

This was a special dog, and not just to Bud. Local people were used to knowing which county pickup was the sheriff's because the little black Lab had her nose stuck out the window, ears floating in the breeze. And somehow the dog sent a message that the sheriff was one of the good guys and not just some hard-nosed cop.

Brenda patted Doc's meaty shoulder. "I'll take care of this tabby. You take care of our sheriff."

Bud followed Doc to a room in back. Molly was laying on a stainless steel examination table, too sick to do more than try to wag her tail. Bud stroked Molly's head, watched another listless twitch of her tail and listened to a quiet whimper.

Without being asked, Doc said in a quiet and sympathetic voice, "She's in pain and probably won't live more than a few more hours. You should let me put her down. It's the kindest thing we can do now. And if you want, I can have her cremated."

Bud said, "Damn," and then nodded. He said flatly, "No, no cremation. I'll pick her up this afternoon and take her back to the cabin … bury her down by the lake."

The vet started to say he was sorry, but the look of sorrow in Bud's hazel eyes stopped him. "I'll have her in a nice box suitable for burial."

Without another word, Bud petted Molly one more time, then turned quickly to walk briskly out the door and back to his pickup.

Doc looked at Brenda and shook his head. "Bud didn't cry, but I think I'll cry for him. He hasn't had a good run this year."

Brenda nodded and smiled, her blues eyes twinkling. "I think he's going to be a lot happier soon."

Doc frowned and asked, "What do you know?"

"Nancy Sixkiller is back living in town. You see, Doc," she said patiently, like a mother instructing a fairly dense child, "Bud never got himself a new girlfriend, which tells the ladies of the town he's still carrying the torch for Nancy.

"So, he grieves for Molly, Nancy consoles Bud, Bud likes being consoled, and then Mother Nature takes over. Ergo, I'll bet you twenty dollars Nancy marries our sheriff … and soon."

"Soon?"

"Pregnant ladies like to marry the fathers. Especially unmarried pregnant ladies."

Doc shook his head, his gray eyes amused, and asked, "How do you know all this?"

"Well, she's been gone almost six months, and she looks to be about six months pregnant. Now, she's back. So, we think our sheriff is the daddy."

"You ladies sure spend a lot of time digging into other people's business."

Brenda laughed. "She isn't the only woman in the county who finds Bud attractive. If I wasn't happily married…"

9

Rescue

C LETUS HELPED THE OLD WOMAN CARRY her packages to the front door of an older, well-kept single-story home a block off Fremont. She said, "Thank you, young man. Your mama raised you right," but she didn't invite him in. And in truth he didn't want to bring trouble to her door.

He trotted back to Fremont, caught the first bus heading east, and got off on 57th. He started walking south on 57th, then ten minutes later he caught a short hop on the southbound TriMet bus towards the Hollywood District.

A neon "Open" sign over the entrance to Mary's, a mom and pop café sitting just south of Sandy Boulevard, looked to be the best bet for getting off the street and out of sight.

He nodded to an apron clad, gray-haired woman who was pouring coffee into a big white mug that was parked in front of an elderly man.

Cletus heard her say, "Stan, Evelyn's been gone a year now. You need to get out and meet some new people, maybe even a nice widow woman."

Cletus slid into a booth where he could watch the door. "Be right with you," she said across the room.

Cletus waited until she took his order for coffee and a cinnamon roll, then he pulled out his wallet and thumbed through a collection of business cards until he found the one he wanted.

FBI Special Agent Sara Watkins answered on the second ring. "Special Agent Watkins. What can I do for you?"

"Sara, this be Cletus, Cletus Falls. I hope you remember me."

"Yes I do, Cletus. How have you been?"

"Well, I was pretty good until Reggie got hisself killed. You know the dude I'm talking about?"

"Yes. The informant who gave you the pictures of all those guns in the mosque we raided last year."

"Yeah. That one. You know he's dead?"

"Yes. I know."

"Good. No, I mean it's good you know about it, not good that Reggie's dead. Now listen, Sara, I had a black dude shooting at me about half-hour ago. Never saw him before. Came at me. Asked if I was Cletus. Pulled a gun … and I ran. Got a bus between him and me and ran all the way to the Lloyd Center.

"I think they made Reggie talk before they killed him. Probably told them who I was. Maybe told them about taking the pitchers in the basement of the mosque."

"Hold on, Cletus. I'll be right back."

He nodded as the waitress set down his coffee and a china plate cradling a hot cinnamon roll coated with warm icing that worked hard at dripping on the table. A smaller plate held two little tinfoil-wrapped squares of butter, a butter knife, and a fork. "Thank you," he mouthed.

Sara came back on line. "Cletus, how would you like to spend a couple of days at our safe house in West Hills?"

He had a flashback to the first time he saw this attractive FBI agent. He was sure he would never forget the pull of her teal-colored blouse against a shapely bosom. "You going to be there?"

She laughed and said, "No. Someone else is in charge of the house now, but if you'd like I can come by for a visit. Now, where are you?"

"I'm in a café called Mary's. It's on 57th near Sandy in Northeast. Don't know the number."

"That's okay. You sit tight. We'll send a car for you. Agents Brandt and Wilcox will pick you up."

Ten minutes later he dabbed his icing-coated lips with a paper napkin and watched a black Ford Expedition pull up against the curb in front of Mary's. Two suits got out. *FBI for sure. One black dude and one white.*

The two agents studied the street and then walked into the café.

Without preamble, they slid onto the bench opposite Cletus. Special Agent Brandt showed Cletus his ID and asked, "Mr. Falls, do you have any picture ID?"

"How do you know who I am?"

Special Agent Wilcox, who somehow reminded Cletus of Dell BeBe, said, "Well, we don't. But we were told to look for a black man in Mary's café." He swiveled his head to look at the nearly empty café. "You're it."

Cletus opened his wallet and showed them his Portland State student body card before saying, "You guys need a little imagination. I mean, a black SUV? You might as well paint 'Cop' on the sides."

Agent Wilcox grinned and said, "But that's who we are. Shall we go, Mister Falls?"

Cletus put a five-dollar bill on the table and, sandwiched between the two agents, walked out to the big Ford Expedition.

When Wilcox headed for the on-ramp to get on I-84 West, Cletus was comfortable, but when he took the exit to I-5 North, Cletus said, "Hey. This isn't the way to the West Hills. Where we going?"

The white dude, Special Agent Brandt, turned and looked back at Cletus. "Sorry. We want to take a statement about what happened when the perp shot at you. And we want you to look at some mug shots. See if you can identify the man. We'll do that at FBI headquarters. Then we'll take you to the safe house. Okay?"

"Okay. Where is FBI headquarters?"

"Out by the airport."

10

The Gathering Storm

BUD BACKED THE COUNTY'S WHITE PICKUP with a gold "Lake County Sheriff" shield on each door into his reserved slot on E street, then shut the diesel engine down. By habit he studied the street and, satisfied no threat was visible, took a deep breath, picked his tan Stetson off the passenger seat, and settled it on his head.

His cell phone rang before he opened the pickup door. "Sheriff Blair," he answered.

"Listen, Bud," BB said without preamble, "an FBI agent will be landing at the Lakeview Airport in about two hours. I'd go myself, but I need to be here at the house."

"And you want me to pick him up?"

"Yeah. I do. But it's a her, not a him."

"And do what with her?"

"Bring her out to the lake, to my house."

"What's going on, BB?"

"Do you remember TJ Wildish?"

"Sure. The little guy who got himself straightened out several years back. And then became a reverend of some kind."

"Right. He helped the FBI identify the stud duck on the Portland terrorist pond and gave the FBI the information needed for a warrant to search the mosque in Northeast."

"Okay," Bud said. "What else?"

"The informant who gave my snitch, Cletus, all the nice pictures of arms in the basement of the mosque? He was killed in a hit-and-run accident. FBI forensics is saying it wasn't an accident. And I'm afraid he was tortured for information before he was 'accidentally' run down. I got word some radical Muslims are after TJ. I'm going to hide him out here until we get this sorted out."

"Judas Priest!" Bud said.

"Dutch is sending this FBI agent down here to interview TJ, if he ever gets here, and try to work it in reverse. You know the drill … TJ heard from somebody, who heard from somebody else, who… Anyway, the FBI is hoping to gather enough information to make some arrests, and then TJ can go home again without fear of anything worse than a random mugging."

"All right. Does this FBI agent have a name?"

"You are not going to believe this, Bud. Her name is Miranda Wright."

Bud Chuckled and said, "Wow. I'll bet she takes a lot of ribbing from her cohorts."

"Her boss says she's one of the best."

"When will she be here?"

"Her plane is due at about one-thirty."

"Miranda Wright. Okay. I'll be there. Will she need a ride back to the airport?"

"No. She'll stay overnight out here at the lake."

Bud's cell phone chimed twice, telling him another call was coming in. "Gotta go, BB. See you this afternoon."

Bud picked up the call. "Sheriff Blair."

"Bud, this is Nancy. I just heard about Molly from Brenda Brown, the vet's assistant. I'm so sorry."

"Yeah," he said, "I am, too. I'm going to bury her down by the lake." He took a deep breath and, without really meaning to, said, "I just can't imagine not watching her run down to the dock to bark at the mud hens."

"Don't you do anything before I get there," she ordered. "I'm coming out right after my shift."

Bud nodded and said, "I'll wait."

"I love you, Bud Blair."

He could hardly speak past the lump in his throat, and despite his best resolve to remain indifferent to Nancy, he whispered into the phone, "I love you, too."

11

Homeward

B UD KILLED THE CALL AND TOOK another deep breath. *Pride be damned. I'm not going to fight it. I want her back. Besides, it isn't like she left me for another man. That makes a difference … at least to me.*

He opened the pickup door and suddenly felt better than he had in a long time. Not even the shadow of Molly dying could totally eclipse his sense that maybe life was worth something after all.

He pushed through the entrance to the Lake County Sheriff's Office, took note of the red roses perched on the booking counter, and grinned—knowing he was forgiven.

"Karen, locate Lonnie and Bea and find out when they'll be back. I need coverage. And I'm bringing Sonny home."

"Home?"

"Yes. Back here as our undersheriff. He and Carol Connor are getting married. Roger says Sonny wants his old job back."

"Wonderful! Now if you can just get Michelle back…"

"Not in the cards. But the thought of having Sonny here sure brightens my day," he said over his shoulder as he hurried to his office.

Bud's office door slammed shut and Karen said quietly to herself, "That's the most energy I've seen in months." She knew she and Bud were not destined to be more than good friends, but she still felt protective of her sheriff.

Bud picked up his office phone, punched in the number, and waited until he heard Sonny say, "Officer Sixkiller."

"Hey, you old rattlesnake. How's life in Bend?"

"Is that you, Boss?"

"One and the same. The sagebrush telegraph says you and Carol are getting married."

"Well, we finally worked it out … I mean a cop married to a reporter. At least I hope so."

"Congratulations. I also hear you plan to live in Lakeview."

Sonny laughed. "You've been talking to Roger, haven't you?"

"You need to know I was planning to bring Roger back to town as my undersheriff. Now he says he doesn't want the job. Lonnie Beltram has been filling in, but it's makeshift at best."

"Boss, are you offering me a job?"

"Want to work for me again?"

Sonny said, "Well, I'd have to take a cut in pay…" And then he laughed. "You bet! I'll need to give notice. I'll try to talk Sheriff Reynolds into letting me go in two weeks, but it's likely to be more like a month."

Bud offered, "I'll call Reynolds and see what I can do."

"I like it up here in the big city of Bend. But it's just not as personal. Too many people live in Deschutes County to get acquainted with anyone outside of the sheriff's department. By the way, how's old man Peale doing?"

"Still alive as far as I know. Still lives all by himself. Officer Beatrice Tusk stops and checks on him about once a week, takes him his mail, makes sure he has something in the fridge to eat … sort of like you did when you were here."

"Good. I'm glad to hear that. How is Bea working out?"

"I think she's a good hand. But, hell Sonny, I don't know that for sure. I've been a bit … distracted."

"Don't worry about it, Boss. You can make it up to her."

"Okay then. I'll call Sheriff Reynolds and see what he says."

"Looking forward to working for you again, Boss."

"Me, too."

The knock on his door was followed by Karen Highsmith, who was holding a folder against her breast. "Well?" she said.

Bud nodded. "He's coming back. Now, I want you to work with HR and make this a formal offer."

She stepped to his desk, opened the folder, and handed it to him. "Sign and date at the bottom of the form."

Bud looked surprised, then said, "I should've known…"

"Yes. Now, you go talk to the judge, touch base, let him know you're bringing Sonny back, and I'll do the rest."

12

Miranda Wright

BUD LEANED AGAINST THE SIDE OF his pickup and watched the aircraft, a bright blue twin-engine, propeller-driven plane of some sort, circle to the north and then line up on the runway.

His conversation with Judge Lynch had been enlightening and brief. The tall, silver-haired rancher, turned county judge and chief county administrator said, "Yes. By all means, bring Sonny back."

Lynch also gave Bud a hard look and asked, "Where have you been spending your time? You do know the new owner of the Z-BAR is talking about running his foreman for sheriff?"

Bud nodded. "I did hear that, just this morning."

"I'm going to suggest you start circulating again. Go visit with people. Have coffee in the Homestead Restaurant in Paisley. Buy gas at the Summer Lake Store. Give talks to the schools, meet with the Chamber of Commerce, join the Lions … hell, I don't know, but you need people to see that you are on the job."

Bud just stared at him, until the judge finally said, "It isn't being political to let people know you like your job and that you've been there for them in the past. If you drop out of sight, the message is … you don't care."

Bud nodded. "The way a man does his job should count for something, but I guess I need to do more. Thanks. I guess."

"Welcome. I'll grease the skids for you to get Sonny Sixkiller back over here. And I'll publicly endorse you for sheriff – if you get off your behind and start acting like a sheriff again."

Judge Lynch stood up and held out his hand. "I like you. I think you've been good for this county, but there is no resting on your laurels."

***

BUD LISTENED FOR THE CHIRP OF the tires as the plane touched down, but couldn't quite hear it over the noise of engines revving and propellers reversing as the plane quickly shed speed, then taxied in his direction. When the engines died and the props stopped turning, the cabin door opened and a set of steps dropped down.

He walked to the aircraft and waited until a tall, slender black woman wearing designer jeans, cowboy boots, and an unzipped USC sweat shirt protecting a white blouse stepped to the tarmac. She had a daypack in one hand and a briefcase in the other.

Bud wasn't sure why he was surprised, but he'd just never connected the FBI with beautiful women. He stepped forward and held out his hand. "Agent Wright?"

She set the daypack down, gave him a dazzling smile and shook hands. "Yes, and you've got to be Sheriff Blair. I've read quite a bit about you. It's nice to finally meet you in the flesh."

"Can't have been all good."

She grinned and said, "Mostly. We in the FBI do think you could use some coaching when it comes to dealing with the press."

"Maybe. I do know one reporter I like and trust."

"Just one?"

Bud smiled and reached for her daypack. "Just one. Although there is a TV anchorwoman in Klamath Falls I might learn to trust."

"Well, I didn't say trust. I said, 'deal with.'"

"Same thing for me. Why deal with them if you can't trust them?"

Bud opened the passenger door to his truck, waited for Agent Wright to settle into the seat, and then closed the door. He put her daypack in the back seat of the Quad Cab Ram and then settled behind the steering wheel.

He started the rumbling diesel engine and drove across the parking lot to the main road. To be polite, he asked, "How was your flight?"

"Loved it. The peaks of the Cascades still have snow on them. Just beautiful. And the air was so calm that we didn't bounce around much."

He nodded and said, "There's something I have to do in town before we head to Dog Lake."

"Okay by me. You know, Lakeview surprises me. I mean, you don't think of the high desert as full of lakes, mountains, meadows, trees … or towns for that matter." She pointed at the big peak a few miles southeast of the tree-shaded town tucked in against the west flanks of the Warner Range. "What's the name of that mountain?"

"That's Crane Mountain. Rugged looking, isn't it, with all its fault scarps?"

"And that little peak in behind the town, that must be Black Cap. I read about Lake County as I was flying down. I guess hang gliders use it for take-offs?" She laughed and said, "I don't think I'd have the nerve."

Bud shook his head and chuckled, liking the sound of her voice. "I like my feet firmly on the ground."

She laid her briefcase on her lap and opened her electronic notebook. "I did some research on my trip down here. It told me Lake County is big – really big – over eighty-three hundred square miles big."

He slowed as a rooster pheasant skittered across the road and dove into the cattails lining the ditch. About fifty big geese, wings set, coasted into a field next to the highway, hungry for the tender green shoots of wheat carpeting the fertile soil.

Bud glanced at her and said, "Yep, and pretty empty. Less than one person per square mile. I always tell visitors we run long on timber, cattle, and high lonesome."

"I took a nice shot from the airplane of Abert Lake and Abert Rim. Wow. I read the rim is at least thirty miles long, stands about twenty-five hundred feet above the valley, and the basalt rim is about eight hundred feet of sheer cliffs. I've never seen anything like it."

Bud nodded, pleased somehow that she had taken the time to be interested in one of his favorite places. "Hooked me, it did, on my first trip down here. I mean the whole country, not just Abert Rim."

She smiled, her hazel eyes lighting up in amusement. "That was after you got the boot from the Portland Police Bureau. Right?"

"What are you talking about?"

"I'm talking about a Portland Police Bureau detective who got himself shot by a punk with a pistol and then divorced because he dedicated more time to his job than his marriage. A little too much drinking was in order, until your captain suggested you stop drinking and maybe try a new job in Lakeview."

"How do you know all that?"

"Let me see now. I must have read your file, but most of it I got from our SAC."

"I don't know what you are doing with a file on me, but Dutch talks too much."

"Yes, he does, but he admires you nonetheless. Said he's going to recruit you if you ever decide to leave this little corner of paradise."

I would, too, she suddenly thought.

Bud eased up to the stop sign on the Klamath Falls highway, put the gearshift in neutral, and then turned to look at her. "I'm doing this as a favor to Dell BeBe, not to hear an analysis of my past mistakes."

A bright red Ford F-250 pulled up behind Bud and honked. Bud glanced in the rearview mirror and waved, put the pickup back in gear and pulled out on the highway, heading east into town.

"One of the Arnold brothers," he said nodding at the pickup behind him. "They have a nice cattle and hay ranch on the north end of Goose Lake."

Changing the subject, she thought.

He turned left just past the railroad tracks and pulled into the veterinary office parking lot. "I'll be right back," he said, "so don't go away."

She watched him walk through the front door, nodded, and thought, *I wasn't prepared for this. The photos and the reports don't do him justice. He's not pretty-boy handsome, but he has rugged good looks. I even like that little scar over his left eyebrow. And he has charisma. I'll bet he stirs the heart of every single woman in Lake County. I know he stirs mine.*

She opened her laptop and scrolled to the video she'd watched of an angry Bud Blair giving the television media the "What for" after the run in with the terrorists who blew themselves up someplace near Fort Rock.

Bud carried a waxed cardboard box that looked heavy. He opened the rear passenger door on the driver's side, wedged the box through the opening, and then slammed the door.

Miranda looked at him quizzically, but Bud just shook his head and backed the pickup around to head for Five Corners.

Miranda had the good sense to say nothing.

13

Safe Harbor?

SPECIAL AGENT WILCOX EXPERTLY PUSHED THE big SUV up a winding, narrow West Hills street through the sun-dappled tunnels of fir, alder, and maple trees, past houses perched on piling driven into tree-covered hillsides that might, or might not, be stable.

Every few years, the news shared pictures of a house riding a mudslide downslope into someone's back yard. The hillsides might not be stable, but the view of the city and the green expanse of fir-covered hills to the east, with Mount Hood in the background, was enough to encourage the risk.

After two hours of looking at the FBI's file of digital mugshots of black men known to have radical Muslim connections, Cletus managed to ID two who might have been the shooter. "The problem I see," he said, "is the dude who shot at me had a beard, and most of these pitchers show men with beards."

He pointed to one photo and said, "This dude sort of looks right, and he's about the right age and height, while this other dude looks like the guy who shot at me, but you say he's only five-feet-seven. Too short. You got more pitchers?"

Wilcox shook his head. "No. That's all we have.

Brandt looked over the top of Cletus' head and shrugged. He said, "I guess we better take you to the safe house. If you think of anything else, like a scar maybe – anything that would help us identify this man – have the agent at the house put you in touch with us."

***

THE SAFE HOUSE WASN'T REALLY AN ordinary house. It was a late nineteenth-century mansion built by an early Oregon entrepreneur grown wealthy from interests in shipping, lumber, land, and politics. Century-old fir trees cloaked the view and hid all but the turret tower.

Wilcox turned down a narrow lane, followed its winding path through the trees, and stopped in front of an iron gate flanked by red brick gate posts about twelve feet tall. Just beyond the gate sat a nasty row of big, ugly, steel teeth … just waiting to eat unwelcome tires.

Here we go again, Cletus thought.

Wilcox leaned out the window of the SUV and entered a series of numbers into a keypad. The steel teeth sank back into the pavement, and the big metal gate quietly swung inward. Brandt followed a circle drive and stopped just beyond the front entrance, under a tall breezeway protected by a narrow, brick walk. A side door opened and a tall, gaunt, forty-something man in a dark blue suit stepped through and waited.

Wilcox jumped out and opened the rear passenger door for Cletus. "There's your guardian angel, Cletus." He handed Cletus a business card and said, "If you need me, call me." Cletus nodded and Wilcox held out his hand. "We'll keep an eye on your mama's house, catch any boogers that come by."

Cletus watched the big SUV complete the circle and leave by the same tall gate. He looked up at the turret tower and wondered why the FBI spent so much money on a mansion. What he didn't know was the FBI purchased the property from the last heirs of the timber baron for use as a safe house, a communications center, and a training park for undercover agents. As terrorism grew, so did the FBI's budget.

The tall agent waited patiently in front of the side door for Cletus to finish gawking and start down the walk. "Welcome, Mister Falls. I understand you've been here before. Agent Watkins asked me to tell you she'll be up this afternoon. Miss Wilson, our house mother had to go into town, so I'm filling in for her. My name is Winslow Butler." He smiled and added, "Sort of fitting today, don't you think?"

In spite of himself, Cletus smiled and shook Butler's hand. "Am I under house arrest, like the last time?"

Butler grimaced and said, "Well, you'll have the run of the house, most of it at any rate … and you can walk the grounds. You can leave anytime you choose. But for your own safety, it would be a good idea to stay on the property."

Cletus nodded. "Last time I was confined to my suite, the pool, and the gym. You guys didn't want me talking to anyone until the raid took place."

"That was different. This time, we just want to protect you until we settle the score with some people we think are jihadists. Come on in. I'll show you to your room."

"If I'm not under house arrest, I'd really like to see the view from the tower."

"I don't see any problem with that. Follow me."

As they climbed the winding stairway to the tower, Butler asked, "Where did you stash your preacher friend, TJ Wildish?"

Cletus' warning system kicked in, and he said nothing.

14

Bad News

Bud DROVE ACROSS THE IRRIGATED FARM and pasture land, heading west toward the gap in the hills that carried the swift waters of Drews Creek, before Miranda broke a very strained silence.

"Want to talk about it?"

"Talk about what?"

"Whatever."

"No."

"Okay, then. Tell me about your friend Dell BeBe."

"A fine man. A good cop. A good friend. A good father. I guess he wasn't so hot as a husband."

"That's it?"

"That's all you're entitled to."

Bud's cell phone vibrated in his shirt pocket. He ignored it until it stopped.

"Aren't you going to answer that?"

"Nope."

The vehicle climbed the first hill and up into the pine timber before crossing the Drews Creek bridge.

"I'm sorry about your dog," she said.

"Are you always this damned intrusive?"

"You know, my first and only husband accused me of being too nosy. Although being nosy about him was the right idea. He was a philandering cheat.

"Anyway, I know I have this terrible habit of just blurting out what I'm thinking. I don't mean to offend you, but I think you've been having a bad day."

A big mule deer doe jumped out of the willows along the creek bottom and clawed her way up the steep side slope, in a hurry to get across the pavement and back into the timber. He tapped the brakes and slowed enough to let her scramble on out of the way and leap a barbed wire boundary fence.

"That's just beautiful. What kind of deer is that?"

He shook his head, but she watched a slow smile work on his mouth. "They're called mule deer because their ears are so much bigger than the other breeds. Must have reminded some early explorer of a flop-eared mule."

"That's interesting." She paused and then added, "My mother said when I was a little girl I told her I wanted to know everything."

"But she neglected to tell you that silence is golden?"

Miranda laughed. "I think she did say that. But I never listened."

"How can you be a cop and have so little impulse control?"

"Oh, I have plenty of impulse control when it comes to dealing with criminals. But not with people who are hurting. I saw dog hair on the seat, and I recognized the burial box. My assumption is your dog died."

He growled, "I could learn to hate cops, if I wasn't one myself."

Bud's cell phone buzzed again and this time he answered it. Dutch said, "Has Special Agent Wright arrived yet?"

Bud growled and said, "Ask her yourself, and next time warn me about your very special agent." He handed the phone to Miranda and said, "Your boss."

Bud heard her say, "Miranda," and then nothing for a good two minutes while she listened to whatever Dutch was saying. Bud couldn't hear Dutch, but in his peripheral vision he saw Miranda start to speak and then simply nod.

Finally, she said, "I'll tell him. Thank you, sir."

She killed the call and handed Bud his phone. "Okay. Let me summarize. Our agents checked the rectory of the Rock of Ages Church in northeast Portland. A neighbor can see the door to the rectory from her kitchen window. She told our agents three young men entered the rectory, and a few minutes later they left carrying what looked to be a PC. Our agents failed to find a computer when they searched a short while later.

"The neighbor says she didn't call it in because the Reverend Wildish never locks his door, and people are always coming and going. She did say the men felt wrong somehow to her, so she took pictures of them with her digital camera … just in case."

"Any idea why they wanted the computer?"

"Yes, and it isn't good. Dell BeBe told my boss he sent the reverend several pictures of his new house and the directions to find it. That's why our agents went to the rectory in the first place – to make sure the bad guys didn't find his PC."

Bud took a deep breath and said, "So someone got there ahead of them."

"I'm afraid so."

"Hmm … how much time does that give us to prepare a surprise party?"

"Like you did with the thugs Ortega sent your way?"

Bud frowned. "Something like that. I had a lot of help from your SWAT team that time."

He paused, watching a dark brown Jeep coming at them. The driver waved and Bud waved back. "That's Jake Abernathy. He owns a house on Drews Reservoir."

He took a deep breath and said, "I'm thinking I get the reverend and BB safely out of the way, then we bait the trap with an email from BB to TJ saying he's glad TJ finally decided to come and visit. Finish with something like 'See you this afternoon.' I think they'll be watching for messages, trying to identify TJ's circle of friends."

Miranda nodded in agreement. "It will take them at least twenty-four hours to plan an attack, and maybe another twenty-four to forty-eight hours to execute the plan."

"And what if we're wrong? What if they come earlier?"

Miranda shrugged. "If they think we don't know they're coming, they might get careless. We trap them, whoever they are, and take as many as we can alive." She nodded. "Yes, alive. These are arrogant people and we might squeeze them for some good intel."

Suddenly she grinned. "I've never been on a stake out."

"Never?"

"No. I'm an analyst. I sift intel and try to make sense of it – look for patterns to give us a chance to head off terrorist attacks."

"You any good?"

"If I tell you that, I'll have to shoot you."

"And are you armed?"

She patted the briefcase. "I carry a 9mm Sig Sauer auto."

The big pickup crossed the culvert that carried Dog Creek to Drews Valley, and Bud shook his head. "Ever shoot a shotgun?"

"I have, but I'm more comfortable with one of those," she said, pointing at the AR-15 clipped to the dash, company for Bud's 10-gauge shotgun.

"Well, your job for the moment is to help TJ remember who he told what, and to protect the Right Reverend TJ Wildish, if he's here yet – not get involved in a gun fight."

***

THE DECK OF THE BIG WHITE house perched halfway up the West Hills of Portland overlooked the downtown skyline and a piece of the Willamette River. Al-Alwani, tall and bearded, in his mid-thirties, watched distant traffic roll across the Ross Island Bridge … before his gaze settled on tree-covered Mount Tabor.

He thought about the open reservoirs on the west flank of the small mountain, huge open cement pools that stored part of the city's drinking water, and then turned to the small slender man who was his personal servant.

"What do you think, Ali? Shall we poison their water supply?"

The little man shuddered and shook his head. "No. We have to drink the same water, and we might kill our brothers and sisters if we did that."

"Tempting, though, isn't it? So easy. They don't even guard their water utilities."

He gave the little man an affectionate hug and kissed the top of his head. "Go see if they have had any luck with the Christian's computer."

His cell phone buzzed and he opened to a text message. *They have pictures of your men who searched the Rock of Ages Church.*

"Infidels," he snarled and threw the phone across the room. The phone smacked a framed picture of the Ayatollah, glass shards spraying across the soft white wool carpet.

"Ali," he shouted. When Ali poked his head back through the door, he said, "Get the vacuum and clean this up. I have a call to make."

15

Dog Lake

A T THE SIGHT OF THE CLEAR WATERS of Dog Lake, Miranda was her voluble self. "Oh, perfect. I can see why Dell BeBe likes this place. Are those pelicans? And look at that green A-frame. It just fits the scenery somehow. Do you know who owns that?""Yes. Yes, I do."

"You actually get to live out here?"

"I have another house close to town, but I spend some of my off-time out here."

He drove past the driveway to the A-frame, and then turned down a second gravel lane that wandered out through a stand of pine trees to a reddish-colored two-story log home on a point of land pushing out into Dog Lake. BB had the house oriented to catch the morning sun, and to give him a splendid view of the lake.

"Oh, my," Miranda said. "This is Dell BeBe's? It's simply gorgeous."

Bud pulled up beside a plain green Dodge Neon. *A rental*, he thought. "Well, it looks like TJ made it."

The garage door powered up and BB came walking out of the garage. He didn't wave – just stood there until Bud and Miranda stepped out.

He waited until Miranda closed the pickup door, then said, "You must be Special Agent Miranda Wright."

"She is," Bud interrupted. "Talks all the time about everything – non-stop – and asks really personal questions. You two should get along just fine."

BB raised his eyebrows in question, but all that earned him was a frown from Bud and a smile that made Miranda's eyes twinkle. She winked and said, "You can learn a lot about a person by their reactions to intelligent questions."

Bud shook his head and suggested, "It's the FBI's new interrogation technique. Talk until the perp confesses just to have some peace and quiet."

BB smiled. "Pay no attention to the grouch. Welcome to the back of beyond, Agent Wright. TJ is upstairs watching the ducks and complaining it took him a week to make the trip down here."

He glanced at Bud. "I think you should write him a ticket. He doesn't even have a driver's license."

Bud shrugged. "The car doesn't look like he hit anything. In Lake County, kids drive before they are old enough to take the driver's test."

"TJ said he just followed the slowest car he could find. And the rental car is almost out of gas. He said he gassed up in La Pine, but forgot to gas up in Lakeview."

Bud laughed and said, "I've got a couple of extra gallons in my garage. We'll get him back to town."

"Detective Blair," TJ said when Bud walked into the living room. "It's been a long time, but I have seen your name in the Oregonian a time or two."

Bud smiled and held out his hand. "I haven't been a detective for quite a few years, Reverend, but it's nice of you to remember me. Let me introduce FBI Special Agent Miranda Wright."

The sight of the slender, attractive woman had TJ standing as tall as his sixty-seven inches would allow. He thought she was the most beautiful woman he had ever seen: unblemished mahogany complexion, hazel eyes, gleaming white teeth behind lips that even the Right Reverend TJ Wildish thought he might like to kiss.

Miranda smiled and held out her hand. "Reverend. How has your day been going? I understand you drove down. That must have taken quite a few hours. Glad you didn't get lost getting out here. I was lost from the time we drove into the timber until we found the lake. I was thinking Sheriff Blair might have nefarious designs."

She took a breath and TJ rushed in with, "Nice to meet you. I understand you've come a long way to interview me. I'm working on that," he said and pointed to a writing tablet open on the granite island, a list of names running down the left side of the page, "trying to remember who I talked to about the Muslim community."

"That's a good place to start, but right now I'd die for a good cup of coffee."

BB said, "I can't guarantee you'll like it, but I just brewed a fresh pot."

Bud smiled and said, "He's gone Western. Reads too many novels about coffee strong enough to float a horseshoe."

"You're just jealous, Honky, because you don't know how. That weak coffee you brew won't even float a toothpick."

Bud just shook his head and walked to the black, granite-topped island. He turned TJ's notes so he could read the list of names penciled there. One caught his eye and he said, "Tyson James. I remember him. Did some time for a gang shooting."

TJ nodded. "And converted to Islam while he was in prison. I know a great many people in the black community who have left the true faith. The name BB gave to the FBI came to me anonymously, so I'm not sure who helped us."

BB slid a cup of coffee in front of Miranda. "Thank you. That smell's wonderful." She pulled a stool out, sat down, and retrieved the notebook. "Well, Reverend, let's go over it. Maybe you can remember something or someone you might have overlooked. So … start from the beginning."

***

BUD CAUGHT BB'S EYE AND POINTED to the deck that overlooked the lake. When they were outside, Bud said, "We have a problem. Our old friend, Dutch Vanderlin, called. Said the people looking for TJ searched the rectory before the FBI could get there.

"A neighbor said three young men took what looked to be a personal computer away with them. So, it's likely they have copies of your emails, photos of this place, and directions on how to get here."

BB took a deep breath and frowned. "I was afraid of that. And for some more bad news, I included a photo of your A-frame as a landmark. Never crossed my mind any bad guys would ever see that email."

Bud shook his head. "Never mind that. What's done is done, and it might work to our advantage. Now then, I have an idea."

BB shook his head skeptically, then growled, "You always wind up in a shootout."

"Do you want to hear this or not?"

BB stared, eyes boring into Bud's, then finally nodded. "All right, but I think we need to find safe harbor for TJ, and this ain't it."

"Agreed, so here is what I think we should do…"

16

Warning Bells

PORTLAND'S FBI JOINT TERRORISM TASK FORCE (JTTF) leader, Joseph Smith, said, "Enter," to a knock on the polished mahogany door that carried a brass plaque which read "Deputy Special Agent in Charge for Anti-Terrorism." He looked up from the file he was reading as Agents Wilcox and Brandt pushed through the door.

They each thought the lean-faced Smith was a politically driven asshole, and a martinet who liked to sit in a plush captain's chair behind his desk, with his back to a west-facing window, while his agents stood on a strip of carpet in front of the desk to make reports. It made it hard to see his face or to read his reactions, and was taken by the agents to be an attempt to intimidate them.

Consequently, Brandt and Wilcox avoided Smith as much as possible, but when days like this came along, and they could not avoid him, they always quickly plopped into chairs before sharing their reports. They knew it was childish, but they enjoyed irritating their boss.

Wilcox, who had been in line to head the Portland JTTF, never voiced his private opinion that ass kissing worked well in the J. Edgar Hoover building.

Agent Brandt said, "Mister Falls is in the safe house. Gutsy little bastard, but someone took a shot at him. Scared him, I think."

"Does he have family?"

"A mother. He sent her to stay with an uncle. Said the uncle keeps a loaded shotgun behind the closet door."

Smith opened a file, turned it around, and pushed it across his big, uncluttered mahogany desk. "A neighbor took pictures of these guys coming out of Reverend Wildish's living quarters. She said they were carrying what looked to her like a PC. And Dutch says Dell BeBe emailed the reverend pictures of his house and directions to find it. That means they probably know where the Reverend T. J. Wildish is hiding."

Wilcox muttered a quiet "shit" and got out of his chair. He spread the photos on the desk and tapped the second one with his index finger. "I know this guy. He's on our watch list. Hangs out in a big white house up in the West Hills."

"You're sure?" Smith asked.

"Dead certain."

Brandt got out of his chair and walked to the desk. "Yep," he said after looking at the photos. "His name is Muhammad Ali, just like our old boxer friend Cassius Clay. I like this. It should be enough for a warrant to search that place. And we could arrest him and his buddies for theft."

Smith nodded and said, "I have a warrant for a wiretap and close surveillance. And our watchers are already in place. We are also listening to their cell phone calls."

Wilcox shrugged. Stake out wasn't high on his list of fun things to do. But he had to admit to a twinge of jealousy that Smitty was ahead of him … and doing a good job (so far).

Brandt asked, "Do we know how to get in touch with the reverend?"

Smith nodded. "Miranda is with him as we speak."

"You're kidding," Wilcox said. "Not Motormouth Miranda?"

Special Agent Joseph Smith tried to suppress a smile and failed. "I never heard her called that before."

Wilcox shrugged and said, "I'll give her credit for being a good analyst, and I decided some time back she thinks by talking out loud. But it can be a little irritating at times."

"So, where is she?" Brandt asked.

***

HIGH ATOP WEST HILLS, A NERVOUS Cletus Falls, seated in a stuffy, windowless interview room – actually a remodeled broom closet – avoided giving direct answers to Agent Winslow Butler's questions. *There's something wrong with this guy*, he thought.

When Agent Butler asked him if he knew who Reggie hung out with, Cletus stood up and lied. "Look, Mister Butler. I work the streets, and I don't poke into the social life of my snitches.

"Sit down," an impatient Butler demanded. "How do you expect us to help you if we can't tie Reggie back to the bad guys?"

"No, Agent Butler, I'm going to my room. I'm tired. I haven't had a good night's sleep ever since Reggie was killed. I'm going to rest awhile and wait for Sara before I answer any more questions."

Butler glared at him for a bit, then shrugged. "Okay, Mister Falls. I'm just trying to help. We'll talk later."

No, we won't, Cletus thought. *I'm calling Sara when I get to my room. This guy is just plain spooky.*

17

To Work

NANCY SIXKILLER BUILT A REPUTATION FOR never making a mistake when she first worked as the coordinator of the Lake County Emergency Services Center. She was composed in stressful situations, knew where all the resources were, and always got it right.

Most dispatches were routine, but on some occasions, they were life-threatening situations that called for a cool head and clear judgment. If a dispatcher sent an officer or an ambulance to the wrong address, or without adequate information, people could get hurt or a rescue could go wrong.

Nancy Sixkiller did not make mistakes, unless you called her busted marriage to "old what's his name" a mistake, but that wasn't exactly job-related.

She was happy to be back and grateful the county had rehired her, but she was anxious – nearly desperate – to repair the damage she had done to her relationship with Bud.

One of three phones on her desk rang, and she picked up. "This is Nancy Sixkiller."

Bud quickly said, "This is Bud. I'm afraid tonight won't work. I think you'd better stay in town."

"What's going on?"

"It's kind of complicated, and I don't have time to explain it right now."

"What about Molly?"

"I'll have to do that alone, I'm afraid."

"All right," she said quietly. "Can we set another time?"

She heard Bud take a deep breath and then say, "I wish I could, but I'm going to be busy for the next few days. I just don't know right now. Gotta Go."

***

Bud slipped the phone into his shirt pocket and shook his head. He took a deep breath and walked to the railing of BB's deck … staring out across the lake, cursing the timing of TJ's problems.

Dell BeBe walked over and lightly punched Bud's shoulder. "Efficient is what I'd call that. Not a single hint of better times ahead."

"Don't go there, BB. I know you don't like Nancy, and even though I'm still mad at her, it doesn't mean I don't damn well love her. You do know the difference between not liking what someone does and loving them anyway?"

"I don't dislike her, Honky. I just don't like the way she treated you.

***

Nancy listened to dead air, then set the receiver back in its cradle. "Well," she whispered, "that didn't go well. I wonder if it will ever go well again…"

She thought about it briefly, then called her backup dispatcher. "Could you relieve me in about thirty minutes, Colonel? I have something I need to do. I'll be gone all afternoon."

***

Bud studied his friend, Dell BeBe, and then asked, "What are you going to do with TJ?"

"Do?"

"Yeah. Do."

"Well, I'll have to find a new place to hide him for a while, but unless we do something about the assholes who want him dead, he'll never be safe. So, I'm going back to Portland to figure out who's after him. Until I do that I won't know exactly how to deal with it."

"You're retired. You don't have any official status."

"Maybe Dutch will swear me in. Or maybe you'll deputize me."

"That's thin, BB."

BB frowned, rubbed the salt and pepper stubble on his chin, and nodded. "I know, but I'm not going to let this go."

"Okay. I have friends in the Klamath Falls Police Department. I'll see if they can find a hidey-hole for TJ … temporarily." Bud took a deep breath, "Agent Wright can take him over there in the rental car, then catch a flight back to Portland from the Klamath Falls airport."

BB shook his head. "Okay, as a first step. What comes next?"

"Well, we bait the trap again. I'll gather my officers and we'll wait for the bad guys to show up – take 'em alive if possible – and see if we can identify the stud duck."

BB's cell phone chimed and he answered. "This is BB."

Bud waited until BB nodded and said, "All right. Thanks, Dutch." He hung up, and eyebrows raised, shook his head.

"And?"

"Dutch says the FBI is watching a high muck-amuck in the Muslim community: wire taps, cell phone communication, on-site surveillance. He thinks they'll send someone here to try and kill TJ. But he says he thinks the FBI will know who and when.

"So, when the bad guys make a move, he'll helicopter a SWAT team down here to work with and for you. Miranda will be your FBI liaison. Dutch is calling it 'Operation Midnight.'"

Bud shook his head. "Operation Midnight. Yippee."

"Don't look a gift horse…"

Bud interrupted, "I know, and I don't mean to sound ungrateful. FBI SWAT teams are really, really good. But Operation Midnight?"

18

One Blind Mole

CLETUS THUMBED IN SARA'S NUMBER, BUT stopped short of hitting send. He killed the call, pulled Special Agent Wilcox's business card from his sweatshirt pocket, and stared at it, trying to think clearly.

What do I tell him? That Butler's creepy? That won't work. You got nothing, Cletus, nothing. But I know I'm right. Butler asks all the wrong questions. Gotta be on the take. I'd bet my life on it.

He took a deep breath and said in a whisper, "And I am betting my life on it either way. The question is who to trust."

He walked into the bathroom, turned the shower on, turned the water in the sink on, and flushed the toilet to muffle his call – just in case Butler had the room bugged. *And, why wouldn't he?*

And then Cletus changed his mind … again, but he left the shower running. He turned the TV on, brought the volume up to normal listening range and then as quietly as he could, slipped out the door of the suite and down the hallway. *Butler can't watch and listen at the same time. I hope.*

At the top of the stairs he stopped to listen for movement, and hearing none, walked as softly as he could down the stairs and toward the side entrance. The stairs were solid oak. No pop or creak of old wood gave him away. Cletus scooted across the landing, ducked through the side door, and walked around the corner of the big mansion. From there, he jogged across the big lawn and into the trees.

When he was satisfied he was out of sight, he pulled the gray hood of the sweat shirt up over his head and looked back at the big house through a screen of ground hugging fir limbs. Nothing. No sign of Butler. Cletus thumbed in Special Agent Wilcox's cell number and waited for him to pick up.

He heard, "Wilcox," and then said, "This be Cletus. I need to boogie out of here, man! Maybe you can come get me?"

Wilcox asked, "What's going on?"

"I know it's thin, but your man Butler asks all the wrong questions. Wants to know stuff that could get the reverend killed and maybe some other dudes too. Wants to know where I hid the reverend, and things like who Reggie hung with. I told him I didn't know. Not my job to keep track of my sources.

"So, he leans over me and tries to scare me, but I still don't say anything. Then he gives up and tries to make it okay. Says he's just trying to help. And I'm thinking, 'No you're not.'"

"But you trust me and Brandt?"

Cletus hesitated before speaking. "Yes."

"I guess why you do doesn't matter. Where are you right now?"

"I be in the trees on the north side of the big house."

"Okay," Wilcox said, "here's the deal. Keep going north. You know where north is?"

"I got a good sense of direction," Cletus said, with a bit of huff in his voice.

"Okay, then. Go north until you hit a tall cyclone fence. Don't worry about it. It isn't electrified – just tall. Climb the fence and walk down the outside of it about two hundred yards. For you city dudes, that's about two football fields. You'll find a trail that goes left and slightly downhill. That takes you into Forest Park. Follow the trail for maybe half a mile … maybe a bit more. That will take you to a parking lot with a restroom and picnic tables. Stay there. Brandt and I will pick you up. We'll be there in about fifteen minutes, depending on traffic."

"So, you believe me?"

"I didn't say that."

"Shit."

"Didn't say I don't believe you either, Cletus. Best I can do. Now, do you think Butler knows you're gone?"

"No. I turned the TV on and snuck out. Don't think he saw me."

"Well, then," Wilcox said, "you best get the hell over the fence and head for the parking area."

***

Wilcox walked down the hall a short distance to Brandt's office and stuck his head in the door. "Hey, let's go."

"Where?"

"I'll explain after we get moving."

Brandt slipped his dark blazer off the back of his chair and slid his arms in the sleeves as he hurried after the longer-legged Wilcox. They'd worked as partners for over three years, which meant countless hours together and a degree of trust that defied explanation. It just was.

Wilcox hit the basement button in the elevator and waited for the doors to close before saying, "Seems Butler spooked our little friend, Cletus, who just took off through the timber. We'll pick him up in Forest Park."

"What did Butler do?"

"Cletus said he asked the wrong questions, tried to get Cletus to tell him who the dead snitch, Reggie, hung with. Where he had hidden the reverend. Stuff like that. Cletus said Butler just asked the wrong questions."

"That's strange."

"Yes. And I'm inclined to believe Cletus."

"In the absence of proof?"

"Yep."

Brandt shrugged. "Okay."

They were on I-5 headed south before Brandt said, "What do you think of Agent Butler?"

Wilcox hit the emergency lights hiding in the grill and accelerated, the big Ford fishtailing slightly, before he said, "I don't like him."

Brandt nodded and braced his elbow against the armrest as Wilcox swerved around a white delivery truck that suddenly slowed when the driver saw the red and blue strobe lights flashing.

Brandt opened his cell phone and made a call. When Jenny Jackson, Miranda Wright's analyst buddy, answered her phone in her familiar husky voice, he said, "Jenny, this is Brandt. Butler may be dirty. Take a hard look at his bank records … quietly. And anything else you can think of. Okay?"

Jenny snapped, "You don't do your own dirty work anymore, Douglas?"

Brandt grinned at the vision of Jenny squaring her thin shoulders and leaning forward, green eyes snapping in anger whenever someone interrupted her concentration.

"This just came up. I'd do it, but I'm on a call, and I need your help. And it needs to be done soon." He paused, then grinned when he added, "It's worth a dinner … on me."

She said, "You certain about Butler?"

"No hard evidence. But my gut says we need to look. Okay?"

"Boy, oh boy. If I get caught, I'll blame it on you. That's a pretty serious accusation."

"It's not an accusation, just suspicion."

"Lobster. I like lobster … eaten alone."

"Well, damn it to hell, Jenny, I thought this might be a new beginning."

She laughed and said, "Okay. If you buy – and if you promise to behave yourself. We can try dining together … again. Just dining out, but that's all."

"Marry me, Jenny. Then we won't have to do all this bobbing and weaving. Thanks. Gotta go."

Brandt glanced at Wilcox who was trying unsuccessfully to smother a laugh. Wilcox broke into a full belly laugh and damned near drove into the barrier separating the I-5 southbound lanes from the ones running north.

"What's so funny, Leroy?"

Wilcox wiped a tear out of the corners of his eyes with his left hand and then said. "Well, she's smart, she's kind of pretty, and she has a nearly perfect figure: eighteen, eighteen, and eighteen. I just can't figure where you find magic in all that."

Brandt looked out the passenger window at the blur of cars Wilcox was passing, and said, "I wish you could understand what that husky voice of hers does to me."

Wilcox chuckled, and then said, "Rubenesque. That's how I like my women: 'Rubenesque.'"

19

Loved and Lost

DELL BEBE LEANED BACK AGAINST HIS deck rail. A light breeze brought him the gift of the subtle scent of dry pine needles. He studied Bud, knowing his friend's mind was working on something hard.

A cloud slipped between the sun and the lake, blocking the light and then gliding away to leave the lake blue, open, and sunny again. Breeze-driven waves sparkled with reflected light. A dozen geese flew at tree top level up the lake, honking and talking to each other in a language BB didn't understand. But he appreciated it. *Somehow, they give me a sense that all is right in the world despite human evil.*

Bud was watching a dozen or so small mud hens diving and then popping up in open areas in a bed of water lilies, feeding on something. He turned his back on the lake and glanced at BB. "I had to let the vet put Molly down."

"Well, damn. Sorry, Bud. I figured something was wrong when she wasn't in the pickup. I just didn't want to say anything."

"I know. She's in the back, boxed up. I need to take care of that before long. I think I'll bury her by the trail down to the boat dock. She loved running down there just to bark at the mud hens."

He stopped a few seconds and then gave BB a thin smile. "You know, I think the ducks sort of looked forward to hearing her. There were times when they would gang up and start swimming towards the dock.

"You want help?"

"No. I might cry, and that wouldn't do for a tough guy. Western sheriffs don't cry."

"The hell they don't."

Bud gripped BB's offered hand, nodded his thanks, and then walked across the deck to the slider, his boot heels loud on the cedar planks. "Let's see what Miranda and TJ came up with."

"Doing any good?" Bud asked as he walked to the island counter where Miranda was filling a yellow legal pad with notes. A cell phone was switched on to record their conversation, but Miranda was more comfortable capturing special points by hand.

She shut the phone off and said, "Maybe. We do have a lead … maybe."

BB closed the slider with a slam and then asked, "How is that?"

TJ started to answer, but Miranda rode right over the top of him. "One of TJ's friends from grade school, one Hamas Abdul-Kallus."

"Formerly, Benjamin Green," TJ butted in. "I've known him since first grade."

"Yes, and he's the one TJ asked to find the name of the most prominent of the radicals," Miranda added. "So … we find him and see who he talked to."

"The name he gave me," TJ said, "was used on the search warrant which led to the raid on the big mosque. That's when the trouble started."

"Anything else?" BB asked.

"Yes," Miranda said with a look of satisfaction, smiling directly at BB. "Hamas has a wife, Basma, who works for the water bureau. I searched water bureau records, and we found an address in the St. Johns area of north Portland. Which means the FBI will talk to Hamas and his wife. Convince them to tell us who is after the reverend – and after your friend Cletus."

"If they know, and if they'll share it," Bud said.

BB looked at Bud and shrugged. "Only one way to find out."

TJ got off the tall stool at the island counter and carried his cup to the coffee pot. He filled his cup and took it back to the island before saying, "I feel like a coward."

BB shook his head and wrapped a long arm around TJ's shoulder with enough force to make TJ spill coffee on the pale-yellow tiles in

BB's kitchen area. "Reverend, you can be brave later. We need you to help us figure this out."

"But I feel like I've betrayed my Lord and Savior. I let him down by not trusting him to protect me."

BB shook his head. "Not to be cynical, Reverend, but the Christians that were fed to the lions in Roman arenas might have been too trusting."

Bud appreciated TJ's dilemma and added, "Reverend, God sent an angel to guide and protect you. This angel's name is Cletus Falls. Cletus got you out of town for good reason."

Thomas Jefferson Wildish hitched his skinny butt onto a tall stool. He looked at Bud and frowned. "Sounds like a rationalization to me, but I'll choose to believe you. I certainly need your help."

Silence descended on BB's kitchen, a silence nearly physical in its intensity.

20

From Beginning to End

Miranda called FBI headquarters and asked for Special Agent Smith. TJ and BB listened in as she briefed her boss. When she gave him the address for the home of Hamas and Basma, TJ shook his head and sighed. He realized he'd been holding his breath. "I need to pray," he said quietly to BB, "for God's protection of my old friend Hamas and his wife … even if they have strayed from the path."

***

While Miranda made her report, Bud drove to his A-frame and parked on the gravel in front of the little garage. He shut the engine down, and stared through the windshield at the narrow path from the front door of the cabin that wandered past the willows to the boat dock. "Crap."

He was angry, and he knew his anger was irrational. But he didn't care. There was strength in anger. It was a whole lot easier to be angry that Molly had died than it was to wallow in sorrow. "It isn't like a human being died," he grumbled, "but it sure feels like it."

He took a deep breath and said, "Well, it's got to be done."

He stepped out and slammed the pickup door with a little more force than the well-oiled hinges required, then walked to a shovel leaning against a downspout attached to a corner of the garage.

Shovel in hand, he trudged to the edge of the willow patch hiding his small boat dock and started cutting the sod in a square slightly larger than the burial box provided by Doc Saunders. The damp, earthy smell of fresh dirt underscored how temporary life could be and how totally consuming the earth was of mortal remains – man or animal.

He had the hole down two feet when he heard a vehicle slow and turn into his driveway. With mixed emotions, he watched Nancy's Toyota pickup, tires quietly crunching gravel, ease up beside the county's pickup. The glare of sunlight on the windshield made it hard to see the driver, but his heart was beating a little faster. And when she slid out of the pickup and closed the door, he thought, *Too much sorrow for one day. Broken hearts should have time to mend.*

She just stood there and waited. She was in blue jeans, red tennis shoes, and a woolen car coat with a Navajo pattern that dropped to mid-thigh. Bud thought she looked simply gorgeous. A sunbeam lit the auburn highlights in her shiny black hair.

Nancy put her hands in her coat pockets and, with her head slightly bowed, started a slow walk toward Bud. When she was within about six feet, she lifted her chin and said, "Howdy, stranger."

"Howdy yourself."

"I think I'm lost," she said, "could you give me directions to the love of my life?"

Bud blinked and said, "Why on earth would I do that?"

"Because I'm a lost soul drowning in sorrow. Besides," she said pointing to the hole he was digging, "I thought you could use some help."

He stomped the shovel deep into the damp, soft earth, walked to where she waited, and wrapped her in his arms

"Oh, Bud," she said and hugged him. "I'm so sorry. I'm sorry about everything. And right now, I'm sorry about Molly."

He set his chin on the top of her head, a faint odor of shampoo tickling his nose. He took a deep breath and said, "I keep trying to understand why you broke the engagement. I mean, we could have stayed engaged even though you needed to take care of your mother.

"And I keep talking to myself, wondering why I would ever take you back. Then I think, well Bud, at least she didn't leave you for another man. Which gets me to thinking some more and figuring I just wasn't the man for you after all because you *didn't* leave me for another man."

Nancy squeezed him hard enough to push air from his lungs, then she stepped back to look into his eyes. "I don't think I understand it, either. I don't know how I let fear rob me of my courage. That was totally out of character … or at least what I believe my character is or should be.

"But after I left, every time Sonny told me some tale about you, I found myself worrying as much as if we were married after all. I couldn't chase the worry away. And then I thought, "Why should I worry about him out of fear for a someday sorrow?" I want time with the love of my life, risk and all. My hope is you can forgive me and let me back in."

He gave her another hug, stepped back, and held her at arm's length, hands on her shoulders. "Nothing has changed. I'm still a cop. And people might shoot at me again. That's the nature of the business. And I like being a cop. When I retire in about ten years, I'll be as safe as any man. But no man is entirely safe in this life. Life is full of landmines. The trick is to not step on one."

"I understand all that. I'm not asking you to give up police work. I'm asking you to forgive me for hurting you. And I'm asking you to take me back."

He let his breath ease out slowly through pursed lips.

Nancy figured he was leading up to saying, "No."

"Listen Bud, I know you have a high-risk occupation. You could get killed. You accept that chance as part of the job. But you won't take a chance on us? I knew you were going to be an asshole about this!"

Bud snorted. "Look who's being an asshole." And then he laughed and said, "Come here, damn it."

She stepped into his arms and broke into tears, but she managed to choke out a few words. "My name isn't 'damn it.'"

***

WHILE BUD FINISHED DIGGING THE HOLE for Molly's box, Nancy unlocked the cabin with the key she had never given back to Bud, and started the coffee pot. She was nearly overcome by nostalgia at the familiar odor of cold wood smoke clinging to the hard fabric of Bud's recliner, and by the array of bird photos hanging on the walls, Bud's photos taken at Summer Lake Wildlife Refuge and at Dog Lake during his years in Lake County.

And as suddenly as her nostalgia hit, it was gone, replaced by happiness bordering on euphoria. "I'm back. Oh, thank you, Lord. I'm back," she whispered.

***

THE BURIAL WAS SHORT AND SWEET. Bud filled the hole, set a big rock on the mounded earth as a marker, and then said a prayer for his old canine partner that ran somewhat along the lines that dog was born of dust and to dust returns, loyally waiting to meet its master in the afterlife.

Nancy glanced at Bud and said, "Do you really believe that? Some Indians think that way."

Bud shrugged. "Maybe. I don't know. But what else are you going to say over an old dog you loved?"

Nancy took his hand and said, "I think the coffee's done."

She set cups on the small kitchen table and poured. "Why did you tell me to stay away?"

"For the same reason that I want you back in town. I believe some really nasty people are about to descend on us – right here at quiet, peaceful Dog Lake."

Nancy's brow furrowed as Bud brought her up-to-date; about last year's raid on mosques in Portland and Seattle, all because Cletus bought photos of military-style weapons in the basement of the mosque; about TJ finding the name of the imam leader behind it; about someone killing Cletus' informant; about some jihadists wanting to kill TJ out of revenge; and about TJ hiding next door with BB.

"Why would they look for him here?"

"Because, the FBI tells me the bad guys took TJ's computer, and because BB sent TJ – who happens to be one of BB's oldest childhood friends – photos of his new log home. BB says he also emailed directions on how to find him out here."

"Good Lord."

"Agreed. I don't know how long it will take them to plan a raid on BB's house, but these dudes are big on revenge."

"How soon do you think?"

"I don't know. By tomorrow maybe. The FBI has surveillance on them, and Dutch Vanderlin, Portland's FBI SAC, thinks he'll have enough warning to get a SWAT team here before the bad guys show up."

Nancy nodded and took a deep breath. "Well, good. That gives you some time to get ready."

21

Forest Park

Because the road was narrow, Wilcox drove slowly once he entered Forest Park. "It's not much further," he said.

"That's okay. I'm enjoying the ride. I've heard about this place. I just never took the time to come and see it." Brandt thumbed his smartphone and pulled up information about Forest Park. "I didn't realize it was so big."

He read aloud from the screen, "Five thousand acres; largest urban park in the world; lots of different critters – including cougars – and one rumor of a wolf sighting. Glad I'm armed."

From behind the ground-level limbs of a fir tree, a nervous Cletus Falls watched Wilcox back the SUV into a parking spot and kill the engine. *Can't see through the tinted windows. I'm not coming out until I see who's in there.*

Wilcox opened the door and grinned back at his partner, "Douglas, one look at your ugly mug, and a wolf or cougar would die of fright."

A small green Subaru Outback rolled in and parked three slots away. The two agents watched until a young bearded man and a blonde woman got out of the Subaru, and popped the back door to grab daypacks and polished hardwood walking sticks. The hikers slipped arms through the straps on their packs, took the right fork in the trail through a thicket of wild rhododendrons, and then they were out of sight.

Wilcox said, "Cletus should've made it here by now. I'll bet he's hiding. People like Cletus are survivors, always wary."

Brandt nodded. "If I were Cletus, I'd be suspicious, too. But he trusts us. Wonder why?"

"He does. And I don't know why either, Douglas."

"Got to be your winning smile, Leroy."

"Must be it.'

Brandt said, "I'll go check the restroom. Just in case. But why don't you walk up the trail and see if you can find him.'

Two minutes later, Wilcox walked back to the parking lot, Cletus close behind.

Brandt had claimed a concrete picnic table and was pouring lukewarm coffee into a steel cup from a battered thermos that looked like it came from an archaeology dig.

"Found him, I see."

Cletus said, "I didn't know who was in your vehicle. So, I waited."

Brandt dug into a wrinkled paper bag that could've come from the same archaeology dig. He held out a trail bar and asked Cletus, "You hungry?"

Cletus shook his head. "No. But I'd sure like to get the hell out of here."

"This a good place," Wilcox said. "Not a chance in the world of being overheard. Let's sit right here, have a cup of coffee, and then maybe you can tell us why you ran."

Cletus glanced back over his shoulder to make sure Butler hadn't followed him, then slid onto the bench seat. "That dude is plumb spooky. Looks like Boris Karloff from the old movies. But it ain't just that. He asks all the wrong questions. And I didn't sign on to give him my life story. I just strung him along. When I said I was tired cause I hadn't had any sleep since Reggie was murdered and that I was going to take a nap, he looked madder than hell. And then he asked for my cell phone."

"But you didn't give it to him?" Wilcox asked.

"I gave him a burner phone and kept the other one."

Wilcox laughed. "I told you he was a survivor, Brandt." He shook his head and asked Cletus. "And that's the one you used to call me."

Cletus nodded without saying anything.

Wilcox looked at Brandt and said, "That's what we do to people we stash up there. We take their phones. People get bored, they miss their girlfriends, they want pizza delivery, all kinds of odd things. So even when they ask for help, that's the protocol. No phones unless an agent is with them."

"I know the protocol, Leroy."

"I'm just explaining to Cletus that we need something a lot more solid than his suspicions."

"Okay," Cletus said. "How about this? He kept asking where I had the reverend stashed. Now, how did he know I'd stashed the reverend anyplace? Where did that information come from? How did he even know the reverend was gone? Gotta be a tie to the bad guys … someplace. They be the only ones, other than you and me, who know he's gone." Cletus shook his head. "Nope. Boris Karloff's on the take."

Wilcox and Brandt looked at each other. Wilcox raised his eyebrows in question, and Brandt shrugged. "Maybe."

"Well, damn," Wilcox said. "We need a safe place to hide Mister Falls until we get this sorted out."

Brandt looked at Cletus and said, "I'm not saying Butler is dirty, but in your shoes, I'd feel the same way."

Cletus said, "I tell you what. You drop me near the Justice Center. I got a place."

Wilcox frowned and said, "How sure are you about this?"

Cletus nodded and said, "You let me make a call. I'll be right back." Cell phone to his ear, he walked around the back side of the restroom.

BB answered on the second ring. "That you, Cletus?"

"Mister BeBe, I need a new place to stay. I might come down to your place. How do I find you?"

"That won't work. The bad guys know the reverend is here. What's wrong with the FBI's safe house?"

"It's not safe. We be thinking the den mother is crooked. Been bought."

"Well, how about my apartment then? I still own that."

"How am I going to get in?"

"I'll call the manager. He'll give you a key. And there's a small convenience store on the second floor. You can get some basic groceries there. Charge it to my account."

"Okay, Mister BeBe. Who would think those pictures would cause us this much trouble?"

"Not me, but if there's a rat working for the FBI, it might explain how they got onto us. Where are you?"

"Forest Park. I'm with two FBI agents, Brandt and Wilcox. They'll get me to the apartment. Gotta go, Mister BeBe. Been in one place too long."

22

A Moving Target

BB LISTENED TO DEAD AIR, THEN SHUT the phone off. Shaking his head, he said quietly, "Forest Park. You do get around, Cletus."

TJ looked up from the island counter and asked, "Cletus?"

"Yeah. He's in trouble again, but a couple of FBI agents are looking after him."

Miranda said, "Who are they?"

"Brandt and Wilcox."

Miranda nodded. "I know those two. They're very good. In fact, Wilcox was in line to be a Deputy SAC, but politics got in the way."

BB raised his eyebrows and said, "Is this Wilcox guy sour on the agency?"

She shook her head. "No. He's fairly young and he knows he'll be a SAC somewhere before his career is over."

"I hope you're right. It's for sure that someone tipped the bad guys off. Cletus thinks your man in the safe house is bent. "Bought" is the word Cletus used."

"That seems unlikely," Miranda said.

"You don't know Cletus," BB said. "His street instincts have kept him out of trouble until now. If I was to bet, I'd bet on Cletus."

***

Al-Alwani's cell phone buzzed, and he picked up on the second ring. "Yes?"

"This is Yoseph."

"Make it quick."

"He's gone. Sneaked away … through the woods, maybe. I can't find him in the house."

"You better find him." Al-Alwani became deadly serious. "Osama won't like this, and you know what happens to people who disappoint him."

23

Listeners

THE TWO MEN LOOKED AT EACH other and shook hands. "Gotcha, you crooked sonofabitch," listener one said.

"Got them both," listener two added. "We best get this to the boss. I mean right now. Send someone to pick up Butler."

Listener one sighed and said, "How does a longtime agent go bad?"

"Divorce."

"What?"

"Divorce," listener two said. "Butler's wife divorced him. The agency doesn't like divorce, so that sidetracked his career. And a judge gave her alimony until he retires, and then half his retirement and his entire house. He lives on a small cabin cruiser moored at Guy's Marina on the Willamette Channel."

"How do you know all this?"

"Butler and I were partners once upon a time. He calls me now and again at night, especially when he's drunk, and tells me all about it … over and over."

"You never mentioned it."

"I told his supervisor. Suggested counseling."

Listener one nodded. "That might open a guy up to temptation. But how would the bad guys know he was vulnerable?"

"Somebody on the inside, maybe," listener two said. "The bad guys have so much money they buy judges, police chiefs, politicians, and maybe even FBI agents."

"Well, time's a wasting," listener one said, then picked up his phone and entered a direct-dial number. The call was answered by Linda Barnes, secretary to Deputy Special Agent in Charge, Joseph Smith.

"This is Delaware. I need the boss."

"He's busy," she said.

"This won't wait," Delaware said impatiently.

"An emergency?" she asked.

"Time sensitive, Linda, so stop messing around."

When Agent Smith answered, Delaware said, "Smitty, we got something really hot."

"What?"

"We got ourselves a dirty agent."

"You sure?"

"Dead certain. Just recorded it."

Listener one heard a deep sigh and then Smitty saying, "Send it." In micro seconds, the recording was in the FBI's central computer.

Four minutes later, Linda Barnes, Smith's secretary and gatekeeper handed him a paper copy of the conversation between Butler and Al-Alwani.

Smith read it and then reached for his cell phone. He punched a number and waited until Brandt answered.

"Special Agent Brandt, I want you and Special Agent Wilcox to arrest Butler. He might still be at the safe house.

"I'm also concerned about the safety of Cletus Falls as well. Pick him up and we'll stash him in one of the downtown hotels. And I'm sending a SWAT team to Butler's boat in case he tries to boogie by water."

"On it, Boss. Our friend Cletus is with us. He didn't trust Butler. Cletus called us and we picked him up."

"At the safe house?"

"No. He hiked to Forest Park. Wilcox and I picked him up. We plan to stash him in another location."

"Where?"

"Can't say for sure. He wants us to just drop him downtown. Says he has a place to hide."

"Well, crap. We need to maintain communications with him."

"We got that worked out, and I don't want to talk about it over the phone. We'll drop him and head for the safe house ASAP. Gotta go, Boss. We'll keep you informed." And he hung up.

Smith shook his head. "I don't like Brandt or Wilcox, but I darned sure trust them." And then it struck him. Brandt had never called him Boss before. *I like it.*

He hollered through the open door to his secretary, "MiZ-BARnes, get Woodson on the line."

Donald Woodson, Supervisory Agent for the Portland FBI SWAT Team, picked up on the first ring. "Woodson," he said.

Linda Barnes, in a prim voice that almost always sounded disapproving, said, "Deputy Special Agent Smith would like to talk to you."

"Okay. Put him on."

"Woody," Smith said, "I have a sensitive mission that calls for a tactical element. I need you to watch Guy's Marina on the Willamette Channel and arrest Special Agent Butler if he shows up."

"Okay. Do you expect him to resist?"

"It would seem likely. Hence, the need for your team."

"When?"

"Right now. Do you need a photo and an address?"

"No to both. I can pull his picture from our files, and I know the marina. I'll keep you posted."

24

The Devil in the Details

BUD SET HIS CUP ON THE scarred surface of his wooden kitchen table and said to Nancy, "I need to get back over to BB's. I think we'll be safe for another twelve to twenty-four hours, but I want TJ and BB out of there. And I want the mother of my child safely out of here too."

Nancy shook her head and grinned. "I know what the ladies are saying, but while I may look pregnant, the truth is I simply ate myself into an extra twenty pounds while I mourned over you."

"Well, damn. I had hopes."

"Is that what you want, a baby?"

"Yes. Marriage first, though. We'll boogie for Reno as soon as I get this business cleared up."

"No."

"What do you mean?"

"Let's get a license here and have a small ceremony with our friends. Maybe your father can come down. I don't want to give the ladies of Lakeview anything more to speculate about."

Bud grinned and said, "And you don't suppose they'll be counting the months?"

Nancy smiled back and said, "Of course, but maybe we'll fool them."

"Bud said, "Stay put. I'll be right back."

She watched him bound up the stairs. *I wonder what that's about?*

It was nearly two minutes before he returned and thrust a small velvet box into her hand.

He almost growled when he said, "Keep the ring on this time. Okay?"

She stood, put her arms around his neck, and pulled his face down to hers. She gave him a long, hard kiss, and then stepped back and stared into his hazel eyes. She reached up, smoothed his left eyebrow, touching the small scar running through it and said, "Okay."

Bud nodded. He pointed to her pickup and said, "Good. Meet me at the courthouse."

"Today?"

"Yes. I want to get us a marriage license, and then I want you to stay in town. I'm not sure when, or even if, we'll have unwanted visitors, but I'd feel a whole lot better if you were in town. And I'd also feel a whole lot better if you were working dispatch when the proverbial substance hits the fan."

"You mean it? About the marriage license?"

"Take it to the bank, Nancy. Take it to the bank."

Nancy kissed his cheek. "I will."

"I have this business at BB's to take care of first. Why don't you follow me over in your truck?"

***

BUD OPENED BB'S BACKDOOR AND SAID, "Anybody home?"

BB hollered, "Come on up."

Miranda frowned when Bud and Nancy climbed the stairs and walked into the big airy living space on the second floor.

TJ caught Miranda's look out of the corner of his eye. *I'll be darned. I think Miranda is jealous.*

Bud introduced Nancy to TJ and Miranda. "Nancy Sixkiller, my soon-to-be bride."

BB shook his head and grinned. Arms outstretched, he walked to Nancy and gave her a hug. He whispered, "I guess I won't have to shoot you after all."

"I love him too, you big lug."

"Then don't hurt him again."

Nancy kissed BB's stubbled cheek and said, "Never again."

"All right, BB. She's marrying me, not you."

TJ said, "Congratulations. The Good Lord finally sent me something to be happy about today."

Miranda shook off her disappointment and echoed TJ with, "Congratulations."

Bud said, "Thank you. Now then, Miranda. As I was leaving, you said you had a plan."

Twenty minutes later BB sent TJ an email saying he was happy to hear TJ would be down later in the day.

It was also agreed that BB would drive TJ back to Portland, but leave Miranda in place as liaison with the FBI SWAT team should that become necessary.

"How sure are you that we'll have advance notice?" Bud asked.

Miranda shrugged and said, "We have watchers in place. We should have at least the same amount of time as it will take any bad guys to get here … whatever that is. If they come by helicopter, we'll know it before they leave the ground. If they come by vehicle, we'll know that too. That should give us plenty of time to have our SWAT team in place.

"Now, I've studied an aerial map of this area. There are only three major roads to Dog Lake, so it shouldn't be too hard to watch and block the roads after the bad guys are in the bottle, so to speak. I think we place the SWAT team in hiding close to the house and leave covering the roads up to Sheriff Blair's team. What do you think?"

Bud nodded. "It's good as far as it goes. But there is another summer home on up the lake. We'll need to evacuate anyone using it."

Miranda nodded.

Nancy added, "And the Goodnights own a ranch about ten miles west of the lake. They use the Dog Lake road to go into town. The ranch is actually in Klamath County, but they do a lot of their business in Lakeview. They'll need to know. In the meantime, they can use the back road to Bly. They don't need to come this way."

Bud nodded. "The devil is in the details."

BB said, "I hate to leave you here, Bud, but I think you're better protected than Cletus or TJ."

Bud put a hand on BB's big shoulder and smiled. "Thank you, partner, but don't worry. I'll be all right." He glanced at Nancy. "I have a lot to live for."

Miranda looked pensive. *I wonder what it would be like to marry, have a child, and live in a small town.* She almost snorted at her temporary loss of career focus. *Nah. It's not for me. I like what I'm doing.*

25

Confession

S PECIAL AGENT WILCOX PULLED THE BIG SUV in against the curb
and turned to look at Cletus in the back seat. "You sure about
this, Mister Falls? We can hide you in a nice hotel not far from our
headquarters."

Cletus shook his head. "No. I got a place."

Special Agent Brandt opened the center console and pulled a small
flat box out from under the standard issue owner's manual. He offered
the small box to Cletus.

"Here's my card and a burner phone you can use to call us."

Cletus shook his head. "No way, man. You'll just use it to find me."

Brandt grinned. "Hell, Cletus, we can do that anyway. Leroy and I
just don't want anyone else doing it. Take it. If it makes you feel better,
find a place away from your hidey hole and call from there, then move.
The bad guys won't find you that way. And please check in once a day.
Okay?"

Cletus looked skeptical, but stuffed the box in the pocket of his gray
hoodie. Without another word, he stepped out on the curb, slammed
the passenger door, and scooted around the corner of a downtown
office building.

Wilcox looked at Brandt who just shrugged.

"Think he'll be okay?" Wilcox asked.

Brandt nodded and said, "If anyone can survive, it's Cletus Falls."

Wilcox nodded. "If he wasn't so damned small, I'd feel better about him being on his own."

"You mean it – about recruiting him, in spite of his size?"

Wilcox nodded. "Yes. Yes, I do. We can use his instincts and his brains. Brains over brawn, Douglas. Brains over brawn."

Wilcox fished a ringing cell phone from the inner pocket of his dark blue sports jacket and looked at the number. "Smitty," he said to Brandt and held the phone so Brandt could see the screen.

The phone rang again and Brandt said, "You going to answer that?"

"No. He'll get tired of waiting for me to answer, and then he'll call you, and you can talk to him."

"Shit."

Brandt's cell phone chimed before Wilcox's phone stopped ringing. Brandt raised his eyebrows and answered the call. "Who's this?"

"This is very, very Special Agent Winslow Butler. You got the kid?"

"Why do you ask?"

"It's logical."

"That doesn't answer the question. Why do you want to know?"

"I'm going to make your careers, you and Wilcox, and then I'm going to disappear."

"Why?"

"Why make your careers, or why disappear?"

Brandt looked at Wilcox and pointed at the phone. "Why disappear?"

"I'm in too deep to do anything else. I'm sorry about the whole business, but if I go to jail, I'll die there, and if Al-Alwani finds me I'll wish I was dead before he kills me."

"You on the take, Butler?"

Special Agent Butler snorted and then started in on a slightly hysterical sounding laugh. "You wouldn't believe how much I've been paid. And I'm not the only one. Watch the analysis section. At least one of them is feeding the bad guys information."

"Who?"

"Hell, you're the FBI. You figure it out."

"Why don't you let us take you in? You can say you were freelancing … working undercover. Give us enough information, and we can get you a lighter sentence."

"No. No sentence. I won't do jail time. Come to think of it, if I don't retire my bitch of a wife won't get a dime. What a nice thought.

"Anyway, here's to your careers … have you been paying attention to the local news? Stories about missing women – all hookers, by the way?

"Anyway, the girls aren't dead. Instead they'll soon be on their way to that great big sandbox in the Middle East, traveling in a well-provisioned, comfortable shipping container. It is my understanding the container is sitting on a dock awaiting shipment to Yemen.

"Judas Priest," Brandt said. "You sure about this?"

"Absolutely. By the way, don't bother coming to the safe house. I'm not there."

"Wait, wait! Which terminal?"

Brandt shook his head, "Damn it, he hung up."

26

Big News

BUD TRAILED NANCY'S PICKUP TO THE courthouse, pulled into his reserved parking spot. and walked back down the sidewalk to where Nancy parked.

She put her purse strap over her left shoulder, slammed the pickup door, tugged the tail of her car coat into place, took a deep breath, and listened to her pounding heart. Bud ginned when she unconsciously tried to pat her hair into place.

He offered her his arm and pulled her close. "What's that old song?" he said. "Up, up and away we go?"

"I don't know that one."

"I'm not sure I do either."

The attractive middle-aged blonde behind the counter smiled when they pushed through the front door. "Good afternoon, Sheriff. How can I help?"

Bud glanced at Nancy and then back at the clerk, a big grin on his face. "Good afternoon, Missus Withers. We'd like a marriage license."

"My goodness, yes. Just wait right here while I get the form."

Judy Withers hurried through an inner door and closed it behind her. "Ginger," she almost whispered, "you'll never believe this. Sheriff Blair and Nancy Sixkiller are out there asking for a marriage license."

Ginger Callaghan, a prim, grey-haired woman looked up from behind her desk, blinked, then took her gold-rimmed glasses off and set them on the file she was reading. "Oh my. That is big news. And it'll break a lot of hearts." She gave Judy a conspiratorial smile and whispered, "Stall until I can get Carol Connor here. She'll want a picture for the paper, and she'll want to run a story. Oh my, this is big." She picked up her phone and dialed the Lake County News. "And about time, too," she added.

Missus Judy Withers took her time getting the proper form and deliberately took an old worn out ballpoint that was out of ink back to the front desk. "Okay. I'll need some personal information from each of you. And I'll need picture IDs. I don't suppose you have your birth certificates? Now then, Miss Sixkiller, I'll need your full name."

Nancy said, "Nancy Louisa Sixkiller."

"Oh darn," Judy Withers said, frowning at the ball point. "This thing seems to be out of ink. I'll be right back."

Four minutes later Carol Connor, managing editor of the Lake County News, followed by the newspaper's photographer, Samuel Adams, a tall, thin young man with a blonde ponytail and a world of computer and digital photography expertise, pushed through the door in time to hear Bud Blair's exasperated voice saying, "How long is this going to take?"

Carol grinned, held out her hand to Nancy and said, "Congratulations!"

Impulsively, Nancy gave Carol a hug. "Thank you. How did you … oh, I see now. Missus Withers was stalling, weren't you Missus Withers?"

Judy Withers curtsied like a little girl and said, "Yes. Ginger and I thought Carol would like a nice picture for the paper. And it isn't every day our sheriff gets married." She hurried to the inner connecting door and peeked in. "You can come out now, Ginger. Carol Connor is here."

"Do you mind, Sheriff?" Carol asked.

Bud glared at her and her photographer. He was about to say something about a female conspiracy, when Nancy tugged on his arm and said, "We'd love to, wouldn't we?"

Deputy Hildebrand's telephone call echoed through Bud's mind – Roger's report about the oddsmakers saying Bud Blair and Nancy Sixkiller would be married within the month. His frown smoothed into a smile. He chuckled and said, "I guess we would at that."

Bud held out his hand to Carol, but she brushed it aside and gave him a hug. She whispered in his ear, "Dad will want to say congratulations in person, but I want to thank you for bringing Sonny back. And I'm sorry I've been such a pain for your department. I think I've been jealous that you and my father had such a close friendship. That's rare for a newspaper editor and a police officer."

Bud hugged her back and said, "Not a problem. Tell Asa hello. I intend to have coffee with him soon."

The photographer had them stand in front of the counter holding the marriage license out at arm's length, told Bud (as opposed to asking) to take his Stetson off … and could he take his equipment belt off … to which Bud said "No."

Carol said, "Just take the picture, Samuel."

The camera flash led to cheering, and a booming voice said, "Congratulations, you two!" as District Attorney Howard Finch walked in, followed by a half-dozen courthouse employees.

Bud did his best to smile over the attention, shook hands and nodded at offered congratulations.

Nancy smiled and almost blushed. But when the DA held out his hand, Bud clamped it in his big paw and dragged Finch over to a corner. Bud said, "I might have some business for you in a day or two."

Finch pried his hand loose from Bud's grip, rubbed his hands together, and grimaced. "Damn, but I hate it when you do that."

He looked up at Bud, and ran his hand through an unruly mass of curly blonde hair in a failed attempt to look a little neater. "Something interesting, I hope. I'm sick of this trespass case I'm trying."

Bud smiled and shook his head. "How about attempted murder?"

"Who?"

"Hasn't happened yet."

"No?"

"Not yet."

"In that case, who is going to try and kill whom?"

Bud looked at his friend and nodded in the direction of the hallway and said, "Let's talk in my office."

Bud gave Nancy a hug and said, "Duty calls."

She shook her head, and said, "Of course," a touch of disappointment showing.

When Howard and Bud pushed into the Lake County Sheriff's office through the interconnecting door from the courthouse hallway, Karen Highsmith looked up. She didn't smile, but she did manage to say "Congratulations," without too much disapproval in her voice.

Bud raised one eyebrow, very much aware of her unspoken censure, but settled for, "Word gets around fast, doesn't it?"

She nodded, then stood up and walked around the booking counter to give Bud a hug. "Ginger just called me."

He pushed her gently away and said, "Howard and I will be in my office." He glanced at his watch and added, "Get with dispatch and have all of our officers here at five o'clock. That includes Roger."

Coffee cups in hand, the two old friends sat across from each other at Bud's scarred wooden desk while Bud brought Finch up-to-date. When he finished, Bud stared at him and waited.

Finally, Finch rocked the wooden chair back on two legs and said, "I have to wonder how a remote western county can attract so damned much attention from the evil elements of this world."

He dropped the front legs of the chair back on the floor, slapped the desk top and said, "Okay, Bud. You catch 'em and I'll put 'em away. This time I want TV coverage and the world watching. It's time the citizens of this country woke up to what's happening. I swear to the Lord above, the people of our country don't believe in evil, and it's going to cost us dearly if we don't wake up."

27

Human Trafficking

IN PORTLAND, SPECIAL AGENT LEROY WILCOX GLANCED at his partner in the passenger seat of their black SUV.

Cell phone to his ear, Special Agent Douglas Brandt listened to another of Smitty's rants about Wilcox not answering his calls, and when Smitty asked what they had done with Cletus Falls, Brandt said, "We don't want to talk about Cletus over the phone. I'm not sure you need to know where Cletus is hiding, but since we don't know either, we can't tell you anyway."

Wilcox could hear Smitty shouting when Brandt held the phone away from his ear. The words, "Are you listening?" were clear to Wilcox.

Brandt shook his head in disgust and said into the phone, "Sorry, Boss. You're breaking up," and killed the call.

With raised eyebrows Wilcox said, "So?"

Brandt shook his head. "Well, Leroy," he always made it sound like "Lee Roy," instead of the "Lah Roy" like Wilcox's mama wanted it to be, "your ass is grass as far as Smitty is concerned. You really should take his calls. It would make my life a lot easier."

"Someday, I will," Wilcox said, "like when he calls from D.C."

"Okay, then. Smitty knows Butler is on the take. And he knows Butler is likely to run."

Wilcox nodded. "Our watchers, probably."

"Yep. Smitty says they have a recording of a really nasty conversation between Butler and Al-Alwani which pretty much nails Butler's hide to the wall. Smitty has a BOLO on Butler out to all FBI units on the West Coast. And he said a team is watching Butler's cabin cruiser down on the Willamette Channel."

Brandt took a deep breath, paused and shook his head. "And he said we are to look for Butler at the safe house."

"We know he's not there." Wilcox said.

"Yeah, I know, but let's go look anyway … keep Smitty happy."

"You didn't say anything to Smitty about Butler's call."

"I know. If you'd answer your phone…"

"Damn it, Douglas, what did Butler say?"

"Temper, Leroy. You drive and I'll talk."

Leroy Wilcox made a strange guttural sound deep in his throat that could only be interpreted as negative. But he started the engine, dropped the gear shift into drive, and left a streak of tire marks on the pavement.

Brandt braced his right elbow against the door as Wilcox made a sliding turn onto a left side street. "Better, Leroy. Better. Anyway, what Butler said after letting me know he was gonna boogie, is that Al-Alwani is trafficking in humans. And he said we should look for a container on the Portland docks – one full of kidnapped girls destined for shipment to Yemen.

"He got to laughing in a really crazy-sounding way, and then told me he was going to make our careers. The jihadists aren't only stockpiling weapons, they're snatching women and shipping them to the Middle East. I think he wants us to find that shipping container."

Brandt hit the emergency lights hiding in the grill of the SUV, accelerated, blew through a red light, and said through gritted teeth, "Why us?"

"Said he likes us, and he thinks you got screwed when D.C. sent Smitty out here. Wanted to do something right for a change."

"Oh, goody," Wilcox said with a cynical growl.

"You can slow down now, Leroy," Brandt said as Wilcox powered his way into the first of the short, tight corners of the streets leading up to the safe house. "You're making me car sick."

Wilcox eased off the throttle and said, "Douglas, you are turning into a real pain in the ass."

"I know, but I'm the only one who can stand to partner with you."

"So, who are we going to share this with?"

Brandt took a deep breath, his blue eyes looking into the distance, not seeing the flash of maple and fir trees guarding the narrow street. Wilcox waited … and Brandt finally said, "I hate to admit it, but even though Smitty is a genuine asshole, I don't see how he could possibly be dirty."

28

To Err is Human

TJ WILDISH LEANED ON BB'S DECK RAIL and just stared at the lake. He took a deep breath and looked at BB sitting in a patio recliner, an empty beer glass on a side table, his camo Cabela's cap over his eyes. Miranda was sitting in another patio recliner opposite BB, sipping a Diet Coke and studying BB's Audubon Guide to Western Birds, comparing pictures in the book to those on the internet.

The drone of a small single-engine airplane accented the quiet, and TJ said, "You know, I don't think that even once in my life, not once, can I remember not hearing the noise of the city or to not feel the vibrations Portland gives off.

"It feels strange. I mean, it's like the world just stopped turning. But, I think I'm as relaxed as I've ever been."

BB pushed the cap back on his forehead and looked at TJ. "I know what you mean, Wildman. That's why I go fishing – to get me some peace and quiet."

"Dang it, BB, you know I don't go by Wildman anymore, not since I was saved." He glared at BB for a few seconds and let his breath out. "Well, as for peace and quiet, you sure have that here. I wish I could just stay for a while."

BB raised his eyebrows and smiled, "I thought you'd be sick of fresh air and silence by now, but we don't have to head out until morning, if that's what you want. Won't anybody bother us tonight."

TJ said, "Do you have a boat?"

"I do. A big canoe."

"I'd like to get out on the lake."

"Okay. If you and Miranda sit very still and promise not to tip us over, we'll do some perch fishing. Might catch enough for supper."

Miranda put the book on her lap and looked at BB. "You sure that's wise?"

BB said, "I don't see why or how any of the bad guys could even get here before tomorrow. In the morning, TJ and I will take the back way out of here – follow the forest roads to Bly. We won't even go through a real town until we hit I-5 at Roseburg. I've got it all mapped out."

"Well, a canoe ride sounds nice," she said. "I'll bring my camera."

"And your pistol?"

"What kind of a question is that? Of course. Rule number one: don't leave home without your cell phone and your pistol. It isn't ladylike."

29

Of Mice and Men

A GENT WINSLOW BUTLER, NOW ON THE run from his own people, had planned well. The money Al-Alwani paid him over the past five years was hiding in three banks, with an extra fifty thousand of his own money hidden in a second boat he'd bought in secret. He knew the FBI would be watching the small cabin cruiser he rented from the owner of Guy's Marina. But he didn't need to go there again. Never.

His 'legend,' built carefully over a three-year period was as foolproof as he could make it, complete with legitimate credit cards, a birth certificate that would pass at least cursory inspection, and a passport identifying him as an American citizen named David Kojak. It would take a forensics accountant to find him.

He knew they would try, but he planned to be living in plain sight in Homer, Alaska. With a beard, new glasses, and a black watch cap. His mother wouldn't have been able to recognize him. Slowly, he would transfer money from the three banks into a new bank account in Homer – at about five thousand dollars per month. Nothing very extraordinary about that for a retired policeman weary of the population pressures of life in the States.

He regretted the loss of his retirement, but there was nothing to do about that now. He took some bitter consolation that his ex-wife wouldn't get any of it either.

The taxi he hired stopped in front of a locked iron gate flanked by a discrete bronze sign proclaiming the land beyond the gate to be The Columbia River Yacht Club. The driver looked at the meter. "That's thirty-seven-fifty."

Butler handed him two twenties and a five. "Keep the change."

Boogie bag in hand, Butler watched the taxi turn around and head back upriver towards Portland. When the taxi was out of sight, he punched the key code in the pad by the pilgrim gate.

It wasn't until he walked the ramp down to the docks, and then to his boat slip, that he realized his heart was pounding and his breathing was heavy. He eyeballed the marina, checked out the boat, and stepped aboard. He tried the latch and breathed a sigh of relief when the cabin door was still locked. *They aren't on to me … yet.*

He spent the remaining daylight hours running through his checklist: fuel levels, batteries, running lights, GPS, radio, radar, flare gun, survival suit, AR-15, ammo, first aid … the whole nine yards.

He fired up the twin diesels and let them idle for a good five minutes, then shut them down.

Anxious, he watched the news on the small TV set mounted on the wall above the bed in the little state room, knowing the whole time the FBI wouldn't announce to the world they were looking for a rogue agent. But it made him feel better, anyway, that he hadn't made the news.

He ate a trail bar, drank a soda, listened to a sudden rain shower pounding the cabin roof, and waited for dark. The clouds thickened, the sky turned blue-black, and he became impatient with the waiting. He donned his rain gear, started the engines, and set them to idle. Rain pattered the hood of his storm jacket as he slipped the mooring lines and stepped back on the deck.

He eased the boat back out of the slip, spun the wheel and headed quietly and slowly down the marina channel to the Columbia.

"A good start," he said to himself. And then he laughed and said, "Find me if you can."

He was below St. Helens, running lights on, radar feeding the screen in the wheelhouse, when the lights quit and the engine stopped. He turned the key, but nothing happened.

"Shit." He fumbled to find a flashlight on the dash and hurried to find his emergency running lights. He attached the emergency lights to the antennae and then walked to the back of boat to open the hatch to the engine room. The flashlight failed to give him a clue as to what was wrong.

He was taking the battery terminals loose one at a time and cleaning each when he heard the "slush" of a bow wave. He climbed back up to the deck and looked downriver in time to see the bow of a container ship riding high over his beautiful boat.

If anyone had been listening they would have heard a resigned voice saying, "The best laid plans…"

30

All Hands

Bud's officers crowded into his small office, coffee cups in one hand and donuts in the other, thanks to Karen Highsmith.

Deputy Larae Holcomb-Bernard smiled and nodded at Bud over Roger's beefy shoulder. Bud remembered first seeing her riding into town astride a black Harley, dressed in a tank top, a hooded Cobra tattoo on her left shoulder – compliments of an undercover assignment several years earlier with a biker gang. For Bud, it almost overshadowed the fact that she was a trim, athletic woman who, when she smiled, was darned near beautiful. He grinned and said, "I thought you quit."

She tilted her head back and looked at Bud. "Is that what you want?"

"Of course not, but Roger said you wanted to be a stay-at-home mom."

"I do, but you seldom call an 'all-hands' meeting. Made me think you might need my assistance. John can watch the baby until I get back."

Bud smiled and said, "How is that little rascal?"

Larae smiled back and said, "If you mean the baby, he's growing like a weed. If you mean John, he's getting restless. He likes horses and cattle, and he likes haying, but I think our six hundred forty acres is beginning to feel a bit small."

"I'll send him to Monmouth for academy training any time he wants."

She shook her head. "That would be redundant. They have nothing to teach him."

"Except which laws he might want to break," Bud said with a grin. "You tell him I'll hire him in heartbeat."

Bud saw Lonnie Beltram frowning and said, "Not to worry, Lonnie. Your grant came through. We can hire another deputy. Good job, by the way."

Wide-bodied Roger Hildebrand said, "What's that about?"

Bud said, "Let's move this to the conference room."

As they walked down the short hallway, Bud said to Roger, "You working out? You look like you've lost some weight."

"Thirty pounds, Boss. I'm working out with Gar ... uh ... I mean John, Larae's husband. He kept nagging me about going to pot, so we started jogging five miles three mornings a week. And we lift a few weights in my garage."

"It will always be Gar, won't it? Anyway, you're looking good, Roger."

"Yeah. Me and Gar – just two old warriors working out."

"I don't suppose he swam to Kuwait with you?"

Roger frowned and walked into the conference room without saying anything.

Deputy Beatrice Tusk, all five-feet-five inches of her, looked at Roger without saying anything, but she thought the big man was nice looking ... dark hair in a crewcut ... not handsome ... just regular features ... maybe five-eleven ... seeming shorter than that because he was so wide in the shoulders. *I wonder if he has a girlfriend. I'll ask Karen. If he doesn't...*

Bud walked to the head of the long table and said, "Before we get down to business, I'm happy to report that Sonny Sixkiller will be rejoining our happy team in about four weeks. I want to emphasize that I'm not at all unhappy with the job Lonnie has done in keeping this outfit afloat. In due time, he will be a good undersheriff, but Sonny will give us experience that only comes with years on the job."

Lonnie nodded and said, "Thanks, Boss."

"No, you deserve the thanks, Lonnie. I'm afraid I've been a bit distracted lately."

"Lately?" Karen quipped.

"Lately," Bud growled. "That said, I will admit to being sheriff in name only for the last couple of months. But that's over and done with."

Karen gave him a sideways look and a smile, then said sweetly, "Does your interest in being our sheriff once again have anything to do with your recent engagement to Nancy Sixkiller?"

Bud shook his head. "No. Well, maybe. It sure as hell doesn't hurt."

Roger grinned and said, "I told you so, Boss. Congratulations."

"How nice," Bea said with a smile. "Who's the lucky lady?"

Karen said, "His once-upon-a-time fiancée who dumped him last fall, Nancy Sixkiller."

"The nice woman who runs the Emergency Services Center?"

"One and the same."

Head cocked sideways, Bea stared at Karen through her dark brown eyes and then said quietly so Bud wouldn't hear, "And I'll bet there's a story in that."

Karen winked and whispered, "For later."

Lonnie echoed Roger's congratulations.

"Okay, enough," Bud said. "Karen, please go cover the desk and find out what's keeping our esteemed DA. I want him here."

"And speak of the devil," Bud said as Sonny Sixkiller walked into the room. "What brings you to the fine city of Lakeview? Or is that 'who' brings you?"

The lean six-footer grinned and said, "Well I heard my baby sister was fixing to marry a cop."

Howard Finch sidled through the door behind Sonny and pitched in, "And about time, too. Maybe Nancy can sweeten him up – if that's possible."

Sonny held out his hand. "Nice to see you again, Boss. Congratulations."

Bud grinned. "Thank you. I believe I owe you congratulations as well."

Sonny grinned back, but didn't say anything.

Bea whispered in Karen's ear, "What's that about."

"Sonny is engaged to Carol Connor, the editor of our paper."

Bud steered the conversation away from engagements and weddings. He looked at Roger and said, "Before we get started, do you have anything new on the drive-by shooting in Christmas Valley?"

"The people living in the trailer won't talk to me. Scared, I think. But something is hinky about the whole thing. I put a trail camera on a post near their driveway. I want to see who comes and who goes."

Karen frowned. "Hinky? What in the world does that mean?"

Sonny laughed and said, "You don't know 'hinky?' I thought you white-eyes knew everything."

Roger thought Bea's laugh was about the sexiest sound he ever heard. If Bea noticed, she didn't let on. "I know hinky," she said. "It means out of whack."

Roger smiled. "Yeah. The civilian version of SNAFU without the 'normal' in it."

"Okay.," Bud said. "Let's focus on the reason I called this all-hands meeting."

***

AN HOUR LATER THE WALLS OF the conference room were papered with flip charts that included diagrams of Dog Lake and the road which ran along the west side of it, possible surveillance positions, estimated times – down to seconds – to BB's house from the eye-and-spy locations, surveillance schedules, equipment, tactical channel settings for the radios, weapons, likely route of ingress for the bad guys, vehicles, medical backup, and after-action plans.

Bud held a magic marker in his right hand and asked "What else?" Just then, the phone started ringing. Bud ignored it until Karen's voice rattled the intercom. "Bud, you'd better take this call."

"Who is it?"

"The FBI. Somebody named Dutch Vanderlin."

"Okay. I'll take it in my office." Bud looked at his team and said, "Break time. I'll go see what Dutch wants."

Dutch listened to Bud's recap of the plan to trap any thugs sent by Al-Alwani. "Sounds good, but you're a little thin on manpower."

"How many can they send?" Bud said. "We can cover the roads and trap anyone who shows up."

"I'm sending you a SWAT team – a short team – four people and a helicopter. My best people. ETA about three hours."

31

Contrition

BUTLER'S AWARENESS COINCIDED WITH DAYLIGHT AS a weak sun poked a hole in the scattered clouds drifting upriver from the Pacific.

Flat on his stomach, right cheek kissing the hard deck, head throbbing, and chilled to the bone, he felt like every joint in his body had taken a pounding. He pushed himself up and rocked back on his knees. A big knot on the side of his head pulsed against his black watch cap. He tried pulling the cap loose, but dried blood glued it in place.

He sat for a full twenty seconds, his mind blank, unable to recall how he had come to this place. He reached for the rail that had taken a blow from his hard skull, and pulled himself upright.

A breeze riffled the surface of the big river and broke sun beams into bouncing shards of light. Rows of cottonwood and alder muted the noise from distant traffic on I-5. A puff of wind carried the rank odor of mud flats. And then memory came flooding back – the heavy rain storm, the nighttime loss of power and lights, and the unexpected dark menace of an upriver container ship rising bow-to-bow over his boat. He remembered the deck tilting under his feet as The Runaway rode the bow wave generated by the freighter, causing him to fall across the slanted deck and run head long into a metal rail.

"I'll be damned," he said aloud. "Missed me … sort of. I think I know what "Kiss your ass goodbye" means now. I knew I was dead."

He walked to the port side rail and looked down at the side of the boat. Not a scratch in sight. "If I believed in God, I'd say the hand of Providence spared me, but I think I'm beyond salvation."

A quick survey told him the bow of The Runaway was stuck on a sand bar, but the stern was parked over much deeper water.

"Just drifted in and parked. Damned lucky."

The warmer air in the wheelhouse welcomed Butler and somehow fueled a bit of optimism. He pulled a first aid kit from a cupboard and headed for the shower to doctor his bloody head.

Twenty minutes later, his cut cleaned and sprayed with antiseptic, followed by a cup of warm coffee from the thermos in the galley, Butler was feeling a bit better. He changed into dry clothes, slipped arms in the sleeves of a red mackinaw, and then went out on deck. He opened the hatch to the engine compartment. "Judas!" he said. "Who is trying to kill me? Not the FBI. They would just arrest me. It's gotta be Al-Alwani."

The small bomb, wrapped in plastic bags and taped to the power junction, had failed, but the detonator had not. Instead of destroying The Runaway … and killing Butler … it simply burned wires and killed the power instead, leaving Butler adrift.

Thirty minutes of cutting, stripping, and insulating bare wires with black electrician's tape saw the engines running again and all navigation and radio systems operable. Butler put both engines in reverse and pushed the throttles to max rpm. The water foamed and boiled and then The Runaway broke free. The sudden movement caught Butler off guard and slammed his sternum against the brass wheel, but the pain was softened by the relief of getting off the sand bar and on his way down river again.

Five hours later, he eased The Runaway into the boat basin fronting the Red Lion in Astoria. He tied off, and then headed up the dock to the marina office. He used a bogus credit card to pay for two weeks of moorage.

Sometime between breaking free of the sandbar and the five hours it took to reach Astoria, salted with a great of deal of guilt and sorrow for his lost life, Winslow Butler resolved to try and make things right again.

32

When Things Go Awry

BB LED HIS GUESTS TO THE GARAGE, punched the control button, then watched the garage door rise and coast to a stop on the overhead rails. He pulled three self-inflating life preservers from a gunmetal gray cabinet and handed one to each of his guests.

Miranda fumbled with the shoulder straps, and he reached to pull the bottom strap around her waist. A hint of scented soap stirred memories of earlier, happier days.

He hadn't thought about his ex-wife in a long time. He'd felt like a failure in the early days of the divorce, but after a year or two he finally admitted he was glad she was gone ... and that she had taken her emotional instability with her.

He snapped the buckles and said, "There, Miranda. That should keep you afloat."

Miranda smiled and said, "Thank you." The sensation of BB's arms reaching around her hadn't been at all unpleasant. "Do you have any children?" She asked.

A frown creased his forehead as he stepped back and looked into her light brown eyes. "A son. Brian Dell BeBe. A career Marine."

"Was that his picture in the family room?"

"Yep."

"He's a handsome young man. He looks a lot like his father."

"That's too bad," BB said with a grin. He closed the cabinet, and pulled two paddles loose from the clip hangers on the wall.

"You carry these and I'll bring the tackle. Follow the path. The canoe is down by the lake. I'll bring the rest of the gear."

BB watched until they were out of sight, then he rolled a set of metal cabinets away from the wall to expose a large gun safe hiding in a cutout there.

He punched a series of numbers into the keypad and pushed the locking handle down. To call the guns in the safe an 'arsenal' was to exaggerate, but he did own a respectable number of weapons, including two AR-15's he'd personally modified to shoot either three-round bursts or a fully-automatic stream of fire.

BB selected one of them, slipped two thirty-round clips in the side pocket of the black canvas gun case, then closed and locked the safe. He rolled the cabinet back in place and shook his head. "Paranoid, I guess."

***

REVEREND TJ WILDISH FROWNED WHEN HE saw Dell BeBe carrying a fishing pole and a tackle box in one hand … and what was obviously a rifle case in the other.

BB said, "I know what you're thinking, Reverend, but it never hurts to be prepared."

"You said they wouldn't get here before tomorrow at the earliest."

"It's not likely, but those assholes aren't the only source of evil in the world."

Miranda nodded and said, "He's right, Reverend. It seems that any town with more than ten thousand people has at least some gang activity."

TJ looked sad and shook his head. "What do you suppose has gone wrong?"

Miranda said, "I think when families fall apart, the gangs offer friendship and protection. Call it love, if you'd like. And a lot of young people, far too many, have nowhere else to turn."

"If only they could find faith in Christ and the love of his Church."

BB ignored TJ and pushed the canoe into the water. He steadied the canoe and said, "You get up front, Miranda."

***

BB PADDLED THE CANOE QUIETLY ACROSS the lake to a weed patch he hoped might hold some yellow perch. A mallard hen with a dozen ducklings matched the speed of the canoe, marking the still water with tiny wakes, not letting BB close the distance between the canoe and her brood, but not moving with any sense of panic either.

He shipped the paddle and let the canoe glide. It lost headway close to the weed bed, and he eased a cannon ball anchor over the side.

"Lovely," Miranda said.

"God's great wonders right here in front of us," TJ said in a quiet voice. "I'm not given to jealousy, BB, but I might admit to a hint of envy that you live in such a wonderous place."

BB laughed and said, "You should visit during the winter when the lake is frozen and the snow is ass deep to a tall Indian."

"Every rose has its thorn," Miranda said, "but the rose always smells as sweet."

"Not when it pricks you," BB chuckled.

***

AN HOUR LATER, THE SHADOWS OF the tall pine on the shore were reaching across the still surface of Dog Lake. BB had six nice perch on the stringer, and Miranda had at least fifty digital photos of ducks – including one bright northern shoveler that flew down the lake at about three feet off the water. "Beautiful," she had murmured.

TJ, binoculars on his lap, was half upright on the bottom of the boat, leaned back on a cushion propped against the center strut. A quiet snore told BB and Miranda he had gone to sleep.

BB smiled at his childhood friend, and shook his head. "Worn out, I would guess," he said quietly.

Miranda nodded and mouthed silently, "Tired."

Something about their jointly-shared protective feelings for TJ drew the two law enforcement officers into the realm of intimacy. Both felt it, and both wished it was of more substance than only of the moment.

The muted sound of car tires crunching gravel in BB's driveway carried across the lake. "What's that?" Miranda asked.

"Looks like someone pulling into my driveway." BB unzipped a pocket in his green safari vest and pulled out his cell phone. Bud answered on the third ring. "Bud, this is BB. Did you send someone out here? Or did you just get back?"

"What's going on?"

"Someone just pulled into my driveway. We aren't at the house. We're across the lake in my canoe, catching perch and shooting bird pictures."

"No. It's not me, and I didn't send anyone your way yet. We plan to."

TJ sat up and blinked. "What's going on?"

Miranda put her index finger across her lip in a hushing gesture.

"Well, I'm not liking this," BB said.

"It can't be the bad guys," Bud said. "They haven't had time to get there, and Dutch would have tipped us off."

"TJ has my binoculars. I'll take a look."

TJ handed the ten-power field glasses to BB and raised his eyebrows in question. "Nothing to worry about, TJ. Probably just a traveling salesman ... or the Watchtower people."

"Out here? No way."

BB pulled his log home into focus, just as a bearded man carrying a rifle walked out on the deck, a pair of binoculars in his hand. BB watched the man focus on the canoe. When the man set his binoculars on the top rail of BB's deck and then slipped an elbow through the rifle sling, BB knew they were in trouble. He dropped the cell phone in the bottom of the boat, grabbed an oar and shouted, "Get down!"

He pulled a short Gerber dagger from his boot top and slashed the anchor line. He was digging hard on the paddle before a slug slammed the water a good twenty yards short of the canoe, the slug ricocheting over the canoe between BB and TJ.

BB turned the canoe end-on to the shore and paddled as hard as he could for the bank where a thick grove of alders sheltered a small cove. *If we can get to the trees...*

The faint sound of Bud's voice could be heard on BB's cell phone. TJ picked it up and said, "Sheriff. This is TJ. We're out on the lake and someone is shooting at us. BB is trying to get us to shore."

"Which shore?"

"Across the lake from BB's house."

"Help is on the way. You guys okay?"

"No one's been shot … yet."

Miranda's paddle was dipping in rhythm with BB when the wooden handle exploded a split second before the sound of a rifle shot carried across the lake. Stunned, she just stared at the large splinter sticking through her left hand.

About thirty feet from the bank, BB deliberately tipped the canoe over and hoped the water was shallow enough for them to walk to shore.

When his feet touched bottom, he reached under the overturned canoe and pulled the Velcro straps loose from the gun case.

"Stay low and head for the trees. Miranda go left into the trees. TJ go right. Got it?"

TJ sputtered and thrashed in the water, more scared of drowning than of being shot. BB grabbed him by the collar of the life vest and said, "Damn, it, TJ, quit that! Put your feet down. You can reach bottom now. Stay low and crawl in behind that big alder tree over there."

BB pushed TJ in the direction of the shore in time to watch Miranda duck behind a small pine, dragging her daypack with her good hand. The sound of another shot followed a slug that punched a hole in BB's canoe.

"He's starting to get the range dialed in," he muttered, as he pushed a dripping TJ up on the bank and in behind a good-sized alder. "Stay here," he said.

"Miranda. You okay?"

"No," she said through gritted teeth. "I have a big splinter sticking out the back of my hand."

"Okay. Stay low and head further into the trees. When we have enough cover, we'll hook up, and I'll see what I can do about your hand."

33

Round Up

Bud LOOKED AT HIS DEPUTIES AND said, "Dell BeBe just called. He's in trouble. He's on Dog Lake in his canoe, and someone is shooting at them – 'them' defined as BB, FBI agent Miranda Wright, and the Reverend TJ Wildish. That's all I have. And BB's cell went offline. He's not answering my calls.

"Karen, you keep trying his number. If he answers, relay anything useful he has to say. And call Dutch Vanderlin. Tell him what's going on. The SWAT team won't get here in time."

"Lonnie, I want you and Bea to head for Lofton Reservoir. Take both vehicles. Plug the back road into Dog Lake. And hustle. Let's see if we can trap these guys."

"Larae, take Roger's vehicle and follow us. I want you to block the Dog Lake road when we get beyond the houses on Drews Reservoir. Keep travelers out until we get this cleaned up.

"Roger, you ride with me. Everybody armor up. Use tac channel one. Let's move it, boys and girls!"

"What about me?" Sonny asked.

"You got a rig?"

"Yeah, Deschutes County."

"You up to a helicopter ride?"

"Oh, shit. You know I hate those things."

"Yeah, I do. But I need some eyes in the sky. I'm worried about that Forest Service road running south from Dog Lake toward the California border. And if there's any shooting, you duck this time."

Sonny gave Bud a grim smile, and involuntarily rubbed the nasty scar on the top of his head, compliments of a chunk of lava blown his way by terrorists who blew themselves up and were trying to take some American infidels with them.

"You don't need to remind me."

Lake County District Attorney, Howard Finch, perhaps for the first time in his entire life, listened until Bud finished his torrent of orders. When Bud stopped talking, Howard looked up at the officers, all of whom were taller than he – with the exception of Beatrice Tusk – and said, "Bring me pictures, maps, fingerprints, ID's, reports, any and all physical evidence … the whole nine yards. Let's collect ground-floor evidence on this. And for Christ's sake don't get hurt!"

***

THE SOUND OF FOUR POLICE VEHICLES, emergency lights pulsing and sirens screaming, had citizens of Lakeview rushing to store windows or stepping out of doorways to see what the racket was about.

Carol Conner, managing editor and chief reporter of the Lake County News, rushed to the front window of the newspaper office and watched. Her heart rate increased, and before the caravan turned the corner at the north end of the business district, she was on the phone with Karen Highsmith.

"Karen? This is Carol Connor. What's going on? I think I just saw the entire Lake County Sheriff's department go by at a very noisy, very high rate of speed."

As his vehicle crossed the railroad tracks on the west edge of town, Bud grabbed his mic and said, "Control, this is County One. We have an emergency situation at Dog Lake. Shots have been fired. Switching to tac channel one.

"I want eyes in the sky. Sonny Sixkiller is headed for the airport. Hire the Forest Service helicopter out there. I need Sonny in the air and headed for Dog Lake ASAP."

"Copy. Control out."

Bud hesitated for minute and glanced at Roger. "What am I forgetting?"

"Ambulance."

Bud nodded and keyed the mic. "Control, this is County One. Roll an ambulance. The EMT's can rendezvous with Officer Holcomb just beyond Drews Reservoir. Have them use this channel."

Nancy's voice carried a hint of tension when she broke protocol and said, "Bud. What's going on?"

He answered, "I don't know. Dell BB called. He said someone was shooting at him, and then his phone went dead."

"You be careful."

He nearly smiled when he said, "Yes ma'am."

Recognizable voices chimed in, one at a time, saying "Yes, ma'am. Yes, ma'am. Yes, ma'am."

Gus Hildebrand was chuckling when he keyed his mic and said with his good ol' boy drawl, "County One, this is Lakeview Police Chief Augustus Hildebrand. You guys and gals need any help?"

Bud thought for a minute, and then said, "You could post a car on Drews Creek at the bridge and stop traffic until we get this sorted out."

"I'm on the way, Mister Sheriff."

"Stay out of trouble, Gus. County One out."

34

Major Crimes Unit

S PECIAL AGENTS LEROY WILCOX AND DOUGLAS Brant sat in padded
office chairs, a big mahogany desk between them and Special
Agent Richard McDonald – a thin, wiry middle-aged man wearing
gold-rimmed spectacles, his hair grown long on the sides and then
combed over to hide a growing bald spot.

His slight stature and academic look belied an iron will. A keen in-
telligence, coupled with an eidetic memory made him, in the opinion of
almost every agent who ever worked with or for him, "One hell of an
FBI agent."

Special Agent McDonald, head of the Portland FBI Major Crimes
Unit, rocked back in his expensive five-point, ergonomically engineered
chair and said, "So … you have a tip from an anonymous source."

Brandt and Wilcox glanced at each other and nodded. They weren't
quite yet willing to give Butler up.

Wilcox said, "Yes."

"I'm a suspicious man, Agent Wilcox. On the one hand, I see a BOLO
for Agent Butler. On the other hand, I hear you have an anonymous tip.
It makes me wonder if the two are connected."

Brandt frowned and snapped at McDonald. "You want to hear what
we have to say or not?"

Special Agent McDonald rocked forward in his chair and placed
his elbows on the desk, hand clasped under his chin. He glanced from

Wilcox to Brandt and then down to the surface of his desk. He closed his eyes for a couple of seconds, then took a deep breath. He straightened up and pulled a blank note pad across the table from a nearly empty inbox. Pen in hand McDonald said, "Okay. Tell me."

When Wilcox finished the story he and Brandt had agreed upon, McDonald stopped writing, put his pen down, and asked, "What do you need from me?"

"Okay," Wilcox said. "Do you have anything on human trafficking? Could it be true?"

McDonald, animated for the first time, said, "Yes. There is human trafficking going on. Primarily young women. We have insider information, but we have yet to figure out how it's being done. The capture part, we understand. Teenage girls are particularly vulnerable, easy to lure. I think a fifteen-year-old girl may be about the dumbest animal on the planet. But how they are smuggled out of the country is still a mystery. Trucks to Mexico, and then air to the Mideast maybe."

"How about ships?" Wilcox asked.

McDonald shrugged his shoulders. "Maybe. We spot check invoices, make unannounced inspections, pay dockworkers under the table. All we really have are rumors."

"What if we gave you a solid tip? Would you go after it?"

McDonald rocked back in his chair again and said, "Have you talked to your boss?"

They both shook their heads.

"Why not?"

"Our snitch tells us there's a leak inside this office. That may be why you never find anything on the docks."

"You don't know who to trust?"

"That's it."

"And you don't trust your boss."

Brandt leaned forward and said, "Yeah. We do. But he's so damned naïve, and so political, we don't know if he can keep it to himself."

"And if he doesn't?"

"We might lose a boatload of young women."

McDonald rocked forward and reached for his phone. "Let's get your boss in here, and let's get Dutch involved. I think I can convince very Special Agent Smith to keep the circle small. But you may have to give up your source."

35

Hunters

ANOTHER ROUND FROM THE RIFLE ACROSS the lake ricocheted into the timber, the slug pulling a small fountain of water from the surface before clipping a low-hanging branch from a small pine tree. BB watched the branch float to the ground, then dragged TJ behind the largest tree he could find. "Get out of that life jacket, and keep your ass down."

Miranda's three measured rounds of pistol fire startled BB, and then he found himself shaking his head in admiration for her spunk if not her good sense. "Did you hit it?"

"Hit what?" she muttered in exasperation from behind a stump, leftover evidence of logging from years past.

"My house."

"Oh, shit."

"Yeah. Oh, shit. Save your ammunition. We might need it later."

"I'm pissed," she said, holding up her left hand, a thin stream of blood running down her forearm.

"Save that, too. Right now, I need to know if your cell phone is working."

"I can't open my pack."

"Toss it over here."

TJ caught a glimpse of a man running through the small pine trees south of BB's house. "BB," he said, "I see a guy going to our left and maybe another to our right. I'm not sure about the second one, but I did see something moving over there." He pointed in the direction of Bud's A-Frame.

As he unzipped Miranda's dripping daypack, the sound of another rifle shot from the direction of his house told BB what he needed to know. "There are at least three of them."

He pointed behind them and said, "You two boogie on out of here. There's a little meadow about four hundred yards due east. Stay in the timber, when you get there, and wait. I'll be along shortly. And don't shoot me. I'll whistle before I come in."

BB watched Miranda and TJ crouch and run through the trees until they were out of sight. He shook the contents of Miranda's wet daypack out on the ground. "Thank God," he muttered when he saw a cell phone, nice and dry in a Ziploc bag. He crawled in behind a large pine and powered on the phone. When the screen lit up, he realized with mild surprise he'd been holding his breath. From memory, he keyed in Bud's cell number and hit send.

Bud answered on the third ring, the muted sound of sirens in the background. "This is Sheriff Blair."

"Bud, this is BB. I'm on Miranda's cell."

"Are you guys all right."

"No one's been shot, but Miranda has a big ugly splinter through her left hand. A slug shattered her paddle. What do you have headed this way?"

"I have two officers who will sweep the back road from Lofton Reservoir to Dog Lake. Roger Hildebrand and I are headed for your place. We just hit the timber along Drews Creek. ETA seven or eight minutes … if I don't hit a deer.

"And we'll have Sonny Sixkiller in a helicopter in another five or ten minutes. He'll be our eyes in the sky. So, tell me what you know."

"Okay. There are at least three perps. One is still shooting blindly in our direction, every thirty seconds or so, from across the lake. I think he's trying to make us think there's only one shooter, so he's staying put. TJ said he saw a man circling the lake to the south and maybe another circling to the north. We don't know that for sure. Sounds pretty stupid to me … unless they don't believe we spotted them."

"I'm going to give the phone to Officer Hildebrand."

BB could hear muffled voices and then Roger Hildebrand said, "Hello, Mister BeBe. What's your location?"

"Do you know Dog Lake?"

"Yes, I caught a few bass and perch up there when I was a kid."

"Okay. We're on the east side of the lake. Agent Wright and TJ Wildish are headed for a little meadow about a quarter mile due east. They'll hold there and wait for me."

"Are you armed?"

BB nodded and said, "I've got an AR-15, two full clips, and my pistol. And Agent Wright has her pistol."

"Good. I'd suggest you hook up with the rest of your party. Can a helicopter land in that meadow?"

"It's big enough."

"Good. Do you all need a ride out of there?"

BB nodded and said, "Yes. Miranda needs medical attention, and TJ isn't worth a shit if he isn't standing on concrete or asphalt."

BB heard a chuckle. "I know what you mean. And you either have what it takes or you don't. I'd suggest you save battery and check in again when you hear the sirens or the helicopter."

"Okay. I'm going hunting now." He shut the phone down and slipped it into his right front pocket. He took a deep breath to steady himself, unzipped the rifle case, and shook his head at the sour memory of a teenager shooting his partner Bud Blair. BB had reluctantly returned fire and killed the teenager. *I thought I was long past this business of shooting people.*

He worked the action, seated a live round in the chamber of the AR-15, and took a quick peek from behind the tree. "Damn," he said when he saw the bullet hole gouged in the side of his canoe. Only the built-in flotation kept it from sinking.

He stuffed Miranda's clutter back in her daypack and the spare clip in his pocket. *I think I'd better stick with TJ and Miranda and get them out of here. Then I'll catch these sonsabitches. I want to know who sent them. That's the dude I want.*

36

Run

CLETUS WAS RESTLESS. BB'S APARTMENT HAD no TV, no phone, and there wasn't a computer to be had. He paced the small living room in the fourth-floor apartment and watched a white yacht ease into the boat basin below the redbrick high-rise. He wondered what it would be like to own a cabin cruiser. Or what it would be like to live here in this complex of gray-green boardwalks, docks, stores, restaurants, luxury houseboats, spas, beauty shops, and convenience stores – like the one on the second floor of BB's apartment building.

A social animal, on a normal day Cletus was in constant motion. He was on the phone with his sports paraphernalia suppliers, with his umbrella supplier (two-dollars and no shipping charge for orders of five hundred or more), checking in with his sales people, and always checking the weather to see if it was time for umbrellas or Rose City t-shirts on folding tables at the major Max stations.

But this wasn't one of those 'normal' days. The clear memory of a black pistol, and of Agent Butler, who Cletus knew had to be on the take, kept him inside.

Frustrated by his self-imposed restrictions, but knowing it was dangerous to be on the street, Cletus settled for a quick elevator ride to the little convenience store on the second floor. The smell of spices and fresh produce greeted him when he pushed through a glass door carrying the gold inscription of "Chin Lee Market."

A very pretty Eurasian girl behind the counter, long dark hair pulled into a ponytail, smiled and said, "Hello." Cletus straightened his shoulders and smiled back. The only word of Chinese he knew wasn't something you said to young women, so he settled for "Hi."

He pulled copies of The Willamette Bridge and The Oregonian from the open news rack and set them on the counter, walked over to a frozen food case, picked out a couple of Mexican-style frozen dinners and a box of breakfast Eggos, then added butter, syrup, a half-gallon of milk, Raisin Bran, coffee, and a six-pack of Diet Pepsi to the growing pile.

The bill was a little over fifty dollars. He started to protest, but then just shrugged and pulled his wallet from his left hip pocket. He set three twenty-dollar bills on the counter. *I can't afford this for very long.*

But a sweet smile and a quiet "Thank you" eased his rancor. And then he remembered he could charge to BB's account. He shrugged and stuffed the change in a pants pocket. *Next time.*

Plastic totes in hand, he fumbled with the elevator button, waited a few seconds, and was rewarded by the elevator bell. The door slid open and he was staring at a tall, ominous-looking white dude in a light grey security uniform that carried the name of the high-rise in bright blue letters above his shirt pocket. His nametag said, "Tony Jones."

"What you are doing here, boy?"

"I'm staying with a friend for a few days."

"Which apartment?"

Cletus shrugged and gave the man a unit number for the fifth floor.

"Who owns the apartment?"

"Mister Cletus Falls ... my stepfather."

The man pushed by Cletus and held the doors back until Cletus was inside. "I'm gonna check this out. You don't be going anyplace until I do. You hear?"

Cletus didn't say anything, just waited for the doors to close, then punched the "Close Door" button. The cables and pulleys hummed as the car rose to the fourth floor.

He stowed the frozen dinners, put the milk and the soft drinks in the empty refrigerator, and set the rest of his purchases on the counter.

He walked to the big window and stared at the north-south traffic across the river on I-5 while he tried to assess the risk of the security guard. But as much as he tried to convince himself that the kind of people he was hiding from didn't live in luxury high-rises, he couldn't shake his growing paranoia. Something about the security guard didn't ring true.

And then it hit him. The guy had on a uniform all right, but he was wearing dirty tennis shoes. *I don't know what this guy is doing, but it can't be right.*

He hurried to the apartment door and peeked both ways down the hallway. Not a soul was in sight, but the flashing elevator lights showed, floor by floor, an elevator car heading up. He stepped into the hall and closed BB's door, made sure it was locked, and then ran down the hall to the exit.

The hollow booming of the metal stairs in the concrete shaft marked his flight. He paused at the landing of the first floor, shook his head and skipped down one more level to the parking garage.

Outside, he leaned against the wall in the shadow of the big building to catch his breath. *Time to call the cavalry.* His hand shook just a little as he fumbled Agent Brandt's burner phone from his pants pocket. He read Brandt's number from the business card, thumbed it in and listened to the phone ring until it went to voice mail. He hung up without leaving a message.

Records. They checked the records for property owned by Dell BeBe and sent this dude looking for him. That's got to be it. And BB's black. I'm black. He made the connection.

"Damn!" Cletus said aloud as the tall dude stepped out the front door of the building and walked down the steps under the canopy. When he spotted Cletus, he shouted, "Hey, boy," and started jogging down the sidewalk.

Arms pumping Cletus took off. He was fast, but longer legs made the faux security guard faster. Cletus knew it was just a matter of time before the big man ran him down. He cut around a corner, heading for Front Street, when he saw a yellow taxi. He whistled and the cab turned back toward him. Cletus jumped in, just as the big white dude rounded the corner.

Cletus shouted, "Go! Go!"

When he saw the big man run to the side of the taxi and reach for the door handle, the cabbie need no encouragement. He stomped the accelerator, and the old yellow Crown Vic shot down the street. The man lost his grip on the door handle and went sprawling, the asphalt tearing at his hands and knees ... and his right cheekbone. Blood trickling down the side of his face, he watched in frustration until the cab turned a corner and was out of sight.

37

Acrimony

B RANDT AND WILCOX WERE IN VISITOR chairs, and Special Agent McDonald was still seated behind his desk, when Dutch Vanderlin and Special Agent Smith walked in.

McDonald said, "Come on in, Dutch. And you too, Smitty. Have a chair. Brandt and Wilcox have been giving me the third degree about human trafficking." He paused before adding, "and sharing a story you ought to hear."

McDonald waited until Dutch and Smitty were seated before nodding at Wilcox. "Your turn agent Wilcox."

When Wilcox finished talking, Smitty was more than a little pissed, but a warning frown from Dutch told him to keep his mouth shut.

Dutch asked Wilcox and Brandt, "Why didn't you two bring this to Smitty first?"

Wilcox glanced at Brandt, who shrugged his shoulders. *Here we go. Right down the manure chute.*

Wilcox looked at Smith and said, "We know you're honest, but you're damned naïve. You have this Boy Scout attitude. You automatically think every FBI agent is a good guy or gal. Hell, Smitty, you refuse to believe that, if you throw enough money at a person and catch him at the right time, even federal agents can be bought."

Brandt glanced at Wilcox and nodded. He took a deep breath and leaned forward towards his boss, an unstated plea for understanding in his voice. "And we have a pretty good idea that two of our people are on the take, Butler and someone in the analysis group. Look, when you hunt a mole in an organization, you keep the circle of insiders as small as possible. We were afraid your blind faith in the FBI would lead you to trust the wrong people."

Dutch shook his head and gave Smitty a grim smile. "You've just been damned by faint praise, Special Agent Smith."

Smitty stared bullets at Brandt and Wilcox before his shoulders slumped in resignation. "Maybe you're right. But you have to have trust in people. Otherwise we all become cynical … or paranoid."

McDonald chuckled and shook his head. "Hell, Smitty. Here we are, just ordinary run-of-the-mill crime fighters. And we're supposed to avoid cynicism? Doesn't happen. Best we can do is observe and stay alert."

"Amen," said Dutch. "Trust and defend, but don't go blind."

"Does that mean we're off the hook?" Brandt asked.

"Not by a long shot," Dutch growled. "Butler we know about, but you two have to ferret out the other one. Isn't that right, Smitty?"

Smitty grimaced and looked disgusted before finally nodding. He added, "We sure do."

Brandt's cell phone vibrated in his pocket, and he took a quick peek. He glanced at Wilcox and said, "Cletus."

Dutch said, "Find out what my little buddy wants."

Brandt walked out into the hallway and answered the call. "This is Agent Brandt. That you, Cletus?"

Without preamble, Cletus said, "They found me. A tall, white dude chased me, but I hooked a cab and got away."

"Where are you?'

"Hiding in the bushes around the east end of your building. I come in and ask for you and Wilcox, this young Hispanic chick says she never heard of you, but if I wait a minute another agent will help me. I don't like the sound of this, so I say I guess I got the wrong building. Then I boogie and hide. Pretty soon this nice looking blonde lady comes out the front door and looks for me. Least that's what I think she be doing."

Cletus shook his head and asked, "Are all you feds on the take?"

"No, but you seem to have found two who are. I'll come and get you. Hang in there."

Brandt walked back in the door and said, "Somebody go arrest Inez Sanchez, and somebody go arrest Sarah Macbeth. The bad guys found Cletus, so he came looking for us. I'll explain the rest in a minute."

Wilcox was out of his chair and down the hall before anyone could react. He used his pass card to open the door into the public information area.

Inez Sanchez, public information receptionist, GS-7, was talking into a Featherlite microphone attached to a headset when Wilcox entered the lobby. He saw her nod and say, "I'm sorry, but he ran out the door. I did exactly as you instructed."

She saw Wilcox, ended the call and smiled at him. She was startled when he growled, "Inez, who instructed you? I heard you say you did exactly as you were instructed."

"Why, Miss Williams of course. She said I was to look for a small, young black man asking for you or Agent Brandt. I was to tell him you didn't work here. Miss Williams said she wanted to talk to him first. Something about an undercover operation he might have information about.

"But he seemed nervous and ran out the door. I called Miss Williams, and I guess she sent Missus Macbeth to check. That's all I know."

"This is important Inez. You're sure it was Miss Williams, not just someone on the phone giving you instructions."

Inez nodded. "Yes. She came in person to tell me what she wanted me to do. She also said I wasn't to mention this to anyone, because it was part of an undercover sting operation."

"Didn't it strike you as odd? Miss Williams is in the analysis section. They don't run ops."

Tears pooling in her dark eyes, Inez asked, "Did I do something wrong, Agent Wilcox? Will I lose my job?"

Wilcox took a deep breath and sighed. He patted her shoulder. "No. I don't think you did anything wrong. And if you didn't, you won't lose your job."

Through the bulletproof service window, they watched Brandt exit the building, looking for Cletus.

Wilcox patted her shoulder again and said, "You always do a good job, Inez. You'll be fine, but I expect you'll be interviewed again by other agents. Just tell the truth, and everything will be fine."

38

Road Kill and Turkey

BB PICKED UP HIS AR-15, SLIPPED MIRANDA'S daypack over his left shoulder and – wet tennis shoes squishing – headed down a thin, shady deer trail wandering through a stand of small pine trees. BB had grown to like the smell of dry pine needles, but his mind wasn't open to the fragrance of the woods. Not today.

When he was close to the meadow, he stopped behind a thicket of lodgepole pine. It took him fifteen seconds to locate Miranda hiding in the shadows with her pistol pointed straight at him. She was behind a natural crib, formed by two downed pine trees.

He whistled and waved before stepping into the open.

Miranda holstered her weapon and stood up. She walked around the tangle of dead limbs. "I could have shot you."

"But you didn't."

"I know. Now, get this big splinter out of my hand."

He shook his head. "No. A surgeon will have to do that. I might damage the tendons."

"I don't see any surgeons around here," she said.

He pointed at the distant sound of a helicopter. "That ship is going to take you and TJ to Lakeview. First stop, the hospital."

He set her pack on the ground and looked at the reverend. "Use your belt and make a sling for Miranda's arm."

He looked at her pinched face, pain and disgust painted there. "You picked a good spot to keg up. Did your survival training kick in?"

She nodded. "I never thought I'd have to use it. I'm an analyst, not an operator." She winced as TJ worked his belt around her neck and under her left elbow.

"There. How does that feel?"

"Horrible, actually, but thanks."

TJ said, "I'm sorry. If I hadn't come down here, you wouldn't be hurt."

She patted his shoulder with her good hand. "Nonsense. You'd be dead by now if you stayed in Portland. Think of it as the Good Lord working a small miracle."

TJ stood as tall as he could and looked at Miranda, total adoration in his eyes. "The Lord works in mysterious ways. I guess that makes you my guardian angel."

BB grinned at Miranda over the top of TJ's head, but he didn't need to say anything. He knew his small friend was in love again.

"Don't let it go to your head," Miranda snapped.

TJ took a step back, feelings hurt. "Sorry."

Miranda waved his apology away. "Let it go, TJ."

The noise of the helicopter engine grew louder. Windows reflecting the fading afternoon sun, a blue chopper flew over the little meadow. Miranda's cell phone buzzed and BB answered. He heard Sonny Sixkiller say, "I see three people on the west side of the meadow. If that's you, wave."

BB waved. The helicopter turned and started a gliding descent into the meadow.

Three minutes later, minus her cell phone, Special Agent Miranda Wright and the Reverend TJ Wildish ducked their heads and half-ran towards the ship. Sonny Sixkiller hopped out of the copilot door and helped Miranda into a rear seat. TJ climbed in beside her. Sonny pushed the door shut. Bent over, an instinct when walking beneath spinning rotors, Sonny carried his AR-15 and a small daypack to where Dell BeBe waited, then gave the pilot thumbs up.

***

DELL BEBE AND LANKY DEPUTY SONNY Sixkiller, the soon-to-be undersheriff of Lake County – again – turned their backs to a small hurricane of dust, twigs, and dry grass as the rotor speed increased, then pulled the helicopter into the air. Sixty feet off the ground, the pilot turned and headed for Lakeview.

BB looked at Sixkiller and said, "I thought you were to be our eyes in the sky."

"I was. But Bud knew you'd go hunting. He decided we couldn't let a civilian get blown away by the bad guys. And he told me to deputize you. I don't have a badge to pin on you, but that'll be our secret. Now, what do we know, Deputy BeBe?"

"Not much. TJ saw a man skirting the south end of the lake. And he *thinks* he saw one heading north past Bud's cabin. If that's true, then at least two people are trying a pincer movement – coming at us from both sides."

The sound of a distant rifle shot coming from across the lake rolled through the hills and BB shook his head. "That, I believe is an idiot trying to make us think the bad guys are still at my house so we won't suspect two other idiots are hunting us in the woods."

"Sounds like amateur hour," Sonny said.

"I'd say so. Now then, I figure they should be getting close to converging on my canoe."

"Your canoe?"

"Yes. My canoe. The asshole shooting at us from across the lake got lucky and drilled a big hole in my canoe. Sank it. I owe him for that. He also got lucky and broke Miranda's paddle. That's how she got the big splinter in her hand.

"But that's beside the point. I think we have time to set up and ambush these guys. I want them alive. And I want the asshole who sent them after TJ."

Sonny nodded. AR-15 in hand, he shouldered his daypack and said, "Lead on, Deputy BeBe. Lead on."

Four minutes of stealthy single-file walking back down a deer trail led them to within forty yards of the little cove where BB's canoe, water up to the gunwales, gently rocked to the rhythm of breeze borne ripples.

The pop of a dry limb stopped BB in midstride. He carefully eased his right foot back to the ground. He turned to Sixkiller, pointed his index finger at his own chest, and then pointed to his left. He stepped between two trees and out of sight behind a thicket of small lodgepole.

Sonny moved to the right, found an open lane in the timber, and eased forward, alert, listening, wanting to hear the bad guys before they heard him.

Another limb broke directly ahead of BB, and he heard a man with a raspy voice whisper, "Ah, shit. This won't work."

A low-pitched voice off to BB's left said, "That you, Turkey?"

"Yeah. It's me. Where you at?"

"Over here. Hell, that helicopter flew 'em out of here. This sneaking around in the woods is just bullshit. Let's get out of here."

"Okay. I'm coming. Don't shoot me."

BB circled deep and turned into the breeze, following the smell of marijuana smoke.

He heard one man say, "I'm telling you, Starbucks ain't gonna like this."

The second man said, "To hell with him. Let him do his own chasing. I'm done with this."

His AR-15 tight against his shoulder, finger on the trigger, BB eased into the little clearing where he found the two men, rifles leaned against a pine tree, sucking on marijuana joints. He said, "You know, you shouldn't smoke when the woods are so dry."

Then Sonny shouted from behind them, "Hands in the air! Do it! Do it now!"

BB picked up the rifles and broke the stocks on the trunk of a tree. He glared at the men and said, "Bikers! They be sending us dope-smoking bikers!"

He shook his head in disgust, then asked, "How many people did you bring?"

The smaller man, a lean forty-something wearing black cargo pants, a dirty denim shirt with the sleeves cut off, and thick-soled black boots decorated by clunky chains, took a last drag on his joint and said, "Piss off."

BB slapped him hard enough to spin the man halfway around. The joint flew from his mouth, and he grunted in surprise at both the suddenness of the attack and the power of the blow.

BB rubbed the joint out with the toe of his shoe and glared at him. "One last time. How many of you assholes are out here?"

The man spit a little blood from a cut lip and looked at Sonny's uniform. "Cops can't beat on people. I got rights!"

"Ah, hell," Sonny said. "They aren't high enough on the food chain to know anything. We're wasting our time. Let's just shoot em. We can always say it was self-defense. Or we could just let the coyotes and the buzzards pick their bones. You know, like we did last time."

Turkey, the smaller of the two, sounded incredulous when he said, "You can't do that! We got rights!"

BB wrinkled his brow like he was thinking about it, then nodded. "Of course, we could just arrest the one who cooperates and shoot the other one."

Sonny glared at the bikers and said, "Enough of the bullshit. Cops get really pissed when assholes shoot at other cops. The woman you injured is an FBI agent. When that happened, you brought the wrath of God down on your heads.

"I don't know what the sentence is for attempted murder, assault on a federal officer, trespassing, and killing a canoe – not to mention the extreme aggravation of getting within smelling distance of you dirty, unwashed assholes, but I'll bet it comes close to the rest of your lives … without parole."

BB nodded at Sonny, pointed his rifle in the air and touched off three rounds. The two bikers stumbled backwards, panicked by the sudden noise.

"There we go. Now your partner across the lake – who is about to be arrested or shot by the way – thinks maybe you got us. Or he thinks maybe we got you. He doesn't know what to do. But I'll bet he sings like a canary, and you take the rap."

Roadkill, the larger man, scalp shaved like his partner's, bare-chested except for a black leather vest, a big sheath knife hanging from his belt, glanced at his partner and said, "I thought this was stupid from the beginning, Turkey."

Turkey looked up at his partner and nodded. "Hell, Roadkill, I don't believe for a minute these dudes are gonna shoot us. But the man makes sense. Starbucks is gonna sell us out. Go ahead. Tell 'em what they want to know."

Roadkill said, "Can I put my hands down? My arms are getting tired."

"Drop the knife with your left hand first. Just ease it out of the sheath and drop it on the ground. And then both of you slip off your boots and take off your pants."

39

Starbucks

B UD NAVIGATED THE CURVE BEYOND THE culvert over Dog Creek, accelerated, and said, "What do you think, Roger? In fast and hard or on foot? BB's driveway is about two hundred yards long. We might be able to block the road and go in through the trees."

Roger said, "I like stealth."

Bud's cell rang and he hit the hands-free button. BB's voice boomed through the speakers in the big pickup. "We caught ourselves two little pigs, but the big boar is still at my place. What's your location?"

Bud said, "About to pull into your driveway."

"Watch yourselves. We're across the lake bringing these guys in. It's going to be another twenty minutes before we get there. They say this is a three-man killing team."

"Thanks, BB. Sonny with you?"

"Yes. And we're both fine. I did shoot three rounds off to make their buddy, the one at the house, think they had gotten us."

***

AFTER BB'S RIFLE SHOTS, THE BIG bearded man known as 'Starbucks' kept his binoculars sweeping the far shore of Dog Lake.

He muttered, "What the hell is going on? This is making me nervous. First the big black dude gets his friends ashore and out of sight. Then the lady, whoever she is, starts shooting back. Then the helicopter lands and takes off again."

He shook his head. "We didn't sign up for this. This was supposed to be an easy job. Walk in and shoot a preacher. That's all.

"And where the hell are Road Kill and Turkey? They're supposed to walk back to the lake and wave. Let me know they got 'em. Ten minutes, and then I'm gone."

***

BUD EASED THE BIG PICKUP OFF the pavement into BB's driveway and blocked the road.

He muted the radio, activated his whisper mic and said, "Control, this County One. We're at the BeBe residence. Send officers Beltram and Tusk as backup." When he heard Nancy say "Copy," he pulled his 10-gauge shotgun loose from the Velcro straps, and stuffed a handful of 00 buckshot shells in his jacket pocket. "If BB's right, there are only three bad guys. He and Sonny have two. That leaves one, assuming the perps are telling the truth."

Roger stepped to the ground, pulled the slide back on his pistol to make sure a round was chambered, and then slid it back in the holster. He pulled his .308 rifle free of the gun case, chambered a round, and said, "Okay. I'm ready." They each stepped into the trees on opposite sides of the driveway and started a slow, watchful walk to the big log house.

They were within thirty yards of the red crew cab Ford F-250 parked beside TJ's rental car, when the sounds of footsteps brought them to a halt. Bud raised his shotgun to his shoulder and waited.

A barrel-chested man carrying a black AR-15 rifle in his right hand and binoculars in his left walked around the corner of the garage. When he saw Bud, he stopped dead in his tracks. The big bore of Bud's shotgun was pointed straight at his head. Bud shouted, "Drop your weapon! Now! Hand's in the air!"

Starbucks looked startled, but he didn't need any further instruction. He dropped the rifle and the binoculars and raised his hands. Roger moved in from the man's right and said, "On your knees. Hands on your head."

"Shit," was all the man could say as he sank to his knees. Roger circled around and kicked the man's rifle out of reach, and then handcuffed his arms behind his back.

Bud said. "I'll check the perimeter." A careful search of BB's house and the outside yard convinced Bud the man was alone. He walked back to where Roger had the man sitting on the ground.

"Who are you?" Bud said.

"I ain't talking," the man snarled. "I want a lawyer."

"How many are with you?"

"I said, I ain't talking."

Bud looked disgusted and moved closer to the man, the bore of the shotgun looking bigger with each step. "I want to know how many people you brought with you. And you might as well talk. We have two of your asshole buddies in custody. I'm sure one of them will sing to save his ass. And whoever sings first … you know the drill. I want to know how many people you brought, and I want to know who sent you."

The man just shook his head.

Bud shrugged. "Your funeral."

Fifteen minutes later, Starbucks, whose driver's license read "Gary Gentle" and listed a Klamath Falls address, was safely confined in the cage in Bud's pickup. He had been properly Mirandized and arrested for attempted murder, assault on a federal officer, trespassing, and whatever else DA Howard Finch decided on.

Deputy Beatrice Tusk, with Deputy Lonnie Beltram riding in the passenger seat, drove the county's white pickup down the open driveway and pulled up next to Bud's rig.

He was on the phone when Beltram and Tusk walked up. They heard him say, "Dutch, the way we see it, a bigwig Muslim from Portland put out a contract to a The Romans biker gang.

"That means the people who took TJ's computer found directions to Dell BeBe's place on Dog Lake and figured TJ might be with BB." Bud paused to listen and then added, "I don't have an update on Special Agent Wright. I'll call you as soon as I know anything. I'm hoping we can trace back from Gentle's phone and find out who ordered the hit."

Bud looked up to see Deputy Sixkiller and Dell BeBe prod two scruffy looking men around the corner of the house. Their hands were cuffed behind them, and they wore nothing but their shorts and socks. Bud chuckled and said, "Gotta go, Dutch. My guys just brought in two more bikers."

Bud raised his eyebrows as Sonny told the men to sit against the garage door. Sonny shrugged. "They got lippy, so we made sure they couldn't run. Skeeters loved 'em." And then he laughed. "But we know who orchestrated this. Some guy called Starbucks."

Bud nodded. Loud enough to be heard by the two bikers leaning against BB's garage door, he said, "Yep. Roger is talking to Starbucks now. He's singing like a bird. How about those two?"

40

A New Winslow

BUTLER LOOKED AT AN OLDER TOYOTA pickup on a used car lot in Astoria, list price three thousand dollars. The tailgate wouldn't open, the rear bumper was sagging from a blow that had to have come from a sturdy pole or a tree, the seats were dirty, and the passenger window was cracked. About the only thing in good repair was a fairly new set of tires. But the engine still sounded strong, the tags were current, the spare tire held air, the lights all worked, and the oil was clean. So, he bought it. The owner of the car lot was only too happy to take cash.

Butler stopped by a small convenience store advertising bait, fishing tackle, beer, and fresh seafood. He bought a paper carton of warm clam chowder and drove back to the marina. He lit the stove in the small galley to re-heat his chowder, listened to the chatter of commercial fishermen on the CB radio, and made a mental list of what gear he needed to take with him. Soon after sunset, a gentle rain dimpled the black waters of the marina, raindrops dancing in the pools of light from lamps spaced along the docks.

He pulled the curtains on the dockside of the main cabin and gathered the gear he thought he might need. He rejected the rifle as too conspicuous and settled on his .9mm service pistol. "I'm not going to shoot anyone if I can help it, anyway," he mumbled to himself and then realized he spoke his thoughts aloud more and more often. "Symptom of living alone too much, I guess."

He pulled a small, olive-drab daypack from a storage locker and began to fill it. He zipped night vision binoculars in a front pouch, stowed a penlight in a side pouch, stuffed black, packable rain gear in the main compartment, and added trail bars, a water bottle, and a bottle of buffered aspirin in a side pouch.

He set out a pair of black Gore-Tex ankle high hiking boots. "I think that's all I'm going to need. Now…to shave or not to shave…that is the question. Beards are in. All the Hollywood stars seem to think two-day stubble is the way to go. Okay, Winslow, stubble it is."

At 10:00 he watched a local news channel, gratified there was no public alert for a rogue FBI agent, or a copy of his picture on national or local television. He lifted a whiskey bottle from a cupboard and started to pour a nightcap. He hesitated, held the amber liquid up to the light and grimaced. "Hell, whiskey is what got me in this mess in the first place." He opened the cabin door and threw the bottle into the night.

At 10:30 he went to bed and killed the light. And then he did something he hadn't done in years … he prayed. Tears spilled down his cheeks from the burden of sorrow and guilt he carried, and he said, "Lord, I know I'm beyond salvation, but please help me do the right thing. Help me save those young women, if nothing else."

Five a.m. saw the Toyota pickup, headlights cutting through a light layer of fog, speeding upriver, back towards Portland, the driver filled with a new sense of purpose.

41

Cleaning House

S PECIAL AGENT BRANDT ROUNDED THE CORNER of the Portland Office of the FBI and saw Cletus slide out from behind a tall Irish yew, one of two dozen lining the east wall of the big building. Cletus brushed dead yew needles from his closely-cropped curly hair and stared daggers at Brandt.

"Took you long enough."

Brandt grinned and shook his head. He turned his wrist and glanced at his watch. "Yep. Twenty-two seconds."

"Felt like an hour.

"I'll bet it did."

"You know, Special Agent Brandt, I bet I'd be safer if I was an FBI Agent. Carry a gun. Wave my badge around. Scare the bad guys off."

"Come on, little buddy, let's get you off the street."

They walked back toward the front entrance and Brandt asked, "How did you get out here?"

"In a cab."

Brandt nodded. "Good thinking. Even if they got a cab number, they won't come looking for you here."

"Yeah, just some white chick who is already here."

"We're getting that sorted out as we speak. How do you feel about spending a couple of days with your Uncle George in Seattle? We'll take you up there and provide security for all of you. And I don't think this will take too long. Couple more days maybe."

Cletus nodded and blinked back unwelcome tears.

***

WILCOX TROTTED DOWN THE HALLWAY AND back to Special Agent Richard McDonald's office. He ignored McDonald's secretary who said, "He's busy."

"Yeah. With me."

***

ALONE IN A STARK, GRAY INTERVIEW room, Miss Verna Williams, analyst, FBI, Portland, Oregon sat in a hard metal chair bolted to the concrete floor in front of an equally hard metal table, both wrists handcuffed to a big eyebolt welded to the table top. Her breathing was rapid and shallow. Sweat beaded her forehead. She was screwed and she knew it.

After thirty minutes, her breathing slowed to a more normal rate. She felt better after concocting a strategy she hoped would help her make a deal. If she helped trap her controller, a handsome young Arab who had swept her off her feet and then moved into her apartment over a year ago, maybe the FBI would go easier on her. *Yeah. Sure girl. Dream on, fool…*

42

Push Back

IMPATIENT AT THE CONSERVATIVE SPEED OF the police caravan taking Road Kill, Turkey, and Starbucks to Lakeview, BB waited for the first long straight stretch through the farm fields, and then powered his bronze Lexus SUV around the line of police cars, the speedometer reading ninety before he passed Bud's pickup. Bud hit the lights in the grill, but didn't speed up.

Roger raised his eyebrows and looked at Bud. "Where does he think he's going?"

"I'd guess," Bud said, "he's headed to the hospital to check on Miranda. And to hook up with his friend TJ Wildish."

"Gonna write him a ticket?"

"Nope."

The vehicle radio crackled and they could hear Sonny's voice. "I got his license number." And then he laughed. "You want me to catch him, Boss?"

Bud chuckled and keyed his mic. "I think I know where to find him."

***

Under the watchful eye of Deputy Roger Hildebrand and Deputy Beatrice Tusk, Technical Deputy Karen Highsmith processed Calvin Culpepper, aka Road Kill, Anthony James, aka Turkey, and Gary Gentle, aka Starbucks into the Lake County Jail. Fingerprints, mug shots, proper

ID including given and surnames and home addresses from driver's licenses … bright orange jumpsuits concluded the process before the handcuffed bikers were walked one at a time down the hallway and locked in individual cells.

BB, TJ, and Miranda Wright, her left hand heavily bandaged, were talking to Bud, District Attorney Howard Finch, and Police Chief Gus Hildebrand when Roger and Beatrice walked back to the booking room.

Roger nodded to Gus and said, "Hi, Dad."

Gus held out his hand and said, "Howdy son. I see you've been busy."

Roger grinned and said, "Now and then."

Bud said, "Everybody coffee up, and then let's go the conference room. You too, Special Agent Wright. How's the hand?"

She held her left hand up and peered at it like it was some kind of foreign object. "Buggered, it is.

"Sorry about that."

"Why? You didn't shoot at me, and you didn't ask for all this trouble. No, this goes back to Portland. Speaking of which, I need a ride back up there. Have you talked to Dutch Vanderlin? He'll want to know what's going on down here. And…"

Bud cut her off and said, "I'll talk to Dutch and get you back to Portland." They watched the others walk into the conference room, and Bud added, "By the way, BB says you did good out there."

She smiled and pulled Bud close to whisper in his ear, "I'm flattered. That one is a warrior."

***

They crowded into the small conference room, and Bud nodded at Roger. "Okay. Let's hear what Gary Gentle, aka Starbucks, has to say."

Roger keyed the prompt on his cell phone, turned the volume as high as it would go, and placed it on the conference table. They heard Gentle's gravelly voice describe a phone call from someone in Salem with the street name Shooter, and how Shooter gave Gentle directions to BB's cabin and orders to kill TJ.

The recording carried Roger's voice asking, "What's Shooters real name?"

They heard Gentle say he didn't know.

Roger then asked, "How much were you paid?"

"Five thousand each when the job was done."

At this point, Special Agent Wright slipped quietly out of the room and into the hallway. She awkwardly thumbed in a text message to FBI *Special Agent Wilcox*, wincing each time she used her left thumb: *Hit hired by a Salem biker named Shooter, a member of The Romans gang.*

Wilcox texted back almost immediately: *Will track this guy down. Who have you told? We have a mole in analysis. Don't trust anyone but me, Douglas, and Dutch.*

Miranda texted back: *Just found out. Haven't told anyone else.*

Wilcox sent: *Good. Keep it that way. How's your hand?*

43

Turf Wars

Bud's cell phone vibrated and he stepped into the hallway in time to see Miranda put her phone in a pocket of her vest. He turned his back on her and answered the call. "Bud Blair."

"This is Dutch. Our little buddy, Cletus Falls can't get ahold of BB. He's worried the bad guys killed him."

"BB's phone is on the bottom of Dog Lake. He lost it when his canoe tipped over. Tell Cletus BB's okay. Right now, we're all listening to a recorded confession by one of the bikers. One of the hit men, a Gary Gentle from Klamath Falls, says he was hired by a man called Shooter, a member of a Portland biker gang called The Romans. Gentle doesn't know Shooter's real name."

Dutch hesitated and finally said, "We'll work on that. Now, then. Because the thugs in your jail assaulted a federal officer, the Assistant U.S. Attorney wants to prosecute them in federal court."

"You can't do that until we finish with them. First, we prosecute for attempted murder, trespass, murder for hire, and for assault on a police officer. Then you can have them."

"Listen, Bud, if I have to I'll send a couple of US Marshals down there and bring them back forcibly if necessary. We want 'em!"

Suddenly, very angry, Bud said, "Let me make myself clear, Dutch. Friendship aside, I will see them prosecuted here in Lake County, and

I will send a message to the criminals that law enforcement in Lake County is swift, stern, and certain."

The phone carried the sound of a deep sigh, and then Dutch said, "Is your DA any good?"

"Bright, seasoned, and dedicated. He's good."

"Don't mess it up, Bud. I'll keep the Assistant U.S. Attorney off your back as long I can. And I'll hold you to the swift and certain part."

Bud nodded into the phone, turned and took a step or two down the hall before saying, "Thanks, Dutch."

"How is my analyst?"

Despite himself, Bud grinned and then laughed. "She's standing right behind me, trying to eavesdrop on our conversation. This woman is a real buttinsky, but gutsy as hell. BB said she did a good job…for an analyst. You're lucky to have her, Dutch."

"Put her on. I want to talk to her."

Bud handed Miranda the phone and stepped back into the conference room. He saw Beatrice Tusk stifle a yawn and take a quick peek at the digital wall clock which read 10:00 p.m.

"Okay, my friends. I don't know about you, but I'm bushed. It's been a long but productive day. Let's call it quits. I'll see you all in here at eight o'clock. Okay? Let dispatch know where you're staying."

***

Bud nodded at BB and motioned to his office. "Where are you going to bunk tonight?"

BB said, "I'm taking Miranda and TJ back to my place. I don't think anyone will come after us tonight."

"And tomorrow?"

BB frowned and said, "I need a safe place for TJ. I need his rental car turned in at the K-Falls airport. Then I'm going back to Portland. I need to put a stop to this, and I can't do it from here."

"I'll go with you."

"Nope. You stay here, get yourself re-elected, get married, make some babies, and keep Lake County safe. I got this."

"You sure?"

"Yes. You mentioned a safe house in Klamath Falls. Can you get that set up? I'll have Miranda drive TJ over there in the morning, turn the rental in, and then she can fly back to Portland. I'll need some wheels, so I'll drive up."

"You want to travel as a deputy sheriff?"

"What I have in mind might have some blowback. No. You stay clear of this. I got it."

Bud shrugged and said, "I'll make a call."

Michelle Trivoli, former Lake County Deputy Sheriff, sounded sleepy when she answered her phone. "Yes?"

He would always picture his former deputy in a shooters stance, her pistol jumping with each shot as she banged away at William Casey, the man she thought had shot her sheriff. Bud missed her.

"Michelle, this is Bud. I need a favor. Can you play host for a couple of days to one of BB's friends? He is a Reverend TJ Wildish from Portland. He needs a temporary hiding place."

"Why? What's going on?"

"Some very bad people are looking for him. We need a couple of days to run them to ground. Then he can go home again."

"Tonight?"

"No. Tomorrow. An FBI agent named Miranda Wright will bring him over in the morning."

"The FBI can't handle this?"

"I wouldn't ask if I thought so, Michelle."

"I don't like it. I'm not a cop anymore, and I have Mariah to think of. Why not ask our sheriff?"

"Because we don't know who to trust." He briefed her on the efforts to kill TJ, the arrest of three Bikers from The Romans gang, and the suspicion of an FBI mole in Portland.

He heard her sigh and then say, "Give me a few minutes. I think I know someone who might help. I'll call you back."

"How is Mariah doing?"

Michelle's voice strengthened. "Bud, she is thriving. Starved! She was simply starved for affection. She's growing like a weed, getting straight A's in her classes, joined the choir, and has me going to church on a regular basis."

"Do you see Detective Harmon?"

Fully awake now, her voiced carried a laugh, and she said, "We're engaged."

"Wow! Congratulations."

"Thank you. We plan to be married in June. I want you at the wedding. And bring Nancy with you. I hear congratulations are in order for the two of you."

"The word gets around fast, doesn't it?"

"Karen called me."

"Well…how about that."

"She also said you were bringing Sonny back."

"Yes. I had to do something. I don't have you to be my undersheriff."

"I always thought you should give that job to Roger."

"You know, I did ask him, and he said he didn't want it. Said he liked it in North County."

"Oh. Okay, let me wake somebody up. Stay by the phone."

Five minutes later Michelle called back. "Sergeant Booker KFPD will hide TJ for a few days. Let me give you his number."

Bud wrote Booker's number on the back of his business card and handed it to BB. "Here you go. K-Falls has had a black community since the first railroad pushed into this country. He'll just be one more face in the crowd. No one will notice."

BB glanced at Miranda and TJ. "In that case, let's saddle up. It's been a long day." He turned to Bud and held out his hand. "Your deputies did a good job today, Bud."

"I'll tell them what you said. Now, I'm for bed."

44

Scout

A T 10:40 P.M., WINSLOW BUTLER DROVE HIS Toyota pickup through
the open delivery door of a small abandoned warehouse just outside the cyclone fence marking the perimeter of the docks.

In the headlights, he saw a bundled figure rise from a pallet in the
corner. Hands shielding his face from the light, a man hollered, "Get
out of here! These are my digs."

Butler opened the pickup door, a heavy 4-cell flashlight in his left
hand, studied the bearded man for a few seconds, and then said, "Not
any more. I'll give you a hundred dollars to boogie."

The man hesitated before saying, "Let's see your money."

Butler held a bill in the headlights and then dropped it on the grimy
concrete floor. "Gather your stuff and get out of here."

"It's raining," the man whined. "Ought to be worth more than a
hundred."

Butler shook his head and then added another fifty. "Now, either take
the money or I'll just shoot your ass." He pulled his badge wallet from
an inside pocket and flashed the light on the badge. "This is official
government business."

"Okay, man. Okay. No rough stuff." A grimy hand with long dirty
fingernails reached into the pool of light and snatched the bills off the
old, cracked concrete floor. "Give me a minute to pack my stuff."

The man's eyes flicked past Butler, and Butler turned in time to see a young woman, eyes wild in the light, coming slowly at him, a raised club in her right hand. He punched the flashlight on and when the beam of the flashlight blinded her, she dropped the club and shielded her eyes from the light. "Don't shoot, mister! Please don't shoot!"

Butler decided she wasn't much over fourteen or fifteen years old and probably didn't weigh a hundred pounds. "What the hell you doing here, girl? You with that asshole over there?"

Trembling, eyes downcast, she nodded.

"Both of you … get over in the corner and sit."

He shook his head as the girl stumbled and nearly fell before she reached the corner.

Butler asked the man, "Is she sick?" The girl's deep cough was all the answer he needed.

Butler told the bum to get going and watched him stuff both bills in his pants pocket, bundle his gear, and hurry off into the night without so much as a "goodbye" to the sick girl.

Butler helped her up off the pallet, put an arm around her shoulders, and helped her to the pickup. He started the engine, then turned the heater on and set the fan on high. He wrapped her in a thin space blanket and said, "Stay right here." She could do nothing more than nod and shake from a chill that was coming from someplace deeper than the cold air.

By the time a Portland police cruiser, siren going, lights flashing, led an ambulance to the warehouse, Butler had his personal gear packed and the vehicle wiped down for fingerprints. *Damn. I'll have to find another rig*, he thought. But he was feeling better about himself than he had in a long, long time. From the shadows of a willow patch growing along a drainage ditch, he watched the EMT's load the girl into the ambulance and head back to the freeway, lights flashing as it headed south on I5.

The police turned the engine off, then spent fifteen minutes searching the vehicle. Butler hadn't transferred the title, so there was nothing to trace his ownership or his new identity. A computer search by the officers found no warrants or stolen vehicle reports. They looked at each other and then simply left the key in the ignition and drove away. There was no legal way to do anything else.

***

HANDS COLD FROM HOLDING BINOCULARS, BUTLER watched the security gate to the four hundred plus acres of the Terminal 6 compound, the huge Port of Portland container dock on the Columbia River. He was back in the deserted warehouse only fifty yards or so from the gate, but floodlights backlit the guard shack, making it almost impossible to identify the man inside.

Butler needed to know who was on duty. If it was Dantonio Jones, it meant easy access to the containers. Two years earlier, Butler formed a mutually beneficial relationship with Dantonio, a numbskull who had an arrangement with certain members of the crews on the container ships which periodically tied up to the dock.

In exchange for the services of freelance hookers, a car to drive, and some money for marijuana or booze, Dantonio was the front man for a smuggling business. When Al-Alwani sent Butler to find a corruptible dock worker, two nights of surveillance and video of a money-for-drugs exchange turned Dantonio from small-time hood into a full-time snitch with keys to the gate. Butler paid Dantonio well.

Butler pulled his cell phone from a zippered pocket and hit a saved number. He watched the shadowy figure in the guard shack put a cell phone to his ear and thought, *That's Dantonio.*

Dantonio said, "Yes?"

Butler laughed and said, "I'm watching you."

"Where you at?"

"Across the road. I'm coming in." He kept his head down because of the security cameras, and walked to the man-gate where Dantonio waited to let him in.

"What you want, man?"

Butler pointed and said, "Let's get inside."

Dantonio made a show of checking a list on his clipboard, opened the gate for Butler, and then pushed through the door to the guard shack with Butler right behind. Butler worked the screen on his iPhone and pulled up a picture of Al-Alwani. "I want to know if he's been here recently."

Dantonio nodded. "Last night. He was in a big fuss about something. He asks if I seen you lately. I tell him no, I ain't seen you. He said to call him if I do. Then he drove to the container in his van. That's all."

"Which container did he go to?"

"The blue one at the far end of the docks … downriver. Sits by itself."

"Here's what I need you to do…"

45

Trust

Hɪs ᴄᴇʟʟ ᴘʜᴏɴᴇ ʙᴜᴢᴢᴇᴅ ᴀɴᴅ ᴠɪʙʀᴀᴛᴇᴅ on the bedside table a half-dozen times and then went to voice mail. A few seconds later it started up again.

Groggy, Brandt glanced at his bedside clock and wondered who in the hell was calling him at 11 p.m. He shook his head to clear the cobwebs and punched the on button. "This better be good," he growled.

The sound of Winslow Butler's voice brought Brandt fully awake. "Oh, it is, Special Agent Brandt. It is."

"What the hell do you want, Butler? I figured you would be out of the country by now."

"Remember when I told you I was going to make your careers, you and Wilcox? Well, get your pen ready."

Brandt swung his legs and sat up on the bed. He turned his lamp on and fumbled a pen and a note pad from the little drawer in the bedside table. "I still think you should come in."

"Nah. I'm having too much fun. I don't think you can have any fun in jail. In fact, I'm sure you can't." And then Butler laughed. "I'm the masked crusader now, protecting the weak, righting the wrongs and dealing out justice. Never had this much fun before." *Or liked myself as much*, he thought.

"Enough. What have you got for us?"

"Take a SWAT team. Go visit Terminal 6, the container dock on the Columbia. Arrest Dantonio Jones for criminal conspiracy. Right now, he's on duty at the guard shack. He has orders to let you in without any fuss or bother, but not before midnight. The swing shift shuts down at midnight. You need to let the terminal clear out and the big yards lights go dim.

"Look for a blue freight container sitting all by itself at the far end of the wharf. I'm sending you a picture of the container. You can figure it out from there. After all, you are the FBI." And then he cackled and laughed like a crazy man.

Brandt asked, "Is that where the women are being held?" All he heard was Butler hanging up.

Brandt shook his head. "Judas priest. He's crazy as a loon." He punched at his phone and waited for Wilcox to answer.

Fifteen minutes later, a black SUV pulled up to the curb in front of Brandt's apartment building. Brandt slid into the passenger seat and slammed the door.

While he read the address for Terminal 6 aloud, Wilcox fed it into the GPS mounted in the dash. "Okay," Wilcox said, "Let's go see if Butler really knows something … or if the crazy bastard is just playing with us."

"Do we want backup? Maybe let dispatch know?"

"No backup," Wilcox decided, "but we should let dispatch know we're on a call and where to." Traffic was light, so Wilcox pushed the big SUV at a steady eighty-five miles per hour up I-5.

Brandt used the radio to let their dispatcher know they were on a call to the Pier 6 terminal, and then checked his watch. "Butler said a guard named Dantonio Jones would let us through the gate after the swing shift left at midnight. He was very specific about the time. Not before midnight."

"Why?"

"He said the place cleared out at midnight. Maybe he didn't want to tip off the bad guys."

Wilcox drove into the big parking lot outside the terminal, reversed and backed into an open parking spot with a clear view of the gate. He killed the lights and turned off the wipers. "And now we wait?"

"I think so. Butler always leaves me guessing … like it's some kind of game."

***

AT MIDNIGHT, THE HUGE GANTRIES UNLOADING containers from the open decks of three container ships shut down, and the rhythm of the work simply stopped.

Five minutes later, Wilcox and Brandt saw a dirty white shuttle bus make its way from the docks to the gate and drop off a busload of longshoremen. A guard stepped out of the shack to unlock the man-gate and to compare each man's TWIC (Transportation Worker Identification Credentials) against a checklist. The last man through the gate was the bus driver who maneuvered the shuttle bus into a parking spot alongside the guard shack, and killed the engine. He waved and said, "Have a good night, Dantonio. Don't let any buggers get you."

Dantonio waved back, checked the driver's name off on his list and thought, *They already have.*

In a cost-cutting measure, the Port of Portland ordered the floodlights shut off as soon as the longshoremen on the swing shift filed through the small man-gate to their vehicles. A string of weak, solar powered lamps lined the fence, but the storage areas were almost totally dark.

46

Busted

S PECIAL AGENTS WILCOX AND BRANDT SLID down in their seats, trying to make the FBI vehicle look unoccupied. They saw a line of
weary longshoremen in battered hard hats, some carrying lunch pails,
trudge across the parking lot and climb into cars and pickups or onto
motorcycles.

The sound of engines filled the night, and the traffic started lining
up at the stop sign on Marine Drive. The line of tail lights marked their
progress towards I-5, where some headed south and others north across
the Columbia for home on the Washington side of the river.

"Well, Leroy," Brandt said. "How do you want to play this? Butler
said to arrest the guard for criminal conspiracy."

Wilcox started the engine and drove slowly toward the gate. "Let's
just leave him in place, and use him … for now."

Sweat started beading Dantonio's forehead when the headlights on
the SUV in the parking lot came to life. He didn't start shaking until
the vehicle pulled up to the gate. As instructed, he punched the remote
and watched the gate roll back on its track, parallel to the fence.

When the SUV was inside, he keyed the remote and watched the gate
close again. As instructed by Butler, he stepped out of the guard shack
with his hands empty and his arms out, wide of his body. "I'm Dantonio
Sims. Butler, told me to help you guys. Says he works for the FBI."

Hand on his pistol, Brandt said, "I need to search you for weapons. Please turn around and place your hands behind your back."

"I didn't do nothing," Dantonio said, "except let a van in to go visit a container down at the end of the docks."

Wilcox pulled his pistol and said, "Turn around, just like my partner told you."

"All right. All right. I'm doin' it. I'm doin' it." Dantonio turned his back to the agents and put his hands behind his back, knowing full well he was about to be handcuffed and arrested.

"I don't have no weapons other than my pistol," he said.

Brandt snapped the cuffs shut, pulled a 9mm handgun from Dantonio's holster, and dug a wallet from a rear pocket. He flipped it open and read aloud, "This Port of Portland security card identifies this man as Dantonio Jones."

He finished his pat down and asked, "Then what's this?" Brandt pulled a knife from Dantonio's left rear pocket.

"That just what my grandpa would call a whittling knife."

Brandt dropped the knife into the right pocket of his windbreaker and said, "Turn around."

Wilcox lit Dantonio's face with his Maglite and said, "What's the security set-up here?"

Sweat dripped off Dantonio's nose. He nodded and said, "Oh, man. Let me think. Ah … we have motion-activated lights along the fence, security cameras on the dock, a Coast Guard marine patrol on the river, and a roving patrol with two security people in a Jeep … like mine over there. And in the main building, we have a couple of people who monitor the cams during work hours."

"Can you trust the security patrol?" Brandt asked.

"Honest as the day is long," Dantonio answered.

"Hold still," Brandt said and produced a key to unlock the cuffs. "Now go call them. Tell them the FBI wants to talk to them. Tell them the truth."

"You ain't gonna arrest me?"

Wilcox snapped off the flashlight and snorted. "Not yet. For now, you belong to us. Whatever we ask, you do. Mind your manners and we'll think about letting you skate. So, you be good. But just for the record, what would we arrest you for?"

The first smidgen of hope blossomed in Dantonio's mind. "Nothing, nothing at all."

"That's what I thought," Wilcox grumbled. "Now do as my partner told you."

Three minutes later the SUV was lit by the headlights of a white Jeep Cherokee with a light rack on the roof. Two women got out, and walked cautiously toward the SUV, hands close to their weapons.

Brandt held his badge in the headlights and said, "We're Portland FBI. Got a tip we need to check out. I suggest we use the guard shack. We can see each other that way. Okay?"

A woman's voice answered. "You first."

In the brightly lit interior of the guard shack, a roomy fifteen by twenty-foot concrete building, Wilcox and Brandt produced their credentials and badges. The taller of the two women, a husky thirty-something redhead with a marine security badge pinned to her blue shirt and a nametag that read 'Sue Allison,' said, "We get shippers in here at all times of the day and night, so nighttime activity isn't all that unusual. To gain access, a person needs a TWIC number. Dantonio, or whoever is on shift, checks the number against a list of people authorized to be in the terminal. If he gets a match, he lets people in."

Wilcox frowned. "You don't keep track of why they want in?"

The smaller woman whose name tag said 'Donna Martin,' a slim brunette with a stunning figure, at least in the eyes of Wilcox, shook her head. "Not our business."

Brandt looked skeptical. "You trying to tell me you don't ever get curious about what the shippers have in the containers?"

Officer Donna Martin said, "We help DEA when they bring sniffer dogs to look for drugs. And TSA has some dogs who are trained to smell explosives. Other than that, we don't do much inspecting."

Wilcox looked at Brandt and shook his head. He didn't say, "Idiots" aloud, but Brandt heard him anyway. "Well, on that happy note, let's go look for a blue container with these numbers on it." He held his phone out for the marine security guards. "This is the one."

Officer Martin said, "Just a minute." She turned to the PC on the desk and typed in the numbers from the container. "Yes. We know where that one is." She started for the door. "Follow us."

Brandt said, "Mister Sims, you stay here. We might need you to let the cavalry in. If you see an ambulance and police vehicles, you let them in and give them directions to the container. Got it?"

Dantonio gave a shaky nod and a weak, "Yessir."

Outside, Officer Allison – the big redhead – asked, "Do you know something about Dantonio we should know? I'm the night supervisor, and I like to know what my people are into."

Wilcox shook his head and gave a non-committal "No."

Brandt stifled a grin and said, "Shall we go?"

"It would be easier to help if we knew what you two are looking for."

Brandt gave into his urge to grin and said, "We're about to find out ourselves."

***

THE MARINE SECURITY GUARDS LED THE way in their Jeep, down the rain-slick asphalt. Nearly a half-mile later they stopped in front of a blue container sitting in isolation near the end of the wharf. Brandt guessed it to be maybe fifty feet long and at least eight feet wide. *Big sucker*, he thought.

Officer Allison lit the doors to the container with spotlights from the Jeep's overhead rack, and both women stepped into the light drizzle, flashlights in hand. A big steel padlock and a metal ribbon sealed the door.

Wilcox inspected the lock and pulled on the handle … just because that's what one does to locked handles when one works for the FBI. Or maybe it was just a 'guy thing.' When the lock held, he slapped the door with his big hand and yelled, "FBI! This the FBI! Anyone in there?"

A startled yell penetrated the steel walls of the container, followed by women's voices crying for help. One voice, stronger than the rest carried over the top of the screaming and crying. "Get us the hell out of here!"

"Bingo!" Brandt yelled. He turned to the guards and said, "You know how to break into one of these things?"

Officer Martin said, "Well, sometimes we have to change the locks. I have a master key in back." Grinning she opened the back hatch of the Jeep and dropped a toolbox to the ground. She unsnapped the latch on the toolbox, flipped the lid open, and produced a cordless drill with a carbide cutting wheel. "We use this."

A few seconds later, streams of sparks from the carbide wheel lit the night as Officer Martin cut the lock and the metal seal. When the lock hit the ground, Wilcox unlatched the doors and pulled them open.

47

Rescued

A TALL, ATHLETIC-LOOKING WOMAN IN BLACK SWEAT pants and a dark, hooded sweatshirt, blonde hair looking like it hadn't seen a comb in a month, pushed hard against the door and knocked Wilcox back.

She stood blinking in the headlights, tears masked by the rain. In a choked voice, she asked, "FBI?"

Brandt moved to the doorway and said, "Yes. We're with the FBI." She nodded, choked back a sob, and then crumpled in a dead faint.

Brandt caught her before she hit the pavement and carried her to the SUV where Officer Allison helped him slide the woman onto the rear seat.

Brandt closed the rear passenger door, climbed into the driver's seat and started the engine. He put the heater fan on high and set the temperature on 80 before walking back to the container.

Wilcox, controlled fury in his voice, stepped out of the container. "Douglas!" he shouted, "we need back-up. I want at least four rescue teams, about eight ambulances, trauma counselors, forensics, and a dozen agents … like right now. Make sure they understand we need immediate help. And stress we want some women agents in the mix. And we'll need traffic control." He looked at the marine security guards and said, "Why don't you set up at the gate and direct traffic? And see about getting the yard lights back on. Okay?"

His emotions barely under control, Brandt used the radio to call for help. He sounded calm, efficient, and in control – the perfect example of a professional in a high stress setting. But he didn't feel that way.

After he put the mic back in its dashboard clip, he pounded on the padded dash with a beefy fist. "Those sonsabitches. Those dirty, rotten sonsabitches."

He went back to help Wilcox calm the young women in the container. "Ladies, Brandt said, "I know you want out of here, but it's raining and it's cold. So just sit tight. Help is on the way. We'll get you to safety."

Wilcox pulled Brandt by the sleeve and motioned him outside. "We got one scrawny little gal comatose in the back bunk. Hell, she can't be fourteen. She has a slow pulse, and I can't get her awake. Another woman is totally incoherent … just babbles and cries like a baby. Lord Almighty, what a mess!"

Through clinched teeth, he growled to Brandt, "I'm gonna kill Al-Al-wani. Take it to the bank."

***

FROM THE DARKNESS BEYOND THE FENCE, flat on his stomach in the wet grass under a thorn-infested blackberry thicket, former FBI Special Agent Winslow Butler watched the caravan of first responders race through the gate, vehicle lights pulsing and counter pulsing, overlapping each other with strident red, white, and blue strobe lights. The Terminal 6 lights came back on, flooding the area with glare and stark shadows. Butler pulled his black watch cap down a little lower on his forehead.

He recognized Special Agent McDonald, leader of the Major Crimes Unit and Special Agent in Charge Dutch Vanderlin when they stepped out of matching black Ford Expedition SUV's. Wilcox and Brandt greeted the senior agents and led them to the open door of the container.

After the last of the eight women had been triaged and rushed to Legacy Immanuel Hospital, a short distance south on I-5, Butler saw a white van, with "FBI Forensics" stenciled in six-inch black letters on the side, pull around the cluster of vehicles and back up to the container. A short while later, Butler could see camera flashes from inside the big metal box as the forensics team documented the evidence.

Cold and cramped after two hours of lying on wet grass, Butler crawled out the backside of the blackberry thicket. Hunched over to keep his silhouette low to the ground, he walked slowly below the berm of a drainage ditch and back to the abandoned warehouse. Safely inside the derelict building, he eyeballed his pickup and thought, *Why not? I'll wait until the fuss dies down, and just boogie on back to The Runaway. Safe enough. No one is looking for this vehicle.*

He slid behind the wheel, racked the seat back as far as it would go and locked the door. The faint odor of the girl's unwashed body lingered in the cab. Amused by the thought, he wondered if he would catch something. And then he was asleep.

***

AT 4:10 A.M., THE FBI FORENSICS experts finished their work. Every surface had been tested for fingerprints and DNA, the food packages had been photographed and labels removed from boxes to preserve any information telling them when and where it was made. It was hoped the purchases could be traced to specific individuals.

The team took every scrap of physical evidence and boxed, bagged, and tagged it. Pillows, sleeping bags, hair brushes, toothbrushes, an old pair of tennis shoes, used tampons, fingernail clippings ... whatever could be collected was loaded into the Forensics van, hopefully to tell the FBI who had been held in the container. On the back wall, hidden by a mattress, they found a list of names and dates scratched into the paint. Some of the dates were two years old.

Dutch turned to the forensics team leader, "I want your guys back here in the daylight to work this container all over again. Your team is good, but I want them to be better than good. Don't overlook anything that might help us identify the poor women who took a sad trip in this thing."

Doctor Ivan Warf, a tall blonde Norwegian, nodded ... emotional pain visible in his face. "I agree, Dutch. All our work is important, and this is too important to hurry. We'll check and double check until there just isn't anything left to do. We'll be back at 0700 with some fresh eyes – new people who haven't seen the box yet."

"Thanks, Ivan. I know you'll do it right. Didn't mean to sound critical."

"No offense taken. And now then, may I suggest you put some people here to guard this abomination until we get back?

Dutch said, "You may so suggest. SWAT is on the way."

Without another word, Doctor Warf climbed into the driver's seat of the van and drove away.

Dutch gave Wilcox and Brandt his thermos and said, "To keep you warm until SWAT arrives. They'll make sure this box stays put. And when they get here, go home. Get some rest. I want you in my office at 0700."

After Dutch drove away, silence settled around the blue container. Wilcox looked at his partner and said, "It's an evil thing, Douglas. Slavery still exists. Only these are white, unlike my ancestors."

Brandt was silent for almost thirty seconds, then he opened up. "I feel damned helpless some days, Leroy. There's so much evil in the world. My mind just can't encompass it."

He set Dutch's thermos on the hood and was greeted by the strong aroma of whiskey-flavored coffee when he filled the cup. He took a drink before handing the cup to Wilcox who sniffed at it and said, "I'll say this much, Douglas, Dutch makes a fine cup of coffee."

48

Debrief

Seven-thirty a.m. saw Wilcox and Brandt sitting at a conference table with Special Agent Smith, Special Agent Richard McDonald, Dutch Vanderlin, and a PR specialist Brandt thought of as "that nice looking woman from Information Management." A stenographer, a video recorder, and Dutch's yawning secretary were there to take notes.

Dutch nodded at McDonald. "Your show, Richard."

McDonald put his elbows on the table and clasped his hands under his chin. He stared at the wall behind Wilcox and Brandt for a few seconds, wondering if they were going to protect their source … again. A smile tugged at his mouth. *Loyal bastards, they are. But loyal to whom?*

"Okay," he said. "For the record, Special Agent Leroy Wilcox and Special Agent Douglas Brandt, what led to your search for a container at the Port of Portland's Terminal 6?"

Without hesitation, Brandt said, "A phone call."

"Any idea who the caller was?"

"Yeah," Brandt said. "I'm positive it was FBI Special Agent Winslow Butler."

McDonald asked, "Why would he do that?"

"You want me to speculate?"

"Yes. Speculate. I know you can't tell us what Butler was thinking, but you are the last person inside the FBI to hear from him. So … what did he say, and what do you think his motivation was?"

"You want the long version or the short version?"

"Short version."

Brandt looked at Wilcox before saying, "I think he's suffering from guilt. He took bribe money – a lot of bribe money, according to him – and then he discovered Al-Alwani was into human trafficking. I think it offended him, so he called us."

Wilcox nodded and said, "And a good thing he did. I'm not sure we would have found the women without him. He said he wanted to do the right thing for a change."

Brandt glanced at his partner and nodded. *Left out the part about Butler thinking Leroy got screwed by D.C. politics*, he thought. *Good for you, Leroy. It isn't relevant.*

McDonald nodded and opened a file. He spread a stack of photos on the table, copies of the ones taken by the forensics photographer of the interior of the container and of each woman … or child in the case of the comatose teenager on a rear bunk.

"Take us through it from the time Butler called Special Agent Brandt right on through to calling for backup."

Taking turns, Brandt and Wilcox led them through each step as they checked out Butler's information. When they were through, Dutch Vanderlin asked, "Why didn't you arrest the terminal guard, Dantonio Sims?"

Wilcox said, "We thought about it. But we think there is more to gain, than to lose, by leaving him in place."

McDonald nodded. "Maybe. Somehow key players at the terminal are notified in advance of our spot checks. I'd bet containers concealing contraband are shuffled or reloaded back on ships to keep us from inspecting the right ones. We need to find who those people are, and Dantonio could be our link."

"Okay," Dutch said. "He stays, but I want him watched twenty-four-seven, both to protect him and to make sure he plays straight with us."

"What about the marine security guards?" Dutch asked, "What do you think is going on there?"

Almost in unison Wilcox and Brandt said, "They're clean."

Wilcox appended, "But dumb as a board. Either that, or not well trained."

Dutch cocked his head sideways and then nodded. "Okay. But sic Forensics Accounting on them. Find out if they are on the take."

***

BACK IN HIS OFFICE, MCDONALD'S SECRETARY handed him a faxed copy of shipping invoices from the Port of Portland for the past year. He murmured his thanks, accepted a fresh cup of coffee, and took the invoices to his office.

The manifests from the Port of Portland showed the blue container, tracked by its cargo number, had made nine regular trips to Yemen and back during the past thirty-six months. It was obvious to him what was going on. Kidnapped women were shipped out, but it was unclear as to what was shipped back. *Just an empty container, perhaps?*

McDonald placed a phone call to CIA Special Agent Candice Palumbo, an old flame from his Stanford University days. McDonald knew people aged and their looks changed, but he always envisioned Candice as the tall, energetic co-ed she had been, a person whose whole face lit up when she smiled. *I suppose her hair has turned gray by now … like mine.*

They had gone separate ways, but stayed in touch to remain good friends over the years. The receptionist who answered the phone asked for McDonald's phone number and said, "If that person works here and is available, she will call you back." Three minutes later his desk phone rang.

"Richard," Palumbo said when he answered. "How nice to hear from you. How is life in the FBI?"

When he finished describing the container and the women, Candice provided the motivation. "Yes. We know it happens. And we have one hell of a time stopping it. INTERPOL tells us that Yemen is a stopping place only. They are sold to wealthy men.

A blonde like the one you described might bring a hundred thousand dollars from the right person. And twelve women could mean as much as a million dollars. Say ten deliveries a year … it might mean twelve million dollars annually. That's just from one source. And they don't just ship girls."

He swore. "Damn them."

"Yes," Candice echoed. "It makes my stomach turn, but it's the world we live in. So, stay cool and get those sonsabitches, will you?"

***

McDONALD READ THROUGH HIS REPORT AGAIN and nodded before his calm, professional facade turned to anger. *Patience, Richard*, he thought to himself. *We'll clean out this nest of vipers before we're done.*

His report described a completely self-contained shipping container, heavily insulated, equipped with bunk beds, solar lights, a porta-potty, and a wash basin. FBI crime scene techs estimated it was stocked with enough water and foodstuff to feed twelve people for thirty days.

Wilcox reported that the blonde woman who was first out of the blue container refused to be identified. When asked why not, she said the men who kidnapped her had shown her photos of her mother and her sister. Said they would wipe out her whole family if she didn't cooperate. Other FBI interviewers had come up against the same wall.

McDonald included his suspicion as to how the scheme worked, as well as speculation that a Kuwaiti citizen, living in the United States and going by the name of Al-Alwani, was the kingpin.

When he finished the body of his report, he appended: *From CIA sources, it is possible that some of the young women kidnapped are being sold in the Middle East for as much as one hundred thousand dollars.*

49

Dog Lake

WRAPPED IN A BLUE WOOL BLANKET, Miranda walked out on the deck to sniff cool, pine-scented morning air. She was surprised to see BB walking the path along the lake, his brown canoe on his shoulders. "Good morning," she hollered. "Need any help?"

BB lifted the canoe and raised it in the air. "No. It's not as heavy as it looks."

She laughed as BB left the path and headed through the scattered pines up to the house. "First time I ever saw a man wearing a canoe."

He dropped the canoe on the grass and took a deep breath. "I just couldn't leave it out there." He pointed to his pant legs, wet from the knees down. "I guess the wind pushed it off the bank. Had to wade to get ahold of it."

"Can you fix it?"

BB eyed the bullet-gouged hole in side of the canoe. He nodded. "Yes. Yes, I can. I'll tend to it when I get back."

She said, "Good. I'd like another canoe ride someday. For now, the coffee's perked and hotcakes are ready." She borrowed a line from a John Wayne film and smiled, "We're burning daylight."

Showered, shaved, dressed in dry khaki trousers and a deep blue turtleneck, BB soft-footed his way down the hallway to the kitchen. A woman in his house fixing breakfast was something he hadn't seen in years. The warmth of the domestic scene cracked BB's resolve to never be involved again. He was about to put his arms around Miranda from behind, when she said, "You gonna sneak up on a woman, you should forego that aftershave."

He stopped, and then she turned around, hotcake turner in her right hand, a smile tugging at her mouth. "What are you up to?"

He took a deep breath and shook his head. "I don't know. I just had this terrible urge to give you a hug."

She tilted her head back and looked down her nose at him. "You haven't known me twenty-four hours, Dell BeBe."

"I know, but I feel like I've known you forever."

She took a step closer, and without saying a word, she kissed him. She stepped back and shook her head. "This isn't smart."

BB wrapped her in his arms, chin on the top of her head, and was about to say something, when TJ startled them both, saying "The course of true love runs a tortured path ... or something along that line."

BB glared at him. "How about fare thee well? Adieu? Adios? Ciao? Get the hell out of here? Your timing sucks, TJ."

"Really? I thought it was perfect. Two lonely people find each other."

Miranda turned back to her hotcakes in time to keep them from burning, and BB grumped at his old friend, "You mind your own business, TJ, or I'm gonna dump you alongside the road someplace."

Miranda slid two hotcakes on a plate and set the plate on the island. Sarcastically she said, "How do you know I've been lonely, your holiness?"

"I can sense such things."

50

Bandits

TJ PROTESTED WHEN BB INSISTED MIRANDA WOULD drive the rental and follow them to Klamath Falls. BB knew his old friend well enough to understand TJ's protest was more a matter of form than a matter of substance. Not only was TJ a poor driver, he was an unlicensed driver. When BB said, "You were lucky to get here alive," TJ sighed, handed the keys to Miranda, and carried his backpack to the Lexus. When he slammed the passenger door, Miranda just grinned.

BB said, "We'll stop by Bud's A-frame and borrow some gas for TJ's car. We can top it off in Bly."

She eyed the Neon and shook her head. "Don't drive too fast. I don't know if I can keep up. And I don't know where I'm going."

***

MIRANDA'S IPHONE GAVE HER A GOOD map of the route from Five Corners, a spot a few miles west of Lakeview, to Bly, and on to Klamath Falls, but it gave her no hint of the beautiful, open stands of tall ponderosa pine lining the highway over Quartz Mountain. *Gorgeous*, she thought.

On the west side of the pass, the vegetation changed slowly from pine timber, to juniper, and then to a grassy open valley. BB spotted a mini-mart on the east end of the tiny town of Bly and pulled into the parking lot. Miranda pulled the Neon up to the pumps.

TJ said, "Gotta go," and ran inside to find a restroom.

BB stepped out of the Lexus and stretched. *Must be something about getting shot at that tires a man*, he thought. A tall, lean fellow – just the other side of middle age, wearing a Cabela's baseball cap and a white apron – looked through the window, then untied the apron to hang it on a peg on the wall behind the counter. He wiped his hands on a white towel and headed for the pump island. The scent of fresh yeast bread followed him through the door. BB sniffed and thought, *TJ won't be able to resist that. I'm not sure I can either.*

"Good morning. Fill it up?"

Miranda smiled and nodded. "Regular, please." She started fishing for a credit card, but BB shook his head. "I got this." He handed a card to the attendant and said, "Is that fresh bread I'm smelling?"

The man nodded. "Yep. Fresh bread, fresh rolls, fresh donuts, and fresh maple bars every morning."

BB said, "Out here?" It was question, statement, and near disbelief.

"Yes. Out here," the man said, a note of irritation in his voice. "A lot of the Forest Service people at the compound around the corner there," he said, pointing west, "buy our bread. And every truck driver coming or going stops for our donuts and maple bars. Local ranchers buy the rest."

Miranda said, "I don't suppose you could spare a half-dozen maple bars?"

He grinned. "I could, and I would. Go on in. I'll be along as soon as I finish filling your tank."

Miranda followed BB into the store. She took stock of the sparkling white bakery case filled with bread and pastries, of the neatly stocked shelves of basic foodstuff, a wall of fishing tackle, and a half-dozen paintings by local artists. "What a jewel. I'm so glad we stopped here. Who would've thought?"

TJ fished a ten-dollar bill out of his jeans pocket and said, "My treat. I want a couple of those fresh maples bars. How about you?"

The man in the Cabela's cap pushed through the door and handed BB the gas receipt. "You folks come far?" he asked.

BB grinned and shook his head. "Nope. I live on Dog Lake."

The man's eyebrows rose. "I heard about you. You're Sheriff Blair's friend, aren't you? Used to be a Portland detective."

Warily BB said, "One and the same. Why?"

"Well … just … just wondering is all. Any friend of Bud Blair is a friend of mine. You're famous, you know. People talk about the man who built a big beautiful log house on Dog Lake. Most are jealous. Heck, I could be myself."

He stuck out his hand. "I'm Morrison Obenchain. Fifth-generation rancher in these parts. Or I was a rancher. My two sons do all that work now, while I goof off with the bakery and store."

BB shook hands. "Dell BeBe."

"Nice to meet you, Mister BeBe. Now, who are your friends?"

BB pointed at TJ and said, "The Right Reverend TJ Wildish. He has a church in Portland. This nice lady is Miranda Wright."

"I heard about the shootout on Dog Lake." Obenchain said, his blue eyes concerned. He looked at her left hand. "You didn't get shot, did you?"

Miranda pursed her lips and then shook her head. Obenchain let it pass.

"Word is," Obenchain said, "Sheriff Blair and his deputies caught three or four bad guys. Bikers, I'm told." He waited, but no one confirmed or denied.

Finally, Miranda said, "How do you know all this?"

Obenchain laughed, took his hat off and rubbed his nearly bald head. "I don't know how it works. Not even after all these years of living out here. We just call it the 'sagebrush telegraph.' And sometimes it brings us word before anything actually happens."

A muddy pickup pulled into the pumps opposite the Neon, and Obenchain said, "My nephew, bumming gas again. He can damned well pump his own. Now, about those maple bars."

Maple bars in hand, a bag of extras for TJ, they said their thanks and headed for the vehicles. "Nice meeting you folks," Obenchain said. "Come again."

That's when the roar of multiple motorcycle engines caught BB's attention. Around a slight dog-leg that marked the main street through the little town came two dozen bikers on Harley motorcycles. A second group of motorcycles followed a few seconds later. BB counted their numbers as well as he could. *Fifty or so.*

They watched until the bikes were out of sight. "Did you see that?" Miranda said. "At least five bikes carried saddle scabbards with rifles."

"I counted six," BB said, reaching for his cell phone.

"Their leather vests said The Romans," TJ said. "Looks like they're heading for Lakeview."

When Bud answered the call, BB said, "I'm in Bly. We're headed for Klamath Falls and stopped to gas up. Some very nasty looking people from The Romans gang just rode through this little burg, headed your direction. I counted about fifty bikes and at least six rifles in the mix. You best line up some help."

"Come to get their friends out of jail, I guess."

"How much backup do you have?"

"Three from the city. The five of us. A State Trooper. And I think BLM has a new Ranger … their version of a cop. And three reserves. I think they're too green to use on this. I might also get some help from the prison."

"Add me in the mix."

"No. You get TJ to a safe place, and I'll get my shotgun out."

"Luck."

"You too, BB. Hey, I know. Let's fix that canoe of yours and drown some worms on the lake … soon."

When he looked around, BB saw Morrison Obenchain standing in the doorway with a semi-automatic shotgun in his hands. "Outlaws," was all he said before turning back into the store.

BB shook his head. "I'm not sure Mister Obenchain makes me feel a whole lot better."

Miranda nodded. "I know."

He took a deep breath. "You take TJ to Klamath Falls. I'm going back."

"You're just a civilian!"

"No. I'm a sworn Lake County deputy sheriff, and I'm damned if I'm going to let Bud keep me out of the fight."

He grabbed TJ's daypack from the SUV and tossed it through the Neon's open window. He dug through the business cards in his wallet until he found the one with Sergeant Booker's phone number. He handed it to Miranda and said, "Call this guy. He'll take care of TJ. Then you get on a plane and head home. I'll be up as soon as…"

She gave him a hug and whispered, "Don't you get shot. Understood?"

BB hugged her back and said, "Yes, ma'am."

TJ stuck out his hand and said, "Go with God."

BB burned rubber getting out of the parking lot and pushed the Lexus hard, topping the Quartz Mountain pass at nearly one hundred miles per hour, anger running hot through his mind. And then he slowed to a more reasonable sixty five when he thought about the possibility of hitting a mule deer. It wasn't until the highway dipped into Drews Valley that he saw the rolling army of bikers.

He debated running a few of them down, just give them a little bump, but settled instead for accelerating and passing the long line of bikes. His reward was a forest of single digit salutes.

See you in town.

51

Booker

AT 0930, MIRANDA DROVE INTO THE KLAMATH falls Safeway parking lot. She pulled Bud's business card from her vest and turned it over. On the back, he had written the phone number for Sergeant Booker, a senior member of the Klamath Falls Police Department. She keyed in the number and hit the send button.

After the first ring, Miranda heard a baritone voice say, "This is Booker. What can I do for you?"

"This is Special Agent Miranda Wright, Sheriff Blair's friend. I'm with Reverend Wildish. Where can we meet you?"

"Have you eaten breakfast yet?"

"Yes, but TJ's always hungry."

Booker chuckled and said, "Let me give you directions to Applebee's."

"How will we know you?"

Booker laughed and said, "Look for the only black police officer there."

***

WHEN TJ AND MIRANDA WALKED INTO the restaurant, a smiling hostess said, "Right this way" and, menus in hand, led them to a back-corner booth where Sergeant Booker was sipping coffee and working the crossword puzzle in the Herald and News.

Miranda noted his choice of booths. *Back to the wall, clear view of the street and the parking lot. My kind of guy.*

"Sergeant," the hostess said, "your guests are here."

Booker slid out of the booth and stood up. He was tall, nearly six-one, his broad shoulders straining a blue KFPD police jacket. A neatly trimmed salt and pepper moustache finished the statement that he was a cop. Booker was known to tell his trainees, "You're a police officer, first and foremost. No reason to hide it. And no sense in flaunting it. Just be who you are … a proud officer of the law."

He frowned, glancing first at Miranda and then at TJ, an unspoken question in his eyes.

Miranda held out her hand and said, "I'm FBI Special Agent Miranda Wright, and this is Reverend TJ Wildish."

Booker shook hands with each of them. "Benjamin Booker. Have a seat."

The hostess put the stack of menus on the table, asking "Coffee?" They all nodded.

TJ said, "I'd like a little cream with mine. And a short stack."

Booker pointed to the bench seat on his side of booth. "Reverend, why don't you sit here."

While they waited for their coffee, Booker looked at his crossword puzzle and said, "Eleven down. I need a six-letter word for a sea hawk."

Without hesitation Miranda said, "Osprey. We saw a pair of those on Dog Lake yesterday. Beautiful birds."

Booker filled in the boxes, set his pen on the newspaper, and looked up, brown eyes serious. "Okay, now I need several words for why the FBI needs me to hide the reverend."

Miranda nodded, forehead furrowed, and looked around the restaurant.

"We can talk here," advised Booker, "as long as we don't talk too loudly."

She gathered her thoughts and then slowly and deliberately briefed Sergeant Booker…

"Last year, Detective Dell BeBe gave the FBI some photos showing weapons cached in the basement of a Northeast Portland mosque. The man who took the pictures sold them to one of Detective BeBe's snitches. BB brought them to our SAC, Dutch Vanderlin. We took them to a judge and asked for a search warrant. The judge said the FBI needed a name before the court could issue a warrant."

Booker interrupted her and looked at TJ. "How did you wind up in this?"

TJ blinked a few times, then said, "BB knows I'm a member of the Portland Ministerial Council, so when he told me what was going on, I asked around to see what I could find. I have friends who left the Christian faith and converted to Islam. But we still talk.

"Anyway, one of the council members gave me a note. It had the name of a prominent imam. That's all. Just a name. I gave the name to BB, and he took it from there."

Booker frowned. "You didn't think that was dangerous?"

"Of course," TJ said, sitting as tall as he could. With a touch of pride in his voice he added, "But I grew up in a tough neighborhood … and back then, I didn't have Christ on my side. I knew I would be protected this time."

Booker nodded and smiled. "As so it came to pass."

True to her nature, Miranda interrupted. "To continue, the judge issued a warrant. We conducted simultaneous raids on a mosque in Portland and on another in Seattle. The FBI recovered a considerable number of military-style weapons, tons of ammunition, grenade launchers, explosives, detonators, street maps, building plans, and so forth … all a clear indication of terrorist activity, or at least terrorist intent.

"We made about thirty arrests. I need to tell you, we were all very happy. And I was convinced we had cut the head off the Muslim terrorist snakes in the Pacific Northwest. But a few days ago, word trickled in off the streets that some very bad people knew Reverend Wildish was the link to the Portland FBI.

"Someone killed the man who supplied the imam's name. It looked very much like a revenge killing – torture followed by execution.

"When we found out, Reverend Wildish left Portland to hide at Detective BeBe's place, I was sent to debrief him. We thought he might be safe with BB, but the bad guys stole Reverend TJ's computer. On it were pictures of Dell BeBe's house and directions to Dog Lake. They hired members of The Romans biker gang to kill us. That's why Sheriff Blair suggested you."

Booker waited until the smiling waitress left a carafe and two cups on the table. He dabbed at his salt and pepper moustache with a napkin, wadded the paper up, and dropped it in his plate. He pointed to Miranda. "How did you hurt your hand?"

"We had a shootout with three bikers – from a club here in Klamath Falls, I should add. We were on Dog Lake doing some fishing, when they started shooting at us. One shot blew up my cedar paddle and drove a big splinter through my hand. Sheriff Blair and his deputies arrested three bikers, members of The Romans gang. I guess they thought it was okay to kill Detective BeBe and me as well. Collateral damage."

Booker waited until their waitress set a stack of hotcakes in front of TJ. When she was gone, Booker nodded. "I know that gang. Forty or fifty bikers who hang out at a bar called Day's End. We haven't caught them doing anything serious … just some minor traffic violations … and they always pay the tickets without any fuss. But the street tells us they're into drugs and prostitution. Murder seems a bit out of their league."

Miranda looked at Booker and shook her head. "You look like you've been an officer of the law long enough to know what people will do for money. Crime is a slippery slope, and the bottom isn't too far down."

Booker nodded. "Yes, but so far we have no reason to suspect them of hiring out as assassins."

"You do now. And to make matters worse, they sank BB's canoe."

Booker smiled. "That's definitely an egregious act." He paused and looked at Miranda. "Good briefing Agent Wright. I thought it might be something like that. So … I have concocted the story that a cousin is coming to visit."

He studied TJ and said, "Black, about fifty, and close enough to my age. I'll have to tell Ruthie, my granddaughter, what we're up to. But she'll keep it to herself.

"Well, Reverend," he said suddenly, "when you finish your breakfast, let's grab your gear and get you settled into my place." He slid a business card across the table to Miranda. "My personal address is on the back. Guard that information with your life."

Booker slid out of the booth and waited for TJ to wipe hotcake crumbs from his mouth. "Come on, Reverend. Let's get moving."

Miranda managed a "Thank you," before Booker stomped his way to the front door, TJ trailing behind. Miranda hit the unlock button on the Neon's key fob, and watched through the window of the restaurant as TJ grabbed his daypack from the back seat and walked to Booker's police car – a white SUV decked out with gold KFPD shields on the driver and passenger doors. TJ waved in the general direction of the restaurant, then pulled the passenger door shut.

She watched Booker's vehicle drive down the hill and out of sight. Then she took a deep breath. *I suspect Sergeant Booker is not very happy with the FBI. For that matter, neither am I.* She sighed and took a last sip of coffee. *Well, time to turn this car in and book a plane for Portland.*

When Miranda tried to pay for the coffee and TJ's short stack, the waitress smiled and said, "On us. Any friend of Sergeant Booker is a friend of ours."

52

Butler's Revenge

S PECIAL AGENT BRANDT WORKED THE KEYBOARD and watched the big monitor as his after-action report worked its way letter-by-letter across the screen. Writing was the least favorite part of his job, but he knew good reports were key to successful prosecutions.

 In a neighboring cubicle, he could hear Agent Wilcox pounding the keyboard and muttering under his breath.

Brandt called over the partition, "You know what they say, Leroy. Don't kill the messenger. Sounds like you're trying to kill your keyboard instead."

"Douglas, I don't want to do this right now. I need to find Al-Alwani and take him down. And I mean right now."

"Soon as we can," Brandt agreed. "But Smitty wants this on the director's desk ASAP."

"I have an idea, Douglas. Let the director come out here, then we can tell him all about it and skip the paper work."

Brandt picked up his cell phone on the first ring. "Agent Brandt."

"And a good agent he is," Butler said. "How many?"

"How many what?"

"How many women were in the container? I counted eight. Is that right?"

"You were watching."

Butler laughed and said, "And a damned fine job you did. If there is a book on rescuing damsels in distress, you followed it to the letter. I'm impressed."

"What do you want, Butler? You can still come in. And we can all pretend you were working undercover."

"No. I can't come in, but I am working undercover." Butler paused … and then, in a more serious tone, said, "I want you to pull surveillance off Al-Alwani tonight for one hour, like from ten to eleven. Don't watch. Don't listen. I'll give you Al-Alwani and enough evidence to convict him of murder, human trafficking, drug dealing, embezzlement, and sex crimes. You get the credit."

"Why should we? You have to know we can't do that."

"Because I want you to."

Wilcox started laughing so hard he could barely hear Butler. "I knew you were listening in, Agent Wilcox. I'll call you back in an hour." And then the line went dead.

Brandt said, "Wow. Now what?"

Wilcox shook his head. "We can't let Butler just shut us down."

Brandt frowned. "We could give our watchers a break, and then you and I watch Al-Alwani. See what Butler has in mind."

Wilcox nodded. "We could do that. It might get interesting."

***

AL-ALWANI'S CELL PHONE CHIRPED, AND HE opened a text message. They found the cargo. You're next. I'd run if I were you. Yoseph.

Adrenalin kicked in, and Al-Alwani's hands were shaking as he fumbled an answer: Where are you?

Butler smiled at the message, then shut his phone down without answering. His non-descript pickup was parked behind a dark green Mazda Miata convertible half a block up the street from the strong iron gate guarding Al-Alwani's driveway. *Now the wait begins.*

The FBI listener couldn't identify the cause of the noise, but he heard the cell phone bouncing off a wall. And Al-Alwani's shouts were easy to identify.

Listener one called to his partner, who was getting a second cup of coffee from the little kitchen in the apartment rented by the FBI. "We got something."

Listener two hurried to his head phones in time to hear Al-Alwani tell his personal servant Ali to get the money and bring the limo around.

Listener One nodded and said, "He's gonna boogie. I wonder who put a bee in his bonnet?"

"I don't know, but let's call this in."

Ten minutes later a polished black limousine pulled up to Al-Alwani's security gate. The driver honked the horn, and a few seconds later the gate rolled back. The car pulled through the circle drive and stopped at the front door of the big house. A man wearing a hooded sweatshirt that hid his face, carried two large suitcases to the limo and slid inside. The big car drove back through the gate and turned right, heading in the direction of downtown Portland. Two FBI agents waited a half block down the street for Al-Alwani's limo to pass their unmarked Dodge Charger, then they pulled out to follow.

Butler just waited where he was. His patience was rewarded when Al-Alwani drove a silver Audi down the driveway and through the gate. He laughed and said, "Thank you, Lord. I hoped he would decoy the watchers with the limo. And it worked. Now then, what do you have up your sleeve, Al-Alwani?"

Butler followed the Audi to the on-ramp leading to I-405. As far as he could tell, Al-Alwani never looked back to see who might be tailing him. Butler's pickup was three cars back when the silver Audi turned onto I-5 North. A puzzled Butler said, "Where is he going? The airport? Or is he just going to drive to Seattle? I hope not." He glanced at the gas gauge. The indicator was still saying full. "

When Al-Alwani took the freeway exit to Marine Drive and then turned west, Butler started grinning. "If I can catch him in the terminal, he's mine." He touched his daypack, feeling for the butt of the pistol in a side pocket.

The Audi pulled up to the guard shack, and Butler backed into a parking spot to watch. He saw Al-Alwani hand what must have been his Transportation Worker Identification Card (TWIC) to the uniformed guard. Then the gate roll back enough to allow the Audi into the terminal.

Butler pulled through the parking lot to the gate. He flashed his FBI badge and said, "I'm following that Audi. I'm undercover. A sting operation."

The guard raised his eyebrows and said, "Who can I call at the FBI to confirm this?

Without hesitation, Butler recited the number for the FBI's Portland headquarters. "Ask for Agent Brandt or Agent Wilcox."

53

Setting the Trap

IF BUD BLAIR POSSESSED ONE STRENGTH BEYOND raw courage, it was the ability to envision the setting and the players involved and to lay out a tactical plan. BB's warning about the bikers set Bud working on a series of quick steps he and his deputies needed to take. He walked the short hall to the booking counter.

"Karen," he said, "I want all of our deputies here in five minutes. This is a red-flag meeting."

"What's going on, Bud?"

"Looks like some bikers are coming to break their buddies out of our jail."

"Oh, Lord. On it, Bud."

He used his cell phone to call the Lake County Emergency Services Center. When Nancy Sixkiller answered, he said, "I have a red-flag warning for all local police officers. We have a gang of about fifty bikers headed for Lakeview. I think they intend to break their friends out of our jail. I need all county officers, the city police, and any state police who might be in the area in my office ASAP."

Next, he called Bob Blankenship, the superintendent of the Warner Creek Correctional facility. Blankenship wasn't exactly a friend, but he had publicly supported Bud in the last election. When Blankenship's secretary answered, Bud said, "I need to talk to Superintendent Blankenship."

"I'm afraid he's in a meeting right now."

"I'm sorry, but this won't wait. I'm calling a red-flag meeting at my office. I need to talk to him NOW."

Thirty seconds later Blankenship said, "Hello?"

"Bob, this is Bud Blair. I'd like you to take temporary custody of three prisoners. I have a reliable tip that a group of bikers are headed for Lakeview, and I think they're planning to break their friends out of the county jail. ETA in about fifteen minutes."

"Not good. I'll send our van and two correctional officers to pick up your prisoners. And I can send four of my best officers, all trained in crowd control, and all armed."

"I'd be grateful for the reinforcements."

"We're on the way."

He hung up and then called Nancy back. "I think an emergency bulletin to all local and state police agencies requesting assistance is in order."

"On it. For good news, a SWAT team from Klamath Falls is in the air. ETA forty-five minutes, but they'll need a ride from the airport."

"Good, but I don't think they'll get here in time."

"I hope you're wrong. And, Bud. Please remember your vest."

Phone to ear, Bud saw BB's Lexus slide to a stop in one of the county's reserved parking slots on "E" street. He was in the hall leading to the booking desk when BB turned the corner.

"Bud," BB said, "I think you've got about ten minutes before they arrive."

"What are you doing here?"

"Can't let you tackle these guys without my help."

Bud shook his head. "And I can't risk a civilian's life."

"I'm not a civilian. I'm a sworn deputy sheriff for Lake County.

"Who swore you in?"

"Mister Sixkiller."

Bud nodded, smiled, and then held out his hand. BB grinned and shook hands. "Like old times."

Bud chuckled and said, "No. No, it's not, but thanks anyway. We'd better get going."

54

The Waterfront

S PECIAL AGENT BRANDT, PEN IN HAND, his own peculiar hen scratches filling a yellow legal pad, listened to the recording of a woman describing her journey from childhood, to housewife, to hooker, to kidnap victim.

"My trade name is Naomi. I love country western music, and I'm a huge fan of Naomi Judd. My given name is Brandy, probably because my drunk of a mother liked her brandy … but first, I want to know how June is doing."

"June?"

"The little one in the back who was so sick."

"I don't know. I'll try to find out. Right now, I want to hear your story. Who's your pimp?"

"He'd kill me, or have me killed, if I told you."

"Not if we put him away, he won't. I don't know what the sentence is for human trafficking, but he'll be an old man before he ever sees the outside world again."

"He also threatened my mother..."

***

BRANDT'S CELL PHONE BUZZED. "SPECIAL AGENT Brandt."

"This is Dean Williams. I'm a marine security guard at the Port of Portland, Terminal 6. I have a guy here flashing an FBI badge who says he's undercover. He said to ask you for verification."

"What's the name on the badge?"

"Winslow Butler."

"What's he doing out there?"

"Well, he tells me he's following the silver Audi I just let through the gate."

Brandt's excitement grew with each breath. "Can you describe the driver of the Audi?"

"Looked like some type of Arab."

"Okay. I'll vouch for Butler. Let him through. I'll be there in about fifteen minutes."

***

BUTLER WATCHED AL-ALWANI'S SILVER AUDI DISAPPEAR down an alley between tall stacks of multi-colored shipping containers. Out of the corner of his eye, he saw the security guard nod and kill the call.

"Go on through."

Butler pulled the pickup through the gate and drove about three hundred yards before stopping behind the first row of containers. They were stacked four high, nearly a quarter mile long. He put the pickup in park and walked to the corner of the first metal box for a quick peek down the alley ... just as the silver Audi drove into the maw of a red container. Butler counted the rows to make sure he could find the right one, counted again to make sure he had it right, and then waited.

Al-Alwani stepped out, looked in both directions, then pulled the doors shut. *Too easy*, Butler thought. Then he sent a prayer. *Thank you, Lord, for stupid criminals.*

Butler walked to the pickup, slid behind the wheel, and nodded to himself. He was half tempted to call Brandt immediately, but his sense of self-preservation kicked in. "No, Winslow," he said aloud. "Get this right. First deal with Al-Alwani, then get yourself in the clear, and then call Brandt."

He slipped his pistol from the daypack and laid it on the seat within easy reach, then he slowly eased the pickup down the alley, counting containers as he drove. When the count was right, he stopped, got out, and approached the box cautiously. He turned the sliding latch and pulled both doors open.

Al-Alwani turned quickly, reaching for a gun he'd placed on a chair beside him. He stopped when Butler triggered a round that punched through the back wall. Bound by the metal walls of the container, the concussion hammered Al-Alwani, and his ears rang from the explosion of the pistol round.

"What do you want?"

"Keep your hands up and walk away from the weapon, or the next round punches a hole in your head."

Al-Alwani raised shaking hands in the air and asked, "Who are you?"

Butler was suddenly struck by the absurdity of the question. He started laughing and sputtered, "What the hell difference does that make?"

"I know that laugh. You're Yoseph, aren't you?"

Butler eased inside the container, squeezing between the Audi and the wall. He stopped when he was ten feet from Al-Alwani. "I've come to end your career, old buddy. You crossed the Rubicon when you started kidnapping our women."

Butler saw Al-Alwani's eyes shift back towards the gun, and he started laughing again. "Prison or death. Do you want to be a martyr? Go ahead. Either way, you're done. No more cocktails, no more expensive cars, no more sex parties."

Butler set his phone on the trunk of the Audi and started the recorder. "Now then, let's go over it. Tell me how you started. Give me the names of your operatives, and I'll think about letting you live."

"You're crazy, Yoseph. I'll do no such thing."

Butler shot him through the right hand, the concussion hammering them both. Al-Alwani jerked his hand down, grabbed it with his other hand, and yowled. Butler laughed, shaking his head. "Huh, uh. Keep 'em up."

Within five minutes, Al-Alwani was bleeding from both his right hand and his left foot … and he was talking. When he tried to avoid a question, Butler would threaten to shoot him again. To Al-Alwani, blood dripping from two bullet wounds, it sounded more like certainty than threat. And since he wasn't interested in being a martyr, he kept talking.

Finally, satisfied the iPhone carried as much confession as he was likely to get, Butler turned the camera on Al-Alwani. "And this is what you get when you extend student visas. Rock on, sanctuary cities. Rock on."

He left Al-Alwani face-down on a cot, handcuffed to a tie-down welded to a padded railing in the container. He wiped his fingerprints from the phone, placed it on the hood of the Audi, waved at Al-Alwani and said, "Ciao, asshole," before slamming the door and sliding the latch into place.

He fired up the pickup and drove to the alley at the far end of the compound, then parked behind the last row and watched until he saw Brandt and Wilcox slide to a stop at the gate. He thumbed in Brandt's number on a burner phone. When Brandt answered, Butler said, "I left you a little something in the seventeenth container of the second row from the wharf. That's on the right as you travel west. There's an iPhone on the hood of an Audi in there that might be of interest. Better hurry before your gift bleeds to death."

He heard Brant say, "Wait, Butler, you should come in." Butler shook his head, and killed the call.

When he could see Wilcox and Brant, guns drawn, sliding the latch back on the container, he walked to his pickup, drove down the backside of a long row of shipping containers, and stopped at the gate.

The guard saw him coming and stepped out of the shack. Butler stopped, rolled down his window, and said "Let me out, please. My colleagues can handle it from here."

55

Posse

THE SOUND OF MULTIPLE POLICE SIRENS converging on the court-house drew people to the sidewalks and window fronts. Sonny pulled up to the curb in front of the Lakeview News building, after Carol Connor flagged him down.

Without preamble, she said, "Karen called. Said a big gang of bikers is coming to break some prisoners out of jail."

"Right. Can you pass the word and tell people to stay off the streets? They should be here in the next few minutes."

She nodded. "Yes."

He shifted into Drive and shouted, "Gotta go." He hit the siren and pulled back into the street.

The wail of sirens stopped, and Bud's grim-faced deputies trooped through the front door. He looked at Karen and said, "Forward all calls to Emergency Services and go home. Now."

Her hands shook just a wee bit as she picked up the phone and punched in the numbers to forward phone calls. On her way out, she stopped, walked up to Bud, and hugged him hard enough to squeeze the breath from his lungs. "Don't you get hurt, Bud Blair." She turned and ran out the door before he could see the tears in her eyes.

District Attorney Howard Finch and Judge Tom Lynch pushed through the interconnecting door to the courthouse. Lynch said, "What's going on, Bud?"

Bud pointed in the direction of the small conference room that served the sheriff's office. "Let's gather. We don't have much time."

City Police Chief Augustus Hildebrand barged in, followed by his two-man city police force. "Don't start without us," he said and then looked out as a dark blue van wearing the Warner Creek Correctional Facility banner double parked. Superintendent Bob Blankenship and four armed correctional officers jumped out the back of the van and crossed the sidewalk to the sheriff's office, AR-15's at port arms.

Bud looked at Roger. "You and Sonny get our prisoners out here. We're sending them to Warner Creek. The rest of you come with me."

***

BUD DID A HEAD COUNT AND started writing names on the blackboard. Without turning around, he said, "This is what I want each of you to do."

"Roger: rooftop of the courthouse with your .308"

"Sonny and Larae: block F Street at Bullard. Use shotguns. I don't want pistol or rifle rounds punching holes in civilians."

"Gus, stake out the road into town. Let us know when they cross the railroad tracks, and then just follow them into town." Same orders for your team … use shotguns. Okay, Gus?"

Gus nodded. "Okay, Bud."

Howard interrupted. "What are you going to do with the bikers?"

"In a minute, Howard. Let me get this set up."

"Lonnie and Beatrice: block F street at the SW corner of the courthouse. Same drill … shotguns."

"Bob, I want you and your Warner Creek folks to stick with me and Deputy BeBe. Everyone gear up. If you're not wearing your vest, I'll shoot you myself. Guaranteed."

He turned to Howard. "Okay, Mister District Attorney. To answer your question, I'm going to arrest them for any number of crimes, starting with creating a public nuisance, threatening a police officer with bodily harm, spitting on the sidewalk, and for violating the city's noise ordinance."

Gladys McKnight, long-serving Lakeview mayor squeezed into the conference room. "I heard that. We don't have a noise ordinance."

"May I suggest that the city council passed one late last night?"

Gladys' eyes clouded. She frowned and didn't say anything until Tom Lynch, the silver-haired rancher, turned county judge, said, "For crying out loud, Gladys. Do I have to spell it out?"

Gladys brightened and said, "Oh. Oh, I get it. Yes. Yes, we did. Yes. Last night. I'll get the council to go over it again right away. Just to make sure it's in force." The room filled with chuckles as Gladys pushed her way to the door of the conference room and down the hall.

"Howard," Bud said, "see what else we can charge them with. I want to process each one. Odds are good that at least a half-dozen are guilty of parole violations or have outstanding warrants."

Howard nodded, but his forehead was furrowed in a frown. "You can't just make up the charges. They have to do something first."

Bud looked sideways at Howard, eyebrows raised. "Are you getting cold feet?"

"No, but I want something solid to work with."

"You will have what you need, Howard. You will."

He looked at the crowd, pointed at the clock, and said, "That's the best I can do on short notice. Any questions?"

When no one spoke up, Bud said, "Judge, why don't you evacuate the building, let everyone go home?"

"Already underway, Bud."

Bud nodded. "Good." He made eye contact with each officer in the room, trying to determine how steady they were.

One of the officers from the Warner Creek Correctional Facility said, "It doesn't seem real. Out here? In Lakeview?"

Bud said, "Doesn't to me either." He paused and said, "Now then, we also have a Klamath Falls SWAT team on the way … and maybe the state police. But for now, we are it. Set your radios to our tactical channel and get going."

Bud watched the officers head down the hallway, except for the Warner Creek Correctional team and BB. He cleared his throat. "Gentlemen," he said, "this is Deputy Sheriff Dell BeBe. BB and I are old friends from our days working for the Portland Police Bureau. Now, what BB and I are going to do when the bikers arrive is this…"

56

Busted

SPECIAL AGENT BRANDT STEPPED OUT OF the container and called for an ambulance, while Wilcox tended to Al-Alwani's wounds. He used two gauze pads from the big first aid kit and a long strip of tape to bind the shattered hand. But when he started unlacing the bloody shoe on Al-Alwani's left foot, all it earned him was a kick in the shin.

Wilcox shrugged and moved away. "Your funeral. Bleed to death. It's all the same to me."

Incredulous, Al-Alwani shouted, "He shot me! I can't believe it. He just shot me. Twice!"

Wilcox laughed and said, "He must be a terrible shot. Almost missed."

"I need help."

"Listen. You cooperate or my partner and I will just lock you up in this tin can and ship you off to Yemen. And then you can tend to your own wounds. Got it?"

Al-Alwani swallowed, his Adams apple bobbing up and down, and with tears in his eyes, he nodded.

"Good. Now … who shot you?"

"Yoseph. He's FBI, but I don't know his name. He's just Yoseph to us."

"Us? Who is us?"

Al-Alwani stifled a groan and took a deep breath. "Please. If Osama finds what I've done, he'll kill me."

"But you haven't been doing this alone. Who helped you? Tell us and make it easy on yourself."

"You already have the recording. I'm not saying another thing until I see my lawyer."

"No lawyer, stupid. You're a foreign national involved in human trafficking and terrorism. You'll see Gitmo before you see a lawyer."

"You can't do that! They'll kill me in there!"

"Your tough luck. You didn't show any mercy to the women you kidnapped. Why should we show you any?"

"Because I can help you stop the next attack."

Brandt walked back into the container and said, "Ambulance is on the way ... along with your boss and mine." He glared at Al-Alwani. "Just for fun, I thought you should know we arrested your girlfriend. You no longer have an inside contact at the FBI. She'll be going away for a long, long time."

"What about Yoseph?"

Brandt and Wilcox looked at one another and each shook his head. "Nope," Wilcox said. "He's not one of ours."

The sound of a siren drifted up the alley between the tall stacks of containers. They followed it in their minds until the siren stopped. "At the gate," Wilcox said.

Wilcox set his cell phone to record, took out his pistol, and said, "All right, asshole. Talk or I'm going to shoot you in self-defense. What terrorist attack are you talking about? Help us and we might get you a ticket back to the big sandbox."

"Unless I shoot you first," Brandt said.

After Butler's second shot splintered the bones in his left foot, Al-Alwani knew beyond doubt that all FBI agents were crazy – crazy enough to shoot him again. He didn't want to be shot again. Ever. So, in a quavering voice, Al-Alwani told the story of a terrorist plot to kill thousands of people in the Portland metropolitan area, Muslim as well as Christian people. Black as well as white. Arab and American. Anyone and everyone.

When he stopped talking, Al-Alwani looked up, frightened by the rage painted on Wilcox's face and the big black hole of the pistol barrel aimed at his forehead. He didn't know if Wilcox was deciding to kill him or not. A tense thirty seconds passed before a cowering Al-Alwani asked, "What happens now?"

Wilcox shook his head to clear his mind, lowered his pistol, and then slowly exhaled before answering. "And you were going to let this happen? No warning? Just kill tens of thousands of people, including people of your own faith? I should shoot you just for that. For not giving us any warning."

Brandt interrupted, disgust in his voice, "To answer your question. First, asshole, we get you patched up. Then we put you in protective custody. Then you will brief some other not-so-nice agents again. You will name names. And if you don't, we turn you over to the CIA. They have some very unusual methods for dealing with terrorists."

The ambulance backed up to the open door and two EMT's squeezed past the Audi to a distraught, weeping Al-Alwani.

The first EMT, a husky, dark haired man in his early thirties, asked, "What do we have here?"

Brandt held out his credentials before saying, "We have a bona fide idiot who seems to have shot himself in the right hand and the left foot. My instructions are to take him to the ER. I'll ride shotgun. This man is dangerous."

57

Flight

S TAYING WITHIN THE SPEED LIMIT, BUTLER followed Highway 30 past Guy's Marina and the cabin cruiser he had called home, then on past the Sauvie Island Bridge and the Willamette Channel. He kept an eye on his rearview mirror, expecting to see flashing lights at any minute. He knew he had to find somewhere to ditch the pickup … and soon.

A sign on the outskirts of Scappoose marked a bus stop near a mini mart. Butler pulled off and parked behind the store. He wiped the pickup clean and left the keys in the ignition. Hopefully, someone would steal it.

He slipped his daypack over his shoulder, then walked around the corner of the building and across the parking lot to the bus stop. With his black watch cap, beard, and daypack, he fit right in with the group waiting for the bus … three bearded young men, two wearing worn gray-green army surplus jackets, and one wearing a black duster. A disheveled-looking woman hid her face in a tattered green hoody with a worn U of O logo on the back of the jacket. Each carried a grimy daypack.

Homeless, he thought. *And dangerous.* Two of the men were taller than his six-one, their rail-thin faces marked by acne scars. The third looked solid and stocky. Their cold stares kicked Butler's survival instincts into high gear.

He turned his back, shrugged the daypack off his shoulder, and slipped the Berretta 9mm into his coat pocket.

The tallest one, who was obviously the leader and the most aggressive, stepped up to Butler. "You got any money?"

Butler shook his head. "Not much. And I need every dime I've got."

The other two flanked him, trying to box him in. The one to his right said, "Let's see what you got in there," and reached for Butler's daypack.

Butler blocked the man's right arm with his left hand, grabbed the man's sleeve with his right, and pulled him off balance. He tripped him and watched him stumble into the man on the left.

Butler pulled the pistol from his jacket pocket and poked the tallest man in the belly.

The aggressor-turned-victim stumbled back, fear in his eyes, and said, "Hey, man. Hold on! We just need to get a fix. That's all."

Grim-faced, Butler said, "Let's get this right the first time. First, you can't have any of my money

"Second, you can't get on my bus. I'm not going to waste my time with you stinking, thieving bastards.

"That said, around the back of the store I spotted a pickup with the key in the ignition. I know for a fact the owner isn't coming back anytime soon. And I know it isn't stolen. So … you behave until the bus comes. Then you can have the pickup."

He looked at the woman and said, "You with them?"

She glanced fearfully at the three men and then took a hesitant step away from the group.

Butler nodded. "Good. You can ride my bus. And I'll give you the funds to get back home."

***

THREE DAYS LATER, A YOUNG TILLAMOOK cop on the graveyard shift followed a pickup driving erratically through a neighborhood lining the main north-south street of the city. When she switched on the emergency lights, the driver of the pickup chose prudence versus flight and pulled over.

A comparison of the license plate to an FBI bulletin on her dashboard computer prompted the police officer to call for backup. The passenger door popped open, and two men ran across the sidewalk. They jumped a fence into the unlit side yard of a residence, where they were greeted by two noisy, salivating Rottweilers. They jumped back over the fence only to face a scared, but determined, police woman who pointed a black pistol at them and said, "Freeze!" She herded them into the back of her cruiser, charges to be determined.

The driver of the pickup, for reasons to remain forever unknown, pulled the gearshift into drive and mashed the accelerator just as a second police car pulled in front of him. His reaction was one second too slow, and the pickup plowed into the right rear quarter panel of the cop car.

The seatbelt the pickup driver was not wearing did not stop his forward progress, and the air bag did not deploy. In a word, he ate the steering wheel. He would later have his broken jaw wired shut at the local ER, before taking a trip to jail. He would then suck unappetizing meals through a straw for most of the next six weeks.

An internet search by the Tillamook Police Department found outstanding warrants for each of the men. The chief breathed a sigh of relief and personally called the proper jurisdictions to tell them where to pick up the "wanted." He made sure he didn't have to feed the men any longer than necessary. As his honor, the mayor, said: "We all need to work within narrow budget parameters."

58

Texas Style

BUD BLAIR STOOD ON THE AGING concrete sidewalk that led from Bullard Street to the front door of the Lake County Court-house. He wore a black Kevlar vest advertised as capable of stopping large-caliber rounds. A shotgun rode the crook of his left elbow. A medium-sized cardboard box marked "Soft Cuffs" sat on the walk behind him.

The two-story courthouse occupied most of a city block, except for the lawn on the NW corner bordered by Bullard and F Street. Tall one-hundred-year-old deciduous trees arched over the sidewalk and gave shade to the sun-hungry grass.

Dell BeBe stood beside him, a shotgun over his right shoulder, his big hand on the stock and his right index finger resting on the trigger guard. The safety was in the off position. The Kevlar vest he wore was a bit tight, but he found comfort in it nonetheless.

Superintendent Bob Blankenship and his Warner Creek correctional officers stood two-and-two on each side of BB and Bud. They were armored up, and they each carried a .223 caliber AR-15. Bud would have preferred shotguns, but they came equipped with their own weapons. Grateful though he was for the added numbers, he thought they were a little too jacked up. *Trained, but never tested*, he thought. *I want to do this without hearing a single gunshot.*

At the distant sound of motorcycle engines, he turned and spoke his thoughts aloud. "We do this slow, we do this right, and no one gets hurt. You ever hear the old Texas Ranger saying about riots?"

The correctional officers all shook their heads. Superintendent Blankenship said, "Can't say I have."

"Well," Bud said, "it goes like this. One riot, one Ranger. That's all it takes. Makes me feel sorry for the bikers. We have them outnumbered thirteen to fifty."

A few chuckles satisfied Bud.

***

DELL BEBE GLANCED AT HIS OLD partner. The setting pulled his memory back to Portland, his mind still seeing Detective Bud Blair punched backwards, as a slug from a .38 smashed into the center of his vest.

BB fired three quick rounds in response. Much to his regret, those shots ended the life of a fifteen-year-old boy – a street punk who had pistol-whipped the cashier of a small convenience store during a robbery – but it didn't make BB feel any better. He was relieved, however, to find Bud would live to heal from a broken sternum.

BB said quietly, "No heroics today. Okay"

Bud frowned at BB. "Never got over it, did you? You still think I screwed up when I tried to talk that punk in Portland into surrendering."

"Got you shot."

Bud nodded. "I'll give you that much."

***

CHIEF AUGUSTUS (GUS) HILDEBRAND, HIS CRUISER parked beside the veterinary building on the north side of the street that led highway 140 from the east into town, counted the stream of motorcycles. When the last pair of bikers crossed the railroad tracks, he keyed his mic and said, "Sheriff, this is Gus."

"What you got, Gus?"

"They just rolled past me, headed your way. I count fifty-two motorcycles."

"Thanks, Gus. Herd 'em on in.

Gus pulled in behind the last pair of bikers and followed the slow parade on into town.

At the intersection of Highway 395 and 140, he spotted a brown state police cruiser, one of the newer Dodge Chargers. Gus waved and looked in his review mirror as the state trooper fell in behind him. He keyed his mic again. "Sheriff, a state trooper just joined the party. He's following me in. You ready?"

Bud glanced back at the courthouse and watched Deputy Roger Hildebrand settle his .308 rifle stock on a sandbag hugging the top of the eighteen-inch block parapet surrounding the roof of the building. Roger gave Bud a thumbs-up.

Bud waved back and keyed his mic to respond to Gus. "We're about to find out."

He looked across the street at the two-story brick building that housed the Elks Club and some upstairs apartments. He looked at Blankenship and said, "There's a hole in the net. I need your men to cover the doorways across the street. Deny access to the building."

"Understood, but that just leaves the two of you to face these guys."

Bud grinned and said, "One Ranger, one riot. Me and BB might just equal one Ranger."

BB laughed so loudly the officers setting up to block the streets looked at each other with unspoken questions. Beatrice looked at Lonnie Beltram who just frowned and shrugged. "Pre-action jitters?" she suggested.

But it wasn't that.

In their law enforcement careers, they both felt frustrated at times by the constraints placed on police officers. Necessary though they were, there were times when both men felt helpless to stop the tide of criminal arrogance sweeping the Northwest. This was a chance to push back, and they were both eager to get on with it.

The correctional officers from Warner Creek were nearly across the street when the head of the snaking column of bikers turned off F street and onto Bullard. The sight of two armed officers didn't intimidate any of them. The one BB privately identified as Beer Belly drove onto the sidewalk and up to where Bud and BB stood.

Two other bikers followed and parked on either side of the two police officers.

BB surveyed the sea of leather vests, beards, and biker rags, then said to Bud, "Convenient, don't you think?

"Works for me," Bud answered as the rest of the bikers filled the street sidewalk- to-sidewalk. A half-dozen drove up on the lawn, and one cut a raucous three-hundred-sixty-degree cookie in the lawn, throwing sod in a forty-foot arc.

A wary biker in the rear of the group eye-balled the blocked inter-sections, the county pickups, the city police cars, and the state police cruiser – then decided he didn't like the looks of things.

He jumped his bike up on the sidewalk and pulled a wheelie, intent on squeezing by the blockade. Beatrice Tusk waited until he was almost to her county pickup before opening the passenger door … directly into the biker's path. She winced at the sound of the impact, and Beltram laughed. "That'll come out of your paycheck."

Beatrice hopped down, hand on her pistol, and stepped over the heavy motorcycle. The moaning biker was sitting on his butt and holding both hands over his nose. There was too much blood to see how badly he was hurt. She pulled her cell phone from a shirt pocket and called for an ambulance.

The leader gave Bud a look of pure hatred. "We've come for our friends. Let 'em loose, and we won't bust up your town."

Bud shook his head and glanced at BB. "He doesn't get it, does he?"

"Nope. Want me to explain it?"

Bud nodded. "Go ahead."

"Well, how to put this? You … are under arrest."

"For what?"

"Well, for a number of things. First, you aren't wearing a helmet. Sec-ond, you violated the city's noise ordinance. Third, you threatened two police officers … and a whole town. Fourth, you are in trespass. Fifth," and BB glanced at the rifle in Beer Belly's saddle scabbard, "you are most likely a felon in possession of a firearm. We'll work on the rest."

The biker sneered. "Ain't enough of you."

Bud looked at the roof of the courthouse and keyed his mic and said, "Roger. Wave at this asshole."

The biker followed Bud's stare and saw Roger get to his knees and wave. "You see, idiot, if you try to hurt any of us, Roger will punch a hole in your head with about 180 grains of lead. No matter what happens, if it goes bad, you die."

"You're bluffing."

BB dropped the shotgun down from his shoulder. The forestock slapped his left hand, and he said, "The sheriff might be, but I'm not." Anger in his voice, he shouted so all of the bikers could hear him. "I don't like being shot at. I don't like it when one of your kind shoots an FBI agent who happens to be one of my friends. And I don't like it when you threaten to hoorah a whole town."

The biker on his right said something he couldn't understand, so BB put his foot against the bike and kicked it over. When the biker stood back up, he stuck a hand inside his vest. BB took that as a threat and smacked him alongside the jaw with the butt of the shotgun, rendering him hors de combat. A small pistol skittered across the sidewalk. BB walked over and picked it up.

Bud shouted, his anger clear to anyone within hearing. "Now, then. You are all under arrest. You will put any weapons, be they knives, guns, or clubs on the ground. You will line up on the sidewalk in single file, or I will shoot as many of you as I can, starting with this guy right here."

Something in Bud's eyes convinced Beer Belly. He had no doubt Bud meant every word. Reluctantly, he said, "Okay, boys. Do as the man said. I'll have our lawyer here before the day's out."

Bud fished a pair of handcuffs from his equipment belt and said, "Get off that bike and turn around."

Several of the bikers were heard to say foolish things like, "I'll be damned if I will." But the arrival of about a dozen 4x4 pickups packed with armed civilians put a stop to that foolish bravado.

One by one, the bikers lined up on the sidewalk along Bullard, guarded by Gus and his two officers, the Oregon State Trooper, and the four officers from Warner creek. They grumbled and cussed while Sonny searched them for weapons. As each was cleared, Beatrice, Larae, and Lonnie used soft ties to secure each man's hands behind his back and add him to the row sitting single file along the sidewalk.

Roger remained on the roof, a grim reminder that one alternative to capture and arrest was a high-speed bullet. Not one biker wanted to be first.

A red rescue vehicle with flashing emergency lights, a siren, and a Lake County Disaster Unit logo, pulled up to the intersection of Bullard and F. Two EMTs popped the doors open, retrieved two heavy bags from the rear of the vehicle, and hurried to the biker propped up against a light pole, holding a cotton pad against his nose.

He glared at Deputy Tusk and said, "I'll get you for this."

Beatrice shook her head. "You want help or not?"

Sonny walked over and said, "We have another injury. Can you take two?"

A photo taken by Carol Connor, editor of the Lake County News, would hit the airways within the hour and become national news. By noon, all Lakeview motel rooms would be booked for incoming reporters.

Another media circus, Bud thought when rumors of the incoming tide of reporters reached his desk.

And by noon, Deputy Roger Hildebrand would answer a phone call from Buffalo Boggs, innkeeper and owner of the Paisley Saloon. Buffalo just wanted Roger to know the Z-BAR foreman had decided to withdraw from the race.

Roger asked, "Are you sure?"

Buffalo laughed and said, "I called a friend of mine who has a bar in Missoula where the new owner of the Z-BAR is from. My friend told me some interesting things about our new owner and his foreman. I sort of let it slip that I had talked to this friend in Missoula. I reckon that gave them pause. I never said I would leak it, but they chose prudence over bravado." Buffalo laughed and hung up before Roger could thank him.

Roger grinned. "Bud," he said quietly to himself, "you have more friends in this county than you know about."

Several times over the years, Roger had thought about doing a little background check on Buffalo, just to find out if Buffalo Boggs was his real name. His old Forest Service friend, Special Agent Tom Johnson, laughed when Roger told him about his hunch. In typical Tom Johnson fashion, he suggested it might be better to "Let sleeping Boggs lie."

59

Bull Run

AL-ALWANI AWOKE IN A STERILE RECOVERY room, his right hand in a cast and his left foot elevated by a pulley system to support the mid-calf cast on that member of his body. He raised his head and found a large, stern-looking man sitting in a plastic chair. "FBI?" Al-Alwani croaked.

The man's grim smile seemed to crack the flat planes of his face. "You had better hope so."

"Where am I?"

"I'm not at liberty to say."

"Why not? I'm not going anywhere."

"No, you're not." The man rose from his chair, walked over and hit the call button. He gave Al-Alwani a dismissive shake of his head and walked back to his chair. Al-Alwani could swear the chair groaned when the big man sat down.

The watcher ignored Al-Alwani and turned back to his Men's Health magazine. It was clear from the way his shoulders packed his suit jacket he had more than an idle interest in men's health.

"I'm thirsty," Al-Alwani said.

"Tell it to your nurse."

***

DUTCH VANDERLIN LOOKED UP FROM THE head of the long conference table, a cell phone to his ear, as Brandt and Wilcox entered the room. Other than Dutch, the room was empty.

Without saying anything, Dutch pointed at two empty chairs next to him and spoke into the phone, "They just walked in. We'll have this set up in about ten minutes. We'll call you back then, sir."

Wilcox looked at Brandt and mouthed the word "Sir?" Brandt shrugged and shook his head. Never had they heard Dutch be so deferential.

Dutch's secretary walked in and handed Wilcox and Brandt each a coffee-filled Styrofoam cup, cream and sugar for Brandt. "For me?" Brandt said.

She frowned and scolded him. "Don't be a smartass, today of all days." They looked at their coffee and watched her walk from the room.

"Curiousier and curiousier," Brandt whispered to Wilcox.

A tall, thin man with a bald head and a gray ponytail carried an electronic notebook to the table and placed it in front of Dutch.

Wilcox knew him from tech support, Terry something or other, a nerd who defied the FBI dress code, with his tie-dyed shirts and long hair.

Joseph Smith, Dutch's Assistant SAC, slipped into the conference room, followed closely by Miranda Wright, her hand in a light cast. They claimed two vacant chairs across from Brandt and Wilcox.

Terry, from tech support, opened the phone Dutch handed him, pulled the SIM card out, and plugged it into a port on the side of the notebook. He opened the screen and told Dutch, "You just scroll the messages until you find the one you want, and then send it. You can all listen in. I've also set your wall monitors to video conferencing. Would you like me to start it now?"

Dutch shook his head. "No. We know how to do this. Thank you, Terry."

Terry might be a nerd, but he knew a dismissal when he heard it. He nodded and left, but not before saying over his shoulder, "If you need any help…"

Dutch waited until the door closed before saying, "I'm keeping this under wraps until after this conference. We'll be talking with the FBI Director, the U.S. Attorney General, and the Secretary of Homeland Security. I want to keep the circle small."

In spite of himself, Smith glanced at Miranda. Dutch caught the look. "I can almost hear your gears turning, Smitty. Why, you may ask, after finding a leak in the analysis group, would I include Agent Wright?

"Two answers. First, I'm certain Miss Williams was the only leak. Wright was never under suspicion. And second, I asked Agent Wright to listen to Al-Alwani's confession. When she heard him talk about a terrorist attack forthcoming, she connected the dots, based on her earlier interview with Reverend Wildish. We now have a lead on two people who may be connected to a plot to poison Portland's water supply.

"As an aside, I can't understand why the open reservoirs, both Bull Run and those within the city, are not guarded. Talk about a soft target.

"But back to the point. That person and his wife – who actually works for the Portland Water Bureau – are being sought as we speak. We'll send agents to interview these people. I'll get into that after the conference."

Miranda tried not to look smug, but her pleasure at the compliment was visible to Wilcox and Brandt.

Brandt held out his hand. "Way to go, Miranda!"

"Amen," echoed Wilcox.

***

THE AGENTS IN PORTLAND FOUND THEMSELVES, via video conference, being introduced to FBI Director Barnett (Barney) Bidwell, to General Ivan Vance, Secretary of Homeland Security, and to Attorney General Georgia Sherman. It wasn't exactly unexpected, but when Hector Wilson, Vice President of the United States, came on line with an apology from the President, they were all surprised.

All but Dutch.

Wilcox connected the "Sir" to the Vice President and knew to whom Dutch had been so deferential.

"The president," Wilson said, "sends his apology. I'm filling in, but I'm quite positive he'll want his own briefing a bit later in the day. So, what do you gentlemen have for us?"

Dutch nodded and started the recording of Al-Alwani's confession. No one said anything for the next fifteen minutes.

Finally, The VP interrupted. "I've heard enough. Does Portland's mayor know about this? Maybe this'll change his notion about sanctuary cities."

Dutch didn't bite on that bit of political bait. He just said, "We plan to detain and interview our two suspects within the hour and then inform the mayor."

They could see General Vance nod. "Keep us posted. I'll have our agents contact you."

The vice president audibly sighed. They watched a look of deep sorrow paint his face. "I think the president would like to talk in person with the two agents who broke this open." He looked directly into the camera. "Forgive me, but I don't remember your names."

Dutch nodded. "Special Agent Wilcox and Special Agent Brandt."

And former Special FBI Agent Butler, Brandt thought.

The vice president stared directly into the camera again. "I'll have to check the president's calendar, but I know he'll want you two back here … and soon. Thank you, gentlemen. And lady. Good job." His image faded from the screen.

From his office in the J. Edgar Hoover Building, the director saw the group at the table in Portland start to fidget. "Hold on a minute. I'll want Brandt and Wilcox here first. Dutch, get them on a plane ASAP."

Wilcox objected. "With all due respects, sir, we are needed here."

"I understand. Good for you. But I still want you back here as soon as you can pack your gear and get your asses on a plane. Understood?"

Brandt's first thought was the need to call Jenny Jackson and cancel their date. *No fresh lobster tonight*, he thought. *No fresh anything.*

His second thought was to take a different tack. "Something you should know, sir, is that the person responsible for breaking this open is Agent Wright. She put the pieces of the puzzle together."

There was a pause before Director Bidwell said, "Okay. In that case bring her with you."

60

Roundup

S UPERINTENDENT BLANKENSHIP SHOOK HIS HEAD AND waved his correctional officers back across the street to where Bud and BB stood guard at one end of the line of zip-cuffed bikers.

"Well Sheriff, you and your friend have more guts than brains, but it worked." He held out his hand to BB and said, "Bob Blankenship."

BB shifted the shotgun to his left hand and reached out with his right. "I'm Deputy Dell BeBe. Looks like you brought help when we needed it most. Thank you. I know my shorts were in a wad there for a while."

Blankenship took a deep breath and let it out slowly. He shook his head, "Mine, too." He looked down the line at the fifty-two-person crazy quilt pattern of red biker rags, blue bandanas, the red and gold logos of The Romans on leather vests and leather jackets, chains dangling from belts, empty knife sheaths, tobacco-stained beards, and nasty looks.

One biker shouted, "We'll get you for this," only to be told to shut up by another biker.

Blankenship asked, "What now?"

Bud said, "I don't know. It's for sure we don't have enough jail space. You got any room?"

"Short term. I can give you the gym at Warner Creek. Just for a few days, though."

"Good. That'll do." He thought about the grant money coming their way and nodded. "We can pay you to feed them and keep 'em locked up … short term. How do we transport?"

"I can take a dozen at a time in our van."

Bud's cell phone chimed, and he glanced at the screen. *Emergency Services.* "I better take this."

Nancy was on the line, "Bud, a Klamath Falls SWAT team just landed at the airport. They need transportation."

"How many?"

"The man who called said he and three others … plus their gear."

"Turn them around. And tell them thanks, but we've got the situation under control."

"On it," she laughed. "Karen just sent me a photo of all those men sitting on the sidewalk, with all those motorcycles blocking the street. How did you do that?"

"Just luck, I reckon."

She sounded a bit peeved, but proud all at the same time. "You and BB are nuts. That's probably what scared them. Two lunatics armed with shotguns."

"How do you know this?"

"Half the town is watching cell phone videos. I'd say your re-election is a cinch. And I think I'll marry you even if you are crazy." He heard her laugh again, just before she killed the call.

Bud put his phone away and held out his hand to Blankenship. "I owe you big-time, Bob. Give me a minute. I have a call to make. Can you and your men stick around for a bit? We'll process these guys and then start moving them out to Warner Creek."

Roger came down the front steps of the courthouse, his .308 cradled in his left arm. District Attorney Howard Finch was right behind him.

Howard held out his hand. "Nice job, Bud." He looked at the line of bikers and shook his head. "Darndest thing I ever saw. You are beyond crazy – right up there with plumb loco. I know it for a fact because I saw it. Otherwise, I wouldn't believe it. And your friend Dell BeBe isn't any saner than you." He took a breath, "What now?"

"First, we process this group. ID, fingerprints, check for outstanding warrants, and arrest each of them for disturbing the peace. Then we move them to Warner Creek."

He looked at the leader of the gang and added, "All but him. He stays." The big biker didn't say anything, but if looks could kill, Bud was in for it.

He looked at Roger and pointed at the man. "Put him in our jail. He is under arrest for threatening a law enforcement officer … me."

61

Come and Get 'em

IT TOOK THE LOCAL TOWING COMPANY TWO hours to load the motor-cycles on trailers and haul them to the horse barn at the fairgrounds for safe keeping. Four hours after the arrests, the Lake County Sheriff's office sent out a list of the names and photos of each biker in custody. Sheriff Blair was very clear in his message: If you want them, come and get them.

Within minutes, Karen Highsmith was swamped by phone calls, email messages, and photos. She was busy matching names and photos sent by police agencies from San Diego to Seattle with the mugshots she took as each biker was processed.

The arrival of Sergeant Booker, from the Klamath Falls Police Department, signaled what would become a flood of lawmen coming to retrieve criminals wanted on a variety of charges.

***

SERGEANT BOOKER WALKED INTO THE STATION, spotted Bud talking to a nicely dressed woman, and heard Bud say, "That's all I can tell you for now, Mayor. Didn't the council pass a noise ordinance last night?"

Gladys McKnight nodded, a mischievous grin tugging at her mouth. "Yes we did, Sheriff."

"Good. And thank you. We'll write each of these miserable specimens a citation accordingly. Now, Gladys, I've got my hands full. If you feel compelled to talk to the press, please do so."

He turned, spotted the name tag and held out his hand. "Sergeant Booker, it's nice to finally meet you."

"And nice to meet you, Sheriff. Reverend Wildish can't say enough nice things about you."

"How is TJ?"

"Anxious to go home."

"I imagine that should be possible before long."

Booker nodded and chuckled. "You know for a big-city dude, he is genuinely naïve. But I think it works for him. He just oozes sincerity, and people respond. If I could talk him into staying and helping our church I would."

Bud gave him a tired grin, "He might be safer."

Booker nodded, "How can we help?"

Bud handed the sergeant a list of names and addresses – or at least names and addresses from the ID each prisoner provided. The truth wasn't often a close companion of The Romans.

"Any of these guys yours?"

Booker scanned the list and nodded. "We have a warrant for the arrest of Bobby Lee Jones. And one for Sheldon Moncrief. I wouldn't mind taking them off your hands."

"Good. Those two are out at Warner Creek. Know your way out there?"

"I do."

A phone rang and Bud heard Karen answer. "Lake County Sheriff's Office." A pause followed, then she said, "Yes, he is. I'll put him on."

She looked at Bud and whispered, "The governor."

He shook his head. "Not now. Take a number and let her know I'll call back in half an hour. And copy these warrants for me. The originals go with Sergeant Booker."

"Bud! It's the governor!" she protested.

"Good for her."

Booker was grinning when he turned and held out his hand. "Sergeant Booker, thanks for being so prompt. Give TJ my regards. When we get more news from the FBI, I'll let him know."

The two men decided they liked one another.

Karen Highsmith watched and shook her head. *Like two peas in a pod*, she thought … before a new message drew her attention back to the job of matching felons with outstanding warrants.

62

Crossing the Bar

A WHITE BUS, WITH "THE CONNECTOR" PRINTED in large blue letters along its white sides, pulled up to the bus stop sign in front of the mini mart in Scappoose. It was headed west, Butler's preferred direction, so he followed the young woman he'd rescued from the three homeless bandits up the steps and into the bus.

They settled into a seat near the back, away from the five other passengers, then Butler took in a deep breath and let it out with an audible sigh.

The woman looked sideways at him, blinked twice and asked, in a nearly inaudible whisper, "Why did you do that?"

"Do what?"

"Help me get away."

Butler frowned and shrugged. "You looked like you wanted help."

She shook her head. "I'm not used to that. You sure you just didn't want to keep me for yourself?"

He studied her dull brown hair, the smudge of dirt on one cheek, her broken fingernails – long past dirty – and shook his head. "I don't think you're my type."

"Why not? I clean up pretty good."

He laughed, "I'll bet you do, but you're young enough to be my daughter."

The hour it took to reach the Astoria Transit Center was enough for Butler to pump the girl for information. Millicent Andrews, age twenty-four, orphaned at age seven – thanks to a fatal car crash that took her mother, father and two brothers. Adopted by an abusive couple, on the streets by age fifteen, picked up for prostitution and placed in foster care until age eighteen. "I peddled drugs, stole food and whatever else I could get my hands on, but I stopped taking drugs, and I quit selling sex."

She plucked at her dirty coat and laughed. "Believe it or not, I have a germ fetish."

Butler shook his head and chuckled. "Well, Milly, it's hard to see that."

"Do you mean it, about giving me enough money to get home on?"

He nodded. "I do. Where's home?"

She shrugged. "I don't really know." She looked up at him, her blue eyes speculative. She studied his gaunt features, sensed his kindness, saw the sadness in his eyes, and reached over to touch his arm. "Where are you going? You don't look to have anyone either."

"Why do you say that?"

"I'd say you were running from something. I saw you hide the pickup behind the store. The one you told them about. And then you pulled a gun on Les. And you are riding the bus with a complete stranger. I think I'm just your cover … your camouflage. And you don't wear a wedding ring. I'm right, aren't I?"

"And nosy."

"It's key to survival on the street. You learn to observe, to watch people, figure out who is okay and who is dangerous. You are dangerous, but only to bad people."

The bus pulled into the transit center. The driver opened the front and side doors to let the passengers disembark. Butler and Milly watched until the others left, and then they exited through the side door.

She said, "Astoria or Warrenton?"

"Why do you ask?"

"Well, if I was to run, I'd use a boat."

He looked uncomfortable and she gloated. "That's it, isn't it? I know I'm right. So, take me with you … or I'll start yelling 'rape'."

"That's no way to say thanks."

"Look, I'm good company, and I can cook. Can you cook? Anything?"

"Girl, you don't know what you are asking. Yes … I'm on the run. There's a group of very nasty people looking for me. And there's another group of very efficient federal agents looking for me. If you have any sense, you'll take the money and run."

She shook her head. "Nope. You need me, and I need you."

***

AT DAWN THE NEXT MORNING, THE Runaway rode the swells over the Columbia River Bar and motored out onto a rain-coated sea.

Milly, wearing new jeans and a new hooded sweatshirt, hair brushed and smelling of scented shampoo, stood beside him in the wheelhouse. Butler concentrated on piloting the boat, but he smiled and asked, "Do you get seasick?"

63

Left and Right

Tᴿᴜᴇ ᴛᴏ ʜɪꜱ ᴡᴏʀᴅ, ʙᴜᴅ ʀᴇᴛᴜʀɴᴇᴅ the governor's call thirty minutes later. His voice lacked warmth, but he managed to be polite and to give her a brief overview of the situation.

"Governor, other police jurisdictions are already bringing warrants for the arrest of some of these individuals. We've received several calls from bail bond skip tracers wanting to let us know they are on the way to take custody of bail-skippers.

"I think that, before this is all over, most of these miscreants will be in the custody of other police jurisdictions and behind bars where they belong."

When asked if they had benefit of counsel, he said, "Governor, you don't want to go there. Your prior association with the ACLU precedes you. I urge you to leave your biases out of this. But yes, they have an attorney – one attorney for fifty-two bikers. If we find they have no priors, they will be free to pay their fines and leave. Please keep in mind, their stated intent was to break their friends out of our jail."

When he heard her say, "You don't know that," Bud hung up.

***

Bʏ ᴅᴀʏ ᴛʜʀᴇᴇ, ᴏɴʟʏ ꜰɪᴠᴇ ʙɪᴋᴇʀꜱ were left in Lakeview. Sixteen others had been released to the custody of a variety of police agencies from four states: Washington, California, Idaho, and Nevada.

Thirty-one of the original fifty-two paid their fines for public nuisance and were released. A convoy of civilian pickups followed them west to the first hill out of the Goose Lake Valley.

When Bud heard about it, he was angry. "Whose bright idea was that?"

Sonny Sixkiller just laughed and said, "Your sheriff's posse. Conway Singleton to be exact."

"Not good! They're just supposed to help me find lost hikers, not mess with nasty people."

Sonny raised his eyebrows and smiled. "I think their message was very clear. 'Don't come back.'"

The only sour note was the arrival of two rather large US Marshals with an order signed by a federal judge for the custody of Gary Gentle, aka Starbucks, Calvin Culpepper, aka Road Kill, and Anthony Hames, aka Turkey.

"There goes your chance at fame," Bud said to District Attorney Howard Finch.

"Or infamy. Think about losing that case. I'd have to move or hide."

"You still have Michael Moore to prosecute. The one BB calls Beer Belly."

Howard nodded. "Not as juicy."

"I think it is, Howard. He threatened to tear the town apart. And he threatened both BB and me. And I don't think this feud with The Romans is going away in a hurry. I want him to serve some time."

"How does charging him as a felon in possession of a firearm, threatening police officers with bodily harm, and accomplice to a conspiracy to commit murder for hire sound? That should get him put him away for the next twenty-five to thirty years."

"I'll buy the steaks."

***

BUD CALLED HIS OLD FRIEND DUTCH Vanderlin. When Dutch answered, Bud said, "I thought you gave us the green light to prosecute the bikers who hurt Miranda Wright and shot at BB and Reverend Wildish."

"I did, but the Attorney General overruled me. She said attacks on FBI agents would not be tolerated. Not a damned thing I can do about it. Besides, from what I see on TV, you sent a strong message that law enforcement in Lake County is swift and sure. Fifty bikers … and you and BB stared them down."

Bud couldn't help but add, "Fifty-two."

Dutch snorted and then laughed. "Okay. Fifty-two."

"What the news didn't show was three city cops, a state cop, four correctional officers, and the seven of us. BB and I weren't exactly alone."

Dutch nodded into his phone and said, "I know. But you two were the most exposed. I understand you arrested all of them and told the law enforcement community to come and get 'em."

"I did. We are waiting for the last few to be picked up."

Dutch said, "Why do you suppose so many weren't arrested before this?"

"I've been thinking about that. Maybe it's because they don't stay put and they run in large crowds. And they are mean sonsabitches. I know I wouldn't want to walk into any bar they take over and try to arrest one of them. Too damned dangerous. I'd have to have one of your SWAT teams behind me."

64

East to West

AN FBI EXECUTIVE JET LIFTED FROM THE National Airport runway and banked sharply west out over Reston, Virginia, climbing rapidly, chasing the setting sun.

Miranda, belted into a comfortable lounge chair, turned and stared out the window, trying to identify some landmark other than the Appalachian Mountains.

She swiveled her chair back and faced Special Agents Wilcox and Brandt. "Well," she said. "That was short and sweet. I mean, a short night's sleep, like they can't remember eight o'clock is still five o'clock our time. I think I only slept about two hours last night. It was a nice hotel, but this girl needs her rest. And then there was the tension of briefing the president. And why did our people grill us for hours and hours? It's like they think we're the bad guys."

Wilcox stifled a yawn and shook his head. "Nah. That's not it. The Bureau just wants to make sure we keep the CIA out of this. When you start talking terrorism, the CIA wants in. And there's nothing like a CIA operation to mess up the prosecution."

Brandt nodded. "Yep. As soon as we identify offshore operations, like Al-Alwani's human-trafficking, the CIA tries to take over."

"I thought that was the split: U.S. territory is FBI, and foreign territory belongs to the CIA."

"In theory," Brandt said. "Doesn't always work that cleanly. Gets to be the chicken-or-the-egg kind of question. And we do post FBI agents at foreign embassies."

"Well then," she said, "where does that leave us regarding Al-Alwani?"

A crewmember opened the cabin door and walked the short aisle to the passenger area. He smiled. Miranda could hear a touch of Georgia peach in his voice when he said, "Howdy, I'm Andy, your copilot. Y'all okay back here?"

Wilcox grinned. "I haven't used a barf bag yet."

The tall young man, late twenties maybe, nodded, his appraising dark eyes fixed on Miranda. "Well, we might just have to do something about that. We haven't practiced our loops or rolls lately.

"Anyway, I came back to let you know we'll reach cruising altitude, twenty-five thousand feet, in about six more minutes. Air time to Portland is about five hours and thirty minutes. I'll be back to fix y'all something to drink. Coffee, tea, soda, water. And we have some deli sandwiches Captain Franks and I brought along. Be back in a little bit."

Wilcox looked at Miranda with a grin. "Mister Andy, your copilot, just about devoured *y'all* with his eyes. I'd watch that one, Miranda."

She looked disgusted. "Men! Is that all you think about?"

Wilcox laughed and said, "Not me. That's Douglas. All he can think about is Jenny Jackson. Hey, Douglas, you think your new medal will help in that department?"

"Jenny Jackson?" Miranda asked.

"He's in love. Says her voice sends chills down his spine."

The notion of love set Miranda's mind on a path back to her brief time with Dell BeBe. *Why,* she thought, *do I find an immediate connection to a person I've never met before? And why does my dedication to my career suddenly seem a little frivolous? And why do I think I'd like to be married again? It wasn't so great last time. But BB doesn't strike me as a bully. I wonder why his first wife left? Maybe for the same reason cop marriages don't last. Too much job and too little home life.*

She realized Wilcox was talking to her. "What?"

"I said, I'd like to see your FBI Star. I've never seen one before."

"Oh. Well, it's in my briefcase."

"So, get it."

Brandt unbuckled and stepped to the closet where their bags were stored. "I'll do it."

Wilcox smiled and said, "Did you have any idea what the director had up his sleeve?"

"No. And I think it was last minute at best. He wanted just you and Brandt – then you opened your big mouth – so here I am."

Brandt handed her the briefcase and said, "Nope. Your medal was in the works already. The director just took the opportunity to have you come back here for the ceremony."

She set the briefcase on her lap, but didn't open it.

"Miranda Wright, you let us have a look," Wilcox demanded.

She unsnapped the locks and opened the case. The medal was tied in a velvet pouch. She undid the slip knot and poured it into her bandaged left hand. All three agents stared at the single blue star surrounded by gold leaf and a round blue medallion.

Brandt took a deep breath and said, "I never gave medals much thought, but this one gives me the shivers. Congratulations, Miranda. Well deserved."

Wilcox picked the citation from her briefcase and read aloud. "In recognition of her courage in the line of duty, leading to a serious injury inflicted by criminal adversaries while defending the Reverend T.J. Wildish and Dell BeBe on Dog Lake, Oregon, said injuries resulting in emergency room sutures and prolonged medical treatment, it is with great pride and my personal privilege to award Special Agent Miranda Wright the FBI Star. Signed, Barnett Bidwell, Director, FBI"

A voice from behind them said, "Wow. I'd like to hear about that, ma'am."

They all turned to see copilot Andy, his eyes wide in admiration. "I didn't know we had a VIP aboard. I'll have to bring out the champagne."

Miranda said, "I'll have you know Agents Wilcox and Brandt were also honored by the director. Each was awarded the FBI medal for meritorious achievement."

Yeah, thanks to Butler, Wilcox thought somewhat cynically.

"Wow again. Congratulations! It makes me proud to know y'all."

Miranda nodded and said, "Thank you."

He sat down in the fourth swivel chair, looked at her bandaged hand, and said, "Now, then. How did you get shot?"

65

Time and Angst

LATE ON THE SECOND DAY OF what came to be labeled "The Biker Invasion," Bud held his only press conference. Carol Connor, editor of the Lake County News arranged the use of the high school gym. A half-dozen television network camera were up and running, including one from Klamath Falls.

Radio stations from Bend, Klamath Falls, Medford, Alturas, Eugene, Salem, and Portland had sound technicians and reporters in place, ready to broadcast live.

The entire country was fixed on the erroneous, but sensational, story of two country cops stopping fifty-some bikers from devastating the small western town of Lakeview, "devastating" being the current buzzword on the major network channels. And people wanted to see what the heroes looked like.

Bud didn't see any reasonable way to avoid the press conference, but Dell BeBe was free to avoid the press if he wanted. He chose not to be interviewed.

"And leave me on my own?" Bud growled when BB said he was going back to his log home, then on up to Portland.

"They've subpoenaed me to testify before a federal grand jury," he explained. "You have no complaints coming, Bud. I was there when you needed me."

"And you don't like the press any more than I do. Right?"

"I like to keep my mug out of sight. You don't have that privilege. Gotta go."

"Drive safely, old friend. And say hello to Miranda for me."

BB surprised Bud when he stopped and frowned. He turned to look at Bud, and in a serious tone he seldom used, said, "You think there's something there for me?"

"If that's what you want, then I certainly hope so. She's a beautiful woman. She's smart. And she's cool under fire. She does talk all the time, but I don't suppose an old bachelor like you would mind." Bud grinned and added, "Maybe then you'll stop pestering me. By the way, let's talk about this cold case I mentioned when you get back."

BB nodded. "I'd like that." Bud shook his head and smiled at the sight of his officers armored up, guarding the doors to the gym. He nodded when Sonny said, "Boss, just remember to keep your cool."

There was thunderous applause as Bud, dressed in starched khaki pants, mirror-polished boots, and a Lake County Sheriff's short sleeved shirt, walked through the side door and into the Lakeview High School gym. The bleachers on each side were filled to capacity with onlookers. About two dozen who couldn't find a seat leaned against the walls. The bright hardwood floor was covered with scuffed white canvas to protect it from folding chairs, light tripods, cables, tables, and foot traffic.

A podium with a microphone was parked under one of the basketball backboards. Bud headed for the podium while Judge Lynch tested the microphone with, "Could we have it quiet please."

When all but a few side conversations stopped, Lynch said, "It is with great pride and deep respect that I give you Sheriff Henry Blair. I don't think it is any exaggeration to say that Sheriff Blair, assisted by the law enforcement officers of Lake County, saved our town."

The applause reached a deafening crescendo, then faded as Bud walked behind the podium and faced the crowd. Someone yelled, "Give 'em hell, Bud." A rumble of laughter chased the silence and then petered out.

He cleared his throat and let his eyes wander the crowd, making eye contact with people on all sides of the gym before focusing on the reporters in front of him. When an anxious reporter said, "Sheriff, how did you know..."

Bud interrupted and said forcefully, "I have a prepared statement I'd like to read before taking any questions. He looked directly at the reporter and said, "So hold that one for a bit."

He took a folded piece of printer paper from his left shirt pocket and smoothed it on the podium.

"Let me begin by saying no one does anything as important as law enforcement alone. I certainly can't. And I didn't. Thanks to a tip from an unidentified source, we knew large numbers of people affiliated with The Romans, an outlaw biker gang, were headed for Lakeview. We had previously arrested three members of that gang for attempted murder for hire, and we were holding them in our jail.

"I enlisted the help of our three city police officers, led by Chief Augustus Hildebrand, and four officers from the Warner Creek Correctional facility, led by Bob Blankenship, and one state trooper." Bud stopped for a split second when he realized he didn't know the trooper's name. *Got to fix that*, he thought, and then continued.

"With the six-person force of the Lake County Sheriff's Department and myself, we all, emphasis on ALL, confronted and arrested fifty of the fifty-two members of The Romans who had come – as stated by their leader to me directly and openly – to free their friends from jail … or else. The "or else" was a threat, clearly stated, and readily understood by the officers within hearing of the man. He said, 'or else we will tear your town apart.' Our answer to this was to subdue and arrest them all."

An impatient reporter shouted, "Sheriff, what did you do with them?"

Another voice asked, "Who was the big black guy with you?"

And with that, Bud's carefully prepared statement flew out the window. The press did not want to hear a carefully written statement. The press wanted immediate answers to the questions viewers were asking via social media. How long have you been sheriff? Are you married? Who is the big black deputy? Are you wearing a bulletproof vest?

He took each question in turn, but it was clear to those who knew him, he was miffed. The questions reinforced his dislike of the press.

Bud finally took control when a young female reporter asked, "What happened to bikers fifty-one and fifty-two?"

"One was hospitalized due to a vehicular crash. He has since been cited for riding a motorcycle on a sidewalk and returned to prison for parole violation. He is also being charged as a convicted felon in possession of a firearm.

"The other is waiting to be transported back to Yakima, Washington, for trial in connection with a homicide."

"Sheriff, isn't it true he was struck with the butt of a shotgun and injured?"

Bud took a deep breath and shook his head. *Here it comes*, he thought.

"That one was reaching for a pistol. Rather than shoot him, which we had the right to do, my deputy hit him with – as you say – the butt of a shotgun. I have the pistol carried by the man in our evidence locker."

"Didn't you actually plant the pistol on him? A "throw down," I believe it's called. We have film that proves it."

Bud looked at the man and asked, "Which news team are you with, son?"

"The Eugene Register-Guard."

"May I suggest your employer have your eyes checked. It happened as I reported it. May I also suggest that if you have an agenda other than the truth, you just trot on home and write whatever you damned well feel like."

A roll of laughter filled the gym, and the young reporter turned beet red.

When another reporter started to ask a question, Bud said, "Copies of my statement are available on tables by the door. What I would like to do now is turn this press conference over to Carol Connor of the Lake County News. She may actually know more about this than I do. Thank you."

A scattering of applause followed Bud through the nearest exit and out onto the sidewalk and his truck. He recognized Carol Connor's voice on the public-address system, but he couldn't understand what she was saying over the hum and hubbub of the crowd.

The short drive from the high school back to his office cooled his anger a bit, but when he parked his ire spiked again. Standing by the door of his office was the attractive blonde anchor woman from the Klamath Falls TV station.

"How in the hell did you get here ahead of me?" He asked.

"While you lectured that young goofball from Eugene, I beat feet. Managed to park and run to your door so I could look cool and nonchalant when you drove up. Beat you by maybe ten seconds."

"And you want what?"

"To interview the real Henry Bud Blair. If you remember, about two years ago you said you would consider letting me do a story about a rural county sheriff. So here I am."

Bud studied her, thought about how fairly she had treated him during the Gooding murder investigation, and then he smiled. "You drink coffee?"

She nodded. "Yes."

Bud stuck his head in the door and hollered to Karen, "I'll be right down the street at No-Dunks Donuts."

They crossed Bullard and walked to the donut shop. "I'm sorry," Bud said, "but I've forgotten your name."

"Now that really hurts," she said. But she smiled. "I'm Anna McBride."

"Right. Now I remember."

"And you don't watch my show very much, do you?"

He looked a little embarrassed. "I know it's a crummy attitude for a cop, but I hardly ever watch or listen to the news. So far as I know, when something important happens, someone always tells me about it. Saves time and angst."

66

Miranda Blushed

MIRANDA OVERSLEPT, TIRED FROM THE EXCITEMENT of meeting the president, the awards ceremony in the J. Edgar Hoover building, the briefing she was asked to give over and over, and the long flight home. She was twenty minutes late for work.

Walking into the entry of the FBI building, she was startled by an easel supporting a big 24x36-inch photo of Wilcox, Brandt, Miranda, and the beaming FBI Director Bidwell. In the photo, the medals hanging from ribbons around their necks were clearly visible. On another easel were posted the written citations for each medal.

Still tired and morning-cranky, she grumbled, "Crap. I don't need this." But she was secretly pleased, nonetheless.

She used her security card, waved a greeting to Inez Sanchez, their information receptionist, then, heels clacking and echoing down the hallway, headed for her desk in the analysis section. Dutch's secretary, Janet Long, a tall, distinguished-looking woman, short hair turning a proud gray, was standing midway down the hall by the door to the big conference room.

She was dressed as she always dressed: black skirt and jacket, white lacey blouse, sheer stockings and polished black flats. She looked like a consummate professional. That she was also pretty, in a severe sort of way, enhanced her professional appearance. The only anomaly today was a red rosebud pinned to her jacket lapel.

Janet smiled. "About time you showed up. Dutch has everyone assembled and the three amigos are late. I think he is slightly miffed."

Miranda shrugged. "Overslept."

"Understandable." The sound of footsteps drew her gaze back down the hall. "Ah, I see the other two amigos have arrived. Now we can get on with it."

"It?" Miranda asked.

"Yes. It. The SAC wants us all to share in his appreciation for what you three have done."

Wilcox said, "I heard that, Janet. What is it we have done?"

"Dutch will enlighten you. Get in here."

Brandt grinned, gave a half bow and said, "Yes, boss. Right away, boss."

Janet frowned before saying, "None of your smartass comments today, Douglas. Dutch is serious about this."

When they followed Janet Long through the conference room door, Dutch said, "Ah, ha. The prodigals have finally arrived. Let's give them a big hand." He started clapping and ninety-plus others filled the big room with applause. A few whistles were heard, then someone started singing to the tune of "He's a jolly good fellow." Only the words were a bit different. Miranda heard, "For they are jolly good agents, jolly good agents, for they are jolly good agents, and nobody can deny."

Miranda blushed.

Heaped with praise, rosebuds, and handshakes, they were finally released from the trials of good-natured ribbing and unwanted celebration, but not before Dutch said, "I'll see you in my office right after this is over."

Wilcox looked at Brandt and then at Miranda. "What?"

Brandt just shrugged. Miranda said, "I don't have a clue."

***

As special agent in charge, Dutch had the privilege of an office on the third floor in the northwest corner of the building.

It came equipped with a view of Mount St. Helens to the north and the city of Vancouver, Washington, on the other side of the Columbia River. In his opinion, the only drawback was the noise of jet aircraft coming and going from Portland International Airport, a short distance east. The building was designed to be quake proof, but Dutch swore he could feel the building shake when a jumbo airliner roared by at eye level.

While he waited for his agents to arrive, Dutch swiveled his chair and watched about two dozen sailboats tack back and forth across the river, trying to catch enough wind to move upstream. As far as he could tell, their forward progress was neutralized by the heavy current. *Some kind of race, I suppose*, he thought. *Seems silly to call it a race. Sometimes they hardly move. A contest might be a better description.*

Janet knocked and, without waiting for an invitation, announced, "Agent Smith is here, sir."

"Come in Smitty. Have a seat. Our honored guests should be here soon. Before they get here I wanted to let you know I'm sending Wilcox to Seattle. It's a six-month acting assignment as your counterpart in the Seattle office.

"And I'm going to ask you to step up our operations regarding gang-related crime. It seems some of the biker gangs have started working for terrorist groups … in addition to the drug cartels."

"Bad business, Dutch. What do you want me to do?"

"I'm assigning six additional agents to your task force. Use them as you see fit, but first focus on The Romans. I want them brought down, Smitty … and soon."

"Amen."

Janet opened the door and ushered Agents Wright, Brandt, and Wilcox in. When they were seated, she said, "Coffee, anyone?" There were no takers.

Dutch looked at Smitty and nodded.

Smith took the hint. "Okay," he said, "here's the deal. Wilcox is going to Seattle on a temporary assignment as acting leader of their joint terrorism task force."

Wilcox frowned and then said, "First I heard about it. Do I have a choice?"

Dutch looked disgusted. He shook his head and took a deep breath. "Agent Wilcox, I would take it as a personal favor if you would accept this assignment."

"What about Douglas. Does he go with me?"

"No. I haven't had a chance to discuss this with Smitty, but I have something else I want him to do. He'll partner with Agent Wright. And that's all I'm going to say on the subject."

Dutch rose from his chair and reached his hand across the desk to Wilcox. "Congratulations."

Wilcox took his hand and said, "Thanks, Boss."

Dutch pointed at Smith and Wilcox, "That's all I have for you two. I want to talk to Brandt and Wright in private. Leroy, see Janet. She has the paperwork."

Smitty looked a little put out at being excluded, but he had the sense to be quiet.

When the door closed, Dutch said, "This is a direct order. Your job is to find Winslow Butler. For the time being, that's your first and only job."

Miranda watched the silent interplay between Brandt and Dutch and then asked, "Are you giving me a field assignment?"

Dutch nodded. "This may call for more analysis than for fieldcraft."

Miranda looked at Brandt and said, "Are you okay with this?"

Brandt suddenly grinned and said, "You know, it might be just the trick." He then looked at Dutch as asked, "And when we find him?"

"I don't know, Agent Brandt. We'll cross that bridge when we get there. But get us there first."

Brandt said, "You do know we might never have stopped Al-Alwani without Butler. In my book, he gets credit for saving those girls in the container. And for delivering up Al-Alwani."

Dutch nodded. "Doesn't make it easy, does it?" He paused and a smile tugged at his mouth. "Find him and we'll work on the details after that."

Brandt said, "I hear we offered Al-Alwani witness protection. Seems strange we would to that for a terrorist and then arrest Butler."

"You are beginning to try my patience, Douglas. Have a little faith. Now get out of here and get to work."

As they reached the door, Dutch called out, "Nice work, you two."

They stopped and looked back.

He said, "Agent Brandt, you can shrug off your part in bringing down Al-Alwani and stopping his slave trade if you want to, but your character and your honesty led Butler to trust you with key information. In his own perverted way, Butler holds you in high esteem."

Brandt looked skeptical, but he nodded without saying anything, then held the door open for Miranda. When the door closed, Dutch took a deep breath and said quietly, "I hope you two learn when to lie."

When they were in the empty hallway, Miranda grabbed Brandt's sleeve and stopped him. "What did you mean when you said it might just be the trick?"

Brandt grinned and said, "Miranda, you are a beautiful woman. So, I'm thinking that if we're paired up, Jenny might be jealous and start paying attention for a change."

In a disgusted tone she said, "Men," like it was a cuss word.

67

Finding A Good Butler

EXCITED BY THE NOTION OF A field assignment, Miranda insisted on developing a good plan on which to base their search for Winslow Butler. She reserved a small conference room, then took her laptop and set two chairs side-by-side so Brandt could look at the screen with her.

Brandt just listened and nodded, amazed by how fast she could talk, how easily she was sidetracked by new thoughts, and then how quickly she would bring herself back to the main topic – which in this case was simply where to start their investigation.

Now I know why she's called Motormouth Miranda. Talks non-stop when she gets excited. But I have to admit she's really smart.

As he knew she would … eventually … she said, "I think we should start by combing the last place he lived."

Innocently, Brandt said, "The cabin cruiser, the one he rented on the Willamette?"

"Precisely. In my work as an analyst, I've found some of the cleverest criminals tend to get sloppy when at home. Perhaps Butler was sloppy as well. We might uncover a clue to help us know where to look next. Like following bread crumbs."

Brandt stood up and said, "Well, let's get to it. Let's go see if Butler left any bread crumbs. And see if the birds haven't eaten them all."

***

THE SHORT, STOCKY, BLUE-EYED MAN IN his early forties, hair just turning gray, a tight salt-and-pepper beard hiding his face, refused to let them search Butler's cabin cruiser. He stood behind the blue, vinyl-topped counter in the office of Guy's Marina, blinked his eyes a couple of times, scratched his beard, and then stared at them after saying "No." Just stared without saying another word.

The two agents stared back, until the man nervously said, "He pays his rent six-months at a time. There is two months to go. That makes it his private residence. I can't let you do that. Not without a warrant, I can't. Not even if you are with the FBI."

Brandt looked disgusted. "I don't need a warrant. He's a fugitive. If you don't cooperate I'll have to arrest you for interfering with our investigation."

Miranda read the name plate on the counter and smiled. "Are you Bobby Moore?"

"One and the same."

"You played ball for the Portland Beavers, didn't you?"

"Yeah."

"Batted .284 your last season."

He puffed his chest out and said, "Right. You a baseball fan?"

"I am," she said. "I always thought you had a shot at the majors." She turned to Brandt and said, "Bobby has an arm like a rocket. Played second base. One time, he picked off a runner who was half way to home plate before Bobby threw the ball."

Moore smiled and said, "Sure glad to hear somebody remembers."

She returned his smile and said, "Let me show you something." She pulled a copy of the wanted poster from her shoulder bag, a clear picture of Butler front and center under a banner practically shouting WANTED. "Maybe this will help," she said and slid it over the counter.

"Oh. Okay. I just thought you were like those two other dudes who wanted to search his boat."

Startled, Brandt said, "Two others?"

"Yeah. They were in here a few days back. Showed me phony badges they must have found in a Cracker Jacks box. They threatened me, but I told them he was gone and so was the cabin cruiser. They sweetened up and said there was a reward if I called them when he got back."

Brandt said, "You still have the number?"

"Yeah. And I didn't call it either."

Miranda asked, "What did they look like? Can you describe them?"

"I don't know. Arab-looking, black beards, young, mean eyes. Each was five-ten or so. They drove a white Mercedes. Now, I ask you, do cops drive white Mercedes? I got their faces and the vehicle license number on our security camera if you'd like to see what they look like. Thought about calling it in, but for what? Asking questions?"

Brandt nodded. "Yes. Emphatically, yes. These are dangerous times. We need tips like this."

Miranda said, "Bobby, can we see what you have?"

An hour later a copy of the security video rode safely in Miranda's shoulder bag, companion to her 9mm pistol. Bobby unlocked the cabin cruiser, a twenty-six-foot Starcraft. The small living area was spotless, not a scrap of paper or a single clue that Butler had ever lived there. It was totally empty. Not even a water bottle in the small fridge.

But when Miranda searched the breakfast nook, she found a Homer, Alaska, flyer wedged between the cushions. She held it up so Brandt could see it. He shrugged. "If he was the only one to ever live here … maybe."

Once he started talking, Bobby Moore couldn't stop. He said Butler seemed like a really nice guy. Stayed to himself. Didn't have any visitors. Took the boat out most week-ends.

"'Practicing,' is what he told me. Came in one time when I was down on the dock. It was a Sunday evening. He was gone all weekend. The wind was blowing pretty hard from down river, so I helped him tie off. I noticed what looked like salt spray on the windshield. I asked him where the hell he had taken my boat. He just laughed and said he'd crossed the Columbia Bar. He said he wouldn't try that again, unless he had a bigger boat." Moore paused, "Come to think about it, he asked a lot of questions about boats. Navigation gear, that kind of thing. And one time he said if he ever bought one, it would have to have long legs."

Miranda frowned. "Long legs?"

Brandt said, "It means able to travel a lot of miles between fuel stops."

Moore nodded. "That's right."

"And you're sure that's what he said?" Miranda asked.

"Why? Is it important?"

"It could be." She looked at Brandt and nodded. "He's bought himself a boat with 'long legs.' I'd bet money on it."

"How does that help?" Moore asked.

Brandt nodded, "If he had another boat, it had to be close by. Mister Moore, where is the closest private marina?"

"That would be the Columbia Basin Yacht Club at the northwest end of Sauvie Island. Lots of spendy boats there. Cross the bridge and stay left. It isn't marked very well, but the road doesn't go anyplace else."

"Thanks, Bobby," Miranda said. She tore a page from her notebook and said, "Would you give me your autograph?"

***

IN THE EXPEDITION, WAITING FOR A break in traffic, Brandt said, "Where did you learn so much about the Portland Beavers?"

"I grew up here. My grandma was a big Beaver fan. We would listen to all the games on Gram's radio."

"And you happened to remember his last season and his batting average."

"I just have that kind of memory."

"I'll bet you win at Trivial Pursuit, too."

She nodded and said – without any touch of humility, "Yes, I do." She paused and added, "I wonder if that had anything to do with the demise of my marriage? I never thought about that before. I always beat Walter at Trivial Pursuit."

Brandt pulled the Expedition out on the highway and drove a short distance, before turning right at the Sauvie Island road sign and over the bridge.

Miranda looked in surprise at the farm fields, the narrow, single-lane paved roads, the red barns, and the herds of black and white milk cows. "It's like driving out of one world and into another. Or maybe like stepping back a hundred years. I had no idea it was like this."

Brandt nodded. "Me either.'"

The road ran parallel to the Willamette Channel, a fork in the river that wound around both sides of the big island before joining the

Columbia. She saw a green tractor busy plowing black, rich-looking earth alongside a big pond.

An armada of ducks and geese rose from a narrow waterway, their noisy wingbeats filling the air. The geese honked and gabbled, protesting the tractor's intrusion, and then set wings and landed a few hundred yards down the long finger of the pond.

"Beautiful," Miranda said.

***

A BARITONE VOICE ANSWERED THE INTERCOM in the key pad set on a ten-foot, black iron post, one of a matching pair built to support wing gates that swung back and out of the way … if you knew the combination. Brandt did not. He pushed a call button and waited.

"Yes?"

Brandt said, "This is Special Agent Brandt, FBI."

"Please hold your credentials up to the camera."

Brandt curbed his impatience and complied. A few second later, the gates quietly swung open.

They drove through an alder grove and into the marina parking lot. A forest of masts from dozens of sailboats backdropped the sky. A dozen powerboats, so large they deserved to be called yachts, filled the slips or were tied to anchor buoys.

"Wow," Brandt said. "Talk about conspicuous consumption." He parked in front of the marina office, then they both stepped out of the black SUV and slammed the doors shut. A tall, gray-haired man in a red cashmere sweater opened the office door and stepped out onto the raised deck.

He waved and said, "Come on in."

Inside, he ushered them into an office that was utilitarian, neat, and nautical, the walls covered with pictures of yachts and sailboats. He held his hand out to Brandt and said, "Welcome to my world. I'm Commodore Winston Moorhouse."

Brandt shook his hand and said, "I'm Agent Brandt, and this is Agent Wright."

Miranda nodded and pulled a photo of Butler from her shoulder bag. She handed it to Moorhouse. "Do you know this man?"

68

Transfer

WILCOX CALLED HIS OLD FRIEND WILBUR Sandstrom, owner of Sandstrom's Property Management Service for the greater Portland Metropolitan area. When Wilbur answered, Wilcox said, "Hey, Wilbur, how you been?"

"I'm cool. How about you?"

"Not so cool. I'm being transferred to the Seattle office for six months. I don't want to give up my place, but I don't want to leave it empty either. Can you find me a house sitter … maybe a college student?"

He heard Wilbur shuffling papers, and then he came back on line. "Let me see. There's lots of demand for housing in northwest Portland. How about a twenty-four-year-old graduate student? Female. Unmarried. Colleen Wilson. Working on her master's degree in theology at Western Seminary."

"Did you vet this one?"

"Yes. She appears to be a very serious student. Nothing on her record more serious than a couple of parking tickets. Desperate for housing. Right now, she commutes from Forest Grove. Says the cost of commuting is eating her up."

"Sounds like a good prospect to me. Would you check and see if she wants to house sit for the next six months? She pays utilities and keeps the house neat and tidy, I pay the rest."

"Glad to. Text me the address, Leroy. I know where you live, but I don't remember the number. I'll contact her and set up a meeting."

"Thanks, Wilbur. See you later."

Smith knocked and then walked in. Without preamble he said, "Congratulations. I know you'll do a good job."

"And it'll get me out of your hair."

Smitty shook his head. "Dutch surprised me as much as he surprised you."

"In that case, thank you."

"Check in on Cletus while you're up there. Let him know we're getting this business wrapped up down here."

Wilcox nodded. "You know, Boss, Cletus is a straight A student. Working on his bachelors in criminology. I think we should recruit him. He's a bit small for field work, but he's damned sharp."

"Okay. When you get him back down here, bring him in and let me talk to him. Do you think it's something he wants?"

"I believe so. And I know he'd be an asset to the FBI."

***

A FRUSTRATED CLETUS WAS PACING THE carpet in Uncle George's home in Seattle, a cell phone to his ear. He stopped pacing long enough to nod and say wearily, "Okay. I'll take them."

He shook his head and shut his phone off. He looked at his uncle, who was watching with curiosity from his recliner, a copy of the Seattle Times in his lap. He picked up his coffee mug and took a sip, but didn't say anything.

Cletus frowned, and by way of explanation said, "Uncle George, the man wants a dollar more for umbrellas this year. At five bucks, they sell like hot cakes. And five dollars is an easy bill. Everybody got a five-dollar bill in his pocket. But now we got to make change … unless I eat the extra dollar."

Uncle George, raised his eyebrows and asked, "How many can you sell in a year?"

"About four thousand. You'd be surprised at how many Portlanders forget to carry an umbrella.

"And how much do you make?"

"I pay the man one dollar, shipping included. I pay my guys one dollar, and I get three."

"Can't make it on two dollars?"

"Would you like a four-thousand dollar decrease in your retirement?"

69

Tracks on the Water

COMMODORE MOOREHOUSE STUDIED THE PHOTO CAREFULLY, before handing it back to Miranda. "Yes. I do believe I know him. David Kojak. Tall, thin man, a bit gaunt. Nautical, in a way. Quiet man. Keeps to himself. Owns a very nice Krogen Express. Built in Florida, I believe. Fifty-two feet. He's been a member of the yacht club for the past two years."

Miranda asked, "Long legs?"

Moorhouse raised his eyebrows and smiled. "I never noticed his legs, but if you mean The Runaway, his yacht, I think you could say that. Depends on how fast you wish to go. Cruising at eight knots, it'll run about sixteen hundred nautical miles or so."

Brandt shook his head. "That's plenty far."

Moorhouse nodded. "You wouldn't want to head for Hawaii in that model, but any place up or down the Pacific coast is easily doable."

Brandt nodded again, his mind kicking into overdrive. *If he stops to refuel, he'll leave tracks.* "Can you tell us when he left?"

"Yes. He left two days ago."

Miranda looked at Brandt and said, "It fits."

She looked at the commodore and said, "And you know him as David Kojak?"

"Yes. Can you tell me what is going on?"

Brandt looked at Miranda and shook his head, so she settled for saying, "Just a routine background check."

Moorhouse raised his eyebrows and shook his head. "No. I doubt that, but I don't suppose you're free to discuss it right now."

Miranda asked, "If you were to plan a cruise to say Homer, Alaska, where would you go and where would you stop?"

"I've been to Homer. Nice trip … when it isn't raining. Basically, there are two choices. Either outside Vancouver Island, or cruise the inside passage. Much nicer water inside. And there are several places for taking on supplies. Neah Bay is a likely place. Port Angeles is another possibility. Anacortes is another, or Vancouver, BC. Let me get my charts." He heaved himself up out of his chair and walked into a side room.

While they waited, Miranda looked at Brandt and said, "Okay, he was in Portland two days ago. That means his yacht was someplace close by."

"Warrenton or Astoria are possibilities," Brandt said.

"All right. Assume he left Astoria two days ago, and assume he traveled at an economical eight knots, and assume he went north, where would that put him?"

"Probably off Vancouver Island," Moorhouse said as he walked back into the room. He spread a chart on his desk and said, "Look here. Possible stopping points: Neah Bay, Port Angeles, Port Townsend, Oak Harbor, Anacortes. And across the strait is Victoria."

"No further than that?"

"Possibly. It's only 173 nautical miles to Neah Bay. If he traveled at eight knots, that would take about twenty-two hours. But if he runs top speed, he could reach Neah Bay in one day."

Miranda said, "He was so careful to clean the boat he was living on, it seems strange he would have overlooked the flyer for Homer. You don't suppose it's a red herring … that he wants us to look north, while he boogies south?"

Moorhouse tapped the photo of The Runaway, "You could just send a picture of his yacht to each Coast Guard station. And to each harbor master. Have them keep watch."

"What if he changed the name of the boat?"

"Yacht," Commodore Moorhouse corrected. "He could, but he couldn't change the color or the configuration, not unless he put it in a ship yard, and even then, it would still be a Krogen 52."

70

Song of the Road

AGENTS BRANDT AND WRIGHT STOOD BEHIND the one-way glass in the viewing room, waiting for the arrival of Gary Gentle, a biker known on the street as Starbucks. A rather imposing police officer, whom Brandt judged to be a good six-feet-four or five inches tall, biceps straining the seams of a short-sleeved khaki shirt, opened the door and prodded Gentle into the room. The officer pointed to a chair bolted to the floor in front of a heavy stainless-steel table, also bolted to the bare concrete floor.

He said, "Sit."

Gentle, dressed in an orange jumpsuit with PRISONER stenciled on the back, took a two-handed roundhouse swing at the officer. He quickly learned what a foolish move it was. The bigger man caught the chain of the handcuffs and slammed Gentle against the viewing window.

Startled, Brandt and Miranda both took a quick step back, but the window did not break. Gentle said some unkind things about the big officer's parentage, but the guard ignored him and snapped a second handcuff around the chain on Gentle's handcuffs, then locked the other end to an eyebolt welded on the top the metal table.

When Special Agent Smith pushed through the door, Brandt and Wright heard Starbucks say, "I want a deal."

Agent Smith shook his head, slapped a file on the table, set a tape recorder beside the file, and sat down on a hard metal chair across from Starbucks. Without a word, Smith turned the tape recorder on and watched Starbucks fidget as his confession to Sheriff Blair rolled through the speaker.

They all listened carefully to the recording, nodding affirmation when the sheriff read Gentle his Miranda rights. On the recording, Sheriff Blair asked Starbucks if he understood his rights, and when he heard Starbucks say, "Yes," Smith smiled and nodded in the direction of the one-way glass. Sheriff Blair was also heard to ask if he wanted an attorney present while being questioned. His voice registering resignation, Gentle had declined legal representation.

Brandt nodded in unison with Smith and nudged Miranda. "Got him."

When the recording ended, Smith shut the recorder off, stared at the ceiling and drummed his fingers on the table top. Finally, he looked at Starbucks and said, "You are charged with assaulting a federal police officer, with inflicting bodily harm on a federal police officer, with attempted murder, and with murder for hire. You will also be charged as a felon in possession of a firearm and illegal possession of an opioid.

"What I am prepared to offer is a promise to keep you away from the general prison population and to keep you alive long enough to serve your sentence … providing you give us the name of the person who hired you to kill Reverend Wildish."

Agent Smith tapped the tape recorder and said, "Remember, we have your confession. Admissible in court…" Smith shrugged his shoulders. "Your accomplices are singing like birds. You know the drill. He who sings loudest and longest gets the prize."

Starbucks just seemed to sink lower in his chair, and when his shoulders sagged, Miranda said, "There he goes."

Brandt nodded and said, "Yep."

Forehead furrowed, brown eyes narrowed, Starbucks looked across the table and said, "If I cooperate, will the judge give me a lighter sentence?"

"I can't promise that, but I will tell the judge what a good citizen you've been … if you give me a name."

"I don't know his name. But his street name is Shooter. That's all I know him by. Runs the Salem chapter of The Romans."

"You sure?"

"Yeah. I know Shooter's voice. He's the one who ordered the hit."

Agent Smith said, "Will you testify to that in court?"

Starbucks nodded.

"Good man. I promise to do what I can for you."

Smith stood up and nodded to the guard. "Please return Mister Gentle to his cell."

***

SMITH MET MIRANDA AND BRANDT IN the hallway. In spite of himself, Brandt held his hand out and said, "Nice job, Boss."

Smith grinned and nodded. "Yes. Yes, it was, but we can blame it all on Sheriff Blair. He did a good job. Everything Gentle said to the sheriff is admissible in court." He smiled again, a rarity for Special Agent Smith, "I'm going to call the Salem office and see if they have a name and an address for this Shooter guy.

"Now then, what did you find out about Butler?"

71

Mountain Point

AFTER FOUR LONG DAYS OF 10-KNOT cruising, Butler was ready to hunker down and rest a day or two. He wasn't lost … exactly. The Runaway's GPS showed him creeping along in the east-west channel south of Mountain Point. The dense fog made it hard to see more than thirty feet. It was getting on toward dark, and he was anxious to call it a day.

Not confident enough to totally trust his charts, he willed the fog to open. In exasperation he muttered, "Lift, damn it!" He shook his head, and then said, "That's totally irrational, but I need to see where we are."

He had Milly keeping lookout on the high bow. In the deck lights, he could see her orange life vest, a bright contrast to the gray of her hooded rain jacket. All the running lights and every light in the wheelhouse were on. His close call with the big container ship on the Columbia was still fresh in his mind. He knew being seen was as important as seeing.

A gust of wind stirred the fog and gave him a look at the channel around the point just south of the port docks. He welcomed the sight of a row of house lights visible along the shore. "Now we know where we are," he said to himself. He turned the wheel to starboard and eased The Runaway up next to a mooring buoy just as the fog settled back in.

With the engines in neutral, he ran to the bow of the boat and grabbed a boat hook. He snagged the buoy chain on the second try and breathed a sigh of relief. He was tired. The trip through the inland passage was reasonably safe – except for the occasional floating log sent to remind him the sea is unforgiving of the unwary.

Butler tied the bow line to a big eyebolt and dropped the chain back through the slot in the buoy. "And there we have it," he said to Millie. "Tomorrow we'll take the dingy to town. You can do some shopping. Maybe buy yourself some new clothes, while I shop for groceries. And maybe we'll find a big, juicy burger someplace."

"And a beer?"

He shook his head. "Not any more. I can't do it. I just turn into a drunk … and then I make really bad decisions … and sometimes do really bad things. You shouldn't drink either."

She slipped an arm through his and said, "Is that why you won't have sex with me? Because you're afraid you'll make a bad decision?"

He shook his head. "No. I won't have sex with you because you are young enough to be my daughter. You need to find a young man and build a life together. That's what young people are meant to do."

They stepped into the wheelhouse and closed the door to block the cold fog. She caught his arm and turned him. "Am I so unattractive?"

He looked at her upturned face, her blues eyes, her shiny auburn hair, and her pert up-turned nose … a dusting of freckles on her cheeks. She was close to being pretty again. He studied the acne scars from years of drug abuse and decided the scars were fading, her skin taking on a healthier glow. He shook his head, and a grin tugged at his lips while he formed a proper reply.

The problem he had was twofold. First, she was still in withdrawal … and scared. Their first night in Neah Bay, she woke in a panic, ran down the companionway to his stateroom, and crawled into his bed – shivering and crying. She curled up against him, and he held her until she fell asleep. That had become the pattern. Start the night in separate staterooms. Wait for her to have a panic attack. Hold her until she fell asleep.

Second, he hadn't made love to a woman in over two years. The booze and the lack of female companionship had kept his frustration at the bay. But now he was staying sober, and a warm young body was keeping him company at night. He was tempted, but he didn't feel right about it.

He never asked her, but he was sure she had been molested as a young girl. The psychology of that was morbid. Wrong as it was, the abused felt inadequate and guilty. Sex became acceptance and love. He'd never thought it through, but instinctively, he knew the last thing she needed was sex – especially sex with an older man.

He put his hands on her shoulders and nodded. "You are very pretty, and I like you very much, but it would be a grave mistake for us to become sexually involved. And I think deep in your heart you know that also. So, let's just be friends while we are on this boat. Okay?"

She shook her head. "I don't get it."

72

Summoned

A REGISTERED LETTER MOVED VIA OVERNIGHT DELIVERY through the USPS system and found its way to the office of Lake County Sheriff Henry (Bud) Blair. His unofficial administrative assistant, Technical Deputy Karen Highsmith, did what all trusted AA's do throughout the world: signed for it, opened it, read it, and started to put it back in its envelope.

He's not going to like this, she thought. *Generally, a sworn deposition from a law enforcement officer is enough.*

The envelope contained a summons from an Assistant U.S. Attorney to appear before a federal grand jury. Two days from now. In Portland. People did not ignore a grand jury summons, not with impunity. Especially law enforcement officers.

She knew, without question, the court was hearing testimony and reviewing evidence in the case of the United States versus Gary Gentle (aka Starbucks). You don't shoot FBI agents without serious kickback.

Technically, you could argue he did not shoot Special Agent Miranda Wright. He merely shot "at" her. But when the high velocity rifle round smacked her cedar paddle, it essentially exploded, and the impact drove a sharp splinter about the size and length of a pencil all the way through the palm of her hand, a wound defined as grievous bodily harm.

Technical Deputy Highsmith shook her head and thought it would have been a whole lot better and a whole lot faster to let Lake County

District Attorney Howard Finch prosecute Gentle in the fine city of Lakeview. But the feds ignored Sheriff Blair's protests, so the Lakeview jail reluctantly turned Gentle over to the custody of two rather large men from the U.S. Marshals Service.

She looked at the phone number on the letterhead and dialed the number. After the second ring, an official-sounding woman answered, "Assistant U.S. Attorney Anthony McRae's office. This is Kathy."

"Hi, Kathy. I'm Deputy Karen Highsmith, Lake County Sheriff's Department. We received a summons for Sheriff Blair to appear before the grand jury day after tomorrow. I'm wondering if he could submit a sworn deposition instead. We're running a bit shorthanded down here. Depositions have been sufficient in the past."

"Hold please. I'll ask."

The wait seemed like half an hour, but in reality, it lasted only a long six or seven minutes. When Kathy came back on line, she said, "No. Mister McRae wants to see him in person."

"Even if he has other duties?"

"Assistant U.S. Attorney McRae insists he appear in person."

"He's not going to like this."

Kathy softened enough to say, "I know. But he really doesn't have a choice, does he?"

Karen hung up without saying goodbye. "Assholes," she muttered, just as Bud pulled the office door open and walked into the booking area. Karen heard him whistle a tune she didn't recognize, but she smiled anyway. It was nice to see her sheriff happy for a change. *Maybe it will work this time*, she thought. *Maybe. If Nancy doesn't change her mind again. Cynical thought.*

She smiled and said "Good morning, Bud."

"Hi, Karen. Sorry I'm late. I ran BB over to the Ford dealership. He needed to get a vehicle, and I had business at the newspaper ... an interview with Carol Connor."

"How did that go?"

He pushed his Stetson back on his forehead and frowned. "I don't know. Fine. I hope. She tells me that now the new owner of the Z-BAR is going to run for sheriff in place of his foreman. She wants to do a series of interviews with each of us."

Karen frowned in return. "I wonder what happened, Bud? Why would he do that?"

He shook his head and leaned an elbow on the booking counter. "I don't know. Carol's sources say the foreman quit his job and left the state. She doesn't know what's going on either. The owner will be a tough contender. He has money, he has Hollywood good looks, and I hear he's an excellent speaker."

"You'll beat him, Bud. You have lots of friends." *And you're handsome yourself. At least I think so.*

Bud shook his head, a worried furrow on his forehead. "It isn't going to be easy. I've always run unopposed. Makes me an amateur. And a lot of people are telling Judge Lynch they think the drug dealers and biker gangs would leave Lake County alone if I resigned. That doesn't sound too damn friendly to me."

She handed him the USPS envelope. "You won't like this, but it might take your mind off the problem of running for sheriff."

"Did you read this?"

"Yes. It's a summons to testify before a grand jury in Portland. Two days from now."

"I've been expecting that, but the timing is crummy."

"Yes, I know. I called the Assistant U.S. Attorney's office. I asked if a sworn deposition would do. No dice. They want you in person."

"In two days, huh? Well, get Lonnie in here. He's sheriff for a couple of days." And then he grinned. "I know just what to do about this." Without explanation, he walked the short hallway to his office and closed the door.

He made a phone call, listened to the first ring, and heard Nancy say, "Emergency Services."

"Howdy, ma'am. This bachelor I know is looking for a beautiful woman to end his solitary way of life. You know anybody?"

She laughed softly. "I thought we had that solved already."

"Yeah, but I'm not getting any younger. You busy along about this afternoon? I thought we might tie the knot and head to Portland for a brief honeymoon."

"What's going on?"

When he filled her in about the summons, she responded, "And I'm supposed to drop everything and run away with you? Is that it?"

Her lack of enthusiasm stopped him dead in his tracks. "I just thought, you know, we could get married and work in a honeymoon."

"We will, but I want to stick with the original plan. I want my family here, Mom's friend Verna, Sonny, Mom if she's able to travel … my family. And your father. And your brother and his family, if he'll come."

"What happened to a small, quiet ceremony?"

"This will be small, but I want our families here. Okay?"

"Well, hell. I suppose I don't have a say in the matter."

She choked back a laugh. "You sound like a little boy who lost his ice cream cone. Of course, I'll marry you. And today is just fine. We'll have a big reception later.

"Let me call Jenny Latimore and see if she can marry us this afternoon. And I'll have to get the Colonel to sub for me. Let's see … wear your best uniform, and I'll wear my white sheath, and … oh, my … I suppose BB will be best man … and I'll ask Carol Connor to be my bridesmaid … and I'll need a bouquet."

Bud breathed a sigh of relief and said, "I'll take care of the flowers."

***

AT NOON, REVEREND JENNIFER LATIMORE SMILED at the couple standing before the altar. She knew Nancy slightly from the few times she'd attended services, but all she knew about the sheriff was what she read in the Lake County News or heard through church gossip.

Reverend Latimore thought Nancy was one of the most striking women she had ever seen, and in spite of the worry lines creasing his face, she thought Bud looked handsome in his blue dress uniform. But he seemed a bit uncomfortable. She contained her impulse to laugh. *Strange behavior for a man who just bluffed fifty bikers.*

She nodded at Nancy and said, "We are gathered here in the sight of God to unite Henry Blair and Nancy Sixkiller in holy matrimony. If anyone knows of any reason why they should not be wed, speak now or forever hold your peace."

She paused and BB said quietly, "Well..."

That earned him a nasty look from Bud and a chuckle from Sonny. It ended with a frown from Reverend Latimore.

Samuel Adams, photographer and digital expert for the Lake County News, snapped pictures for the paper when the brief ceremony was "sealed with a kiss."

Bud turned to look at a sea of faces. He whispered in Nancy's ear, "Well, so much for a small ceremony. Half the town is here."

Near the back of the chapel, Doc Saunders, reached into his wallet and handed his longtime veterinarian assistant, Brenda Brown, a twenty-dollar bill. She smiled sweetly. "I told you so."

73

Shooter

THREE HOURS AFTER SMITH CALLED FBI Special Agent Stanley Johnson, SAC of the Salem office, a ten-person FBI SWAT team joined an eight-person Salem Police Department tactical team at the Salem police department armory. Chief of Police Roger Littlefield waited until coffee cups were filled and the team members had each picked a chair, before calling the meeting to order. There was noticeable tension as the two units sized each other up. None of the officers liked working with strangers when there was the possibility of a shootout.

From the rear of the room, Special Agent Johnson leaned against the wall and watched Littlefield. He knew about Littlefield from reading an FBI briefing file, but this was his first chance to meet him in person. He was impressed. Distinguished looking, wavy hair turning silver, dressed in a dark blue uniform with four stars on his epaulets, Littlefield carried the aura of command.

The chief looked around the room at the officers, almost all were men in their early thirties, though the group also included two tall, athletic-looking women. All were lean and tense, their serious attitudes mirrored by their black uniforms.

Chief Littlefield said, "Before we get started, I want to say the Salem Police Department welcomes the help of the FBI. We've been working to take down The Romans for the past couple of years." Johnson smiled at that. *The Chief is making his territorial claim … and very neatly.*

"Introductions." He pointed to a man sitting at the head table on his right. "This is Marion County District Attorney Justin Black. And this gentleman," nodding to his left, "is Assistant U.S. Attorney Robert Hall. At this point I'll turn the briefing over to them."

Hall, a lean thirty-five-year-old dressed in a dark blue suit, white shirt, and red tie, claimed the right to go first by standing up and frowning at the assembled officers. He made eye contact with as many of the officers as he could, cleared his throat, and said, "We want clean arrests. Make sure there are no grounds for dismissal based on sloppy procedures. The chain of evidence needs to be tight. And these citizens are entitled to hear their Miranda rights. We're bringing in additional prosecutors in anticipation of multiple arrests, but the main target is Henderson, also known as Shooter."

He opened a file folder lying on the table and handed out a stack of photos. "Pass these out, please. He held up one and said, "This is Shooter. We want him for a range of crimes, including murder and murder for hire. Our FBI profiler says he is a sociopath with psychotic tendencies … in other words, he's a cold-blooded killer. It would be very useful to bring him in alive."

Hall looked at District Attorney Black and sat down. Black was a husky six-foot, broad-shouldered man. Women loved his intense blue eyes and dark curly hair. Chief Littlefield privately thought Black's election was based on good looks, not competence, but the DA's office was staffed with young, bright prosecutors, so maybe Black best served the citizens by making the DA's office look good.

DA Black, in contrast to Hall, smiled and said, "Good afternoon, gentlemen … and ladies. This is a terrific opportunity to deal a blow to crime – not only in Marion County and Salem, but in the rest of Oregon. The city of Portland Police Bureau lists over three hundred gang members in that fine city. They perpetuate drug use, prostitution, murder, and extortion on a grand scale. You have an opportunity to hit back. The Romans are not the largest criminal gang on the West Coast, but they are among the most dangerous. Bring them to me, and I'll see they are prosecuted to the full extent of the law. Thank you."

Agent Johnson shook his head and watched the handsome Black sit down. *I wonder if he expected applause?*

Chief Littlefield nodded and said, "Thank you, gentlemen. I'm sure our officers will take that to heart. For those who don't know me, I'm Roger Littlefield, Chief of Police for Salem. The gentleman in back is FBI Special Agent in Charge Stanley Johnson. I thank you all for being here. And now, let me introduce Officer Wallace, who has spent the last seven months working undercover to infiltrate The Romans. I suspect he'll be looking for a new job after tonight."

That brought the expected round of chuckles. "Wally," the Chief said, "tell us what we're up against."

Officer Wallace was a medium-sized man, bearded, with sleeve tats on his muscular arms and diamond studs in his earlobes. He wore a black leather vest with The Romans logo. Standing there in his leathers, he looked like the real deal … a bona fide, mean-assed biker. *A warrior,* Chief Littlefield thought.

Wallace cleared his throat and scanned the crowd. "The Chief asked me to brief you about what we'll be up against. Every Roman is armed. Most prefer a 9mm handgun. They all carry sheath knives and know how to use them. Our primary target, street name Shooter, birth name Larry Henderson, carries a sawed-off shot gun loaded with buckshot. He keeps it behind the bar when he isn't on the road. Do not take these people lightly. They live by intimidation and cruelty. And there are lots of them.

"Forty or fifty gang members gather most evenings at the Stone-Cold Tavern on South Commercial. Ostensibly, it's a public bar – but outsiders have the good sense to stay away. The gang likes that location because there are three roads they can use to boogie if they need to. Shooter has an office in the back of the building to keep books and take care of 'special business.' There's a back exit from that room. Here, let me show you..."

Officer Wallace used a white board to sketch the floor plan of The Stone-Cold Tavern: one entrance, three exits, with a bar running down the north wall. "The front of the bar is made of oak planks backed by a sheet of quarter-inch steel. That makes a good barrier, especially for lighter pistol rounds.

"There is a boogie door at the west end of the bar. It leads to the bathroom hallway and to a back exit. One thought is to chase them out that exit and trap them there."

A hand went up. Wallace pointed and said, "Go ahead."

"Do they have an evening ritual? A recurrent pattern?"

Wallace nodded. "Yes. They drink, smoke dope, gamble, and generally get drunk or stoned into the wee hours of the morning."

A member of the FBI Swat team held his hand up and asked, "So you think we hit them after midnight?"

Wallace nodded. "There's one complication. Two bikers we call 'soldiers' are posted to guard the bikes. They stay sober, because Shooter is liable to kill any soldier who gets drunk or stoned on duty."

"So, we need to take care of those first..." the leader of the Salem Tactical Team observed.

Wally nodded. "My pal Sloppy Joe and I will take them down. They know us. The real risk is if the bartender – who also stays sober – is watching the security cameras when we engage."

A voice from the back of the room said, "Sloppy Joe?"

Wallace smiled. "I guess you could say I 'turned' him. He's a long-time biker who wants out of the life. But he's scared of Shooter. Says Shooter has no qualms about killing people who try to quit. I convinced Sloppy Joe to help me in exchange for a new identity and some traveling money. He's solid. He'll help me tonight. And he's kind of scary himself. Imagine a giant red-headed Viking with a skull helmet coming at you swinging a broadaxe. That's Sloppy Joe. Please don't shoot him ... or me ... tonight."

That brought a few chuckles.

Special Agent Johnson pushed away from the wall to enter the conversation. "Let me get this straight. They get drunk and stoned almost every night. And then they ride off into the night?"

Wally shook his head. "No. If they get too messed up to ride, they walk a short half-block to the bunkhouse."

"How many?"

"Depends, but as I said, generally there are forty to fifty bikers in the place, and sometimes more. Shooter never sleeps at the bunkhouse. We'll have to engage him at the bar."

Chief Littlefield interjected, "Okay. Listen up. We want you to work on a plan to pick them up one at a time as they walk to the bunkhouse. Quietly. Patrol cars will block the streets and divert traffic away from this den of inequity. Maybe we knock out the power to the tavern and bunkhouse, then round 'em up. What do you think Agent Johnson?"

Johnson nodded in agreement. "Yes, maybe. But not before midnight. We want them as inebriated as possible." He grinned and said, "Chief, why don't we take our attorney friends and go have a quiet drink some-place ourselves … let our teams work out a plan. We'll come back in a couple of hours for a briefing. Agreed?"

Chief Littlefield and Special Agent Johnson turned the action over to their subordinates and left the meeting room. Black and Hall followed them to the hallway and waited until the door closed.

DA Black held out his hand and said, "Thanks. This could get in-teresting. I'm afraid I can't join you. I have a meeting with the mayor I need to get to."

Assistant U.S. Attorney Hall said, "I too have some business waiting for me. Later, maybe."

Littlefield and Johnson watched the men walk down the hall and out the door. Chief Littlefield said, "I'm not sure what to make of this. The FBI making nice and working as equal partners with the City of Salem? What's going on?"

Johnson grinned. "In some cities, three on this coast I can point to, we find very little cooperation. So, when we have a happy opportunity to work as partners with a local agency, we jump at the chance."

"That bad, huh?"

"That bad. In San Francisco, the mayor actually ordered the city police to not cooperate with us. It makes enforcing federal laws very difficult. We can't even use local jails."

Littlefield took a deep breath. "In that case, let's make tonight's effort a showcase for cooperation."

"Agreed. First round is on me."

74

Basma

WHEN BRANT AND MIRANDA BRIEFED AGENT Smith about their hunt for Winslow Butler, he looked surprised … and then envious. He studied the picture of The Runaway, shook his head and marveled. "A black 52-foot Krogen. Wow! Most of us can only dream about owning one of those."

Brandt looked sideways at Miranda, then back at Smith. "Uh, boss? What's it about? The boat or Butler?"

"Oh. Sorry. I dream of owning my own cabin cruiser someday. A smaller one, I'm afraid."

Brandt and Miranda stared in disbelief. Smith's reaction revealed a human side they had never suspected. A dreamer? Smith? Political Smith? Unbelievable.

"Okay. Okay," he said. "Sorry. So, you think he may be headed for Homer, Alaska?"

Miranda nodded. "Maybe. Even likely."

"What are you going to do about it?" Smith asked.

Brandt shrugged. "Running away in a boat is about as dumb as it gets, especially in a Krogen. How do you hide a boat like that? At some point, you need to stop for fuel and supplies. I guess you could lay up in some sheltered bay for a week or so, but not forever. We sent a BOLO out to every harbormaster and Coast Guard station on the west coast. An 'Observe, but do not approach' BOLO."

"Good. And tell the harbormaster in Homer exactly what to look for."

Brandt said, "On it boss," and started to rise from his chair, but Smith stopped him. "Sit down. You can take care of that after we're through. Good job, by the way."

He pulled a file from his top drawer and pushed it across the desk. "Read this and then go interview this lady. She works for the Portland Water Bureau. She and her husband may have been feeding information about Portland's water system to a terrorist cell. I suspect, as does Dutch, they intended to poison our water.

"She lives in a bad neighborhood, so I've arranged for a tactical team to go with you."

Brandt shook his head. "Sorry, but Dutch made it clear that finding Butler is our first and only priority."

"I talked to Dutch. And since you are in a holding pattern for the moment, he said I could use you for this one job."

Brandt looked peeved, but Miranda just opened the file. She read the first name in the file and nodded. "Basma, wife of Hamas … formerly Benjamin Green, if I remember Reverend TJ Wildish's story correctly."

Smith nodded. "There's an address in the file. Agent Woodson, our SWAT team leader, is waiting for your call. Coordinate with him. My source says Basma is at home today … drinking bottled water."

"Source?"

"Yeah. A city inspector. Apparently, someone made an anonymous call about a gas leak."

Miranda smiled and said, "You didn't?"

Smith shook his head, but his smile told the tale.

"That's sneaky," Brandt said, with a hint of admiration in his voice.

***

Their trip through North Portland gave Brandt and Miranda a close look at the once-flourishing area.

Miranda noticed an unusual number of pawn shops. Many of the taverns had bars on the windows, and some of the convenience stores employed security guards to protect the property.

She sighed and said, "This used to be a place people could raise families."

Brandt nodded. "I know. Neighborhoods used to be sanctuaries for families. But now that we are a sanctuary city, our neighborhoods aren't safe for anyone anymore. I don't know where this is going to take us."

Too depressing, Miranda thought. And then out of the blue she asked, "How are things between you and Jenny?"

Brandt smiled and laughed. "You know, this might be working out. She called this morning and reminded me I owe her a lobster dinner. And … assuming we live out the day … she and I are going to dinner tonight."

"So?"

"So, she has turned me down about ten times in a row. Why say yes, now? I think she is a wee bit jealous you and I are partners. At least I hope so."

***

BASMA COOPERATED FROM THE BEGINNING. WHEN Brandt and Miranda showed her their credentials, she nodded and said, "I've been expecting you. Please come in."

She ushered them through a spotless living room to a shiny kitchen. She pointed to the table, saying, "Please sit. Would you like a cup of coffee?"

They each shook their heads and remained standing. Brandt asked, "Is your husband home?"

Tears formed in the corners of her dark eyes. "He hasn't been home for the past two days. I fear for him."

"You know that we have to look," Brandt said.

"I know. Go ahead."

Brandt waved the small tactical team inside and waited until the team leader came back to the kitchen and said, "Clear."

"Why do you fear for you husband?" Miranda asked.

Tears rolled down Basma's brown cheeks, but she brushed them angrily away. "You must understand. He is my husband. When he started asking questions about my job – how the system worked … maps of the system … sources of supply … pumping stations … I didn't think anything of it. At first, I just thought he was interested in my job. But, when I heard whispers of a plot to poison the water supply, I was terrified. I begged him to go to the police, but he wouldn't listen. He kept saying it was in the hands of Allah. And then he disappeared. That's when I knew he had been providing information to terrorists – bad people who would kill Muslims as well as infidels to further their goals."

Brandt asked, "Did he mention any names, anyone he might have been passing the information to?"

She nodded. "He said someone named Osama was curious about the water supply. I don't know him."

Agent Wright said, "Why don't you sit down. I'll get you a glass of water."

"No! I'm afraid of the water. I only drink bottled water."

Miranda nodded. "I guess I would be scared, too. Now … did your husband have any papers? Notebooks? A desk someplace?"

"In the back bedroom. He has an office. I searched the desk. There's nothing there."

Brandt pursed his lips and nodded. "Then you won't mind if we search again."

"Why would I care? My life is over."

She wiped her tears away on a kitchen towel, straightened her shoulders and said, "I have asked my neighbor to keep my cats while I'm gone. I'm ready."

Sadness in her voice, Miranda read Basma her rights and placed her under arrest. Brandt picked up a framed photo of Basma and a tall, bearded young man. Multnomah Falls was in the background. They were both young, smiling, happy … a full life ahead of them.

Brandt said, "Is this your husband?"

Basma nodded. "Happier times."

A restless crowd of people gathered on Basma's small lawn. One angry young man shouted, "Hands up, you pigs!" Others took up the chant until Basma yelled, "It is okay! Go home, but don't drink the water!"

A buxom black woman asked, "What are you saying, Basma?"

"The water has been poisoned by jihadists!"

Miranda watched people frantically dialing cell phones or running up the sidewalk in the direction of the neighborhood grade school while Brandt put Basma behind the cage of the big SUV. She slid into the passenger seat and slammed the door. "Go! Go!" she said. "This will hit the airways in about sixty seconds."

She called a number and waited. When Special Agent Smith answered, she said without preamble, "We need to issue an emergency bulletin warning people to not drink city water. It may have been poisoned."

She heard an uncharacteristic swear word, and then Smith said, "On it."

75

Exodus and Chaos

A POLITICAL ADVISOR IN THE MAYOR'S OFFICE wanted to wait until the water was tested for toxins before declaring a state of emergency. The mayor glared at him and said, "George, you are an idiot. You're fired! Go drink some water and save me the trouble of shooting you."

***

THE PORTLAND METROPOLITAN INTERAGENCY EMERGENCY RESPONSE Team was activated, and the governor used her authority to call up the Oregon National Guard to declare a state of emergency for Multnomah County, Clackamas County, and Washington County.

The president of the United States declared a state of emergency and ordered FEMA to Portland. The major television networks scrambled to send teams of reporters to Portland, and by the second hour of the event, talking heads on local and national television were advising people to stay home, to stay calm, and to remember it could turn out to be just a political ruse by the party currently outvoted by the majority party.

News channels immediately brought in expert consultants to describe how they would go about the business of poisoning the Portland water supply. Computer-generated graphics flashed on HDTV screens showing maps of the Bull Run watershed, pipelines, wells, and the open reservoirs in the city. One well-known newscaster for FOX asked, "Aren't you concerned that you might be spreading needless panic?" He was immediately portrayed as "insensitive" by CNN.

Other talking heads condemned the City of Portland for its open water supply, an effort that died quickly after other experts listed all the open sources of water for other cities like New York, Washington D.C., and Los Angeles.

What ensued lacked the orderly behavior predicated by the emergency response plan. People did not listen to the urgent voices on radio, television, and social media sites telling then to remain calm and stay home.

Instead, they packed their kids and pets into vehicles and headed out of town, creating a mega traffic jam that would take the Oregon Department of Transportation, the Oregon State Police, the Portland Police Bureau, and a bevy of officers from surrounding municipalities days to untangle.

It was a bonanza for towing companies. Hundreds of vehicles were left abandoned. Television newscasts showed thousands of people with daypacks and water jugs walking the freeways and highways away from Portland.

Urgent care centers, hospital ER's, and medical clinics were swamped with people convinced they were dying. The sound of ambulance sirens added to the hysteria, and 911 was flooded with more calls than dispatchers could handle.

Predictably, looters took to the streets. Fires burned out of control, because fire engines could not be driven through the clogged city streets.

As word spread, bottled water became a new form of currency. Vending machines were looted, and convenience stores were robbed of any bottled liquid. The National Guard was ordered out and issued live ammunition. One battalion from Salem was able to drive as close as the junction of I-5 and I-205 before congestion halted progress. They slogged the next nine miles to a staging center set up in the West Linn High School football field. They would wait twenty-four hours for further orders.

Police helicopters fed pictures of cars using southbound overpass exits to escape the congestion, then using northbound exits as on-ramps to get to the less congested half of the freeway ... driving south in the northbound lanes of I-5.

***

Osama Ali, forty-five years old cleric, a hint of gray in his groomed beard, twisted the cap on a plastic bottle of imported spring water and took a sip. "Amazing."

He looked from the Channel 6 coverage of a fire engine – lights flashing, horn and siren blaring – trying to edge up Burnside to a fire a few blocks up the street. Drivers did their best to move into right hand lanes and make room.

A reporter brushed straight black hair away from her face and said, "Panic has turned Burnside into a parking lot as drivers attempt to leave the city. And, as you can see, congestion is making it nearly impossible for a fire engine to reach a blaze just a few blocks up the street." The camera panned south on 4th Avenue and zoomed in on a group of young men, most of them in masks, in time to record two of them using baseball bats to break into a cell phone store.

"And it looks like looters are already at work. Let's hope the police can reach the scene in time to prevent further damage. Amy Chou reporting live from downtown Portland."

The circle of men lounging on couches and overstuffed chairs in the large side room in the mosque laughed at the confusion and panic. Osama studied each face, trying to judge their dedication. "What do you think?"

One older man shook his head and grinned. "We will all be arrested, is what I think. Our brothers and sisters will turn against us."

Osama nodded. "Yes. I think you are right. This did not go as planned, but I am enjoying the chaos nonetheless. Who talked?"

They all looked away, afraid to meet the challenge in Osama's eyes. "No, I don't suppose it was any of you. But someone did."

"The weak link," the old man said, for he was the only one in the room unafraid of Osama, "is Hamas. His wife Basma has been arrested, and I suspect she will tell the FBI everything she knows. They will figure it out from there."

"How long before they learn it was a ruse … that there never was any poison?"

One of the men shrugged, saying, "The FBI agents are very efficient. Hours maybe?"

The old man gave Osama a side glance and studied him for a few seconds. "And you intend to be arrested, don't you?"

"Yes, a small gesture of martyrdom. Besides, can you jail someone for a rumor? I think not." And then he laughed, "This has exceeded my wildest expectations. Now, go with Allah's blessing."

They all rose from the couches except the old man. "What of Hamas?"

Osama said, "By this time next week, he should be sweating in the Libyan desert, training to become a martyr."

He bowed slightly. "Congratulations, Osama."

Osama bowed in turn, lowered his eyes and nodded. "The will of Allah."

76

The World Watches

B UD PULLED INTO HIS GRAVEL DRIVEWAY, half expecting to hear Molly's bark when he opened the driver's door. He slammed the pickup door a little harder than necessary and said, "Molly. I'm gonna miss you."

Her water bowl was dry and her food bowl was empty on the back porch, but he just couldn't bring himself to dump them in the trash. He pushed through the back door and hurried to his bedroom. He pulled a soft-sided carryall from the closet and flopped it on the bed. He was packing socks and underwear, one set for each day he planned to be gone – plus one extra set for emergencies – when his cell phone rang.

He didn't recognize the number, but something told him he should answer. "Bud Blair."

BB's voice growled through the speaker. "Bud, you better turn your TV on. All hell's breaking loose in Portland. Somebody … at least that's what the police think … poisoned the water supply. Thousands are fleeing the city, traffic is all jammed up, and the looters are having a field day. It's a disaster."

"Hold on." He rushed to his living room and hit the power button on the remote in time to see a picture of Burnside Avenue in Portland, fire trucks trying to weave through a traffic jam, looters four or five blocks up the street from the television crew. He recognized Amy Chou and heard her say, "And it looks like looting has already started."

The picture faded and an anchorman Bud didn't know was saying, "Thank you Amy. It looks like total chaos. Be careful out there." He actually sounded like he meant it.

The camera shifted to an overhead shot from a Channel 6 helicopter showing the traffic jam at the junction of I-205 and I-5 southbound. An airborne reporter said, "As you can see gridlock has all but closed most major highways out of the city, making it difficult for our police and our first responders to do their jobs. It looks like total panic from up here. We just checked I-205 where it joins I-84 and it looks much the same. And traffic on the Sunset West is not moving at all. It looks like a number of people are abandoning their cars to walk the shoulder of the freeway.

"Reporting live, this is Gordon Sharp for Channel 6 news."

The scene shifted back to the studio and a newscaster saying, "We're hearing rumors of a plot to poison the city's water supply, so we are urging people to not drink any tap water. Use bottled water instead. I need to add that neither our city officials nor Homeland Security have confirmed the story. They are asking people to please stay in their homes and off the streets. The mayor and Police Chief Henry Meyer have scheduled a press conference for thirty minutes from now. Stay tuned."

Bud turned off the set and called Nancy's cell. When she picked up, he said, "Have you heard the news from Portland?"

"Yes. I'm headed for Emergency Services right now. Radio is our best bet for communication."

She paused and said, "I don't think the Assistant U.S. Attorney is going to expect you to appear any time soon. Oh Bud, do you really think someone poisoned the water supply?"

Bud shook his head thoughtfully. "I don't know. Millions of gallons of water? How would anyone get any type of poison into the system in sufficient quantities to poison the water? No. I don't believe it. Something else is going on. I wouldn't put it past some terrorist son-of-a-bitch to concoct the whole story. And it's working, isn't it? Portland is coming apart at the seams. Look, I think I'd better get back to the office. Keep me posted."

"I love you, Bud Blair. Is this going to interfere with our honeymoon at the cabin? Will you be there?"

"Come hell or poisoned water. Count on it."

"That's not funny Bud."

***

ALL OF THE MAJOR NETWORKS CARRIED pictures of looters shooting at Portland city cops … and losing. One reporter tallied six dead looters and two injured police officers in the first four hours. It made for extremely good program ratings. Networks were buzzing with insinuations about racial injustice and police brutality. Television channels worldwide relayed the pictures from Portland, augmented, of course, by camera shots posted on social media.

In Lakeview, a thoughtless comment by Buck, a local blockhead who allowed that Portland was just getting what it deserved, led to a bloody fistfight between Buck and Charlie Bates, the father of a daughter enrolled at Portland State University … and ended with the father blubbering in fear for his daughter. "I can't get a call through to her cell phone. I don't even know if she's alive or not. And I can't do a damned thing about it!"

Buck wrapped him in his big arms and said, "Ah, hell, Charlie. I forgot. I'm so sorry." The bar crowd was surprised to see tears pool in Buck's eyes. A couple of old cowboys looked away and surreptitiously dabbed at their own eyes.

Denver, the bartender, made a show of pretending to polish his eyeglasses with the open cuff of his flannel shirt.

A man shut his cell phone down and, from the back of the room, said, "I just heard it was some jihadi bastards that did it. They better not come through Lakeview."

Denver put his polished glasses back on and pulled a .357 magnum revolver from under the counter. He slammed it on the bar and said, "They will damned well regret it, if they do."

***

BUD'S EFFORTS TO CONTACT THE ASSISTANT U.S. Attorney's office met with the same success as the rest of Oregon. Calls to Portland were simply not getting through. His cell screen read "No Service" and his landline picked up nothing but a busy signal.

He used the radio in his county pickup to call Deputy Roger Hildebrand, who was driving back to Christmas Valley. "Roger, I'm wondering if any of the Portland refugees will make it this far. What do you think?"

"Maybe. But I don't think it's a problem for us. Bend is more likely to have problems. I think our best bet is sit tight. If Deschutes County asks for help, Larae and I could run up there. Although I don't know how much difference two officers might make."

"Okay. We'll just settle for worrying about our own people for now."

77

Go Forth and Prosper

B Y THE TIME IT TOOK THEM TO bring Basma to the FBI headquarters building, perhaps twenty-five minutes, Brandt and Wright noticed a heavy increase in traffic and cars driving well in excess of posted speed limits.

"It's starting, isn't it? The panic, I mean," Miranda said.

"Yeah. Thanks to Basma when she let the cat out of the bag to her neighbors."

Basma said, "I did not mean to create panic. I just wanted my neighbors to stay safe."

"I think that was the plan all along, Basma," Miranda said. "They counted on your kindness and your compassion to start a panic. And it's working. It's a cunning ruse – nothing but a scam – yet it's terrorism nonetheless."

"Do you think my husband will be arrested?"

Miranda nodded. "Yes," Miranda snapped, "and I hope he goes to jail forever."

Basma began to sob, all composure destroyed by sorrow for her husband.

***

THEY USHERED BASMA INTO A HOLDING cell, took her handcuffs off, and offered her a bottle of imported spring water.

Miranda pulled a notebook from her handbag and pointed to the small table. "Sit here, Basma. I'm going to give you a pen, and I want you to start writing everything you remember: questions you were asked, information you gave your husband, any names he might have mentioned … anything that will help us put an end to this. Okay?"

A tall, clean-cut college intern entered the room and Miranda said, "Kenny here will sit with you until we get back."

***

SMITH'S SECRETARY WAS WORKING THE PHONES and taking notes when they entered the outer office. Smith's door was open and she pointed them in. A large TV hanging on a sidewall was tuned to a local TV station, volume muted. The scenes looked like something out of a movie – people running to catch already overcrowded busses, drivers honking horns and bumping cars in front of them. *It's a disaster movie,* Brandt thought. *Only worse. It's real.*

Miranda shook her head. "Ridiculous. Just don't drink the water. What in the world is accomplished by running away?"

Brandt said, "It's the primitive impulse. Fight or flight."

Smith's chair was swiveled to look out the window overlooking Marine Drive and the Columbia River. They heard him bark, "Can't you make it happen any quicker?" Then, a sigh. "Okay. But we need to know if the water is actually poisoned or not. People … a lot of people … are in a panic. Some poor fool just ran his car off Marine drive into the Columbia. Get those tests done. Right now!"

He turned his chair around and put the phone back in the cradle. "I think we're all going to be insane before this is over."

Smith surveyed the two, "How did it go?"

Brandt said, "Basma is cooperating. We've an intern watching her in the holding cell, and she's busy writing down everything she remembers.

"Good. Agent Wright, you will interrogate her. You, Agent Brandt, are going to Alaska. Find Butler and bring him back."

"Arrest him?"

Smith nodded, "If he won't cooperate."

Brandt said, "What's in it for Butler?"

"You sound like his attorney, Agent Brandt."

"I know we wouldn't have broken up Al-Alwani's slave trade – or found this other person and the plot to poison the water – without Butler's initiative."

"Is that what you call it? Initiative? Taking bribe money is initiative?"

"Okay. But he had a change of heart. And he gave us critical information and help. I think the very least we can offer is witness protection."

Dutch Vanderlin eased into the room in time to hear Brandt's insistence to do something for Butler. "I think so too," he said. They turned in time to see him smile.

"Go forth and prosper, Douglas. Find Winslow Butler, offer him witness protection … but get him back to testify to the grand jury as to what he knows about Al-Alwani's operation.

Brandt pointed at the pileup on Marine Drive. Traffic was at a standstill. "Just how am I supposed to do that?"

"The Coast Guard found his boat. It's anchored a short distance south of Ketchikan. And a helicopter is warming up on our rooftop helipad as I speak. It will take you to Sea-Tac where you'll be joined by your old partner, Agent Wilcox. You will then be flown to Whidbey Island Naval Air Station, then on to Ketchikan. Bring Butler back. Now, get moving."

Brandt nodded and said, "Yes sir. On it."

78

Stone-Cold

AT PRECISELY 12:01 A.M., THE COMBINED FORCES of the eight-person Salem Tactical Team and the ten-person FBI SWAT team moved into position a block south of the Stone-Cold Tavern.

Four members of the team proceeded on foot to the sidewalk of a side street leading from the tavern to what Officer Wallace called 'the bunkhouse.' They waited impatiently behind a dilapidated six-foot wooden fence and were rewarded by two bikers stumbling home from the bar.

The arrest was efficient and quiet. While two officers hustled the inebriated bikers around the corner to a waiting paddy wagon, the other two made a third arrest. This pattern lasted for another forty-five minutes and netted a grand total of fourteen bikers.

Two officers watched the front door of the bunkhouse, and two watched the back door. They were armed with 12-gauge shotguns loaded with buckshot.

Sloppy Joe and Wally entered the tavern at 1:05 a.m. Shooter, all six feet-four-inches of him, was sitting at a back table, a cigarette smoldering in an ashtray made from a cylinder head cut off from a Harley engine. Wally waved and said, "I don't know what's going on, Shooter, but there isn't anybody guarding the bikes."

Shooter said, "Those bastards had better be there or I'll cut 'em." He pushed the table out of the way and stormed outside. He was met by six officers, one of whom poked the barrel of his pistol in Shooter's ear and told him to keep quiet. Shooter complied. One officer tore a strip of duct tape from a silver roll and slapped it over his mouth. Another officer pulled his arms behind his back and snapped handcuffs in place. They hustled him to a second paddy wagon a half-block down the street. A deviated septum and a racing heart made it difficult for Shooter to breathe. No one cared.

Inside, Sloppy Joe and Wally ordered a beer, did a head count and came up with nineteen conscious bikers … plus two passed out in a corner. Wally walked to the back exit and popped the door open. He keyed his whisper mic and said, "The number is nineteen, plus two. We'll handle the bartender. Go."

Sloppy Joe held the bartender at gunpoint, while the Salem tactical team poured into the tavern from the back entrance. The FBI SWAT team, minus a watcher left outside, poured through the front door and fanned out along the wall. All were shouting, "Go! Go!" Team leaders were shouting, "Hands up! Hands in the air!"

The stoned and inebriated bikers were too befuddled to react. All, that is, but one … the one who was in the bathroom and wasn't included in the head count. He pulled a peashooter .25 caliber pistol from a holster hiding in the small of his back and ran out the back exit into the waiting arms of the Salem tactical team watcher.

The biker triggered a wild shot that was rewarded by the sound of breaking window glass in a store next door. The officer immediately returned fire, hitting the biker three times in the upper body with .9 mm slugs. It would be ruled a good shoot, and the biker would soon be shipped home in a coffin.

All in all, it was a classic operation that worked smoothly and efficiently right up to the pistol shots. The gunfire woke some of the bikers in the bunkhouse, where two idiots stoned on meth rushed out the front door, guns drawn. It was like something out of Butch Cassidy and the Sundance Kid … with about the same result.

When they reacted to an order to drop their weapons by shooting at the officers, they were treated to several rounds of 12-gauge buckshot. The rest of the gang inside the building surrendered without fuss. None were interested in committing suicide by cop.

79

Consequences

BUD, BB, DEPUTY BEATRICE TUSK, AND Deputy Lonnie Beltram spent the remainder of the afternoon staring at the wall-mounted TV in the small conference room, sipping stale coffee from white mugs and watched the chaos in Portland.

BB shook his head. "Nuts is what it is. Look at all that water. You have the Columbia River, the Sandy River, the Clackamas, and the Willamette. No way have they been poisoned. Put a few drops of bleach in a gallon of water and get on with life."

Bud nodded, sighed, and put his mug on the table. "I'm sure someone will think of it … eventually."

BB said, "A registered letter brought me a federal grand jury summons? Did you get one, too?"

Bud nodded. "Yep. Supposed to be there day after tomorrow, but that's not going to happen."

The phone on a side desk rang, and Bud reached over to pick it up. "Bud."

Karen Highsmith said, "You have a call from Sergeant Booker in Klamath Falls."

"Okay. Put him through."

Booker said, "Sheriff?"

"In the flesh. How are you, Sergeant Booker?"

"Fussed. Are you watching that mess in Portland?"

Bud nodded, "Yes. We are glued to the TV. BB and I both worked there for several years, so it feels personal."

"I never worked there, and it still feels personal. If Dell BeBe is with you, I'd like to put TJ on the phone. He's been worried about his friend."

"Hold on." He handed the phone to BB and left the room to make more coffee.

Karen saw him coming down the hall and gave him an urgent motion to hurry. She put her hand over the mouthpiece of her phone and said, "I'm getting lots of calls wanting to know what we've heard from Portland. I'm on the line with Carol Connor right now. She wants to know what she can put in her newspaper."

Bud took a deep breath and reached for the phone. "Hello, Carol. I can't tell you much more than what you are seeing on TV. Police channels are telling us that, so far, no one checked by doctors in Portland has shown any sign of poison. Not one."

Carol said, "Wow! A hoax?"

"Darned if I know."

"What do I tell our readers?"

"Well … I guess you can say there has been mass panic in response to rumors someone poisoned the Portland water system. That much is true; there has been mass panic. The rumors about poison in the water have not been confirmed. And I guess you could say the mass exodus from Portland has completely blocked transportation for now."

"Sheriff, how will this affect us?"

"Well, I'd say without normal delivery service, the shelves in our stores will be empty in about twenty-four to forty-eight hours, and our service stations will run through their supply of fuel in a couple of days. And I have no idea how long the whiskey and wine will last. I'd urge people to ration their supplies and get on with life."

"Thanks. And may I suggest that you to talk to KQIK radio? I won't get the next edition of the paper out until tomorrow morning. We plan to pull an all-nighter. Nothing like radio for immediate information."

"I hadn't thought of that. We have plans in place for other emergencies, but not this one. Thanks, Carol. I'll get on it."

He walked hurriedly to his office, looked up the number for Lakeview's only radio station, and dialed. When the station owner answered,

Bud said, "This is Sheriff Bud Blair. I think we need to get something on the air about this mess in Portland."

"Yes. We were just talking about that. Can you come to the station?"

"I'd rather do this over the phone."

Within five minutes, the station was broadcasting their emergency signal followed by a standby bulletin. Bud's voice urged calm, prudence, and self-imposed rationing. The bulletin was broadcast every fifteen minutes for the remainder of the day.

Bud walked back to the conference room. "Are your rigs gassed up? We might not get any fuel shipments for a while."

Lonnie and Bea both nodded. "Mine is full," Bea said. "Mine, too," Lonnie echoed.

"Well, mine isn't. I better go tend to that."

Bea stood up and held out her hand, "Keys, please. I'll go do it."

There was no panic in Lake County, but within minutes of the first broadcast, Martin Conley, Lakeview's druggist, was on the air telling people medical supplies were sufficient to meet demand for the next two weeks.

Bea was gone for over forty-five minutes. "Had to get in line for gas. Everyone is filling up."

Bud nodded and said, "Thanks. Now, besides sitting here watching TV, what else should we be doing?"

Bea laughed and said, "I should be shopping. There's not a thing to eat at my house."

Bud grinned. "Well, if it comes down to it, I have a whole freezer full of frozen dinners. We just might have to share."

"Or," BB said, "we could all run down to Reno."

Bud shook his head. "Nope. I have a date tonight."

80

Dog Lake

BY LATE EVENING, PHONE CALLS TO THE sheriff's office had tapered off, and the necessary meetings with local officials were over and done with. Bud figured it was safe to head for Dog Lake. He ran a mental check list of essentials he kept at the cabin, decided he was good to go, and called BB for a ride out to his house north of town.

When BB pulled up against the curb in front of the sheriff's office … driving a new dark-red Ford F-150, Bud grinned broadly. He slid onto the passenger seat and said, "I never thought I'd see the big city detective, Dell BeBe, driving anything like this."

BB kidded back, "I thought I'd see what driving a pickup would be like. Just until my Lexus gets repaired."

"What happened?"

"During the ruckus with the bikers, somebody sideswiped my car. Had to take it to the beauty shop."

"And lease a pickup?"

BB nodded.

"Uh, huh. You be careful Deputy BeBe. You might catch the Western fever."

"God forbid that should ever come to pass. It's bad enough just living in a log cabin."

"Some cabin," Bud scoffed.

"Where you headed?"

"I want you to run me out to the house so I can get my rig."

"Honeymooning?"

Bud laughed and shook his head. "You know, BB, every time I think I have this business with Nancy lined out, life gets in the way. We have reservations at the Hyatt Regency in Portland for tonight and tomorrow night – for which I will be charged, no doubt – and I can't even get a call through to cancel."

"So, you'll just have to rough it at the cabin, I suppose?"

Bud laughed. "I guess so. It's a tough life, but someone's got to do it."

A short ride later, BB pulled into the driveway of Bud's single-story house and parked. He reached across the seat and held out his hand. "Bud, I love you like a brother. Here's to all the happiness you deserve. Congratulations."

Bud shook BB's big hand and felt a lump in his throat. Voice a bit husky, he said, "I'm glad to have you for a friend BB. Now get your ass out of here."

***

BUD'S MOOD IMPROVED WITH EACH MILE he drove to Dog Lake. By the time he crossed the big culvert feeding Dog Creek to the desert, he felt as content as he could remember ever feeling.

The weather gave blessing to Mister and Missus Bud Blair, inviting them to linger over a tender, grilled T-bone and a glass of wine. A big vase of red roses graced the middle of the picnic table. As the evening shadows edged across the lake, a mourning dove treated them to her plaintive song. Nancy leaned against Bud's shoulders and kissed his cheek.

"I think I'll go take a shower, Bud. See you in a little while."

81

Ketchikan

S PECIAL AGENT LEROY WILCOX SHARED A happy grin with his old partner as the big Coast Guard helicopter lifted off from Sea-Tac airport. They tried shouting over the roar of rotor and engine noise, until a young guardsman pointed to headsets hanging beside each of their seats and mimed putting them over their ears.

"That's better," Wilcox said, his voice a bit tinny sounding through the microphone. "How you been, Douglas?"

"Fine. How's your new job?"

"I don't know … I think I like fieldwork better than I like sending people out to do the fieldwork. You don't suppose Dutch knew that?"

Brandt shook his head. "I'm beginning to think Dutch can be devious at times. I'm sure he thinks Miranda needs some time in the field. And maybe he's right. It might make a better analyst out of her."

Wilcox shrugged, then said, "How are you and Jenny doing?"

Brandt shook his head. "Well, I don't know. We were going to meet for lunch … then the fuss in Portland started."

"What do you know about that?"

Brandt shook his head. "Not much beyond what you can get from the TV. I do know Dutch plans to arrest a prominent imam – some dude named Osama.

"You gotta be kidding me."

"No. Dutch really means it."

"No. Not that. The name."

"Coincidence."

Wilcox grinned. "Shame on me, but I like it."

"By the way, Leroy. Do you have any idea where this rattletrap helicopter is taking us?"

"Yes. We're headed for the Whidbey Island Naval Air Station. A Navy plane will give us a ride to Ketchikan. The Coast Guard reported seeing Butler's yacht tied up to a mooring buoy just south of there. They'll keep an eye on him until we arrive."

"Think about it, Leroy. Given the tools we have, you really can't hide. You can run, but you can't hide. As an FBI agent, I like it. As a private citizen, it scares the hell out of me."

***

A NERVOUS BRANDT WATCHED CAREFULLY AS the Learjet dropped low over the Tongass Narrows. Through the porthole window, he saw patches of evening fog on the shipping channel and houselights slipping in and out of view. The Navy pilot eased the C-21 down smoothly on the runway, braked hard, and taxied to the terminal.

Brandt took a deep breath and unbuckled his seat belt. "You know what I hate about flying, Leroy? You can't see out the front window."

"What difference does that make, Douglas? You can't fly this thing anyway."

"Yeah. I know, but I like to see where I'm going."

The steward, whose nametag read 'Seaman John Perry,' grinned at the exchange. "Spoken like a true ground-pounder."

"Amen to that," Brandt said. "Armor. That's more my style."

"I notice you gentlemen don't have any luggage."

Brandt, whose beard was beginning to show, shrugged. "Snatched from the jaws of victory by a rooftop helicopter. No time to pack."

The steward pushed on a handle to open the cabin door and a set of steps unfolded. He said, "Here comes your Coast Guard escort. I'm told we are to wait for you to conduct your business, then return you to Sea-Tac tomorrow. Please let the Coast Guard dispatcher know if those plans change."

Brandt filled his lungs with cool, sea-scented air and exhaled slowly. "Doesn't that smell good, Leroy?"

"Does what smell good? Dead fish, jet fuel, and rotting seaweed?"

"You have no romance in your soul, Leroy. You should at least be grateful for another good landing. We survived to walk away."

A white Chevy Suburban pulled to a stop, its doors emblazoned with the Coast Guard emblem. Brandt studied the gold shield with crossed anchors, red-white-and-blue center circle, and the words "Semper Paratus" around the edge of the circle. A young officer slid from behind the wheel and walked to meet them.

"Gentlemen, I'm Lieutenant Harrington. I'll get you over the ferry to the Coast Guard station on the main island. The commander said he would meet you in his office. He wants a little more information, before we launch a boarding party. May I please see your ID?"

Wilcox fished his badge wallet from the inside pocket of his dark blue blazer and held it out for Harrington's inspection. "I'm Special Agent Wilcox, FBI, and this is Special Agent Brandt. Thanks for meeting us."

"Luggage?"

"We didn't have time to pack."

"No problem, sirs. We can fix you up, but we'd best get moving. We don't want to keep the commander waiting."

Brandt couldn't help himself and said, "Hard-ass?"

Harrington held the rear door open for them, then smiled and shook his head. "Not really. Just busy at the moment – with trespassers. Our big cutter is scheduled out of port in the next hour." Seatbelts fastened, Harrington started the engine and headed to the ferry boarding area.

"Trespassers?" Brant said from the rear seat.

"Yes. Foreign ships fishing within our maritime borders."

Wilcox was interested. "Does it happen often?"

Lieutenant Harrington nodded. "Every season. They just got the jump on us this year."

***

From the ferry dock on Revillagigedo Island, it was a short drive to the Coast Guard base just south of town.

When Wilcox said, "That didn't take long," Harrington nodded and smiled back at them in the rearview mirror. "Nothing is very far away in Ketchikan."

A clutter of service buildings and a square, white, utilitarian-looking administration building, dating back to maybe the 1950's, stood sentry over a sheltered cove, home port for the Chandeleur, a sleek one-hundred-ten-foot interisland cutter.

A tall boathouse served as home to a second, smaller cutter, and several black and red Zodiacs were moored on the port side of the pier, subject to wind and weather, ready for the next mission. *Busy place*, Brandt thought.

Harrington stopped in a "No Parking" zone and hopped out in time to open the back door, just as Wilcox reached for the handle. He said, "This way, gentlemen," and led them into a foyer with an armed guardsman sitting behind bulletproof glass. Brandt and Wilcox signed in, and the guard pushed the "Pass" button. Inside he handed them each a visitor badge that clipped to their jacket pockets.

Commander James Madison claimed a second-floor office with a view of the Coast Guard moorage and the green waters of the Alaska Marine Highway. Compact, energetic, a man who seldom sat still, he came around from behind his desk, hand outstretched, blue eyes searching the faces of the two FBI agents ushered in by Lieutenant Harrington.

"Welcome to Ketchikan, gentlemen. I'm Commander Madison. I run this place … or maybe it runs me. Which of you is Wilcox and which is Brandt?"

Wilcox held out his hand. "I'm Special Agent Wilcox, and this is Special Agent Brandt." Madison shook hands with each of them.

"Have a seat. Let's talk a bit about the situation that brought you here. Harrington, how about getting us three cups of fresh coffee?"

When Harrington closed the door, Commander Madison backed up and sat on the edge of his desk, arms crossed. "Your fugitive's yacht is about five miles south, tied to a mooring buoy just around Mountain Point. What do you want to tell me about this guy? Is he dangerous? Desperate? Pushing drugs? What?"

Brandt glanced at Wilcox and then looked back at Madison. He said, "Winslow Butler is not actually a fugitive. There have been no warrants issued for his arrest. But we need him to testify before a federal grand jury. And that's about all I can say. We don't believe him to be dangerous. What we need is a ride to his boat, so we can talk him into coming back with us."

"And if he won't?"

"Then our orders are to detain him as a material witness."

Madison nodded and fished for more information. "This must be a big deal, given the trouble you've gone to."

Disgust in his voice, Wilcox nodded. "When foreign nationals kidnap young women and then ship them to the Middle East as sex slaves, it is a big deal. Butler has information that will help us put the ringleader away."

Commander Madison nodded. In his career, he had seen the seamier side of human nature, so the thought of sex trafficking wasn't new. The Coast Guard sometimes interdicts shipments of people coming into the US, but it's rare to find people being smuggled out.

He said, "Okay. We have eyes on him as we speak. One of our guys is an avid fisherman, who just happens to be fishing for salmon a short distance from The Runaway. He tells me it doesn't look like there's plans to go anyplace soon. Your guy dropped a crab pot over the rail, and it looks like he's fishing for halibut. Last report said lights are on in the staterooms, and his mooring lights are lit. I'd say he's camped for the night.

"You two look crapped out. Why don't you let us keep an eye on his boat tonight and then go pick him up in the morning? Go get something to eat.

The two hungry FBI agents looked at each other and nodded. Brandt said, "Sir, we'll take you up on that."

"Good. Lieutenant, take these gentlemen to the chow hall, and get them fixed up at the VOQ."

82

Sunrise

THE WIND PUSHED THEIR NEW GORE-TEX rain parkas hard against their bodies as the open Zodiac sped south on through the Tongass Narrows. Icy sea spray convinced Brandt his new parka was worth every penny. Wilcox, a cold hand holding the peak of his hood in place, turned and grinned at his smaller partner. "Douglas," he shouted over the roar of twin outboards and the noise of the wind, "we got to get ourselves one of these."

One Coast Guard crewman looked back and grinned. "That's why I'm here. I love boats and being on the water. Most days are just plain fun."

Ten minutes later, Chief Jones, skipper of the three-person crew, retarded the throttle and the big Zodiac slowed from forty miles per hour to a more sedate twenty. He brought the throttle back further, toggled a switch on the dashboard to shift the engines to quiet mode, then pointed to a high-prowed green and white Krogen tied to a mooring buoy about a half-mile up the sound. "There's your target."

Even though Brandt and Wilcox were convinced Butler was not a threat, the briefing prior to launch was specific about safety precautions. Chief Jones insisted the FBI agents armor up and wear life jackets. "That's required for all boarding parties. Semper paratus," the Chief said. "Always ready."

***

WINSLOW BUTLER, FORMER FBI AGENT, SIPPED hot coffee and watched through the wheelhouse window as the red Zodiac slowly eased up to The Runaway. With something akin to admiration in his voice, he muttered. "Damned if they didn't find us."

He slid the wheelhouse door open and stepped out on the deck, coffee mug in his hand. He leaned on the rail and took another sip of coffee. *Might be my last one as a free man. Better enjoy it.*

Brandt pulled his hood back and looked up at Butler. Even though Butler had grown a beard and was wearing a watch cap, he was still the same gaunt figure he had always been. "Good morning, Winslow. You got the pot on?"

In spite of himself, Butler smiled. "How did you find me?"

Brandt stood up and said, "We didn't. Miranda did. Or more to the point, she found the moorage for The Runaway."

"Well, damn. And the Commodore ratted me out?"

"Why don't we come aboard," Wilcox said. "We can talk about it over a cup of coffee. It's cold out here."

Butler set his coffee mug on the deck and walked to a boarding ladder tied to the rail halfway down the length of the boat. He unclipped a section of deck rail and slipped the pins of the boarding ladder in holes engineered for that purpose. "Come aboard," he said.

"I'm Chief Jones, United States Coast Guard," the wheelman from the Zodiac said. "May we come aboard to inspect your boat?"

Butler slowly let his breath out. He nodded. "Okay. Do your job, but let me wake Milly up first. She's had enough fright to last her a lifetime."

Brandt climbed the boarding ladder and stepped on deck. "Milly?"

Butler said, "A lost soul I found and sort of rescued … or so I thought."

"You lead, we'll follow," Brandt said.

While Chief Jones and his crew inspected The Runaway, a trembling Millicent, Butler, and the two FBI agents sat at the galley table and talked.

Wilcox looked at Butler and said, "She's kinda young, don't you think?"

Millicent became defensive. "He saved me, but he won't even have sex with me. He's a big prude." And then she smiled. "I love him."

"Like a father, I hope," Wilcox growled.

Brandt studied her. Mussed hair, no makeup, acne scars and all, and thought that with a little makeup, she would be pretty. *And Butler treats her like a daughter. Okay, I'll buy it.* He moved Butler up a notch on his approval scale.

"So, what happens now?" Butler asked.

Wilcox nodded at Brandt, giving him the lead, since Brandt was who Butler placed a call to in the first place. Brandt said, "We want you to testify to a federal grand jury in Portland. You will be in a witness protection program after that."

"No jail time?"

Wilcox looked around the pristine galley and down the stairway to the state rooms and said, "You deserve it, but probably not. I don't know if you'll get to keep the yacht and all the money you took."

Butler shook his head. "The yacht wasn't purchased with dirty money. My father left me a two-million-dollar life insurance policy when he died. I bought The Runaway with that money. And I made damned sure my ex-wife couldn't touch it."

Wilcox frowned and said, "And that should make us feel better?"

Butler shook his head. "No, but I did help you bust Al-Alwani's sex slave business. That makes me feel better."

"Okay," Brandt said. "What are we going to do with Miss Millicent Andrews … and with this yacht?"

Butler looked at Millicent and patted her hand. "I've signed the title to The Runaway over to Milly. I'll give her one of my credit cards and what cash I have on board. That should carry her for a few months. If you don't throw me in jail, I'll be back. I suggest we move The Runaway to the Ketchikan harbor and let Milly rent a slip."

Millicent, tears in her eyes said, "I don't want to be left alone. I want to go with you."

Butler put an arm around her shoulder. "You can do this. Stay clean. And buy a cell phone." He fished a notepad from a drawer and wrote a number on the top sheet. "This is my number. Call me anytime … day or night. As soon as I can, I'll be back."

Chief Jones walked into the galley. "Mister Kojak, your boat passed inspection, but your flare-gun cartridges are getting old. They haven't passed the expiration date, but you need some new ones soon. Otherwise, you are good to go."

Chief Jones looked at Wilcox and Butler, then said "I'd like to say something personal to Mister Kojak and the young lady … if you don't mind."

"Certainly," Wilcox said. "Speak your mind."

Chief Jones looked at Milly. "Okay. Here goes. You're trying to kick a drug habit, aren't you?"

"How do you know?"

"Well, I'm sure it's none of my business, but you look like my daughter did when she was trying to get clean. But, maybe I'm wrong."

"And did she?" Millicent asked.

"Yes, but she works at it every day. Goes to meetings three times a week. If you would like, I think you should meet her. She could help you, give you someone to talk with while your friend is away. It helps her stay clean when she helps others. Okay?"

Milly stared at her coffee cup before looking at Chief Jones. "I'm not sure I can do it on my own. Please introduce us."

Butler held his hand out to Chief Jones. *The Lord works in mysterious ways, he thought.*

An hour later, The Runaway was moored safely in a marina slip. Millicent had tears running down her cheeks. Butler gave her a hug, then turned and followed his companions to a Coast Guard SUV waiting to take them to the airfield.

83

Campaign

THE SMELL OF BACON AND THE sound of domestic clatter woke Bud from a restful night's sleep. It was the second morning of their A-frame honeymoon. Bud wished for a few more days, but he knew he had to get back to the business of being sheriff.

Showered, shaved, dressed in his uniform, Bud walked stocking-footed to the kitchen and sneaked up on Nancy, who was turning strips of sizzling bacon in a big cast-iron skillet. He put his arm around her shoulders, pulled the collar down on her blue terry cloth robe, and kissed the back of her neck. "I know, let's take a leave day. I'm not ready to go back."

A red Ford F-150 rolled to a stop in the driveway, and Bud turned to look.

"Who is it?" Nancy asked.

"BB. He's trying out a pickup … until his Lexus gets fixed."

BB, wearing blue jeans, a short sleeved western style shirt, and polished cowboy boots, rapped on the front door and opened it, without waiting for an invitation.

He grinned and sang, "Honeymooners, at last alone…"

"Or trying to be," Bud said without a hint of rancor. He handed BB a fresh cup of coffee. "What are you up to, BB? Dressed like a cowboy."

BB pulled a chair out and sat down, put his elbows on the table, hands clasped under his chin. "You have the honor of looking at the Henry Bud Blair for Sheriff campaign manager. I figured 'when in Rome,' so if I'm your campaign manager, I might as well be Western. Besides, I think the style fits me."

Nancy smiled. "How does that work, BB? The campaign business."

"Well, first Bud has to file for the office. I have the papers in my pickup. He signs and I run them to town. The deadline is tomorrow, which I know he forgot about. Then I register us as a PAC and raise some money."

BB turned serious and said, "Bud, I think we need to get moving. Your opponent was just on KQIK saying he plans to modernize the sheriff's department and bring state of the art police techniques to Lake County, including the use of drones to patrol the far reaches of the county. And he implied you are old-fashioned."

"He did, huh?"

"Yes."

"Wouldn't that take the cake? Get married and then lose my job."

BB shook his head. "Not going to happen. Now then, I have a debate scheduled between you and your challenger next Saturday at the Lakeview High School gym. News Watch 12 from Klamath Falls will film it. That nice blonde anchor lady will be the moderator. She is developing a set of questions, and she'll email them to each of you ASAP. The debate will proceed from those questions."

Bud frowned. "How did you arrange that?"

BB grinned like a kid pulling a joke on a friend. "I did not. Your secret pal, Carol Connor arranged it. And that really is a secret. Carol does not want to let that cat out of the bag. As your campaign manager, I okayed the debate."

Bud pulled a chair out from the little table and sat. He stared at BB before shaking his head to say, "Self-appointed campaign manager."

BB was obviously enjoying himself. "Yes. You have excellent skills as an investigator, and you're a pretty good sheriff, but you lack political savvy. Think of me as your political body guard."

Nancy slipped around the table to give BB a hug. "Thank you, BB. He's a wonder, he is, but he hates the press. And he hates politics even more."

Bud finally rocked forward and reached across the table. BB smiled again, thoroughly enjoying himself, and shook hands.

"Thanks, BB. I accept your generous help and concern. By the way, what's this guy's name?"

BB's cell phone chimed, and he pulled it from his shirt pocket. "Miranda," he said. "Do you mind?"

Bud shrugged and Nancy raised her eyebrows in speculation.

Phone to his ear, BB pulled the door open and walked outside.

Bud said, "Nancy, I'm pretty green at this. I've never had to campaign for my job. And it sounds like I'd better dig up some money. Maybe we could sell my house in town, and then I'll move in with you."

Standing beside him, Nancy put her arm around his shoulders and kissed the top of his head. "I love you, Bud Blair."

Bud nodded, but still had trouble saying "I love you too" aloud. He slipped an arm around her waist and held her. They stayed that way until BB shut his phone off and walked back inside.

"Miranda says Portland's still a mess. Local authorities are getting things moving again, but looting is still going on. She's been pretty much stuck at headquarters for the last couple of days. Says she wants clean clothes and a shower. She got a call from the Portland Police Bureau to let her know her apartment has been ransacked. I offered my apartment, until she gets hers put back together."

Nancy cocked her head and looked sideways at BB. "Wow. That sounds awful for Miranda, but do I detect a budding romance?"

BB just shrugged, grinned, and said, "I don't know. We'll see. Right now, I'm just helping her out."

Bud nodded. "Good. Now back to business. What's this guy's name again? My opponent."

"Clay Oliver."

"What do we know about him?"

BB grinned again, "Why, Mister Sheriff, Deputy Roger Hildebrand will have a background file on your desk before the day is out. Suffice it to say, what we know at this point is that he's wealthy – but unnamed sources in Montana are saying he didn't get all of his money by honest means."

"Won't that backfire … if I accuse him of being dishonest?"

BB shook his head. "First rule of campaigning: let others do the dirty work. It will come out … but only if you and I say so."

"Disgusting," Bud said.

84

Grand Jury and Return

WILCOX AND BRANDT SPENT A GOOD share of the flight back to Whidbey Island pumping Butler for information, taking notes, refining questions, and looking for any small detail that could be used later for the prosecution of Al-Alwani.

Osama turned out to be just a shadow figure in Butler's world. "I heard him mentioned, but never met him. Good old Al-Alwani often tried to impress me talking about what a badass he worked for. He said Osama would get me if I ever turned on him. And that's all I can tell you about Osama. There is a connection, though."

Brandt nodded. "Do you think this Osama character knew about the kidnaps and sex trafficking?"

"I don't know. What I think is that Osama had bigger fish to fry, and he might have gotten pissed if he had known Al-Alwani was taking chances. These guys like to fly under the radar. Send their jihadi friends out to do the damage and remain anonymous themselves."

Wilcox had decided sometime back he didn't care for Butler, and that Butler should be going to jail – not back to his young girlfriend and his expensive yacht. He shook his head before he asked, "How did you get hooked up with Al-Alwani?"

Butler nodded. "Good question. It was so easy. Or maybe I was so easy. I spent a lot of time in a downtown bar called The White Swan. I was a regular. Had my own special stool at the bar, ran a weekly tab.

"That was after some pasty-faced lawyer convinced a liberal female judge that not only was my soon-to-be ex-wife entitled to half of my retirement, she was also entitled to my house and my car. I walked away with my possessions in two suitcases. I didn't even get to keep my PC. So … wiped out, after twenty-five years of marriage, I managed to drink my way into feeling sorry for myself.

"And one night, I let it slip that I was an FBI agent. The next night, Al-Alwani is buying me drinks and sending me home to Guy's Marina in a limo. A month later, I'm getting cash gifts, nights in the Hyatt with a lovely young woman, and the promise of more. All I had to do was keep my ear to the ground and let Al-Alwani know of FBI surveillance or planned raids."

"So, you sold us out," Wilcox said, disgust in his voice.

"The money was huge … at least to me. Like twenty thousand a month. I gave him limited information about actions I didn't think would hurt us that much. That's about the time when my father died. I'd developed a taste for cruising, including one hairy trip over the bar in that little boat I was living on. That's when I decided spending Dad's insurance money on The Runaway was the right idea.

"And then I found out that Al-Alwani was kidnapping young women and shipping them to a bunch of Arab assholes in Yemen. Somehow, that tipped the scales for me. So, I started watching him, and that led me to the shipping container. That's when I called you guys."

"Oh, goodie," Wilcox said.

Angered by the disregard Wilcox had for his actions, Butler said, "Damn right. I may have been a fool, but I put my life on the line to tell you about that container, and you ran with it. I know I can't make up for what I did. I'm not sure that God himself will ever forgive me, but at least I could do that much and help put a stop to the kidnapping."

"And run away with a woman young enough to be your daughter. How about that, Douglas? He betrays us and reaps the glory."

Stung, Butler said, "Milly is a recovering drug addict. I'm trying to help her. She has no one else in this whole miserable world. You're right. She's not much more than a girl, and that's as far as it goes. You can believe me or not. Nothing I can do about that."

The C-21 intercom broke the tension. "Seat belts, gentlemen. We'll be landing in twenty minutes."

***

THE RETURN TO PORTLAND WAS VIA FBI helicopter from Whidbey Island to the Portland FBI's rooftop heliport. Traffic was beginning to move again, slowly, but any movement was a blessing. A beleaguered Assistant U.S. attorney was once again getting witness testimony scheduled before the federal grand jury. Wilcox and Brandt took Butler to the FBI safe house atop the West Hills to await an appearance at the Justice Building.

85

Debate

CLAY OLIVER WAS AN IMPRESSIVE FIGURE, a solid six-foot-two, dressed in an expensive western-style suit, black Justin boots highly polished, silver hair swept back, piercing blue eyes sweeping the crowd in the high school gym. When Oliver gave the crowd a big smile and waved, Bud thought, *"Damn, but he's a good-looking guy. I'll bet he turns the heads of all the ladies. But I'm in uniform and he's not. That should count for something. I'm a lousy debater, but I know I'm a better sheriff than he would be. Suck it up, Bud. Get this guy."*

Introductions made, Anna McBride, co-anchor of News Watch 12, said "Gentlemen, you have each been given a list of questions to prepare for this debate. There is a copy of the questions on your podiums. I will give you one minute to answer each question. At the end of the half-hour, you will both be given time for a five-minute summary, and then we give members of the audience reasonable time to ask questions. Understood?"

They both nodded, and Anna smiled. "Good luck, Gentlemen. Mister Oliver, since you are the challenger, you will go first. Please tell this audience, what qualifies you to be sheriff of Lake County?"

Oliver smiled and said, "Thank you. In Missoula, where I lived before buying the Z-BAR ranch, I was part of the sheriff's posse and a member of the sheriff's reserves. This gave me a lot of hands-on experience in support of law enforcement officers. I also trained with firearms, and

I took crime scene forensics classes through Montana State. All in all, I'm extremely familiar with police procedures. I'm up to date on current technology … and I'm smart." He flashed a smile and was reward with a smattering of chuckles.

Bud thought, *"Well, here we go."* Heads were nodding as Bud described his nearly eight years with the Lake County Sheriff's office, his master's degree in criminology, and his eleven years with the Portland Police Bureau. A smattering of applause followed Bud's "Thank you."

BB whispered to Nancy, "Round one to Bud."

Anna McBride moved to the next question. "Mr. Oliver, you've said you'll bring new methodologies to the sheriff's office. Would you tell us about that, please?"

"Yes," Oliver smiled. "Glad to. I mean no disrespect to the experience of Sheriff Blair, but I think we could cover more ground and be less intrusive with the use of drone patrols, like the military uses, and do it cheaper than officer patrols. We could track cars, monitor speeds, find poachers, and get video of rustlers. In Montana, our sheriff used a drone to break up a large rustling operation that included on-the-spot slaughter trucks that sold direct to a string of butcher shops. That one saved our local ranchers one-million dollars a year. That's the kind of thinking I'll bring to the job."

"Sheriff Blair, do you agree that using drones to aid surveillance is a good idea?"

Bud rubbed the scar on his eyebrow and then straightened, standing taller without realizing it. He shook his head and scanned the faces of the two hundred plus people gathered in the gym. "I don't like the idea of drones watching our citizens. I don't like it at all. No one else should either."

A few people, mostly older men and women, nodded, and a few just fidgeted. He looked over and directly challenged Clay Oliver. "Mister Oliver, you are Western, so you have to know that most of us live here for the personal freedom and privacy the Western lifestyle gives us. No. I don't like it at all. Too much opportunity for abuse. Honest police work and community cooperation get the job done. And we've all but stopped rustling in Lake County … without a spy-in-the-sky approach.

"Crime will always be around, but we have a proud record as a police department, and I oversee an efficient office when it comes to solving crime. To my knowledge we only have one unsolved cold case on our books, and we're going to tackle that one soon."

He paused and took a sip of water from the glass on his podium. "I can see the use of a drone in search and rescue, but not for routine police work. Nope, not on my watch."

That brought a round of applause, and one man from the back of the room yelled, "Go get 'em, Bud!"

Oliver glowered at Bud and said to the audience, "That's exactly what I'm talking about. Sheriff Blair is blind to innovation."

That comment earned Clay Oliver a chorus of boos, and a sharp rebuke from Anna McBride. "Save your rebuttal for the appropriate time, Mister Oliver."

BB nodded and said quietly to Nancy, "I score a knockout for Bud, or at least a knock-down. Oliver got suckered with that question. He's sure an arrogant sonofabitch."

Clay Oliver never quite recovered, but he was still an imposing, handsome man who relied on charm to try and win people over.

Bud stumbled a bit over his own "special question." Anna McBride tried unsuccessfully to hide a smile when she said, "Sheriff, what role does the news media have in the law enforcement playbook?"

Bud snorted and said, "Anna, I only know two ... no, make that three ... reporters I would trust to know when to suppress a story in the interest of helping the police work a case and catch a criminal. Two of those are in this room tonight, and one is retired. Otherwise, I do my best to stay away from the press. Period."

Anna nodded and said, "Thank you, Sheriff."

***

STANDING APPLAUSE AT THE END OF the debate had both candidates wondering who had won. They met at center stage and shook hands. Bud leaned in close and whispered, "Your Montana past is about to catch up with you."

Oliver pulled back and looked Bud in the eye. "Past is right. I cleaned up my debts before I left. But why didn't you say anything here tonight?"

"Maybe because I'm willing to let the past stay that way. You stay clean, and you'll have no trouble in Lake County."

Oliver laughed and gripped Bud's shoulder with his free hand. He gave Bud's hand a firm grip and then said, "Damn, I might vote for you myself."

86

Aftermath

AT THE END OF TWO GRUELING DAYS of testimony, Butler was dismissed – but not before giving a sworn deposition to the Assistant U.S. Attorney, who said, "We will do what we can with this, but I can't guarantee you won't have to testify in person at trial."

He was released to FBI custody. Two agents he didn't know gave him a ride to the Portland International Airport. Butler stepped out the back seat of the black SUV and walked into the terminal without a word. He used his David Kojak credit card to buy a ticket on an Alaska Airlines flight to Ketchikan. Winslow Butler no longer existed.

After four tedious hours, broken only by a change of planes at Sea-Tac his flight touched down in Ketchikan. He called to let Milly know he was back. A musty-smelling taxi dropped him at the marina. He paid the fare and realized he didn't know the code for the security gate. But it didn't matter. Milly was walking up the dock. She looked healthy, and the smile on her face chased his worry away. She held the gate open and said, "Welcome home." She let the gate latch behind them and then grabbed his sleeve. She gave him a big hug and tried to kiss him on the lips. He turned his face and gave her a cheek to kiss instead.

She took his hand and led him down the dock. "I've missed you. I just got back from my first meeting. I think I'm going to like it. Janice Jones is a wonderful friend, and I have so much to tell you."

And you are high, Butler thought. It made him feel sad. *No one said it was going to be easy.*

***

Al-Alwani was indicted on the charges of murder for hire, human trafficking, and aggravated kidnapping. When June Daniels, the young woman rescued by Brandt and Wilcox from the shipping container, died from complications brought on by malnutrition and pneumonia, murder was added to the charges. Dutch reasoned her death was caused by her captivity. "Because that sonofabitch wouldn't get her any medical help, the deal is off."

***

Homeland Security sent agents to arrest Osama and five of his closest advisors. All were sent to a detention center in Cuba. Four would later be deported to Syria.

While in prison, the old man would die of congestive heart failure. And Osama would be shot while trying to escape. Records of Osama's detention were expunged from all official files. He was buried in an unmarked grave. Rumors among the guards said it was in the middle of a gravel road running around the inside perimeter of the razor wire fence.

***

Former motorcycle gang member, Gary Gentle, aka Starbucks, testified that he had been hired by "Shooter" to kill TJ Wildish, and he described firing at the "black people in the boat on the lake."

Testimony by FBI Special Agent Miranda Wright, who gained sympathy from the five women on the jury when she held up her left hand to show the jury the scars from her injury, reinforced the jury's belief in Shooter's guilt. He was convicted of being an accomplice to an attempted murder and murder-for-hire, then sentenced to twenty-five years in prison.

As one of the women on the jury later explained, "It was clear he ordered his gang members to kill Reverend Wildish, and that nice FBI lady was hurt because of what he did. Besides, he just oozed evil. He sat there in court and glared … like he would kill all of us if he could. Just trying to intimidate us. Make us afraid. He needed to be put away."

***

AT THE PAISLEY TAVERN, CLAY OLIVER bought a round for the house from innkeeper Buffalo Boggs, sipped Crown Royal, and said to the half-dozen men sitting at the bar, "A toast to Sheriff Bud Blair.

I figured he was just a country bumpkin county sheriff. And I had it wrong. He's all man and smart as a whip. That's why I'm getting the hell out of the race. I'm beat before I start. Besides, I like that guy. Square shooter is what he is."

Buffalo peered at the big rancher over the rim of his granny glasses and ever so slightly shook his head. *You were whipped all right. I wonder why Bud Blair didn't tell the citizens of Lake County about your shady past?*

***

WHEN CLAY OLIVER ANNOUNCED HE WAS withdrawing from the race for sheriff, BB resigned as Bud's campaign manager. He walked into Bud's office and said, "Well, that wraps it up for now. I'm going to Klamath Falls to pick up TJ and take him back to Portland."

Bud rocked back in his old wooden captain's chair and looked up. "I'll send my formal thanks to Sergeant Booker through the Klamath Falls Chief of Police, but I want you to give him my personal thanks for his help when you get over there."

"You bet."

"I suppose you'll see Miranda while you're in Portland?"

"Yes. And I admit I'm looking forward to it."

Bud nodded. "Beautiful woman. Smart as a whip, but she sure talks a lot. You think you can handle that?"

"Life is fleeting, old friend. I'm willing to take a chance. Question is, will she take a chance on me?"

Bud rose from his chair and held out his hand. "Go find out, BB."

"I will. Me and my new F-150."

***

SPECIAL AGENT WILCOX, FBI, CAUGHT A short flight to Sea-Tac hired a cab, and rode through the streets of Seattle to Uncle George's house.

When the cab stopped at the curb in front, Cletus and a tiny woman came out the front door and stood on the little porch, two small bags packed and ready to go.

***

A STOOPED BLACK MAN WHO MIGHT have been tall at one time walked out the front door and stood behind them.

Wilcox looked up at him and said, "You must be Uncle George."

"I am. Cletus is joining the FBI, huh?" He looked skeptical. "He's pretty small."

"Brains over brawn, Uncle George. Brains over brawn."

***

THE LADIES OF LAKEVIEW COUNTED THE months down, only to be disappointed when Nancy Sixkiller-Blair failed to produce the predicted child. In fact, Nancy appeared to be slimming down.

Doc Saunders pocketed the twenty-dollar bill from Brenda Brown, his longtime assistant who had bet on Nancy's pregnancy. "Miscarriage?" he quipped.

Brenda scowled. "Not likely. I'd have heard about that."

***

COMFORTABLE, NOW THAT SONNY SIXKILLER WAS once again the undersheriff of Lake County, Bud told Sonny he figured it would be all right if he and Nancy took some time for a real honeymoon. "I think we'll run up into that Northern Idaho country. I've always wanted to see Lake Pend Oreille. Ride the sternwheeler. Catch a fish maybe."

"Go, boss. I've got this under control"

"And hire me a new deputy while I'm gone. Larae sent in her resignation."

***

In Salem, the Oregon Liquor Control Commission canceled the Stone-Cold Tavern's liquor license, and the city canceled the tavern's restaurant license. The bunkhouse was condemned as a meth house … even though the evidence was pretty flimsy. But who was going to object? The Romans were universally detested. Those who escaped jail time rode their bikes to Nampa, Idaho. There, the leader of the Nampa chapter discouraged any talk of reprisal against the Lake County Sheriff. "Leave that man alone. He just keeps winning. Let's not tempt fate."

***

Special Agent Wilcox talked to Dutch Vanderlin about returning to Portland and his old job. "I'm a field agent," he argued. "That's where I belong."

Dutch pushed him hard about turning down his shot at promotion, but Wilcox insisted. Dutch said, "Two weeks. Then come on home. And welcome."

Wilcox said, "You knew, didn't you?" Dutch hung up without answering.

***

Jenny Jackson's lobster dinner at Jakes Famous Crawfish cost Douglas Brandt most of two hundred dollars, including tip. He fumed silently about it, but when she invited him in for a nightcap, he forgot about the expense.

***

Miranda opened the apartment door to BB's knock. On impulse, she pulled him inside and closed the door. When she pulled loose from his embrace and his kiss, she said, "I called for reservations for two at that nice dinner house on the marina dock. My treat. It's the least I can do for letting me use your apartment." But in her heart, she knew there was more going on than gratitude.

Dell BeBe was too smitten to notice.

Acknowledgments

Dedicated to Benny Nork: In all the world, a truer friend never lived.

Vi Collins, whose patience was tested once again.

Jerry Barrowcliff, who is always there with encouragement and gentle, succinct criticism.

Aaron Cooper, my lifelong friend and always faithful keeper of the files.

Dale Casey, off-site keeper of the files.

Sydney and Quinn … who gave me the moon and the stars.

Zach Sturgill, my talented young cover creator. I can hardly wait until he's a teenager.

My special thanks to this cadre of volunteer proofreaders: Rendy Jantz, Ivan Farm, Jim Goble, Sandra Jeter, Ed Monk, and Linda Gibbs.

Much appreciation to my patient publications manager, Eva Long.

And finally, my humble thanks to all of you who posted reviews of the earlier novels.

God bless readers, one and all.

About the Author

R OD COLLINS GREW UP IN A family nurtured by the oral story-telling tradition of rural America. Good storytellers (like his grandfather, Charlie Troop) were always welcome at the supper table or around the campfire.

True to that tradition, Collins created his award-winning, contemporary detective mysteries series featuring Sheriff Bud Blair. *Not Before Midnight* is book five of that collection. The Bud Blair series includes its first novel, *Spider Silk,* followed by *Stone Fly, Bloodstone,* and *Mariah's Song.*

Two more of Rod's books, *Bitter's Run* and *Abiqua* are historical novels set immediately following the end of the Civil War. John Bitter plans a solo trip across the Oregon Trail to his farm on Abiqua Creek, but the Good Lord and the beautiful red-haired lass, Morgan Eagan, have other plans.

Rod is also the author of *What Do I Do When I Get There? A New Manager's Guidebook.* This little book (called a "gem" by one reviewer), was the 2007 winner of the Pinnacle Book Award.

Rod loves to hear from his readers. Get in touch by leaving a comment on the Rod Collins Blog: www.brightworkspress.com/blog/.

www.ingramcontent.com/pod-product-compliance
Lightning Source LLC
Chambersburg PA
CBHW020647120726
47906CB00001B/158